VIPER AND STEEL

MEGAN O'RUSSELL

Ink Worlds Press

For the ones they would diminish.
You are worthy of the freedoms you seek.

WHITE MOUNTAINS
Royal Palace
Map Master Palace
BARRENS
Ilara
Arion Sea
Frason's Glenn
Barrens Bay
Harane
Ian Lioche
ILBREA
Ian Mithe
Ruthin Mountain
Ian Ayres
Mountain Road
Southern Citadel
TE
Pamerane

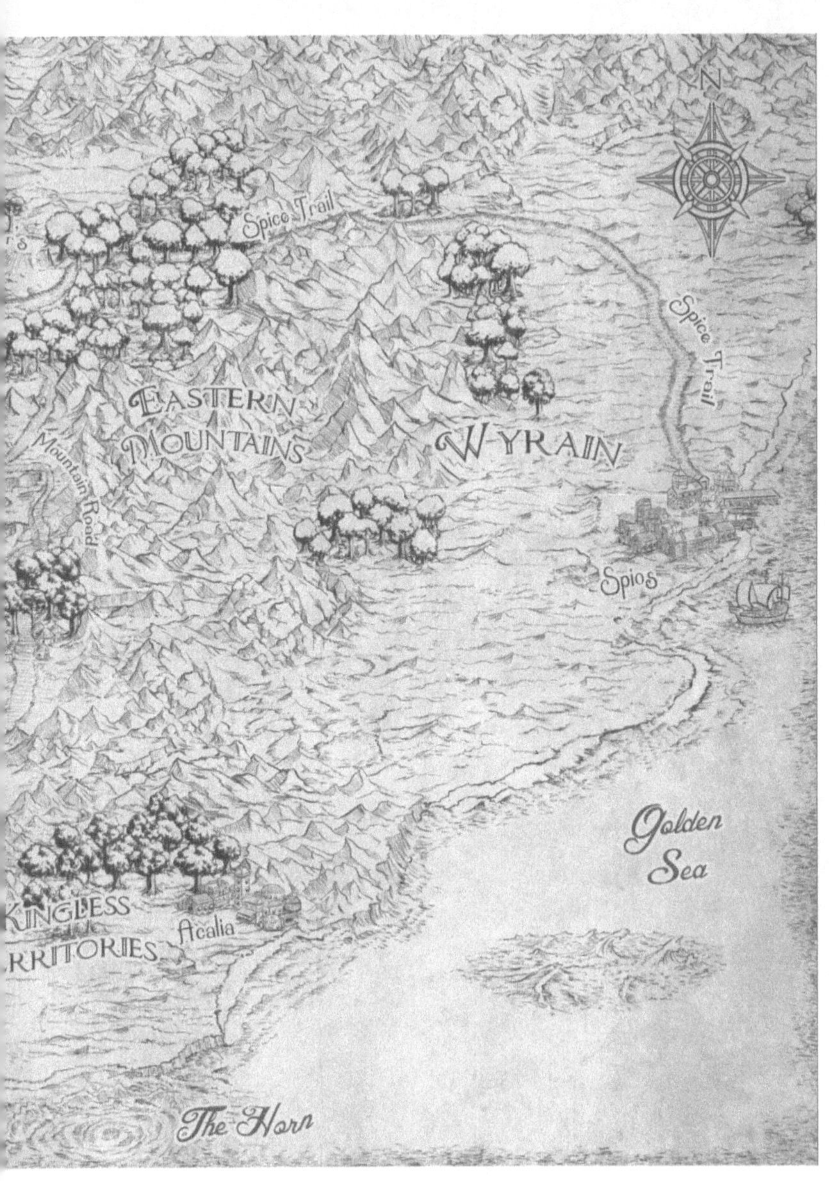

N
Spice Trail
Spice Trail
EASTERN MOUNTAINS
WYRAIN
Mountain Road
Spios
Golden Sea
KINGLESS TERRITORIES
Acalia
The Horn

VIPER AND STEEL

1

ENA

The breeze off the Arion Sea swept in through the open windows, offering a hint of salvation as the afternoon dragged on. The sun gleamed in the clear blue sky in a way the moneyed merchants surrounding me declared delightful and enchanting, a glorious reprieve after the turmoil Ilara had suffered.

But a day so bright and promising shouldn't be spent locked in a parlor listening to demons drone in your ear. I should've been out riding through the woods, or swimming in a hidden pool, or plotting a way to rid Ilbrea of the Guilds and all the golden-cloaked monsters that fed on the torment of the common folk.

A serving girl brought in a fresh tray of cakes, the fifth the gaggle had devoured.

"If the ships continue to be delayed at the docks, we'll have no hope of our cargo from Pamerane reaching the city before the storms blow in at the end of summer." Elaine Zelly paused, looking to me before dragging a noisy breath in through her nose. "Keeping proper track of all the goods that come into the city is certainly important, but commerce must continue."

"Absolutely." Mrs. Quintrell's curls bounced around her well-jowled face as she nodded.

I sipped my tea, watching both women stare at me, feeling the rest of the merchant women who'd crowded into the parlor staring at me as well. A whole flock of laxe just waiting for the head scribe's wife to speak. I twisted my foot, letting the sheath of the knife hidden in the ankle of my boot bring a smile to my lips.

"There are shipments of fabrics I know we've all been dying for," Mrs. Quintrell said. "And if we don't get them soon, our gowns won't be ready for the fall festivities."

"It's not just fabrics," Zelly said. "One of our shipments of fruit was held at the docks for nearly a week. The amount of food that spoiled reduced me to tears."

"You cried at the thought of all the empty bellies that could've been filled by the bounty your ships bring up from the south?" I set my tea aside.

"Of course." Zelly leaned toward me. "My family has been in the shipping trade for generations. Everything my family has, our very legacy, depends on our ability to reliably bring goods into Ilara."

"I agree, Mrs. Zelly, the shipping delays have gone too far," I said. "After the rebellion and the cathedral's collapse and the fresh rounds of fighting in the streets, there is far too much hunger in Ilara. Food that could be given to the poor shouldn't be held at the docks."

"Well"—Zelly chose a cake from the tray—"our produce sells for more than what those who are suffering can pay. We bring exotic fruits from Pamerane, not grain from the farms just south of Ilara."

The gaggle of women tittered.

"Pity." I stood, letting the women all scramble to their feet to mirror me. "The more the common folk go hungry, the worse the unrest will get, the longer your ships will wait at the docks."

Mrs. Zelly's smile froze as though she'd pinned it in place. "I have limitless compassion for those who are suffering, but I must see to the prosperity of my business."

Then you will burn. And the tilk will dance around the pyre.

"I wish you the best of luck as you try to negotiate with the sorcerers," I said.

"The sorcerers?" Zelly spoke through her ghoulish grin.

"Of course." I gave a little giggle to match the laxe's. "Surely, you know the Sorcerers Guild has been charged with protecting the people of Ilara by searching all the goods coming into the city. The Scribes Guild is only assisting at the request of the Lady Sorcerer. My husband's people create lists of inventory. It's the sorcerers who tear through every plank of your ships to be sure nothing dangerous is being brought into the city."

A fresh gust of wind blew in, whisking around the women as each of them drowned in the certainty that there would be no negotiating with anyone in the Sorcerers Tower.

"It's been lovely to spend time with you all, but I'm afraid I must go," I said. "Watching you devour these delightful treats has made me too hungry to wait a moment longer to eat."

"There are plenty more cakes." Mrs. Quintrell offered me her own plate. "Please do stay. I'd love to get to know you better. We've wasted so much time chatting about the appalling state of Ilara, I haven't even asked how you and the head scribe met."

"Your curiosity is kind." I gave Mrs. Quintrell a nod. "But my husband prefers me to only eat food that comes directly from the library kitchens to our room. After the tragic poisonings at our wedding, there's too great a risk in eating anything that could have been made to murder the head scribe's wife."

The horse breeder, who'd tried to pester me into getting the head scribe to push through papers so she could hoard more land, spit her cake out into her hand.

"I hope you enjoy the rest of the treats. The cooks in the library's kitchens are truly talented." I gave them a final sweet smile and swept out of the parlor I'd been trapped in for the last hour.

A scribes' guard shut the door behind me. He kept his gaze stuck over my head as though that might convince me he wasn't waiting to follow me wherever I went.

If the paun would only disappear, I could have one chivving moment to breathe. Or, I could light the parlor on fire and burn all the merchant women who cared more for their precious coin than the starving tilk.

My ankle itched as my knife begged me to stride back into the parlor and slit their laxe throats. It would've been easy, a joy even.

But it wasn't the time. There was too much work to be done.

I strode down the corridor, keeping a demure smile on my lips, careful to look pleasant for all the paun who stopped to stare at me. I pulled my hair over my shoulder, whipping the colorful strands into a tight braid rather than risk my hands straying to my stomach.

I won't let them hurt you, I promised the child. *The Guilds will crumble, and you will live in a world free from their torment.*

Let the paun stare at the beautiful imposter who'd slipped into their ranks. The more they studied the girl who'd stolen the head scribe's heart, the less they'd see the hunter who longed to wade through their blood.

Two scribes' guards waited outside the door of the scribes' shop, or the sad room that had become the scribes' shop after the one out in the city had been so foolishly destroyed.

Both guards nodded to me, making sure the shop door was open before I even asked if I could go in to see the head scribe.

Two rows of desks lined the sides of the room, like someone expected my husband to pace between his scribes, shouting commands as they created the papers necessary to keep Ilara running.

"Ena." Taddy jumped to his feet, giving me a deep bow.

"Hello, Taddy." I winked for the boy.

Red crawled up his cheeks.

The rest of the scribes set down their pens and nodded to me, even that chivving cact of a demon Travers.

"Is there anything we can help you with?" Scribe Tammin stepped out from behind her desk. "Or have you come to see the head scribe?"

I studied the coloring of Tammin's face. The rich bronze hue of her cheeks had returned. She was steady on her feet, too. All traces of the illness she'd suffered after the wedding had faded away.

"I've just come to visit the head scribe." I waved Tammin away as I strode down the row of desks. "I can't make the inks for his vellum if he doesn't tell me what he needs."

"If you'd like, I could—"

I walked into my husband's workroom and shut the door behind me before Tammin could finish whatever her useless offer might have been.

"Ena." Adrial looked up from his worktable. Joy lit his face as though my barging into his space were the most miraculous triumph of all the gods' feats.

I locked the door behind me.

"Are you all right?" Adrial stood, abandoning the image of a flooded valley he'd been working on to worry over his chivving wife. "Do you feel ill? Has something happened?"

"I am going to tear through the library walls with my teeth if I have to be locked in another parlor with chivving laxe women who care more for the coin in their pockets than the fate of those who are suffering in this chivving city." I pushed away from the door to pace beside his worktable. "If I told them they could get their goods into Ilara faster by drowning babes in the Arion Sea, I can promise you the docks would be lined with tiny floating corpses by dawn."

"I'm sorry, Ena." He stepped away from his seat but kept carefully tucked out of the path of my rage. "You don't have to see any more of them. We can have the guards at the gate turn away everyone who tries to visit you."

"But I'm the head scribe's wife. It's my duty to listen to people blather their complaints about the Scribes Guild. Lord Gareth made that quite clear."

"We'll tell him you're not up to it."

"No." I let my hand stray to my belly, to the subtle roundness I couldn't pretend didn't exist. "Anything that might imply I'm ill or tired is too dangerous."

"We could say you're busy making inks for me." He offered me his hand. "Blame your not taking visitors on the vellum."

"It's not worth the risk."

"Then what can I do?" He finally dared to step into my path.

"Nothing." I didn't pull away when he touched my arm.

"Please, Ena. All I want is for you to be happy."

"Take off your robes."

"What?" He backed away from me.

"Take off your robes." I began unlacing my bodice. "If you don't, I'll slice the throat of every coin-hoarding demon who stuffed their face with cakes in that chivving parlor, or climb over the library walls and set fire to their precious goods, or run until I forget the Guilds ever existed."

I dropped my bodice on the floor.

He glanced toward his office door.

I unbuttoned my skirt and let it join my cast-aside bodice. I pulled off my shift.

"Ena, this is my office." Red crept up his cheeks as his gaze flicked from my naked breasts to the door.

"And I am your wife." I took his hands and placed them on my waist. "If you don't offer me a blissful distraction, I will climb over the library walls as soon as night falls." I brushed my lips against his as I unfastened the neck of his robes. "I will search the city for the worst of the fights." His fingers trailed up my sides. "I will stride into battle and let the gods decide my fate."

His thumbs grazed the sides of my breasts.

A shiver trembled up my spine. "Don't reject me, husband."

He kissed me, claiming his longing for me in a way that twisted my wrath into wanting.

Adrial. My Adrial. Mine to have. Mine to protect.

He let his perfect white scribe's robes wrinkle as he threw them aside.

The feel of his skin against mine and heat of his lips on my neck…everything else faded, and it was only us. Locked together in our own world where nothing could reach us.

Even once the flames had settled and we lay on the floor a blissful, sweaty tangle of limbs, it still seemed as though we could build walls strong enough to keep the demons at bay.

I nestled close to him, and he laid his hand on my belly, humming a tune for the child he so desperately longed to hold.

Two broken people clinging to each other, wishing they could hide from the wrath of the gods and the bloody battles to come.

I had seen too much pain to believe we would be spared.

2

KAI

A branch slammed into the side of Kai's face, slicing his cheek. His breath hitched from the sudden spike in pain, breaking the flow of air that had kept him running for so long.

"Above us!" Arto shouted.

Kai looked up at the cliffs to the east just long enough to see the horde of shadows gathering above them. He glanced west, making sure Drew kept pace beside him.

The knife in Drew's hand glinted in the silver moonlight, but the blades he and Kai had been allowed wouldn't do them any chivving good until the beasts were right on top of them.

Kelsea stopped in front of Kai, nocking an arrow and shooting down one of the shadows. She shot a second arrow, striking a second beast.

The shadow tumbled over the edge of the cliff, fading into nothing before it reached the top of the trees.

"What kind of monsters don't even leave corpses?" Drew dodged around a tree to cut behind Kelsea.

That moment Drew was out of Kai's view stole the rest of the precious air from his lungs.

"Keep heading north," Kelsea called to the group, as though

any of them were fool enough to stop and savor the horror surrounding them.

Kai tightened his grip on his knife as he ducked between branches, following the gleam of Isla's red hair shimmering in the moonlight.

The rustling of leaves charged toward them from the east.

Kai pulled out his second knife as he planted himself in front of Drew.

Drew dodged around him, claiming a place by Kai's side.

The rest of their group joined the line—the six fools who'd dared to travel through the southern chivving mountains all standing side by side to face the beasts sent to torment them.

Drew raised his knives, face set, ready to fight creatures he never should have been made to battle.

Kai didn't have time to think of a way to say how sorry he was for every pain Drew had suffered before the shadows burst through the trees and the beasts were upon them.

Whisps of darkness, like tentacles made of demon-forged black, reached for Kai. He sliced through the shadows, ignoring the inhuman cries of pain caused by his blade.

The shadows that attacked them had faces, that much Kai could tell from the way the beast he fought bared its teeth as it slashed its talons for his gut. But the details of its face were somehow beyond Kai's ability to see as he dodged away, raising his knife to block the shadow's next blow.

Perhaps his weeks spent climbing through the southern mountains, plagued by nightmares made real, had somehow ruined his eyesight.

He lunged forward, slicing through another of the beast's tentacles as he stabbed for its gut.

The beast's scream tore at Kai's ears, but his blow hadn't been enough to kill the monster.

He kicked low, ignoring the cold throbbing the contact shocked up his leg as he stabbed the beast's flank.

A sharp pain sliced through his arm. He leapt back, trying to stay within sight of Drew, who fought two shadows at once.

Kai kicked again, hoping the gods would be kind enough to let the strike slow the beast he fought as he drove his knife into the neck of one of the shadows Drew faced.

He wrenched his blade free and spun back around to face his own monster, trying to focus beyond the piercing pain the shadow's screaming drove into his head.

The beast lashed its tentacles at Kai.

Kai sliced through one, but another wrapped around his neck.

Frigid pain gripped his throat, blocking the air he needed to survive.

The beast bared its teeth again, this time seeming to grin, relishing Kai's pain.

One of Kai's knives slipped from his hand. He stared into what should have been the beast's eyes.

There was nothing but barren darkness.

Maybe his ability to see hadn't been stolen by the unending battle with the demons the southern mountains sent to stalk them. Maybe when the mountain had formed these living nightmares, it hadn't bothered to give the beasts eyes. Eyes were not as important to shadows as tentacles and talons.

Kai grabbed the tentacle around his neck and yanked hard, jerking the beast closer to him. He drove his blade into the beast's chin, twisting the knife before the shadow could begin to scream.

The beast dissolved, leaving nothing but the pain in Kai's arm and throat as proof the shadows weren't a horrible trick of his mind.

Kai slipped his toe under the knife he'd dropped, flipping the blade back up into his hand as the next beast's claws slashed at his gut.

The second beast went down more easily than the first.

The third gave Kai a slice on the thigh before he managed to stab the shadow in the chest.

The fourth wrapped a tentacle around Kai's hand hard enough to break his bones. Kai drove his blade into that beast's empty eye.

His knife tumbled from his broken hand as the shadow faded. He didn't bother bending to pick the blade up before facing the fifth beast.

His injured leg trembled beneath him as he lunged toward the shadow.

The shape of the monster pulsed, its form wobbling before fading to nothing.

Isla stood behind the monster, sword in hand. "We need to go," she shouted, her words aimed at Piran though she didn't look his way. "We've made it far enough."

"We can get a little farther," Piran shouted back.

Kai grabbed the knife he'd dropped, tucking it into his belt as he pivoted to stand back-to-back with Drew.

"We're done," Isla said. "We can't win this fight."

"Down!" Drew shouted.

Kai ducked, kicking out at the shadow he fought as Drew's beast swung a tentacle over their heads.

"Go," Kelsea said. "I'll take the back."

"Cliffs to the northeast. We can find a clearing. Move." Arto tore past them, slicing through the shadow Piran fought as he raced into the trees.

Kai kept a step behind Drew as they followed, ignoring the pain shooting through his injured leg as they bolted through the forest.

The twang of Kelsea's bow echoed behind them.

How many arrows does she have left?

Arto reached the base of the cliffs. He stayed twenty feet away from the rock wall as he turned to face the rest of their fleeing party—his sword raised, his feet set apart, ready to stand against whatever monsters followed them.

Piran and Isla dodged behind Arto, each pulling a bag of black rocks from their pocket.

Isla started to the north and Piran to the south, carefully placing the stones, creating an arc against the cliff with Arto at its center.

Drew and Kai reached the arc and took their places beside Arto, waiting for more beasts to attack as Kelsea sprinted out of the trees, a trail of shadows behind her.

Isla knelt at the center of the arc, the final stone in her hand.

One of the beasts reached for Kelsea, raking its claws across her back as she dove into the arc.

Isla dropped the final stone.

A blinding blue light burst into being, slicing through the beast's arm.

Kai fell to his knees as the shadow shrieked in pain and faded to nothing.

"Who's worst?" Piran yanked off his pack, tossing it beside the rock wall.

"Not me," Kai panted. "I can wait."

"Me too." Drew took off his pack and sat beside Kai. "I'll need some help. But I haven't bled too badly."

"It's me." Isla sagged to the ground. "I think it's me this time." She gasped as she tried to shrug free from her pack. Blood seeped from a wound on her left side.

"Let me help." Kai crawled toward her, taking her pack in his good hand, easing the weight off her back.

Drew took her shoulders, helping to lay her on the ground.

"Anyone want to compete for top slot?" Piran knelt beside her.

"It's not a competition." Arto sank down, leaning against the rock wall.

"I'll take that as a no." Piran sat back on his heels, pressing his hand to Isla's forehead.

"Don't take this the wrong way, but we've got to get you

undressed." Kai winked at Isla as he untied the front of her bodice, pulling the laces free with a speed that would have been impressive in a more joyful setting. He lifted her shift, exposing the wound on her side.

The gash was clean. Whatever the beasts had been, their claws hadn't held any poison, but the cut went deep enough only a fool would dare to gamble that nothing necessary for survival had been damaged.

"You're going to be sore tomorrow." Piran closed his eyes as he laid his fingers on either side of the wound.

Isla screamed through gritted teeth as her skin began to knit back together.

The shadows on the other side of the barrier shrieked in unison, as though whatever force had created them was vowing to exact more pain on their party.

"Could you just be chivving quiet?" Drew opened his pack, unloading the wood he'd gathered as they'd walked earlier in the day. Just waiting to be attacked...again.

"They tore through my pack and my quiver," Kelsea said.

"I'll fix them once I've stopped bleeding," Isla said.

"Once you've stopped bleeding and finished eating." Arto winced as he tried to untie his pack with blood-slicked fingers. "The fabric won't get any worse for the waiting."

"I'll need more arrows, too," Kelsea said.

"Might have to wait until our friends leave." Piran rubbed the red skin on Isla's side that had been a life-threatening wound only moments before.

"Then you'd better hope the southern mountains take a rest before sending something else to attack." Kelsea dug a packet of dried meat from her torn bag.

"I gave up hope a few days ago." Drew peeled off his shirt. Red welts wrapped around his right arm, and slashes tore through his shoulder. "I think it was the leaves coming to life and flying off the trees to pluck our eyes out during the middle of the chivving day that really convinced me we're fighting a battle we can't win."

"It's not about winning." Isla tucked her shift back into her skirt. "All we have to do is survive until we reach the northern edge of these cursed southern mountains. Once we get into the eastern mountains, into the Black Bloods' proper home, things will get better."

"And how far from the meeting of the two mountain ranges are we? Do the mountains know exactly where the border is, or will the southern mountains just guess when they should stop tormenting us?" Drew tore a bite from his dried meat.

"Do you really expect any of us to answer when you're just going to ignore what we say and prattle on about the same things the next time we seek shelter?" Kelsea said.

"Could you both stop?" Piran said. "I'm exhausted, and if I'm to mend all your wounds, I'd appreciate a little quiet."

"Better to not take stabs at each other while beasts lurk a few feet away. Let's get the fire started." Arto crawled over to Drew's pile of sticks.

Drew and Arto worked together on building the fire. Kelsea made sure everyone had a bit of something to eat. Piran moved on to mending the wound on Isla's calf.

And Kai had nothing to do but sit and wait for his turn to be healed.

He stared at the beasts lurking just beyond the arc of the shield made by the Black Bloods' magic stones. Shadows prowling through the night, waiting for a chance to attack.

Maybe the beasts would remain even after the sun rose, lingering just outside their magically made safe haven for days. There was no way to know.

But, if whatever magic stalked them through the mountains kept to the cruel routine it seemed to favor, the beasts would vanish eventually, as though the force that had formed them had gotten bored with its toys and tossed them aside.

Their party would be left to run north, covering as much ground as they could before the next attack began.

It's no wonder these mountains are said to drive men mad.

One of the beasts slammed against the stone-made shield. A flash of blue light flared to life.

The barrier will hold, Kai. A mimicry of Piran's voice chirped in his mind. *It's made by the stone magic granted to the Black Bloods, Kai. We're protected by the pact the eastern mountains made with the Black Bloods, Kai. You don't understand the magic that flows through our people—*

"Kai, you're next." Piran wiped Isla's blood from his hands. "I don't like the look of the wound on your leg."

"I don't like the feel of it, either." Kai unfastened his pants with his good hand.

"Is the other hand broken?" Piran asked.

"Feels like it. One of the beasts crushed it."

"Let me." Piran helped Kai pull his pants down. He sighed as he glared at the wound on Kai's thigh. "I've never minded having a talent for healing magic, but I'm not fond of using it on the same people day after day."

"I hate to sound ungrateful, but I'm not fond of being on this end of your magic, either." Kai lay down, fixing his gaze on the moon and preparing for torment.

"It's not right," Isla said.

White-hot pain pinched in Kai's leg. He tucked his tongue between his teeth, forbidding himself to scream.

"What's not?" Drew pressed his hand to Kai's shoulder.

"The number of times I've run through these mountains," Isla said, "ferried sorci children away from the Sorcerers Guild through these mountains, I've never been attacked like this."

"Perhaps the mountains require a greater cost of travel from those who seek to change the world," Arto said.

The pain in Kai's leg shifted, fading to a wrenching pounding that twisted his gut.

"Maybe it's you," Kelsea said.

"I haven't been using my magic outside the stone barrier," Isla said. "I've been torn through the gut while not using my magic to fight the beasts that hunt us. I understand that magic can draw the attention of the creatures—"

"Like I said, your fault," Kelsea cut across.

"You're helping no one," Arto said.

"I'm not saying Isla's secretly using magic to make sure the southern mountains continue to demand we fight our way out of their clutches," Kelsea said. "But if there is any beacon in our party continually drawing the wrath of the mountains to us, it's her."

"I've crossed through the mountains before and been fine," Isla said. "Do not blame your pain on me."

Piran took Kai's hand. "Deep breath."

Kai inhaled, shifting his tongue out from between his teeth as his bones cracked back into place. "Chivving cact of a demon's nightmarish spawn from the chivving depths—"

"I'm not blaming. I'm trying to figure out what we have to do to get out of these mountains alive," Kelsea said. "Our mission is in Ilara. Every day we spend fighting our way through the mountains is a day we're not fighting the Guilds."

"Don't you think I know that?" Isla said.

"Arm next," Piran said.

Kai flexed his newly healed hand, testing the bones before pulling up his pants.

"I'm doing everything I can to help us reach the eastern mountains," Isla said. "I would fight every shadow out there on my own if it would get us to Ilara faster."

Kai sat up to unbutton his shirt.

Isla and Kelsea knelt on opposite sides of the fire, glaring at each other.

"You were never supposed to come to Ilara," Kelsea whispered. "If we fail in our mission because of you—"

"Then I suppose it's a good thing it's not Isla's fault." Kai eased his arm out of his shirt.

"And how would an Ilbrean know?" Kelsea shifted her glare to Kai.

"How about a trade? You tell me what you're going to Ilara to do, and I'll tell you how a Guilded sailor knows so much about magic." Kai offered a charming smile.

"If you know how to stop this and—" Kelsea began.

"Enough," Arto said. "Let Piran work. Most of us are still bleeding."

Kai smiled as Piran mended the rest of his wounds, keeping his gaze fixed on Kelsea as he waited for her to punch him.

But the pattern stayed the same.

Kelsea didn't attack him.

Piran healed everyone's wounds.

Arto stared north, as though waiting for the eastern mountains to welcome him home.

Isla stared at her hands, as though fighting to keep her magic contained.

Drew stayed right beside Kai in their magic stone-made haven, as though waiting for a moment to speak they both knew wouldn't come.

And Kai watched them all, trying to figure out what the Brien had planned in Ilara and why they had decided to help two Ilbrean sailors survive the terrible journey home.

3

MARA

The knot in the rope dug into Mara's back as she dragged herself deeper into the ice. Easing her ribs over a sharp ridge, she inched forward, carefully keeping the flame on her glove tipped up so it wouldn't sputter out.

"Remind me to tell Ronya that having my criolas back would make our work much easier," Mara shouted into the shadows behind her.

"Do you think she'll listen the seventeenth time you tell her?"

Mara could hear the teasing in Tham's voice even though a stranger would have thought it a serious question.

"It could take telling her the exact same thing thirty times. But we won't reach the thirtieth if I don't ask the seventeenth." Mara twisted her hips, trying to minimize the bruising the ice was sure to leave on her side.

She reached her light as far forward as she could. The tunnel narrowed in front of her then curved to the left. If she lay on her side, she might be able to make it just a bit farther.

"Mara?" Tham called.

"I'm fine." She dug the metal spikes attached to the toes of her boots into the tunnel wall and inched forward.

"If she gets stuck in there, how am I supposed to get her out?" Andric said.

"Carefully," Tham said.

Mara laughed, paying for expanding her ribs with a new bruise on her right breast.

She twisted to lie on her right side, accepting it would be entirely covered in scratches and welts as she wriggled her way through the narrow passage.

"Women don't belong in the Map Makers Guild, Mara Landil," she whispered to herself. "Women shouldn't spend their time exploring, Mara Landil." The flame on her right hand wavered as she gripped a ridge to pull herself forward. The ice dug into her palms, threatening to slice through her leather gloves. "I'd like to see a single man in the Map Makers Guild fit through this godsforsaken tunnel."

Bending her knees the scant amount the passage allowed, she shoved herself forward.

The tunnel narrowed again as it twisted off to the left at a steeper angle than Mara had expected.

"Lovely." Mara wriggled forward.

The ice that had tried to cut through her gloves dug into her waist. She gritted her teeth against the ache as the ridge rammed into her hipbone.

Reaching high overhead, she grabbed the edge of the passage's curve, pulling herself forward until the tunnel seemed ready to trap her. She took a deep breath. Her ribs touched passage walls all the way around.

"And this is as far as we go." A familiar longing pulled at her heart as she stared at the twist in the ice she couldn't squeeze past.

If she could just see what hid around that corner.

It could be nothing but more dreadful tunnels of ice. It could be a path that led out of Isfol. It could be something wonderful she'd yet to imagine.

She tipped her hand, pressing the light on the back of her glove to the ice until the flame sputtered out.

Fear sent her heart punching into her throat as darkness surrounded her.

But not total darkness.

Just around the corner, the faintest glimmer of blue begged her to keep venturing onward.

"You are a seductive beast, but I'd rather not be stuck down here forever." Mara opened the pocket she'd had sewn into the wrist of her coat and pulled out her little mirror.

Reaching as far as she could, she angled the mirror to see around the curve.

A gentle blue sparkled in the ice. Not as an ambient glow, but as individual points of light.

"Thank you, Saint Aximander." Mara watched the lights shift, like worms burrowing through the ice.

She allowed herself a full minute to enjoy the bounty that crawling through the tunnel had bought before tucking the mirror into the pocket on her wrist and beginning the unpleasant process of easing herself backward—carefully digging her toes into the ice and bending her knees to inch back while using her arms to negotiate the sharpest sections of the jagged passage.

"Mara?" Tham called.

"I'm coming out." Ice banged into Mara's elbow. She bit her lips together, swallowing the curses she longed to spit, unwilling to frighten Tham by making any sound of pain. "It gets too narrow. I can't go any farther."

"Did you find anything?" Andric shouted.

"Ice," Mara said. "I found lots of ice."

She twisted onto her stomach, working her hips through a tight squeeze, then rotated onto her side again, trying to avoid the ridges she'd met on her way down the tunnel.

A sharp spear of ice jammed against her stomach, dragging her coat up and slicing into her side. Mara gasped through gritted teeth, trying to lift her weight off the ice as it threatened to cut deeper than skin. She pressed her back to the top of the passage, choosing bruises on her spine over more dire wounds.

"I knew crawling into this darkness was a braidic waste of time," Andric said. "The ice will tell us when it wants us to find the ice worms. The miners will begin the harvest when the path appears. We live in a mountain that doesn't like to be hurried."

"Waiting is a wonderful way to waste time." Mara blinked away the heat pooling in her eyes and slid herself past the ice that had tried to flay her. "Especially since there are ice worms down this passage."

"You said you only found ice," Andric said.

"I never said *only*." Mara's shoulders relaxed as the tunnel widened enough for her to press herself up onto her hands and knees. A wave of pain shot through her side, clenching around her lungs.

"You couldn't just say you'd found something worth shoving ourselves into these awful holes?" Andric said.

"Not right away." Mara crawled backward.

Warm light began flickering on the walls.

"Andric, you're so delightful when you're agitated, I didn't want to deny you the opportunity to shine," Mara said.

"I'm here." Tham placed his hand on the back of Mara's ankle.

A bliss utterly contrary to the circumstances eased Mara's pain.

Tham kept his hand on her, protecting her head from the sloped edge where the tunnel met the chamber in the ice where he and Andric waited.

As soon as her head was free, Mara looked to Tham, not seeking comfort, only wanting to see the most beautiful face the gods had ever created.

"What happened?" Tham took her face in his hands.

"What?" Mara pressed her palm to his chest, panic flying through her at the fear in his eyes.

"You have blood on your face." Tham ran his fingers over her cheeks, then moved on to checking her hands.

"It's on her clothes, too." Andric untied the rope around her hips.

"I got caught on some ice." Mara looked down at her side. The ice hadn't managed to cut through her coat, but blood stained her hip. "I'm sure I'm fine."

"That's quite a bit of blood for someone who's fine." Andric reached for Mara.

Tham blocked Andric's hands, shifting to kneel between him and Mara before lifting the bottom of her coat.

A gash eight inches long sliced from her hip to her ribs.

"That's a bit worse than I thought." Mara swallowed the sour that rose in her throat at the sight of so much of her own blood leaking from a wound.

"We need to get you to a healer," Tham said.

"We should bandage it now," Andric said.

"With what?" Tham said.

"I'm fine." Mara got to her feet, grateful for her less than significant height as even she had to hunch to keep from banging her head on the chamber's ceiling.

Her legs were grateful for being able to walk instead of crawl. The rest of her body throbbed its protest at being asked to do anything at all.

"She's losing blood," Andric said.

"Do you have a clean bandage?" The crunch of Tham's boots stayed right behind Mara.

"A torn-up shirt is better than nothing," Andric said.

"Not when a bandage is so close by," Tham said.

Mara dropped back onto her hands and knees, using the metal spikes on the toes of her boots to help her crawl up the tunnel that led to the surface.

The blue light of Isfol sparkled above, the unchanging gleam both a promise of comfort and the bitter proof that her trip into the ice hadn't brought her any closer to escape.

Hands reached down, grabbing her wrists and lifting her to the surface.

Mara stifled a whimper of pain as her guards set her on the street beside the hole she'd been fool enough to climb into.

"She needs bandages and a healer," Tham called.

"I'll go," one of the newer guards—Bran, Brin, maybe his name was Braiden—ran off through an alley, heading toward the healers' hall.

"It's not that bad." Mara pulled off her gloves and tucked them into her pocket. "All my insides are firmly in place. I just need a few stitches."

The guards reached back into the hole, dragging Tham up onto the street.

"Let me see." Lynn knelt beside Mara and pulled off her pack.

"Do you actually have bandages?" Mara lay on her side.

"Some guards carry more than wine, weapons, and rope." Lynn winked.

"Is a healer coming?" Andric asked as the guards pulled him from the hole.

"Brin's gone to the healers' hall," one of the guards said.

"I can walk to the healers' hall," Mara said. "There's no point in making a healer come here for a little cut."

Lynn tsked a laugh as she pressed a cloth to Mara's side.

Mara gasped as the pain from the wound doubled. "I'm not saying I don't need stitches. I'd just rather not have a needle shoved through my skin in the middle of the street."

As though Mara's plea had lured them to her, a team of barking sled dogs ran up the street, heading right for the hole.

"This way's closed," a guard called.

"Whoa!" the musher shouted over his dogs' gleeful racket. "Sorry, didn't know!"

"Sit up." Lynn pulled a roll of bandages from her bag.

Mara sat, trying to ignore the way the road swayed.

"Head back up and cut around," the guard said. "Not safe for anyone to pass."

"Hold her coat up, Tham," Lynn said.

Tham raised Mara's coat, keeping it just high enough for Lynn to wrap Mara's wound.

"Can you still breathe?" Lynn asked.

"Sure." Mara took a deep breath, sending pain shooting through her side and gray drifting through her vision.

"I'll carry you to the healers' hall." Tham carefully lowered Mara's coat.

"You don't have to. I can—"

Tham scooped her into his arms.

"Fine." She kissed the side of his neck. "But only because it's you doing the carrying."

She relaxed in his arms as he carried her through the streets of Isfol, not asking for permission or directions from the flock of guards that trotted along in their wake.

This was what their life had become. Freedom to roam the city they'd been forced to make their home. Their every move tracked by guards who reported to Princess Ronya of Isfol, the demon who kept them trapped in a city of perfect blue ice.

"Someone should go straight to the palace to tell Ronya about the ice worms," Mara said. "If the tunnel keeps growing at the same rate, they might be able to get a few miners in as soon as tomorrow."

"She'll want a report from you," Andric said. "How tightly were the worms packed? How deep in the ice were they moving?"

"She'll give a report after she's seen a healer," Tham said.

"Her Highness is not known for her patience," Andric said. "Best to give her something right away."

"Her Highness has made it clear Mara's safety is a priority," Tham said.

Mara reached up, touching Tham's cheek, trailing her fingers across his smooth chin, which a servant had shaved only that morning.

The glimmer of a smile that should have shone in his eyes didn't appear.

He's worried about me.

I must be worse off than I think.

She tried to reason past the pain in her side.

Her body ached from being battered as she'd dragged herself through the tunnel, but that was to be expected. Her head ached, too, but listening to Andric and Tham trying not to shout at each other always did that. Her fingers were cold. Her fingers and her toes had all gone cold.

Mara tensed, swallowing the odd panic that surged into her throat. She hadn't been cold. Not for weeks.

Ronya had dosed her and Tham with the ice worms' tonic, the very brew that kept the Isfolians from freezing to death inside their city of ice.

If the tonic had stopped working. If she'd become susceptible to the cold…

You've lost blood, Mara, Adrial said. *Too much blood. You need a healer.*

"Oh, that might be it." Mara tried to see the side of her coat.

"What might be it?" Tham looked down at her. The most precious wrinkle had formed between his eyebrows, the one that only seemed to appear when he was worried about her.

"Nothing." She gave up trying to see how much blood she'd lost.

Tham tightened his hold on her, picking up his pace as though she'd confessed how oddly cold she'd gotten.

As they reached the healers' hall, two guards ran in front of them, opening the doors before Tham had climbed the steps.

"We're going to need some help," Andric called.

Two matrons with tight buns and white robes bustled down the hall.

"I'm really fine," Mara said.

"She's got a gash on her side," Andric said.

"Fifth door on the right." The older of the women waved Tham down the corridor lined with identical doors. "I'll be right in to see to her."

"Thank you." Tham hurried down the hall.

Andric darted in front of him, opening the door and stepping inside the room the healers had assigned Mara.

A bed and a chair were the only things in the space not made of ice.

Tham set Mara down on the bed.

She cringed, wondering who she should apologize to for getting blood all over the clean, white sheets.

"Leave." Tham knelt in front of Mara and began unbuttoning her coat.

"It is my duty to ensure both of you are protected at all times," Andric said. "I need to stay with Mara while she's cared for."

"I'm going to take her shirt off," Tham said. "Leave."

Mara watched Andric juggle the choices Tham had left him, distracting herself from what seemed an inordinate amount of pain caused by Tham helping her out of her coat.

First, Andric's chin tensed, as though he were preparing to shout at Tham. Then he pursed his lips, as though wondering what to shout at Tham that wouldn't end with Tham punching him, causing a fight that would delay the matrons' work. Finally, he furrowed his brow, as though realizing Ronya would side with Tham in protecting Mara's modesty.

"I'll be right outside." Andric went out into the hall and shut the door behind him.

"He's a funny one." Mara kept her voice light as Tham peeled her shirt over her head. The entire right side of the fabric had been coated in blood. More seeped through the bandage Lynn had wrapped around her. "It really didn't feel *that* bad when it happened."

Tham tossed her shirt onto her blood-stained coat. He pulled off her boots.

The cold of the floor stung her feet.

The door to the hall opened.

Mara covered her bare breasts.

The younger matron pushed in a metal cart with curved gliders on the bottom.

"You have done a bit of damage then." She frowned as she looked at the bandage on Mara's side. "You've lost more blood than I'd like, but we'll get the wound closed and go from there."

"Thank you," Mara said.

The other matron burst into the room, not giving Mara time to cover her breasts again. She set a basket of bandages beside the bed. "We've got her from here. You can go." She shooed Tham toward the door.

"He should stay." Mara grabbed Tham's hand. "I want him to stay."

"You won't have any idea if he's here or not." The first matron held a cup out to Mara. "We find it easiest to tend to flesh wounds when the injured is sedated."

"I still want him here." Mara took the cup while keeping her hold on Tham with her other hand.

"He can wait in the hall until the blood's cleaned up." The second matron opened the door, holding it wide as she waited for Tham to leave.

Andric stood in the hall directly opposite Mara's door. His cheeks pinked as he plastered his gaze to the ceiling.

Tham stepped in front of Mara, blocking the view of anyone else who might pass by.

"The matter is not up for discussion," the first matron said. "Out. Now."

Tham kissed Mara, squeezing her hand before backing out of reach. He grabbed the door from the matron, snapping it shut behind him as soon as he was in the hall.

"Drink up so we can get to work," the first matron said.

"You should have let him stay," Mara said.

"Drink. Now," the second matron said. "The sooner you're out, the sooner we can stop the bleeding."

"Fine." Mara downed the bitter, milky brew. "Will you make the cold stop, too? Adrial thinks I lost too much blood."

She fell asleep before she could hear their reply.

4

THAM

Tham kept his back to Mara's door, guarding her against any enemy though he didn't have a weapon.

He clenched his fists, willing the strength of his own body to feel like enough to defend her.

They're healers. You brought her here so they could help her.

"She'll be fine," Andric said. "I've seen the matrons bring back a man who had some of his guts spilling out. Mara's strong. They'll have her up in no time."

He should have found a way to go into that tunnel instead of her. It should be him bleeding and wounded.

You wouldn't have fit. She'll say it was worth the pain.

They needed to explore the breaks in the ice. They needed to find the paths to the ice worms before the tunnels were wide enough for the miners to brave.

Finding the ice worms early gave the miners more time to harvest the base of the tonic that protected the people of Isfol from the deadly cold.

A scream carried down the hall. Not one of pain, but of sickening fear.

It wasn't her. She's safe.

Finding the paths to the ice worms pleased Ronya. Which allowed him and Mara more freedom. Freedom they needed to try and find a way to break free.

The scream came again.

There was no sound from inside Mara's room.

The silence sank leaden dread into Tham's chest.

Quiet is more terrifying than screams.

It was a cut. An Ilbrean healer could have helped her.

She bled too much.

"She'll have to stop climbing down into the ice for a while." Andric leaned against the wall. "The matrons will want her to rest."

The stickiness of her blood coated Tham's hands. He should clean them, but that would mean abandoning her door.

"I'd say we could send someone else down into any cracks that appear. But if Mara managed to get hurt, whatever braidic fool dared to try venturing into the darkness would probably get stuck and be taken by the ice." Andric paused, as though assuming Tham would speak. "We'll have to wait for Mara to heal. She's invaluable to Isfol."

They could freeze. Every person in Isfol could freeze if it meant keeping Mara safe.

Mara had gone into that tunnel to find ice worms to protect the Isfolians. Their captors.

But there were children in the city. Innocent babes. Mara wouldn't want the children of their enemies to suffer while she had the ability to help.

Her skills as a map maker held too much value.

Andric was right. If Mara couldn't make it through a tunnel safely, no one in Isfol had a godsforsaken chance.

Sobbing came from the far end of the hall.

"I'll see if I can have her moved back to her room in the palace while she recovers." Andric looked toward the sound. "I can't see why they'd need to keep her here. I don't want Mara to suffer through this grim place."

"One of our party is still here." Tham pointed just down the hall to the door of Elver's cage. "Your healers haven't been able to help him."

"The one who went ice mad?" Andric walked toward Elver's door. "Pity that soul. Haven't heard of many who were trapped in the ice and ever recovered. I can't imagine someone from the south managing it. He should have stayed clear of the ice."

"He was dragged into it," Tham said. "By your people."

"The guards in the ice do what's necessary to protect Isfol. You can't blame them for any damage done." Andric laid his hand on the doorknob.

"Don't." Tham stepped toward him.

"I've been ordered to protect Mara. I'm doing what's necessary." He opened the door to Elver's room. "You, Ilbrean."

"No. No. No. No. No!" The strangled shout came from inside Elver's room.

"Leave him alone." Tham bolted down the hall, shoving Andric away from the door.

"No. No. No. No. No!" Elver lay curled in the corner of the room, his fingers balled up by his scalp as though he wanted to tear out his hair. But someone had cut his hair and beard too short for him to grasp. "No. No. No!"

"I'm so sorry, friend," Tham whispered under Elver's screams.

Elver looked up, meeting Tham's gaze. "You're here." His fingers relaxed. "I thought she'd already gotten you, dragged you far away."

"No, I'm here." Tham dared to step into Elver's room. "Mara and I are both here."

"You found her. That's good." The chain linking Elver's ankle to the wall clanked as he rolled over and sat up. "I thought the blue said you were both gone. Taken by blood and Death. I must not have understood."

"Elle's here." Tham knelt. "Kegan, too."

"No. No, that's a lie. You're a lie. We went into the blue, the light flashed. You went into the blue, too. Then the stories start. Death is coming. Death is the kinder fate. Teeth and claws… they'll tear everyone apart. I was sure you'd been surrounded by blood. Death was there. He waved at me."

"We're all alive, Elver. We made it through the ice. I promise. Kegan is an advisor to Princess Ronya. Mara and I—"

"You're a chivving slitch of a fool!" Elver tore at his too-short hair. "The teeth are waiting. Hiding and waiting. We'll drown in a sea of blood."

Elver threw himself forward, reaching for Tham's throat.

Tham leapt to his feet, dodging out of Elver's reach.

Elver dove for Tham again. The chain around his ankle held him back and he fell face first to the ground. "There is no other story, Tham. Death will ride! She will ride!"

"Keep trying to heal, friend." Tham backed out of the room and closed the door behind him, his guilt at abandoning Elver tempered by Elver having remembered his name.

He let go of the doorknob, leaving a smear of Mara's blood behind. He used the bottom of his shirt to wipe the red away before turning back to Mara's room.

Andric had planted himself in front of her door. "The ice is a cruel foe to battle, but don't worry, the matrons will be able to do far more for Mara than they could for your friend."

"You can guard her door from across the hall. Move."

"And trust Mara's safety to someone who abandons her to visit old friends?" Andric grinned. "I'm the guard assigned to protect Mara Landil by Princess Ronya. It's my duty to protect Mara. If you're bored, you can scurry back to the palace."

"I'm not leaving." Tham stood opposite Andric, tucking his

hands behind his back, giving the getch the perfect chance to punch him in the chin. "I'll be here when Mara wakes up."

"I'm sure your standing uselessly in the hall will be a great comfort to her. Mara does seem fond of her pets."

5

ADRIAL

The doors had been shut tight, barring any chance of eavesdroppers listening in on the business of the Guilds Council. The bright afternoon sun poured through the high windows and skylight above the round table, striking the golden star inlaid in the perfectly polished wood, sending glistening light dancing around the room as though Dudia himself shone upon the gathered Guild Lords, declaring the presence of the saints watching over the leaders of Ilbrea.

"The state of the city can no longer be tolerated." Lady Byrd laced her fingers together, as though barely restraining herself. "The Healers Guild should not be barricaded within its own walls. Twelve soldiers had to escort my carriage to the palace for this meeting. Only Saint Galen knows what I will find when I return to our hall."

"You forget the sorcerers who escorted you to this meeting," Lady Gwell said. "And the sorcerers who will see you tucked safely back into the refuge to which you so desperately cling."

It was not Dudia or any of the saints that bathed the inlaid golden star in a magnificent light. An architect had created the room, and a craftsman had built the table. The whole brilliant display had been created by mortals to make the Guild leaders who sat on the council feel as though they were somehow larger than the people whose fates they controlled.

"We treat more and more soldiers every day." Lady Byrd leaned forward. "We had eleven merchants brought in during the night. Some of those wounded had horrible burns. And the mob outside our gates still tried to keep them out."

"If I send my soldiers against the mob—" Lord Kearney began.

"There will only be more common folk gathered to protest that violence the next night." Lord Karron looked to the King.

Adrial joined the other five heirs, leaning around the Guild Lords they would one day replace to get a better view of King Brannon's face.

The King furrowed his brow as he stared at the glistening seven-pointed star. "The violence in the city cannot be allowed to continue. It is tearing Ilara apart and putting the good people of the Guilds in danger."

"Then let us do more than defend the strongholds of each Guild," Lord Kearney said. "We can block the rotta from breaching the healers' gates as long as you like. But while we allow the rotta to gather—"

"My wedding will take place in a month." The King spoke over Lord Kearney. "I don't care what it takes. I will marry Lady Allora. I will not allow the ceremony to be interrupted again."

"It will not be interrupted," Lady Gwell said. "Now that the protection of the ceremony and royal family has been handed to the Sorcerers Guild, I can assure you that you, your bride, and your sister are safe."

"Do you dare to imply the attack on the cathedral was the fault of the Soldiers Guild?" Lord Kearney pounded his fist on the table.

"Of course not," Lady Gwell said, the faintest trace of a smile curling her lips. "The collapse of the cathedral's dome was not the fault of the Soldiers Guild, only an excellent example of their failings."

"And what of the state of Ilara!" Lord Kearney stood.

"Your bickering does nothing to protect the healers." Lady Byrd smacked her palms on the table.

"We should move on from this nonsense. We need to talk about the disaster at the docks," Lord Nevon shouted over them.

Lady Gwell's smile broadened into a grin.

Adrial shut his eyes for a heartbeat.

Saint Alwyn, give me wisdom.

"If I may." Adrial stood, not allowing himself to limp as he stepped closer to the table.

"The docks are surrounded by angry merchants and filled with piles of goods the Sorcerers Guild wants us to store in warehouses that don't exist. You, Lady Sorcerer"—Lord Nevon dared to point at Lady Gwell—"are bringing the anger of the common folk down on the Sailors Guild."

"Silence." Lady Gwell waved a hand.

A tiny pinch tightened the front of Adrial's throat as the room went deathly quiet.

Lady Byrd gagged. Lord Kearney reached for the blade at his hip.

Only King Brannon seemed unbothered by whatever spell the Lady Sorcerer had cast over the council.

Adrial rapped his knuckles against the table. Gently, as though he were tapping on the door of someone he didn't want to risk waking.

Lady Gwell looked to him.

Adrial knocked on the table again.

"It is not common for the second of a Guild Lord to speak at a meeting of the Guilds Council," Lady Gwell said.

Adrial knocked a third time.

"It would be unwise to waste our time when there is so much

tribulation in our city. I advise caution." Lady Gwell waved her hand again.

The pinching released from the front of Adrial's throat.

He swallowed, making sure he really had been freed from her spell, before trying to talk.

"Thank you for allowing me to speak, Lady Gwell." Adrial bowed to her. "It is my belief that all the measures for restoring peace that have been discussed in this meeting would cause nothing but further unnecessary bloodshed."

"So we should let chaos reign?" King Brannon spoke as though Lady Gwell's spell had never affected him.

"The chaos must end, Your Majesty." Adrial bowed to the King. "But I firmly believe the common people on the streets do not crave violence for the sake of violence. They are rioting because they are afraid. They've grown desperate.

"With the searches of everything coming in at the gates and the docks, the flow of goods has slowed to the point that there isn't enough food entering Ilara to feed all the people in the city. The Guilded are fed, the merchants buy the rest of the food at exorbitant prices, and there is nothing left for the common folk. They're rioting because they're hungry. They're mobbing the gates of the healers' compound because their children are ill, and they are desperate for help."

"I cannot allow their desperation to place members of the Guilds in danger," King Brannon said. "We will continue to search all goods entering the city."

"A wise precaution in these troubled times," Adrial said. "But if we were to create a different registry for wagons and ships carrying only food, those searches could be given priority. We could get more food into the city and into the bellies of those hungry and desperate people."

The King looked to Lady Gwell.

"We could give priority to those bringing food into the city," Lady Gwell said. "But the searches will remain thorough until we find the villains behind the attacks, no matter how much it delays goods entering Ilara. I lost my second to these butchers. I will not allow Sorcerer Clery's death to go unavenged. If all the rotta in Ilara have to starve, so be it."

"The attack that killed Sorcerer Clery and Lady Green happened at my wedding." A new pinching born of fear tightened Adrial's throat. "I could've lost my wife that night. I will be happy to see the murderer's head on a pike in the cathedral square. But allowing the common folk in Ilara to starve for the actions of a few murderous demons will only fuel the hatred of those who are suffering. The more the people loathe us, the more dangerous the city will become for every member of the Guilds.

"We need to feed the common folk. Have the sorcerers create a safe place for the healers to treat the common folk. If we prove to the people that the Guilds care, that we are fighting for not only our safety but theirs, we could truly begin restoring Ilara to what it should be."

Lady Byrd banged on the table.

Lady Gwell ignored her, keeping her gaze fixed on Adrial. "Ah, the hope and promise that lives in the hearts of the young and naïve. To believe food and bandages will cure the city."

"That won't be all it takes," Adrial said, "but if we remove the desperation, every other step we take to restore the city will be more productive. And that is not a thought born of naivety, Lady Gwell. I spent the beginning of my life on Ian Ayres. I know what it is to be hungry and hopeless. We can spare the common folk that pain."

Lady Byrd stood and slammed her palms on the table.

"History will remember what we did during this moment of bloody trials," Adrial said. "Let us at least ensure that the scribes who chronicle the riots in Ilara can say the Guilds did everything within their power to keep from having to use swords against their own people."

"I agree," King Brannon said. "Move more food into the city, make sure its distribution reaches the poorer parts of Ilara. Lady Gwell, I trust you will find a way to safely allow Lady Byrd's healers to treat ailing common folk."

"Of course, Your Majesty." Lady Gwell bowed. "It is the duty of the Sorcerers Guild to protect Ilbrea."

Lady Byrd pounded her palms on the table again and again, glaring at the Lady Sorcerer in a way few would have dared.

"The King has spoken. Do you wish to argue?" Lady Gwell waved a hand.

Lady Byrd cleared her throat. "It is not for the Lady Sorcerer to decide what is safe for my healers. We will not endanger ourselves to treat the very people who threaten us."

"The healers will hide behind their walls while the rest of us work." Lord Nevon stood. "I have sorcerers, soldiers, and angry merchants swarming my docks. And that's aside from the common folk raiding the warehouses. What of the safety of my sailors? Should we refuse to do our work like the healers?"

"Your ships swarm with rotta at the best of times," Lady Byrd said. "Do not forget the filth you allow to work alongside your Guilded sailors."

Lord Gareth took Adrial's hand, guiding him away from the table and back to his seat as Lord Kearney and Lord Karron joined the fray.

Adrial sat, staring at the star on the table, waiting for the fighting to be done so the council might have a hope of moving forward.

Though he felt utterly and depressingly sure of how the rest of the meeting would go.

They would talk of the steps that had been taken to find the villain who'd destroyed the cathedral. There would still have been no trace of the culprit found.

They would discuss the murderer who'd slipped poison into his wedding. There would still be no sign of how that had been accomplished either, despite the searches of the library's kitchens and the questioning of all the scribes' servants.

They'd spent more than a month locked in a desperate fight to find whoever had killed so many members of the Guilds, and they were still no closer than the day of the King's failed wedding to Allora.

But there had to be something. Some clue all of them had missed. Some monster from Cade's rebellion lurking in the shadows.

Unless the rumors were true and a killer who was more myth than man had come to stalk the streets of Ilara. But if the Demon's Torch—

"Enough." The King stood.

The council fell silent just as quickly as when Lady Gwell had used her magic against them.

"We have had these arguments again and again." The King looked to each of his council members. "We are no closer to finding the murderers who have tormented the Guilds or to restoring peace in Ilara. We will ensure the innocent among the common folk are fed and cared for. The head scribe is right. I will not allow the histories to name me as the King who hid in his palace while children starved in the capital city. But food and bandages won't be enough to ensure the safety of my bride at our wedding. I refuse to waste any more time waiting for progress to be made. Lady Gwell."

Lady Gwell stood, leaving her place at the table to stand beside the King.

"I will not sit and listen to this council bicker any longer," King Brannon said. "I want Ilara back in order. I want my kingdom back in order. I want anyone who has threatened the safety of my future Queen executed."

"Of course, Your Majesty." Lady Gwell bowed. "Given the authority, the Sorcerers Guild would gladly put the chaos to right."

"I leave the council in your care." King Brannon's gaze shifted to the star set in the center of the table. "This is Ilbrea, a country Dudia himself created. You will restore tranquility to our great land. Do whatever it takes." He strode toward the door, abandoning his council to the clutches of the Lady Sorcerer.

A jagged stone sank in Adrial's stomach as a fear he didn't quite have a name for sent a chill raking through his veins.

The doors closed behind the King with a thud that echoed around the room.

"Let us begin." Lady Gwell sat in the King's seat at the apex of the seven-pointed star. "You will soon find the Sorcerers Guild has little mercy for those who do not contribute to Ilbrea's goals."

6

____

NIKO

"Where is my daughter?" Light poured through the windows behind the Brien Elder's throne.

The sun warmed Niko's hands. The first proper warmth he'd had since the ground had swallowed him, trapping him in the darkness.

"Do not test my patience, Ilbrean," the Elder said. "You will tell me where my daughter is."

"Daughter?" Niko pulled his gaze from the sunlight gleaming on the white stone of the throne room, trying to focus on the Elder's face.

The Elder wasn't that old. Younger than Lord Karron at least. Her blond hair had been perfectly pinned back in braids and twists more elaborate than any crown. Her purple gown was made of fine fabric.

"The trueborn that was lost. My child," the Elder said. "Where is she?"

"I don't know." Niko tried to see the details of the Elder's face.

Eyes, nose, mouth. All the pieces were there, but blurry. Lacking distinction, as though her face wasn't quite sure what it should be.

"Tell me where they took her."

"I don't know." Niko crawled toward the Elder. The sunlight shifted, pulling away, letting only his fingertips graze its warmth. "I didn't know about trueborns or the Brien Clan until after the ground swallowed me. I've never met your daughter. I don't know what happened to her."

"Liar." The Elder leaned forward. Her face darkened—shifting, blurring, making two faces where there should have been one.

Niko swallowed the sick surging up from his stomach as the room twisted. His legs slipped out from under him as the walls buckled.

"You have to ask the Sorcerers Guild." Niko clawed at the white stone floor, fighting to drag himself into the light. "If anyone knows where your daughter is, it's the sorcerers."

The sunlight vanished. The shadows swirled, winding up the Elder's body, shrouding her face.

"Liar!" The Elder's whisper shattered the throne room.

Stone blasted into Niko's chest, hurling him backward.

He landed in a still-forming chair.

The stone of his seat curled up, coiling around him, locking him in place.

"How did you find your way into the mountain?" The Elder stood in front of him, her silhouette darkening as the sunlight behind her brightened.

"Rocks." Niko leaned to the side, trying to see past the Elder, desperate for another glimpse of the sun. "A rock cairn. There was writing inside. It wasn't a language I know. The words glowed. It was some kind of magic. Amec touched the writing and the ground swallowed us."

The bindings around Niko's ribs tightened.

"I didn't place the magic in the cairn." Niko gasped in a breath as his lungs begged for room to expand. "I don't know who created the entrance to the darkness below the mountain.

Whoever that villain is, I wish them nothing but pain and death."

"If I had them here, they would be bound beside you," the Elder said. "They would share in your fate."

One of Niko's ribs broke with a sharp crack. His scream ripped through the center of the throne room, tearing the walls away as though his pain held the power to crumble stone.

His chair dissolved. He landed on his knees in front of the Elder's throne.

"Tell me where she is and all of this will end," the Elder said.

"I don't know where your daughter is." Niko coughed. A fine spray of blood flew from his mouth. The red stained the perfect, white floor. "Let me go, and I will do whatever I can to help you find her. I know the Head Scribe of Ilara. I can ask him for help. I'll search for any trace of her in the Soldiers Guild's reports. I'll spend the rest of my life searching for your daughter. I swear it. Please let me go."

The Elder tipped her head.

Pain whipped across Niko's back.

"The Map Makers Guild came into the eastern mountains." The Elder gripped the arms of her throne. "They would not have risked venturing into our mountains without good reason. They have come because of my daughter."

"No, they haven't." Niko looked up into the Elder's face.

The blur had gotten worse. Not two faces that fit together any longer. Instead, a vicious darkness where her face should have been.

The darkness called to him, luring him in. If he let his mind drift into that void, he might finally find peace.

"We…" Niko pressed his palms to the ground as the edges of his vision faded. "We were trying to find a path through the mountains to Wyrain. The King wants a new trade route. He ordered a road. That's all."

"The Black Bloods don't recognize your King's orders," the Elder said.

Pain slammed into Niko's chin, cracking his teeth together as he flew up.

The ceiling morphed above him, swallowing itself then growing from the edges back to the center, forming a new ceiling to block out the horror of the barren blackness beyond.

Niko crashed back to the ground, landing on his spine, knocking all the air from his lungs.

The stone of the floor shifted, writhing up to form chains and straps that bound him in place.

There was sunlight nearby. Niko couldn't turn his head enough to see the pool of light on the ground, but he knew it was there, just out of reach.

Always kept out of reach, dooming him to rot in the shadows.

"This is your last chance, Ilbrean." The Elder paced beside him, the swishing of her skirts marking her every step. "I've been patient and gentle. But there is far too much at stake for me to allow sympathy toward a stranger to outweigh my need for the truth."

"This is your gentle sympathy?" Niko laughed. The sound crackled in his throat, his voice damaged from hours spent screaming. "I've told you everything I know. You can dice me to bits, it won't change anything. I've never seen your daughter. Never heard of her before the ground ate me. Kill me or let me go. Everything else is a waste of time."

"I will decide when we have completed our work." The Elder leaned over Niko, her void of a face hovering inches above his. "Pain will drag details from the deepest parts of a man's mind."

"You've already hurt me. Pain changed nothing."

"That wasn't pain, not really." The darkness in the void twisted into a smile. "Don't worry, you'll learn. Now, would you prefer your pain to be caused by magic or more mundane means?"

"That's a trap. Magic might sound like it's better than knives, but it wouldn't be. I hope Amec didn't choose magic."

"A man wise enough to fear magic should be thankful for the mercy of a blade." A knife appeared in the Elder's hand. "Tell me where my daughter is, or my sorcerers will rip the truth from your mind."

"I don't know anything!"

Niko screamed.

Niko watched himself screaming.

The image of his own face vanished as a new scene played out before him.

Smoke rose from Ilara, just inside the city gates. Niko rode away, leaving Allora behind.

He sat in a wagon, young and red-faced, a terrified child leaving home to join the Map Makers Guild.

A storm battered their ship. He cowered in the corner of his cabin, covering his ears to dull the sound of the mast splitting in two.

He knelt in a shelter made of rock. Blue words glowed around him before the world disappeared.

Darkness. Surrounded by darkness. Unending darkness.

Niko screamed.

The darkness faded, and he was watching the image of himself again.

He was bound to a chair. Blood and filth stained his face.

A man stood behind him, staring down at him.

"Show me your secrets." The man's whispered words pounded through Niko's mind.

The Karron mausoleum with the true maps hidden in the wall.

Standing in front of a mirror, practicing telling Allora he loved her.

Dazzling white light beaming through the trees.

"Show me Regan Brien," the man whispered.

Pain wrapped around Niko's middle, clawing at his gut, dragging him back to the beginning of the cycle of horrors.

"Where is my daughter?" The Elder's words tore a sob from Niko's throat.

The sunlight beamed through the windows behind her throne, but the light stayed out of reach.

The light would still be out of reach when the images in his mind looped back around to the beginning and the whole awful show started again.

7

ALLORA

"Are you sure you wouldn't rather sit inside?" Princess Illia flinched as a bolt of lightning streaked across the sky.

Allora took a deep breath, letting a smile brighten her face as the weight of the storm filled her lungs. "It's perfect out here. And I'm sure the roof will hold."

Illia looked up to the ceiling as though unsure the veranda tucked behind the palace had been built to withstand such strong summer storms.

Another bolt of lightning split the sky above the gardens. Thunder shook the tea tray.

Allora laughed. "I was just going to say how much I love the quiet back here."

"If you'd like quiet, we can go to my sitting room." Illia left her own chair to sit on the couch beside Allora.

"But we wouldn't have such a clear view of the rain pounding down on the gardens from inside the palace." Allora poured a fresh cup of tea. "And it's only us and our guards out here. Inside, it's impossible not to feel the buzz of all the people flitting around the palace, even when I'm hidden in my rooms."

"I suppose you are right about that." Illia allowed Allora to refill her cup.

They sat in silence for a few minutes, watching the rain streaming from the edges of the veranda's roof.

"Do you think there are storms like this in Wyrain?" Illia asked. "Where the whole sky splits open?"

"I don't know," Allora said. "My father might. He should be visiting soon. I'll ask him for you."

"Thank you. I think I would miss the rain." Illia leaned forward to choose a cake from the tray a moment too late to hide the tear trailing down her cheek.

"I'm so sorry, Lady Karron." Sorcerer Gillien stepped away from the pillar at the corner of the veranda, her purple robes like a deadly warning against the white marble. "I don't want to interrupt—"

"But it's suddenly desperately unsafe for us to be sitting outside?" Allora asked.

"No, Lady Karron." A hint of humor colored Gillien's voice. "I assure you, I can keep both you and the Princess safe from the storm."

Sorcerer Terin stepped forward from her place on the other side of the veranda, as though determined to prove her vital contribution to the protection of Princess Illia.

Perhaps the sorcerers will lock themselves in a battle of magic and leave Illia and me alone.

"I only felt I should mention that your father will not be visiting the palace. At least, not until the next council meeting," Gillien said.

"Why?" Allora's teacup clacked against the table as she set it down. "Is he ill?"

"To my knowledge, the Lord Mapmaker is well," Gillien said. "But the city is still not safe. The Guilds Council decided yesterday that all members of rank should avoid traveling through the city for any unnecessary reasons until the Lady Sorcerer has quelled the current troubles."

"The city has been plagued with *troubles* since the head scribe's wedding." Allora rested her hands in her lap, forcing her shoulders to stay relaxed. "Has some new horror struck Ilara?"

"No, Lady Karron." Gillien glanced to Terin before stepping closer to Allora. "The Sorcerers Guild has been given charge of restoring peace within the city. With such a large task ahead of us, it's best if the Sorcerers Tower doesn't divide its resources escorting Guild members who could more easily be kept safe at home."

"Yet you're here with us," Allora said. "I promise, I have no urge to leave the palace. If you could be of more use out in the city, please go. Help restore peace. The people of Ilara have suffered long enough."

"The safety of the royal family is the highest priority of the Lady Sorcerer," Terin said. "You will remain guarded by the Sorcerers Guild."

"Good," Illia said. "I prefer to have a sorcerer nearby when there are monsters out for my blood."

"I can assure you, Your Highness," Terin said, "you will remain under my protection until the danger passes."

"In that case, please sit, Gillien, Terin." Allora gestured to a chair for each of them.

"We are quite happy to stand, Lady Karron." Terin bowed.

"But I would like you to sit." Allora smiled for the sorcerers. "If you are going to be our constant companions, I would like to know more about you than your attachment to the Sorcerers Guild."

"Of course, Lady Karron." Gillien took the seat nearest Allora. "Your safety is our primary concern, but your comfort must also be considered."

"How very kind of you." Allora offered Gillien a cake, ignoring the fact that Terin still stood ten feet away. "If my father can't come to the Royal Palace, do you think a letter might be delivered to him at the Map Master's Palace?"

"I'm sure it can be arranged, Lady Karron." Gillien nodded.

"Thank you," Allora said. "It seems strange to ask someone to ferry a question to my father when he's only on the cliffs above the city."

"Within a few weeks, it should be safe for him to move freely," Gillien said. "Then you'll be able to see him more often."

"And will you still be my guard?" Allora said. "Once the city is safe? Once Brannon and I are married?"

"To my knowledge, yes," Gillien said. "That is the honor I have been assigned by the Lady Sorcerer."

"Well then, you shall have to call me Allora." She reached out and took Gillien's hand. "I do hope we'll become the best of friends."

"And you, Sorcerer Terin," Illia said, "will you remain my guard when I marry Prince Dagon?"

"No, Princess." Terin bowed. "Sorcerers are not allowed to enter Wyrain. Your guard will be provided by your husband."

"Alone in a foreign land." Illia's shaky smile appeared more desperate than hopeful. "What an adventure I shall have."

"Indeed," Terin said. "Marrying for the good of your country is an honor and an adventure."

Screaming at a sorcerer helps no one, Allora Karron. You cannot fight a monster by placing your neck in its mouth.

Allora took a breath, cooling her temper before daring to speak.

"You should write Prince Dagon. Though you cannot bring a sorcerer with you, perhaps you could bring a few guards who aren't gifted with magic. Or some of your maids might be happy to venture to Wyrain with you." Allora laid her hand on Illia's shoulder. "Your betrothed may even have a fondness for dogs. Wouldn't it be comforting to take a pup with you across the mountains? A furry friend for you to cuddle and coddle."

"I'm not sure my brother will agree to my having a pup." Illia brushed a tear from her cheek. "But I have always liked dogs. It would be nice to have a loyal companion who can travel with me to Wyrain."

"Then you write to Prince Dagon, and I'll talk to King Brannon." Allora winked. "We'll work on them together."

Gillien met Allora's gaze, giving her a faint smile and a nod of approval.

You and I shall be great friends.

Allora smiled back.

Perfect and peaceful friends.

8

KAI

"Just keep going!" Piran shouted from the back of the group. "We're almost there."

Easy for him to shout for them to run. He had magic to keep the smoke from filling his lungs.

Piran didn't have a damp cloth tied around his face.

Piran wasn't choking in water with every ragged breath as their party fought their way upstream.

Kai splashed more water on the cloth covering his nose and mouth as he kept slogging through the waist-high creek.

His feet slid out from under him as he tried to scramble up into the shallows, sending him face first into the water.

The soothing cold surrounded him, offering such blissful relief.

He could roll over and float on his back and just stop running…

A hand grabbed him under his arm, yanking him back to his feet.

"Come on. You're not allowed to give up." Drew kept hold of his arm until Kai found his footing again.

Kai wanted to reach into his pocket and pull out the token, pass it back to Drew.

But thanking Drew for making him run would have to wait.

With fire raging on either side of the creek, it wasn't the time to show his appreciation for being saved from burning or boiling to death.

"We're almost there!" chivving Piran shouted again. "Keep going."

Kai fixed his gaze on Arto and Isla running in front of him. If Isla could make it through this chivving creek in a skirt that had been weighted down with water and tried to tangle around her ankles every other step, then he could keep moving, too.

The throbbing in his lungs didn't agree.

Crack!

Kai looked toward the sound, grabbing Drew and wrenching him back as a flaming tree fell across the creek, blocking their path.

Sparks singed Kai's hand as he shielded his eyes.

"I've got it." Piran sent a wave to lap over the tree. The water turned into a wall of steam as it extinguished the flames.

The blaze on either side of them grew, as though fed by Piran's magic.

Drew scrambled over the tree then grabbed Kai's arm and dragged him over.

The wall of steam stung Kai's face, and the heat of the tree burned his legs, adding to the pain he fought so hard to ignore.

Another step.

Another step.

Just one more chivving step.

He repeated the lie to himself, focusing his anger on the smoke surrounding him.

The trees should have been beautiful, towering and old and heavy with vibrant green leaves.

The afternoon should have been bright and glorious, a wonderful day to be out in the woods.

But the smoke had stolen every joy from him.

The edges of his vision started to blur as blackness crept in, swallowing the flames that lapped at the sides of the creek.

"We're nearly there!" Piran shouted. "I promise, Kai."

A hand gripped him under his arm, propelling him forward. A hand from a different person gripped under his other arm.

He couldn't make himself look to either side to see who was dragging him upstream through the never-ending fire.

One had to be Drew, logic promised that. But the other person…that, Kai wasn't sure of.

His foot snagged on a rock. His weight tipped forward, but the hands kept him upright.

If he ever got back to Ilara, he was going to find a token crusted in jewels to toss Drew for all the times Drew had saved his life.

A bright, beautiful light shone up ahead, breaking through the shroud of smoke.

He wasn't going to make it to Ilara.

He wasn't going to die at sea as was his right as a sailor.

He was going to be burned to death in the southern chivving mountains.

He gagged on the injustice of it.

Heat flew out of his mouth as light surrounded him.

"Get him onto the bank." A hand pulled the cloth from his mouth.

"No, I—" Kai coughed. Black came up, spattering down his front.

Someone lifted his pack off his back and laid him down on the ground.

The ground wasn't on fire, but the touch of it against his skin sent pain shooting through his leg.

He fought the darkness that tried to consume him.

A bright sky shone above him, but off to the side, smoke tainted the blue. The sharp border between the two colors seemed absurd, like a painter had drawn a streak of gray on the edge of the sky.

"I'm sorry for how much this will hurt." Someone touched his arm.

A scream tore from Kai's throat. He looked toward the pain, trying to see what was finally going to kill him.

His sleeve had been singed away. The skin beneath oozed with burns. The burns went all the way down his side, stopping just above his knee.

Piran pressed his palm to the bubbled skin on Kai's arm.

Kai's second scream ripped another round of black from his lungs.

"You're all right." Drew hovered above Kai. "You've just got to breathe. We've made it past the flames."

The pain shifted down to Kai's side.

"We've reached the eastern mountains." Kelsea leaned into Kai's vision. A triumphant smile lit her face. "Whatever cursed magic chased us in the southern mountains can't harm us here."

"Can't harm us here?" Drew leapt to his feet. "Kai nearly died saving—"

"And he's not out of danger yet," Piran said. "So please take your shouting elsewhere."

Kelsea backed away.

Drew knelt beside Kai, holding his unburnt hand.

The pain in Kai's side reached farther in, searing his lungs. He gripped Drew's hand as agony stole his sight.

Someone screamed.

It was probably him.

Visions of fire danced through his mind.

The flames had burst into being so quickly, Kai had been sure he was hallucinating. But the smoke had stung his eyes and flooded his nose. So when Arto shouted for them to run, he'd followed, ready to battle whatever new monster the southern mountains had sent after them.

But you can't stab fire or shoot arrows at it.

Piran had done something, some magic, to find the stream.

The flames around them had soared. The top of a tree had split from its trunk, falling toward Piran's head. Kai had shoved Piran out of the way. The flames meant for Piran had attacked Kai's side, burning through his clothes, scorching his flesh.

The pain in his lungs ebbed as the agony shifted to his leg.

The weight of Drew's hand gripping his didn't change.

"You should set up the stones." Drew's voice broke through the high-pitched throbbing of the pain wailing in Kai's mind. "We're not going to be able to move him. He needs to rest."

"We don't need the stone barrier for him to be safe resting," Arto said. "Not here."

"We're in the eastern mountains," Kelsea said. "We're safe here. We'll use the stones to protect ourselves from animals at night, but—"

"How do you know we're in the eastern mountains?" Drew sounded angry and exhausted.

Kai wished he could offer his friend a good drink of frie.

They all deserved a bit of frie.

"Just because the fire stopped chasing us doesn't mean we're out of danger," Drew said. "It could just be the demons that have been tormenting us trying to make us feel safe so they can finally kill us."

"I promise you we're in the eastern mountains," Arto said. "I can feel it in my bones."

The pain in Kai's leg focused in on his knee with an intensity fit to make the joint explode. He screamed. Louder than he'd managed before, like his lungs had gained the strength to shove out more air.

"You're all right, Kai." Drew pinned Kai's good shoulder to the ground.

"I'm a Black Blood." Arto spoke over Kai's scream. "I've the stone of the eastern mountains running through my veins. The eastern mountains are etched into my soul, and I promise you, I am home."

The pain in Kai's leg shifted to a fiery peak. He turned his head in time to vomit.

"What have you done to him?" Drew shouted.

"It's expected," Piran said. "With healing this extensive, there's going to be some illness. Let's get him into the cool water, it'll help ease the ache."

Ache.

It would be nice to ache. A bearable ache that would let him feel past the burning that consumed his left side.

The support of the ground vanished as someone lifted him, carried him, and laid him down on something less flat than where he'd been.

A blissful chill swept around his body, pulling away tiny slivers of the heat in his limbs.

"You should get cleaned up," Piran said. "I'll sit with him."

"There's not a chivving chance I'm leaving you alone with him," Drew said.

Something soft slid under Kai's head.

Their words faded away, seeming less important as the pain ebbed and a blissful nothingness surrounded him.

The sound of splashing in the water lured Kai back out of the black. He shifted, trying to move away from the hard thing that dug into his spine.

"Easy now," Piran said. "Don't push too quickly. You needed more healing than I like to do in a hurry."

Kai balled his hands into fists, testing their ability to move.

"Your skin healed just fine, it'll keep any infection out," Piran said. "But the burns went pretty deep. It's the deeper layers that'll be sore for a while."

Kai took a steadying breath and dared to open his eyes.

The sky had faded to the gray blue of dusk.

Piran knelt beside him, his brow furrowed as he watched Kai.

"That's better." Piran's smile didn't reach his eyes.

"Just—" Kai swallowed past the grit in his throat. He bent his elbows and knees, clenching his teeth against agony that didn't come. "Just about anything is better than getting your side seared off by a demon of a mountain." He planted his hands against the rocks, pushing himself to sit. The trees lurched sideways.

Piran put an arm behind Kai's back.

Kai sagged against Piran, trusting the Brien to keep him upright as his mind struggled to understand the scene surrounding him.

Right in front of him, the trees were old and tall and healthy. But downstream, the trees had been burned to nothing more than charred stumps.

But it wasn't the difference between the dead and living trees that made Kai wonder if he was still in some sort of pain-born nightmare. It was the way the fire damage stopped, as though two children had been playing soldier, fighting over a line etched in the mud, and one side of the fight had been ravaged by flames.

"That's not chivving right," Kai murmured.

"It's the boundary." Piran leveraged Kai to sit up straighter. "The eastern mountains can't protect us in the southern range, the southern mountains can't hurt us in the eastern mountains that created the Black Bloods."

"I didn't know mountains were so respectful of borders." Kai splashed water from the stream onto his face.

"From your stories of surviving horrors at sea, the mountain claiming my people as her own is not so very different from the way the Arion Sea names Kai Saso among her beloved children."

Kai rubbed stream water over the freshly healed skin on his arm. "Whatever magic stopped the flames from chasing us, I owe it my life."

"As I owe you my life." Piran took Kai's hand, clasping it in something that was not brotherhood. "Not many men would push someone they hardly know out of the way of danger and accept the pain of the blow themselves." He kissed Kai's hand. "I owe you my life."

"If you want to prattle on about gratitude for Kai saving your life, there's a rather large line you're going to have to join." Drew spoke from just behind Kai.

Kai turned to look at Drew, tipping over as his brain sloshed against his skull.

Piran caught him and pushed him back upright.

"Are you in that throng, or have we moved beyond such niceties?" Kai dug deep in his pocket.

"I'm not one to clamor for attention," Drew said.

"Showing appreciation is not clamoring," Piran said.

"You've healed everyone on this wretched journey enough times, I owe you a barrel of frie and a well-bred horse when we reach Ilara." Kai rolled over and dragged himself up onto the dry bank. "Come up to the Map Master's Palace, and I promise you'll be thanked for every wound you've healed."

"I hope that's not a promise you'll forget," Piran said.

"Never. Piran, I will see you showered with every gift my bonds with the Karrons can offer. You will bathe in luxury while sipping the finest chamb." Kai crawled toward Drew. His fingers fumbled as he pulled the token from the depths of his pocket. He held the bit of silver out to Drew as he collapsed at his feet. "Don't try to toss this back to me too soon. I feel like a chivving corpse and don't want to fail you."

Drew took the coin and tucked it into his pocket.

"We should get you into dry clothes." Piran stood. "I'll get your blankets laid out so you can sleep."

"No, no." Kai waved Piran away. "You already kept me from dying. Drew's got me now. You rest. Do magic. I'll be fine."

"I'll make sure your spare clothes are dry." Piran walked away, heading toward the rumbling of the other Brien's voices.

Kai flopped over to sprawl on his back, looking up at the darkening sky with a wonder one could only feel after being snatched from Death's grip.

"You shouldn't have passed the token back to me," Drew said once Piran's footsteps had faded. "I'm not the one that saved you. It was Piran who healed you."

"I don't give a runted pig's tit for Piran or any of the chivving Brien saving me. Anyone who keeps you alive when you're fairly certain they're planning on killing you later is only saving the delight of seeing you dead for another day." Kai reached over, patting Drew's foot. "I would've lain down and let the fire take me if I hadn't known it would ruin your mood."

"Seeing you half-charred and close to dead did ruin my mood."

"I'll try to stop at a quarter-charred next time." Kai shivered as a breeze swept down from the north.

"Let's get you into dry clothes before you're sick enough to need more Brien healing." Drew took Kai under the arms, hauling him to his feet.

"Just to be clear, I owe *you* two barrels of frie, a horse, and a cottage on the grounds of the Map Master's Palace." Kai didn't fight as Drew wrapped an arm around his waist, helping him toward the crackling fire and the chivving Brien.

"Just don't die and we'll call ourselves even," Drew said.

"Help me out of these sopping clothes, and I'll toss in a dozen barrels of ale," Kai said. "Have you ever thought of raising chickens? I'll surround your cottage with a fleet of fowl."

"You're a chivving fool."

9

NIKO

The Dudia blessed relief of a dull, throbbing ache lured Niko deeper into the blissful nothing of his mind.

They'll come back soon.

He tried to bat the thought away.

The longer they leave you to rest, the worse the next bout will be.

They're going to break you.

Niko scrunched his eyes shut, paying for the movement with a pang of pain in his face. His cheekbone had been broken…at some point. Hard to say how long ago anymore.

Years. It's been years.

She's forgotten you. Allora's moved on.

"Stop it." Niko's voice scratched in his throat. "Just stop."

"Are you awake, Ilbrean?" A woman's voice came from the corner.

Niko froze as fear shot through his chest.

Calm. Stay calm.

He tried to breathe steadily in a sad attempt at feigning sleep.

"It would be a pity if you died now." Soft footsteps moved closer to the bed. "After all you've been through, to let Death take you when you're on the edge of relief."

Niko swallowed, testing the pain in his throat before speaking. "What relief do you think might be kinder than death? A new form of torment? More spells so your elder can root through my mind, viewing my memories like entertaining curiosities? Or will we go back to non-magical means of torture? Are your healers bored now that they don't spend every night patching me up enough to survive the next day's depravity?"

"You're lucky Bryana sent healers to tend to you. She could have let your wounds fester."

"I'll thank her for her compassion when next we meet."

"I'm hoping you're clever enough to realize the wisdom in that decision."

Niko opened his eyes, blinking in the dim blue light that filled his cell.

The woman stood beside his bed, the knives on her hips the only hint that she'd walked into a stone room with an enemy.

"Thanking Bryana for each breath you take would be a good place to begin every thought you have for the rest of your life." The woman cocked her head. Light fell across her face.

She had eyes, a nose, and a mouth, just one set of each. Actual, normal features undistorted by magic tearing into his mind.

The woman was young. Niko's age, maybe a bit older. She wore pants and a loose shirt under her bodice, as though she'd come prepared to haul his corpse out of his cell.

She was pretty, might have been beautiful even, if she hadn't been working for the demon of an elder who'd been tormenting him for however long he'd been trapped with the Brien.

Must be a year now. Maybe more.

He tried to think back through the days of beatings, the times he'd been healed.

But the magic they'd driven into his mind…the healers didn't always come for that.

Maybe it hasn't been a year. A month? Six months?

"Ilbrean." The woman kicked the leg of his bed. "Did you hear me?"

Niko dug back in his mind.

Not years. Six weeks...

"I didn't." Niko gripped the thin cover of his rope-woven bed. "Having my thoughts torn through over and over again seems to have caused my mind to wander."

"Don't goad Bryana," the woman said. "Sniping will get you thrown right back into this cell."

"Thrown back?" Niko pushed himself up onto his elbows. He gasped through gritted teeth as pain thrummed through the ribs that had been broken too many times. "I'm thrown back into this cell every time your precious elder gets bored with tormenting me."

"Bryana sent me to offer you a deal," the woman said. "She's only going to offer it once, and if you place any value on your life, you'll chivving well take it."

"What's the deal? Is she going to cut off something the healers can't grow back?"

"Your freedom in exchange for service to the clan."

"What sort of service does your demon of an elder have in mind?" Niko fell back onto his bed. "I'm assuming it's something I can't agree to. Does that mean you'll slit my throat right here? Finally end it?"

The woman gripped the hilts of her knives. "I never relish the need to kill anyone. Neither does Bryana. The Brien aren't a violent clan."

"Who's the liar now?" Niko shut his eyes, waiting for pain to burst through his skin as the woman used her blades to punish his insolence.

"Things were different before Bryana's daughter disappeared," the woman said. "Her daughter, Regan, was her heir. Losing Regan was a terrible blow for the clan, and Bryana's not been the same since."

"I'm sorry your elder lost a daughter and your clan lost an heir, but it's got nothing to do with me. Whatever torture your elder wants to hurl at me—"

"It's more than just losing Regan." The woman pushed Niko's legs aside and sat on the foot of his bed, perched like a friend while still clutching her knives. "The clans have been at war for almost two years now. Black Bloods fighting against each other is a terrible thing the mountain should never have to witness."

"There's a war happening in the mountains and Ilbrea knows nothing about it?" Niko opened his eyes, wincing at the pain as he pushed himself to sit up. "How is that possible?"

"You're a map maker. You should know how vast the mountains are."

"Of course. But a whole war? That much bloodshed shouldn't go unnoticed by the world."

"No. It shouldn't." The woman loosened her grip on her knives. "If you'd wandered into our territory before the horrors began, things would have gone much differently."

"I would've been allowed to scamper straight home?"

"You'd have been questioned for an hour and met a swift end when we were done."

"Pity I arrived too late to receive such kindness." Niko waited for a laugh of sarcasm to rise in his throat. The truth of his words hollowed out his will to jest.

"Our grief may be what allows you to live. Bryana and her advisors have all agreed that you don't know where Regan is."

A laugh that had nothing to do with humor finally rattled out of Niko's throat. "Which torment was it that finally convinced her?"

"I don't know." The woman turned to look at Niko. "But Bryana has decided she has use for you. Do as you're told, prove your worth, and she'll let you live."

"What use could your elder have for me?"

"Does it matter? I'm offering an end to the torture and a way out of this cell."

Niko looked to the door set into the stone wall.

If he could get out. See the sunlight.

"I'll do whatever the demon asks if I get to see the sun."

"Bryana will be pleased." The woman offered Niko her hand. "I've been assigned as your guardian. I'll be your shadow and keeper while you work on Bryana's behalf."

"And after I do her work, I can go home?" Niko eased his legs over the side of the bed. "How long have I been here? I need to get back to Ilara. There's someone waiting for me."

"I will never lie to you, Niko. I vow to the mountain herself that I will always be truthful." The woman kept her hand out. "I can't promise Bryana will let you go back to Ilara. But I can promise that doing as she asks and earning her favor is the only way you stand a chivving chance of seeing anything beyond the stronghold again."

You're smarter than this, Mara whispered. *Never bargain with a monster. You will always end up in their teeth.*

"I can't survive in here," Niko whispered back.

"No, you can't," the woman said. "Bryana didn't tell me what would happen to you if you refused her offer."

"Death, I assume." Niko looked down at his hands.

The healers had cleaned his skin. They hadn't left a trace of blood or dirt behind. They'd stolen his scars as well. Remade his flesh over and over to hide the horrors committed by their elder.

He shut his eyes, imagining the gentle weight of Allora's hand in his.

He laced his fingers through hers. *I will find my way back to you.*

"I'll take your elder's bargain." Niko gripped the edge of the bed and pushed himself to his feet. "What misery will she drag me through in exchange for my freedom?"

"Bryana doesn't share her plans with me." The woman gripped Niko's elbow as he staggered forward.

Niko pulled his arm free, paying for his obstinance with a stumble to the side.

"Try not to break yourself. You're not on the healers' schedule today." She pressed her fingers to the door, turning the heavy lock without a key.

"My guardian is a sorcerer. I'm honored." Niko lurched forward enough to lean against the wall. "Open the door. We don't want to keep your elder waiting."

"She's not waiting on us. Bryana has no interest in seeing you today."

"Then why are you pulling me from my cell now? And don't say mercy. Your people don't understand the word."

"Recovery. You can't serve the Brien as the mess you are now." She yanked on the handle, leaning her weight back to drag the heavy door open.

Four guards in purple uniforms waited outside Niko's cell.

He recognized all of them—minions who'd dragged him back and forth from his daily torment.

The urge to hit and kick and bite and kill no matter the cost surged energy through Niko's limbs. He clenched his fists, ready to fight.

The woman stepped out into the hall, cocking her head as she looked back at Niko as though she knew exactly what useless battle he longed to begin.

Pain radiated up his arms as he loosened his fists. He sagged against the wall, too tired to stand on his own.

"Do you need to be carried to your room?" the woman said.

"I don't want those chivving bastards touching me." Niko stepped into the hall.

He froze, waiting for a spell to throw him back into his cage and slam the door behind him, trapping him forever.

"This way." The woman walked down the corridor to the right, away from the path that led to the throne room.

Niko licked his lips, hating the bitter taste of panic that flooded his mouth as he followed her.

She kept her pace slow, letting Niko shamble along behind her.

The guards didn't bother following. They'd done too much damage for Niko to have a hope of fighting his way to freedom anyway.

"Your room will be kept locked," the woman said as they passed the dozens of other cells carved into the stone of the mountain. "Everything you need will be brought to you while you regain your strength."

"Strength for what?"

"Whatever purpose Bryana chooses." The woman stopped at a door, opening the lock with a touch.

Niko held his breath, waiting for the door to open into his new cage and the charade of hope to come to an end. But the door led into a hall, wider and better lit than the passage between the cells.

"The other Ilbrean," Niko said, "is he being moved from his cell, too? Can I see him?"

"You are my charge. I have nothing to do with the other Ilbrean."

"But he's alive, isn't he?" Niko stumbled a few quick steps, reaching for the woman's arm.

She spun around, knocking Niko's hand aside and slapping him hard across the face.

"Try to grab me again, and you'll get a punch instead. Or a knife to the gut if I'm in a foul mood."

"I'm sorry." Niko held up both hands as though he had a chance of defending himself. "I'm sorry. I just need to know if Amec is alive."

"Last I heard, he was." The woman started down the hall at a faster pace Niko struggled to match. "If he had finally died, I'd probably have been told."

She turned down another corridor that led up a tall flight of carved, stone stairs.

"Are you a prison guard?" Niko kept one hand on the wall as he climbed the steps. "Or a soldier? There have been women soldiers who've dragged me to the throne room."

"I'm not a guard or a soldier."

"Then why"—Niko dragged down air, ignoring the pain in his ribs—"why are you my guardian?"

"Because I'm the slitch that got stuck with the honored task." She touched the door at the top of the steps.

Niko gripped the doorframe to haul himself up the final stair. The muscles in his legs tensed, screaming their protest at having been asked to do so much. His chest ached. The bottom of his lungs seemed to have forgotten how to fill with air.

"We're almost there." The woman closed the door the moment Niko managed to move out of the way.

"For what—what it's worth"—Niko pressed his knuckles to the pain in his side—"I'm sorry you got stuck with me."

"You should be celebrating. The others considered for the task don't have nearly as kind a disposition."

Unlike the prison's passage, the new corridor only had doors on one side of the hall. The doors they passed were set farther apart as well, as though the rooms beyond were far larger than Niko's stone cell.

"You should have all you need for now," the woman said. "I'll bring you more food tonight."

"Thank you."

"Thank Bryana."

"I don't think I could form those words."

"You'll learn." The woman stopped in front of a door that matched the rest in the hall, turning the handle without any need for magic.

"What's your name?" Niko blurted the question as dread raked down his spine.

"Guardian to you."

"No, your name. Your proper name." Sweat beaded on Niko's forehead. His hands began to shake.

"What's wrong with you?" She furrowed her brow, tipping her head to the side again as she watched Niko panic.

"I'll wake up when you open the door." Fear pinched Niko's throat, cutting off his air. "I'll be back in the cell. They'll bring the knives. Give me a name I can scream when I curse you."

"Danu." A hint of a smile curved Danu's lips. "I'll allow you to use my name as you tell your god to bless me."

She pushed the door open.

Sunlight poured into the hall.

The pain in Niko's throat wrapped around his chest, clenching his racing heart.

He reached out, brushing his fingers against the sunlight.

Blissful warmth caressed his skin.

He limped forward, letting the light wash over him.

Windows lined the far wall, looking out onto the valley beyond where trees with emerald-green leaves shifted in the breeze.

A bed—a real, proper bed—took up the center of the room. The wardrobe in the corner had been left open, displaying clean, well-made clothes. The table had been set with a meal—bread, soup, cheese.

A glass of frie.

There was a tub in the corner and a rug under the bed, and windows. Dudia bless the windows.

Niko's legs went numb as the pain in his chest ebbed. He sank to his knees, tears streaming down his sun-warmed face.

10

ADRIAL

The warmth of the bed lured Adrial deeper into his dream.

He could hear them, just through the door, Ena and their son.

The child wailed, angry over some awful offense only a babe could truly understand the horror of. Ena cooed to the baby, promising him everything would be fine. His mother would protect him.

Adrial tried to focus on the text.

He needed to study.

Maps. No. Battle plans.

He had to study the battle plans.

An account of the battles fought by the Sorcerers Guild. In the war with the invaders from Pamerane. Invaders with no magic of their own.

The baby wailed again, as though he knew the atrocities his father studied.

Adrial wanted to go and comfort his son, but this work had to be done. For the child's sake, Adrial had to understand.

He'd found a few other accounts of the Sorcerers Guild fighting to protect Ilbrea. But there had to be more. More information hidden somewhere in the library.

Why else would the sorcerers be granted so much power? They must have proven their might in an undeniable way. But when? How?

The baby screamed. Not a sound of childish woe, but a shriek of true, soul-tearing fear.

"Ena." Adrial tried to push himself away from his desk. He needed to get to them. No book could matter as much as protecting his family.

"Ena." His chair wouldn't let him go. The wood twisted, wrapping around his legs, pinning him in place as his son screamed. "Ena. Ena!"

With a crack, the baby's cries disappeared.

Fear jolted through Adrial's heart. "No!"

He gasped for air as he tried to break free from his chair.

"Ena!"

He kicked as hard as he could.

His sheets shifted easily with the movement.

He lay in bed, covered in sweat, panting as he tried to convince himself it had only been a terrible dream.

He reached over to Ena's side of the bed. Her place was empty.

"Ena." He felt his mouth form her name. His voice had the rasp of someone who'd just woken. But the assurance that he wasn't dreaming didn't stop his fear from growing. "Ena!"

A strange blue glow filtered in through the window, giving the bedroom enough light to prove she wasn't there.

"Ena." Adrial ran to the sitting room, the pain in his hip barely piercing his panic.

She sat perched on the sill of an open window, her white shift fluttering in the smoke-tainted breeze.

"Ena, are you all right?"

She kept her gaze fixed out the window as she reached for his hand.

A scream carried through the night. Then a blue light flashed out in the city.

"What's going on?" He took Ena's hand.

She laced her fingers through his and wrapped his arms around her, as though anchoring herself against some terrible storm.

A wave of yells like battle cries came from closer than the last scream had.

"The King gave the sorcerers charge of searching the city. This is how the demons do it. With death and terror and spilt tilk blood." Tears glistened on her cheeks.

Adrial tightened his hold on her, brushing his hand across the roundness of her belly where their child still safely grew.

"How many dead common folk will be scattered on the streets come morning?" Ena whispered.

Bang!

Sparks flew into the air in the merchants' section of the city.

"I should be out there." Ena shrugged away from Adrial's embrace. "I should be fighting to defend my people."

"There's nothing you can do." He stepped into her path as she stood.

"A tilk with a knife can kill a sorcerer."

"One sorcerer, perhaps." Adrial took her shoulders. "But you can't stand against the might of the Sorcerers Guild."

Flames leapt into the sky, burning whatever had been destroyed in the explosion.

"The paun are murdering innocent people!" Ena shoved his hands away, cutting past him toward the bedroom door.

"Not everyone out there is innocent." Adrial turned to her, keeping his feet planted, holding her gaze when she rounded on him. "I don't know what chaos the sorcerers are causing in the city tonight. I don't know if they're capable of enough compassion to only target the guilty. But there are murderers lurking in this city, Ena."

"You're right." She stepped closer to him. "In the soldiers' barracks, in the Sorcerers Tower, in the healers' compound, there are even paun who have caused the deaths of innocent tilk right here in your precious library."

"I wish I could say you were wrong. But the sins of the Guilds cannot change the fact that the unguilded murderers lurking out in the city must be found. Before they collapse another building on my head. Before they come near murdering my wife again."

"Cade and his men are dead," Ena said. "They're the only tilk in Ilara who've tried to murder me. Are the sorcerers hunting ghosts tonight?"

"You were almost killed at our wedding, Ena! Two people were murdered. Four others nearly died. If you had taken the wrong drink—" Adrial shuddered as a weight collapsed onto his chest. "One wrong sip and I could've lost you. I could've lost my wife and our child. I have no love for the sorcerers. I take no pleasure in whatever violence they're using to search the city, but I will be relieved and filled with joy when I see the poisoner's head displayed in the cathedral square."

Ena laid her hand over his heart. "Then my place is on the streets with my people. If you want vengeance against the poisoner, I would hate to deny you the joy of seeing my head on a pike." She strode into their bedroom.

Adrial stared at the doorway, waiting for her words to make sense.

"What do you mean?" He made his legs move so he could chase after her. "Ena, what do you mean?"

"If sorcerers are out there hunting for the one who killed the Lady Healer and that chivving Sorcerer Clery, then I might as well walk onto the streets and make the paun's job easier." She yanked a skirt from the wardrobe and dragged it over her head. "I won't let them rampage through innocent tilk to find me."

"You're not to blame, Ena." Adrial snatched the bodice from

her hand before she could put it on. "People were murdered at our wedding. That doesn't make their deaths your fault."

"You're right. It's the poison I dropped in their cups that makes it my fault." She faced him, her chin high, not a hint of fear or remorse in her eyes.

"You can't mean that." Pain surged through Adrial's hip. He sank onto the bed before his leg could give out. "You don't…Ena, you're confused. You're tired. Perhaps the pregnancy has been harder on you—"

"Sorcerer Clery threatened you. She promised she would hurt you to punish Allora." She took a new bodice from the wardrobe and pulled it on. "Sorcerer Clery threatened my husband. Do you think she wouldn't have stooped low enough to threaten the baby? I had to protect my family."

"Ena…" He couldn't make himself stand as she yanked on her boots.

"The Lady Healer was far from innocent." She tucked her knife into the ankle of her boot. "How many common folk have died because her healers treat us like nothing better than rodents? She had the blood of thousands on her hands. I avenged my people."

She walked to the door, like she was going to climb over the library walls and disappear forever.

She'd go after the sorcerers with nothing but a knife as a weapon.

"Ena, don't."

She paused in the doorway but didn't look back at him. "I'll beg for mercy for the babe. See if they can wait for my head until after the child is born."

"You're my wife." Adrial's legs shook as he stood.

"Then perhaps they will spare the child."

"You poisoned Tammin. She's never harmed anyone." An ache dug into Adrial's gut. "And those three soldiers. Had you ever even met those men?"

"It wasn't the same brew."

"What?" Pain throbbed from his leg to his throat as he stepped closer to her.

Ena turned around, keeping her gaze fixed on the window as she spoke. "It wasn't the same brew. What I gave Tammin and the soldiers was never meant to kill. Just make them ill enough to cause confusion. The soldiers were an easy mark, too drunk to notice me slipping something into their bottle. Tammin was necessary."

"Tammin is a good person."

"Who is close to you. Who cares for you. I had to be sure suspicion would stay well away from you and the library. A scribe had to fall ill. One you're close to was even better, and I couldn't bring myself to make Taddy sick even for a night."

Adrial shut his eyes, hoping to hear a whisper in his mind promising him he was still trapped in a nightmare.

"I am not the monster, scribe," Ena whispered. "I protected my family. I have to protect you. I do not regret what I've done."

The floor creaked as she moved away.

He lunged forward, bracing himself against the wall as he caught her wrist. "Don't go. Please don't go."

"I don't have a choice."

"Yes, you do." He wrapped his arm around her waist. "Stay here with me."

"Even if you wanted to share your bed with a killer"—she didn't fight as he tightened his hold on her—"I can't stay here if the sorcerers are out there murdering innocent people as they hunt for me."

"Did you bring down the dome of the cathedral?"

"No." Ena twisted to look at him.

"Promise me."

"I would never risk hurting you." She touched his cheek. "You could've been killed in that attack. If I'd known something was going to happen at the royal wedding, I would've stopped you from going. I had nothing to do with the dome coming down."

"Then you sacrificing yourself to the sorcerers wouldn't help anyone." He dared to loosen his grip on her wrist, sliding his hand down to lock with hers. "They want the one who attacked the cathedral, too. The searches won't stop just because you let the sorcerers take you."

Her shoulders sagged as though a bit of her fight had been ripped away. "Then they may never stop."

"Do you know who brought down the dome?"

She slid away from him.

"There are still rumors about the Demon's Torch flying through the library." He kept hold of her hand. "If there is a man capable of such violence, if you know him—"

"I've already told you the Demon's Torch is not in Ilara." She leaned against the wall, taking a deep breath as though trying to convince her lungs to work. "It's not him."

"How can you be sure?" He dared to touch her cheek, brushing her hair behind her ear. "If you're afraid of him, I will find a way to keep you safe."

The look in Ena's eyes changed, as though she were seeing something far beyond the library walls. "If the Demon's Torch were in Ilara, he would find me. And I wouldn't be afraid of him. I would punch him square in the jaw, and bury myself in his arms, and forbid him to ever leave me again."

Adrial froze, unwilling to risk shattering the closest he'd gotten to seeing the girl that had existed before becoming the woman forged in fire that had swept such beautiful madness into his life.

"If the Demon's Torch were in Ilara, the soldiers would be too terrified to patrol the streets, and the healers' compound would have burned to the ground. But my brother is dead, and not even vengeance against the Guilds can bring him back to me." She pulled her hair over her shoulder and began weaving it into a tight braid. "Someone might've taken up his sword. But I'd have no chance of knowing their name or face."

Boom.

A flare of purple light burst through the night sky.

"The sorcerers will never stop." Ena let go of her hair. The end of her braid unraveled. "This babe will be born into a world the sorcerers terrorize, and I'm not strong enough to stop them. I can't stop the paun from murdering the tilk. My brother might have managed it, but I'm not him." She gripped the black stone pendant that hung just above the neck of her shift. "I can't fight the Guilds on my own."

Adrial wrapped his arms around her, guiding her head onto his shoulder.

"You're not on your own. There is a way to fight back." He brushed his lips against her hair. "We will find a way to stop the sorcerers and make things better for the common folk."

"Then they'll be hunting the streets for you."

"Not if we change things from inside the Guilds." He tipped her chin up. "Your weapons may be knives and poison, but paper and ink can strike mighty blows. You're not fighting on your own, Ena. We can stand together."

"Can you even bear to share a bed with the girl who poisoned people at your wedding?" She held his gaze, truly asking the question.

"You have consumed my entire soul. To turn away from you would be to destroy myself. Whoever you are, whatever you've done, I love you, Ena."

Her body stiffened as though she were preparing for an attack.

"I know you may never be able to love me, at least not in the way I love you." He laced his fingers through her hair. "But whatever scars life has left on your heart can't change the way I feel. I love you. Madly and irrevocably. Without any hope or need for you to ever feel the same. I love you. And if you walk out to meet the sorcerers, I will follow you. I would rather die by your side than face a world without you in it."

She trailed her fingers beside the corner of his eye and over his lips.

"I love you, Ena," he whispered. "Whoever you are, whatever you've done, I love you."

And she kissed him. Claiming what was hers. What she had ended lives to protect.

11

MARA

"It's not enough." Mara twirled the pencil through her fingers. "Weeks of work and we're hardly better off than when we started."

"That's not true." Tham placed a steadying hand on her back.

He was right. She knew he was right.

The massive parchment laid out on the table had been filled with a map worthy of any maker but Lord Karron himself.

She'd spent days meticulously drawing the streets of Isfol by hand, then made charts of the daily changes the ice inflicted upon the city.

The banks of the river had regrown and stabilized. A tunnel cutting under the river on the north side of the city had appeared and vanished all within the same week. Stalactites of glorious blue ice had descended from the ceiling on the western side of the massive cavern that encompassed Isfol, creating a forest of pillars that could muddle the mind.

"It makes no sense." Mara leaned against Tham's side. "The changes in the ice are exciting to explore, but I can't find a pattern or purpose in it."

"Scholars in Isfol have been studying the changes since long before we were born. They've never found any reasoning behind the shifts, either."

"So, I should give it up?"

"If anyone can figure this out, it's you." Tham kissed the top of her head. "But you shouldn't blame yourself for needing more time."

Elle barked and began running circles around Mara's and Tham's feet.

"I don't know if Elle believes I can be patient." Mara tucked her pencil into her curls. "I want to search the streets just north of the royal kennels. I haven't seen any changes in the ice there. Though it is so close to the palace, I'm not sure there's much point—"

Tham squeezed Mara's shoulder.

She took a breath, focusing on the weight of Tham's touch.

"You're still healing. You can't crawl into any tunnels until the matrons say you're ready," Tham said.

"Then I need to convince Ronya to finally let me see the scholars' maps." Mara twined her fingers through Tham's. "Finding the ice worms is too important to waste time waiting to heal. If I can't go into the ice, I could at least be studying the information that already exists."

"I'll make you tea."

She watched him pour her tea from the tray by the fireplace, calm and confident with every move, as though he didn't know Ronya's spies were lurking in the walls, judging every word and action, waiting for any hint of rebellion.

Mara turned her attention back to the map.

She'd found four pockets of ice worms below the city. None of them large enough to be declared a triumphant harvest, but every bit of available tonic could help save a life.

None of the pockets she'd found had come close to offering a path out of Isfol either.

She needed a reason to explore the southern edge of the city, where an escape route would likely lead them closer to Ilbrea instead of farther into the deadly white mountains. She had yet to find any changes in the ice that could reasonably warrant such exploration.

Tham set a cup of tea on the small table beside the desk Ronya had so graciously allowed Mara. With the parchment she'd allowed. The ink she'd allowed. The pen she'd allowed.

Saint Aximander, guide my journey. Let us find a way out of this frozen hell.

She placed a fresh piece of parchment on top of the map and sketched out the river, edges of the city, and placement of the palace.

Elle whined and nosed her way between Mara's legs, insisting on lying between her feet.

"You're all right, Elle." Mara marked the places where she'd seen radical changes in the ice.

The fastest shifts always happened near the river.

But the cold of the water would be deadly even to an Ice Walker. Mara had no hope of surviving an attempt to explore whatever lay at the bottom of the river, let alone swimming far enough to escape.

Elle scrambled to her feet, baring her teeth as she growled at the place where their bedroom door always appeared.

"Hush, Elle," Tham said, even as he placed himself between Mara and the door as though expecting an attack.

They won't attack! The need to scream ricocheted through Mara's chest. *They will trap us here forever, condemning us to live as useful pets.*

Their door formed and swung open without anyone bothering to ask if they might enter the room everyone pretended was Mara and Tham's private quarters.

Andric, Lynn, and two new guards strode through the door.

Mara left her maps to stand beside Tham.

Andric took a moment, examining the room before looking to Mara. "Princess Ronya has requested your immediate presence."

"You'll have to forgive me. I hadn't expected to be summoned by Her Highness this afternoon." Mara tucked her pencil back into her hair.

"Expected or not," Andric said, "your presence is required."

"For what occasion?" Mara swept a hand toward her plain pants and shirt. "If Her Highness would like us to attend a public affair, I'm afraid I'll have to ask you to leave so I can change."

"You're to meet her in her library." Humor glinted in Andric's eyes. "There's no need for you to change."

"Perfect." Mara took Tham's arm.

"Princess Ronya did not request Tham's presence." Andric almost managed a polite nod in Tham's direction. "He'll be staying behind."

Tham stepped away from Mara's touch, meeting her gaze before kissing the back of her hand.

His eyes held more meaning than Mara could fully read.

I love you. Be careful. Stay the course. We're in this fight together whatever danger may come.

There was something else…a warning lined with worry Mara didn't understand.

She brushed her lips against his cheek, trying to convey all the things she couldn't say out loud, couldn't whisper, couldn't even write on a slip of paper without worrying that one of Ronya's spies might discover her words and use them as a weapon.

"I'll be back soon." She let her hand trail down Tham's arm as she followed Andric and the other guards out into the hall.

She hated that those simple words might be a lie. Mara might not return to their room anytime soon. It all depended on the whims of the Princess.

Andric pressed his hand to the ice, waiting until the door to Mara and Tham's quarters had melded with the wall before heading down the hall.

Mara followed him, making it ten steps before stopping to look back.

Lynn had stayed planted in front of where Mara's door had been, flanked by the other two guards.

"Mara," Andric said, "Her Highness is waiting."

"But aren't they coming?" Mara nodded toward the other guards.

"Her Highness has decided one guard is sufficient for your protection when moving about the palace," Andric said. "She's allowed me to claim that position."

"Really?" Mara squeezed her arms against her body, letting the pain of her healing wound drown out the possibilities swirling through her mind. "When Tham and I move about the palace, it'll only be you guarding us?"

"*You* only need one guard." Andric bowed Mara down the hall. "If there is more than one to be protected, more guards will be required."

Mara relaxed her arms and pressed a pleasant smile onto her lips. "It'll be strange not to have the thunder of boots following me."

"I promise I'll keep you safe." Andric winked.

He walked beside her as they cut through the halls of the palace, behaving more like a friend keeping her company than a jailer preventing her from making a break for freedom.

"How's your side?" Andric asked.

"Fine," Mara said. "Still sore, but the matrons closed me up nicely, and I'm not cold anymore."

"You were cold?" Andric looked to her, furrowing his brow.

"I lost a lot of blood. The matrons gave me seven kinds of tonics. They promised I'd be fine."

"Good. That's good." The wrinkles stayed on Andric's brow as they turned the corner, cutting down the staircase that led to the entryway of the palace where the elite Isfolians of the court liked to linger.

The women wore dresses designed to impress their fellow minglers. The men wore coats with fur-lined collars, providing them far more warmth than the women's clothing ever allowed.

Mara longed to weave through the clusters of gossipers—not to join in the leisure of the rich, but to hear what troubles they thought worth whispering about inside the ice palace.

None of you know. You're teetering on the edge of doom, and you can't see the misery you face.

"…if you'll believe it." Andric stopped at the far end of the entryway, waiting for Mara to catch up.

"I'm sorry, what did you say?" Mara pinned her gaze on Andric, forbidding her mind to wander.

"I was saying that guarding you is the most trying of the duties I've been given since I joined the guards."

"Actually, I can believe that quite easily," Mara laughed. "Testing the nerves of everyone around me has been a lifelong pursuit."

Andric kept to an unnaturally slow pace as they climbed the stairs to the royals' private wing of the palace. "You don't test my nerves, Mara. You frighten me."

"I've managed to frighten you? I didn't know I was that intimidating."

"You aren't." Andric shrugged. His shoulders loosened, giving him the look of a normal man rather than an enemy with a sword on his hip. "You didn't scream when the ice cut you. You crawl into dark places most wouldn't face even if offered a fortune."

"You're frightened by my lack of self-preservation?"

"I'm afraid I won't be able to protect you." Andric stopped at the top of the stairs. "I would defend you from any enemy that might storm the palace. For more than a month, I've spent every day making sure you're safe, making sure you aren't lost to the ice. The only time I've had real cause to worry is when you've put yourself in danger."

"I'm not crawling into the ice for fun." Mara reached out,

laying her hand on Andric's arm before realizing what she'd done. "I'm working on behalf of the Princess."

She counted to three before pulling her hand away and tucking it into her pocket.

"I know. Her Highness has instructed me to assist you in your exploration of the fissures in the ice, but that doesn't make the work any less dangerous. I don't want to face a day when I fail to protect you, Mara." Andric rocked back on his heels. "You're an asset to Isfol."

"Thank you." Mara headed down the hall, dipping her chin to hide the heat flaring in her face. "But I'd hate for you to fuss over keeping me safe. Tham worries about me constantly. I think one man's brooding is sufficient."

"I'm not so sure." Andric's long strides placed him in front of Mara as they reached the door to Ronya's library. He nodded to the five guards on either side of the entrance before stopping with his hand on the doorknob. "From what I understand, you've been attached to Tham for a long time. If his caring for your well-being led you to this moment, I can't in good conscience trust him with your safety."

Mara opened her mouth, ready to scream a tirade of curses in Tham's defense.

Gentle, Mara, Allora whispered in her mind.

"Any danger I've placed myself in has been born of my own choices." Mara's voice sounded unnaturally pleasant to her own ears. "Tham understands me well enough to know that safety is not nearly as precious to me as freedom."

Andric held her gaze for a moment before opening the library door.

Unlike the entry to the room Mara shared with Tham, this door swung open without any magical aid.

Andric placed himself just inside the library, bowed toward the hearth, and gestured for Mara to enter.

May the gods give me patience.

As she stepped into the room, Mara glanced to each corner of the space, making sure there was nothing but books lurking in the shadows, before finally looking to the fireplace.

Ronya and Kegan worked at a table in front of the hearth, each studying a different set of papers.

"Your Highness." Mara curtsied, feeling like a fool for not bowing while wearing pants.

"You should learn to walk more quickly." Ronya beckoned Mara toward the table without looking up from her papers. "I need to know about ships."

"Ships? I don't know how much I can help," Mara said. "I've been on ships plenty of times, but only as a passenger. Tham spent his childhood at sea. If you want to know about sailing, you should—"

"No." Ronya grabbed Mara's wrist, yanking Mara to her side. "It would be wrong of me to involve him in this."

"In what?" Mara asked.

Ronya tapped the map on the table in front of her, right on a series of islands reaching out into the Arion Sea. "I don't want to know how to sail a ship. I'm never going to drag a rope or whatever it is they do to make the ships go."

"Drag a rope?" Mara swallowed her laugh. She glanced toward Kegan.

He had his gaze fixed on the map without a hint of humor on his face.

"The Ice Walkers have no fleet," Ronya said. "No ships at all, for that matter."

"Your people are contained inside a mountain. Why would you need any ships?" Mara said.

"Ian Ayres." Ronya tapped the dot on the map again. "The bastards' island created by the demons of the Guilds."

A chill ran up Mara's arms. "What about it?"

"The righteous will be offered victory. My cause must be undeniably worthy." Ronya paced in front of the fire. "My legacy will be one that generations speak of with awe and reverence. I cannot sit quietly waiting to be gifted the crown that is rightfully mine. It is my duty to ensure a prosperous future for my people. The ice is failing us. Even with your help, our harvest is lacking."

Mara glanced toward the door.

Andric stood guard beside the door to Ronya's library, hearing every word the Princess said.

"And not just the ice worm harvest, edible crops are falling short of every marker as well," Ronya said. "I will not be complacent as my city drifts further into decline."

"The food isn't growing?" Mara said.

"We should be a people of bounty, not cowards hiding and hoping for mere survival. My father would keep the Ice Walkers on a path to their doom," Ronya said. "Keep us all huddled inside the mountain, waiting to die."

"Have things actually gotten that bad?" Mara stepped into Ronya's path.

Ronya stopped short.

Mara clenched her jaw, waiting to be slapped.

"I won't wait for starvation to strike my people. Not when I see a path to salvation." Ronya gripped Mara's shoulders.

"The tundra, Mara," Kegan said. "There's nothing between Whitend and the mountains. Barely anything between Ilara and Whitend."

"Don't tell me you found ice worms that far south." Mara twisted out of Ronya's grip, feeling the promise of new bruises on her shoulders even as she moved.

"Not ice worms. Land." Kegan looked up from the map, meeting Mara's gaze for the first time since she'd been dragged into the ice so long ago. "The people in Ilbrea think of everything close to the white mountains as too far north for a village, let alone farmland. But the Ice Walkers could grow their crops on that land. Live comfortably there even during the winter months."

"It would be daring," Ronya said. "My father would never approve. Convincing the people of Isfol to settle south of the mountains would be difficult at best."

"It should be," Mara said. "Settling anywhere outside Isfol would mean revealing the existence of your people, letting the Guilds know the Ice Walkers exist. Right now, you have solid walls of ice no one can break through. If you venture anywhere near Ilbrea—"

"We'll be setting ourselves up for a battle with the Guilds," Ronya said. "I know. It's an awful thing to even consider. But if it's a choice between sacrificing my people in battle or watching them starve and freeze, then I will stain the snow red with blood."

Mara studied the map, the swath of land between the white mountains and Whitend. Even a small portion of the territory would be far more than the Isfolians could fill in generations of settlements.

"There is unused land. Land that could save my people from their doom," Ronya said. "It's right there on the map. We have to take it."

"You can't take it." Mara gripped the edge of the table, willing her heart to stay calm. "Whatever the danger to your people might be, you cannot claim Ilbrean land."

"You would let innocent people starve?" Kegan said.

"No one is starving. You've just said—"

"You would have us wait to act until Isfol's children begin to suffer?" Ronya cut across Mara.

"I would have you keep your people alive," Mara said. "If anyone tries to take land claimed by the Guilds, they will be slaughtered. First, the Soldiers Guild will come and then the Sorcerers Guild. They won't leave any survivors."

"I forget you're Guilded." Kegan pushed away from the table and sank into a chair by the fire.

"What's that supposed to mean?" Mara said.

"You get a fancy mark on your arm and a special color to wear and start to believe the Guilds are almighty and far above the rest of us," Kegan said. "Neither the King nor the sorcerers were born gods. They are mortal."

"And powerful. Even if an army could stand a chance against the Guilds, the cost would be terrible." Mara cut around the table toward Kegan. "There has to be a way to feed the Ice Walkers while staying well away from the Guilds."

"You can't tell people to starve just to keep the Guilds comfortable," Kegan said. "Let the Soldiers Guild come into the white, see how well they do fighting the Ice Walkers."

"Why would you wish the Soldiers Guild into battle against anyone?" Mara said. "You have friends in the Soldiers Guild."

"Who were paid more than I ever was." Kegan leaned back in his chair. "Given privileges I never was. The Guilds' rule only helps the slitches with Guild marks on their arms. The first time I ever slept in a well-made bed was when Princess Ronya saw to my comfort. Years of working for the Guilds and I couldn't even afford new boots. I'm sorry, Mara, and I do regret any pain that might come to my friends in Ilbrea, but I have no loyalty to the Guilds."

"No loyalty to anything, it seems," Mara said. "Princess Ronya, do be careful with that one. Your new Ilbrean pet is a fickle beast."

"Mara—"

"Stop squabbling before I begin to doubt your usefulness," Ronya said.

"Yes, Your Highness." Kegan stood and went back to the map.

"My course is set, sweet Mara," Ronya said. "We must expand the Ice Walkers' territory. The decision must be presented to the people in a way that does not allow for dissension."

"You told me yourself the Ice Walkers rely on secrecy for safety," Mara said.

"Which is why I need ships." Ronya slammed her palm on the table. "I will not be a cowering Queen. The Ice Walkers must thrive. To build our glorious future, we must move south. If I am going to spill any of my people's blood, I must be certain even the Guilds' god would deem it a worthy sacrifice. We will go south to make our new home. We will seize Ilbrean ships, and I will rescue every innocent woman and child the Guilds have condemned to Ian Ayres. When my people hear the tale of that wretched place, none will dare to declare me the villain. The people will cheer as they call me their righteous warrior."

"You're going to tell your people about Ian Ayres?" Mara glanced back to Andric as shame and anger flushed her cheeks. "You may have demanded my darkest secret, but that does not make it yours to tell."

"My pet." Ronya took Mara's hand and gave it a gentle kiss. "I treasure our friendship, but I would slit your throat on the palace steps to protect my people."

"But I've been finding more worms for you to mine." Panic pressed on Mara's throat. "I've done everything you've asked. I've been helping you."

"You will continue to aid our miners," Ronya said. "And you will bow to me when I tell my people of the atrocities of Ian Ayres. And when the day to journey south arrives, you will beg to be by my side. For once people hear how long you knew of the horrors of Ian Ayres and did nothing to save those innocent children from being tormented by the Guilds, you will have no choice but to fight to free the island's victims. If you were to turn your back on their pain again, I don't think even your beloved Tham would forgive you."

"Tham doesn't know what happened on Ian Ayres," Mara said. "Please, he can't ever know."

"Are you afraid he won't worship you anymore?" Ronya said. "If you aren't perfect, he'll realize you aren't worth all the pain he's suffered because of scarred little you?"

"Tham would love me no matter what."

"Liar," Ronya whispered. "Tham's life is the penalty for not telling the truth. I'll give you one more chance. Lie again, and I'll have his heart torn out."

"He'll—" Mara swallowed the fear throbbing in her throat. "He'll see it as a betrayal. I told you but never him. Even knowing how much he suffered as a child, I stayed silent while innocents were trapped in that awful place."

"That's better." Ronya patted Mara's cheek. "You have done a horrible thing, Mara. The path to redemption begins with action. Help me free the children of Ian Ayres."

"I…" Mara closed her eyes, picturing the rocky shore of that terrible island. "You'll need more than one ship. And I don't think there's any port north of Ilara where you'll have a guarantee of any ships being at the docks once the end-of-summer storms set in."

"Then we shall make our way to the Guilds' capital," Ronya said. "How lucky you're so familiar with the city."

12

MARA

A child should never have to endure such darkness.

Lord Karron's words pounded through Mara's mind over and over, an unending echo even years couldn't silence.

A child should never have to endure such darkness.

She sat curled in the corner of the room, letting the chill of the walls seep through her shift. A slit of light peered through the curtains they'd finally been given to block out the unrelenting glow of Isfol.

Tham lay in bed. The line of light cut across his back and Elle's snout. Elle had curled up just behind Tham, hiding the worst of the scars on his back. He'd gained the deepest of those wounds because of Mara, as punishment for saving her life when they were barely more than children.

He'd survived so much, battled so many demons no person should have to face. She had no right to feel broken, no excuse for the fear she couldn't shake.

A child should never have to endure such darkness.

It was always dark in the children's hall on Ian Ayres. Even during the day, the tiny windows set high up in the walls didn't let in enough light.

Mara had learned to be grateful for the shadows—more places to hide from the matrons and older children who thrived on tormenting the weak and small.

She'd hidden under her cot until they'd found her. After that beating, she'd learned to lie on the benches tucked under the tables where the children of Ian Ayres ate moldy food from unwashed bowls.

Silence and stillness. It was the only way to survive the bastards' island.

The screams of the mothers in the birthing house carried to Mara's hiding place. The cries of the infants, too. Wails of misery and pain she could not escape.

Until the day the noise changed.

"Do you understand who you are speaking to?" The powerful fury in the man's voice didn't belong in such a hopeless place. *"You will address me with the respect my position demands."*

"This island is under the matrons' care. There are rules that must be followed."

Mara flinched at the matron's crisp shout.

"If you will not bring me the child, I will find her myself," the man said.

The bang of a door slamming open muddied the matron's reply.

The thump of heavy boots shook the floor.

Mara clung to the bench as the man stormed past.

Other men with their own heavy boots followed behind him.

"How many children do you have living in this filth?" the man said.

"We take all the Guilds send us," the matron said.

"Search everywhere. Find the girl." The man left, heading deeper into the children's home.

Mara closed her eyes, hoping whatever child the man had come to find had a good place to hide, or was one of the older ones who enjoyed causing pain. The ones who kicked hard enough to break ribs might deserve whatever the man had planned for them.

Boots thumped toward the table. The one wearing them paused.

Mara held her breath.

The bench beneath her shifted.

Mara rolled sideways, landing under the table. She scrambled away from the boots, dove into the open, and leapt to her feet.

"I found a redhead!" A man stood between her and the door to the outside.

Mara bolted the other way, running farther into the building, cutting past the rooms packed with cots where the older children slept and into the empty rooms she'd learned to avoid.

"You, stop," another man shouted as she dodged around him.

If she could get all the way to the far end of the children's home, to the place where they stacked the wood for the fires—

An arm wrapped around Mara's waist, scooping her off her feet.

"Whoa now," a man said. *"You're a fast one."*

Mara didn't kick or scream as the man carried her back to an empty room. She froze, unable to do anything but wait for whatever pain might come.

A man in a fancy, map maker green coat waited in the empty room, loathing and anger pulsing from every shred of his being.

"Is this her, sir?" The man who'd grabbed Mara presented her to the map maker.

"What's your name?" the map maker asked.

Mara met the man's gaze.

"Child, I asked you a question," the man said.

"I—" Could she still have a name when no one had spoken it in months?

A bit of the map maker's anger seemed to fade. *"I'm not going to hurt you. I just need to know your name."*

"Mara Landil."

The map maker pushed her matted hair away from her face. *"You're going to be all right now, Mara. I'm going to take you away from here. You're going someplace safe."*

"You can't just take the girl." A matron blocked the doorway. *"She was placed in our care by the Guilds."*

"Your care is a travesty I will be reporting at the next meeting of the Guilds Council," the map maker said.

"I will not be threatened." The matron slammed her fist against the doorjamb.

A whimper came from the shadows.

The map maker turned toward the sound.

A bundle of filth lay in the corner. It twitched as the map maker got closer.

A boy rolled out of the rags. He tried to get to his feet but toppled over, smashing his shoulder against the wall. The boy gasped but didn't cry out.

"What is this?" The map maker stared down at the child.

The boy tried to crawl away, but his arm crumpled beneath him.

"This child is hurt." The map maker rounded on the matron. *"There is blood on his face. Why has no one seen to him? What happened to him?"*

The boy dragged himself across the floor, his breath hitching in his chest as he tried to escape.

"You saw that the boy was hiding," the matron said. *"And that one's been hurt enough times, he should know how to treat his own ills."*

"You're a demon." The map maker scooped the boy into his arms.

The boy whimpered, covering his head, preparing for a blow.

"What do you think you're doing?" the matron said.

"Taking this child before he dies in your care. Now get out of my way before I order my men to restrain you."

"You're not the only one who will be speaking to the Guilds Council." The matron backed out of their path.

The map maker strode out of the empty room, the wounded boy in his arms.

The man carrying Mara cradled her to his chest, holding her more gently than he had before.

"We'll find you some food as soon as we get on the ship," the man said. *"A nice meal. And we'll get you cleaned up. Lord Karron is a good man. He'll take care of you."*

Mara shut her eyes as they passed the rooms packed with cots where the unwanted children of Ilbrea slept. She didn't want to see the faces of the others as they wondered if she was lucky or doomed.

The bright afternoon sun warmed Mara's cheeks as they cut across the island.

She still didn't open her eyes.

She didn't want to see the graves where they piled the women who died in labor on top of each other, muddling the layers of bones.

She didn't open her eyes until the man set her down on a wooden seat in a fancy ship's cabin.

"Get the healer," the map maker, Lord Karron, said. *"Find the children soup and bread."*

"Yes, sir."

A door closed behind Mara.

She wondered if she was trapped.

"You're safe now, Mara." Lord Karron knelt to look into her eyes. *"I was a friend of your father. He wanted me to look after you, but I was away on a journey when he died. I'm sorry it took me so long to come and get you. A child should never have to endure such darkness."*

Mara looked to the boy sitting in the chair beside her. Filth and blood stained his sunken cheeks.

He stared at Lord Karron with terrified wonder, as though he didn't believe someone might be taking him away from Ian Ayres but didn't want to give up the only bit of hope he'd ever felt, either.

A bell rang on the deck, and the ship left the docks, stealing Mara and the boy, Adrial, away from the bastards' island, leaving all the other children behind.

A child should never have to endure such darkness.

How many children had Lord Karron left behind on Ian Ayres?

Mara brushed the tears from her eyes, clearing her vision so she could see Tham and Elle lying in bed.

How many more children had been born into the darkness since she'd been rescued? What had happened to all the other children from Ian Ayres?

The ones who had hurt her. The ones who'd suffered worse beatings than Adrial.

Mara shook out her hands and let out a long breath, willing the panic in her chest to ease.

Elle huffed and resettled her snout on Tham's side.

Mara had been lucky. She had been rescued.

Hiding from the demons was a privilege she did not deserve.

There are still children trapped in the darkness, Adrial whispered. *It didn't stop with us.*

Mara stood, letting the cold of the floor still her nerves as she crept around to Tham's side of the bed.

"Tham," she whispered.

His eyes flew open as he shoved back the covers, instantly alert and ready for attack.

"It's all right." Mara laid her hand on his chest. "Everything's fine. I just…I told Ronya something awful, and I can't…. You deserve to hear the truth from me."

"Mara?" He brushed her curls away from her face.

"There are things I never told you about Ian Ayres."

13

ADRIAL

"Goods are still flooding the docks," Lord Nevon said. "I have merchants showing up wanting to pitch tents over the crates that won't fit into the warehouses. One getch even tried to convince me to let a flock of his men come in to guard his shipment of lace. As though I'm fool enough to allow armed common folk to enter the nightmare my docks have become."

Adrial looked up to the skylight overhead. Rain spattered down on the glass, blocking out the sun, leaving the golden seven-pointed star inlaid in the round table as nothing more than a moderately pleasing decoration.

"The end-of-summer storms will be arriving soon," Lady Gwell said. "That will slow the flow of ships docking in Ilara and allow time for the goods that remain in storage to be thoroughly searched and then released."

"The storms are coming, and there is still no word of Captain Devlin's ship that left the docks with your sorcerer-made sail." Lord Nevon jabbed his finger against the table. "Have you forgotten you're meant to be searching incoming ships for word of my lost sailors, not just whatever weapons you think the monsters who've been attacking us might be trying to sneak in from the Arion Sea?"

Adrial gripped his hands together in his lap, willing his face to stay calm and his mouth to stay shut.

Kai will come home. The best you can do for him is make sure there's something left of Ilara when he finally turns up.

"We have questioned every crew. There has been no news of Sorcerer Roo's lost ship," Lady Gwell said.

"Captain Devlin's lost ship that Sorcerer Roo dragged to its doom," Lord Nevon said.

Not doom. Kai is still out there, making his way back to Ilara. Swimming across the Arion Sea to find his way home.

There was no doubt in the voice that whispered in Adrial's mind. No sorrow or fear. Only a bit of laughter, as though Kai himself were preparing to tell the harrowing tale of his escape from a bitter storm and his seduction of whatever handsome rogues waited for him on the far side of despair.

Adrial let his shoulders relax, grateful that the thoughts of his friend offered some relief from the tension that threatened to snap his nerves.

"We will continue to search for the ship," Lady Gwell said. "I will send another round of messages to every port if that is what you desire. But remember, Lord Sailor, progress cannot be attained without sacrifice. We must thank those brave Ilbreans who willingly dared to push us into the future rather than turn the truth of their heroism into a mockery of the loyalty owed the Guilds."

"Ha." Lord Nevon coughed out a laugh and sat back in his chair, glaring at the Lady Sorcerer as though wishing he could use a knife to demonstrate just what the Sailors Guild owed the sorcerers.

"And what of my ship?" Lord Karron said. "My journey south has been postponed long enough. As soon as my daughter has married King Brannon, the voyage to the southern islands must begin."

"The end-of-summer storms are already creeping into Ilara." Lady Byrd pointed to the rain pattering down on the skylight. "They'll be here in full force by the day of the wedding." She looked to Lady Gwell. "I hope arrangements have been made to ensure the comfort of the guests arriving for the occasion."

"Of course," Lady Gwell said.

"Wet wedding guests should not be a higher priority for this council than the map makers' journey," Lord Karron said. "Preparations for the journey cannot be delayed any longer."

Lord Nevon dragged his hand across the stubble on his chin.

"The King himself ordered the exploration of the islands beyond the southern storms," Lord Karron said.

"The southern storms are unpredictable at the best of times," Lord Nevon said. "With a ship already missing—"

"Lord Karron's journey will set sail as soon as his daughter has wed the King," Lady Gwell said. "The commands of King Brannon cannot be tossed aside. Whatever it takes, whatever the cost, the Lord Map Maker's journey must begin."

"Perhaps the King should be allowed to judge what price he's willing to pay to see his orders followed," Adrial said.

Silence swept around the room.

Lady Gwell stood, making her position in the King's rightful seat even more glaring. "His Majesty's orders must be followed. His desire for the Map Makers Guild to explore the islands beyond the southern storms has not changed."

For the baby. You can face any demon to protect your son, Adrial Ayres.

He reached into his pocket, pulling out a scroll as he stood to face Lady Gwell. "The Sorcerers Guild was given orders by King Brannon to root out the villains who have been attacking the Guilds. In the five nights the sorcerers have scoured the city, your Guild has yet to find any of the rebels who attacked us."

"We are digging further into the muck that taints Ilara than someone in a white robe can understand," Lady Gwell said. "The progress we have made—"

"Progress?" Adrial stepped up to the edge of the table as he unrolled the scroll. "In the past five nights, one-hundred and twelve adults have been killed in the sorcerers' raids. None of these victims have been marked as rebels who had anything to do with the attack on the cathedral or at my wedding."

"Those are not the only two crimes a rotta can be guilty of," Lady Gwell said.

"Twenty-seven children have been killed in the raids," Adrial pressed on, "including three babes too young to walk."

Lord Gareth gasped.

Adrial looked up from his scroll. "Do you think the King would find those numbers worth the cost? Or shall I go on?"

"The city must be secured." Lady Gwell planted her hands on the table, leaning toward Adrial, danger sparking in her eyes.

"Eighty-six injured have begged the Scribes Guild for aid in petitioning the Healers Guild to treat their wounds." Adrial held the Lady Sorcerer's gaze. "None of our petitions have been answered. Seventy-two homes burned. Fourteen shops. Thirteen new orphans have been made, with no family on record to offer them a home. Shall we ask the King what we should do with the orphans the Sorcerers Guild has created in their failed attempt to find the rebels?"

"The orphans will be sent to Ian Ayres," Lady Gwell said. "It's where the unwanted belong."

"It is a hell not even demons should be forced to endure." Adrial pounded his fist on the table, leaning toward Lady Gwell, letting his rage consume his fear. "Your sorcerers have become murderers, and the people of Ilara are watching it happen. Every night, your butchers go out and use their magic to spill innocent blood. Every death at the sorcerers' hands turns the people of this city further against the Guilds. If you continue down this path, there will not be a soul possessing any reason or compassion who won't understand why the common folk loathe the Guilds."

"Are these the things your rotta wife whispers in your ear?" Lady Gwell sneered.

"These are the things being a man with an ounce of compassion and a reasonable mind has taught me. The Guilds are meant to serve the people of Ilbrea, not torment and slaughter them. A tally of the people who have been slain by the Sorcerers Guild has been delivered to the King."

Lady Gwell's lips tightened into a pinched line. "The King approves of my methods."

"Then I hope the King will not be shocked when Ilara runs out of citizens for you to murder and you're still no closer to completing your task." Adrial rolled his scroll back up and tucked it into his pocket. "Even members of the Guilds need boots, so do be careful not to kill the last cobbler." He stepped behind Lord Gareth and took his seat.

Lady Gwell held his gaze.

For a moment, Adrial thought he saw a shimmer of sparks crackle across her skin. He held his breath, waiting for pain to scorch through his veins.

"Such fire from the Lord Scribe's heir," Lord Nevon said. "The young should not be braver than the old. Send the orphans the Sorcerers Guild has made to the docks. I don't care how young they are. The Sailors Guild will take them all. We'll find families for them among my sailors, and they'll join the Guild when they come of age. I'll not have the mistakes of the Sorcerers Guild condemn innocent children to Ian Ayres."

"Thank you, Lord Nevon," Adrial said.

"There will be no cost for burial papers for those killed by the Sorcerers Guild," Lord Gareth said. "Have postings placed around the city. I will not have the people of Ilara thinking the Scribes Guild endorses the ill-aimed violence of the sorcerers."

"Do you think your petty defiance will stop our search?" Lady

Gwell sat in the King's seat. "We will continue our work until it is done."

"Adrial." Lord Karron locked eyes with his former ward. "No one should go hungry because the Sorcerers Guild destroyed their ability to earn enough coin to buy food. There are always tasks to be done at the Map Master's Palace. Send those who need work up to the cliffs."

"Thank you, Lord Karron." Adrial nodded.

"Nicking the paws of a lioness won't maim her, Head Scribe. It only reminds her what annoyances needn't be tolerated," Lady Gwell said. "You are a sweet little dove filled with naïve hope. Be careful not to push too far. You risk drawing the predator's claws to your throat."

14

MARA

If Mara squinted in just the right way, the blue of the cavern's ceiling almost looked like a bright, dazzling afternoon sky. But for all their beauty, the plants on the palace grounds ruined the illusion that Mara had escaped to a garden in Ilbrea.

"No, Elle." Tham nudged the dog away from a bed of silver-bloomed flowers. "I don't know if those will hurt you."

Elle gave herself a shake and began running circles around the flowerbed instead.

"They wouldn't kill her," Lynn said. "But the poor pup would end up having an awful day. The maids, too."

"Thank you." Tham gave Lynn a nod. "Come here, Elle."

Elle barked and sprinted back, weaving a loop through the eight guards who'd been assigned to Tham and Mara, before flopping over at Tham's feet.

She wriggled on the moss-covered ground, staring up at Tham, absolute adoration lighting her charcoal-rimmed eyes.

"Good girl, Elle." Tham knelt and scratched her stomach.

"And you say someone tried to train her as a sled dog?" Andric laughed.

"She is a sled dog," Mara said.

Elle scrambled to her feet just long enough to flop onto Mara's toes.

"I never said she was a very good sled dog." Mara had barely managed to scratch Elle's ear before the dog had taken off again.

"She's stir-crazy," Tham said. "We should take her for a walk in town."

"You're not to leave the grounds today," Andric said. "You can let her run in the gardens or take her back to your room."

"The gardens are delightful." Mara started walking again, barely keeping Elle in sight as she bounded through the trees. "Who could dream of anything more?"

Andric skirted around a tree to walk beside Mara, claiming the place that should have been Tham's.

Mara squinted up through the white leaves dripping from the trees, trying to fool herself into believing she was seeing the sky.

"Are you all right?" Andric asked.

"Just appreciating the beauty of the gardens." Mara moved to tuck her hands into her pockets before remembering the dress the maids had insisted she wear didn't have them. "You know, I've spent so much time exploring the city and searching for caches of ice worms, I really haven't taken the time to enjoy the palace grounds."

"Are there places like this in Ilara?" Andric asked.

"No," Tham said.

Mara looked back at him.

Tham walked behind Mara, his gaze shifting from Elle, to the trees, to the guards—anywhere but in Mara's direction.

"More or less grand?" Lynn's hand brushed against Tham's as she pointed to a patch of deep-pink blooms that seemed to have been dusted with ground-up diamonds.

The muscles in Tham's neck tensed.

"It depends on where you are." Mara pointed toward the cavern ceiling high above. "But every garden I've seen in Ilara is in the open air."

"I suppose that would make a difference," Lynn laughed.

"It would be a wonder to behold." Andric bowed Mara onto a side path.

Mara froze for a moment, waiting for Tham to step forward to walk beside her.

Instead, he leaned over to see past Mara, watching Elle sprint through the trees.

Mara headed down Andric's chosen path, smoothing the curls that fought to break free from her braid, wishing she had something better to do with her hands. "Do you know how long it will be before we can get back to our work?"

"All I've been told is that you aren't to leave the grounds today," Andric said.

"Of course." Mara moved on to brushing out the front of her skirt.

"Try to enjoy yourself," Andric said. "It wasn't long ago the matrons had to stitch your side back together. As grateful as the people of Isfol should be for the work you've done, I'm not sorry Her Highness's orders are forcing you to rest."

"I've had enough rest for a lifetime," Mara said.

Tham should've given a faint, low laugh behind her, but the only sound was the thumping of footsteps trailing in her wake.

She dug her nails into her palms, resisting the urge to fuss with her curls again.

"Elle, come back," Tham called.

Elle froze, so far ahead of them Mara could barely see her through the trees.

"Elle, come," Tham called.

Elle barked and bolted back toward them, bursting through flowerbeds to reach Tham's side.

"At least she understands *come*," Lynn said.

Elle banged into Lynn's legs, as though wanting to prove her worth through affection.

"You are a love." Lynn brushed the flower petals from Elle's head.

"We should be getting back inside." Mara cut around the guards and back onto the path that led toward the palace.

"If that's what you want." Andric reclaimed his place beside her before she'd made it twenty steps.

"You were right to suggest I take this opportunity to rest." Mara lengthened her strides, letting the rustle of her skirt mask the footsteps of the people behind her.

Andric had the sense not to talk as they cut over to the wide walkway that led to the front entrance of the palace.

The usual gossiping elite of the court wandered up the path, stopping to stare at Mara as she passed.

Anger bubbled in her chest, threatening to tear a scream from her throat.

Their whispers could have been about her dress, the fact that she was nearly running, or peevish wonder that Ronya had let her pet Ilbreans loose on the palace grounds.

But in her mind, Mara could only hear one whispered word.

Coward. Coward. Coward. Coward.

A guard walked down the palace steps, cutting through the clusters of gawkers. He locked his gaze on Mara.

It's in my head. It's all in my head. He's not looking at me.

The guard directed his steps straight toward her.

She gripped the sides of her skirt, preparing to run.

The guard bowed to Mara then turned and bowed to Tham. "Her Highness has requested your presence. This way." He bowed a third time before walking back toward the palace.

Mara made herself follow the guard but couldn't convince her hands to let go of her skirt as she tipped her chin up, hoping the people she passed would think she looked more regal than terrified.

The entryway of the palace had far more people milling about than usual. And, instead of tight little clusters sharing hushed gossip before flitting on to the next pack, everyone roamed on their own, as though hoping to find the one person who might have the juiciest news.

Mara clenched her teeth, not allowing herself to flinch at the roar of whispers that trailed in her wake as the guard led her to the stairs that cut up to the royals' private wing of the palace.

The guard stopped at the foot of the steps, held up a hand to keep Mara from passing him, and nodded to another guard at the top of the stairs.

An ache tightened in Mara's chest as Tham stepped around her, placing himself between her and the guard who'd been sent to fetch them.

If she could just reach out and take his hand, feel the warmth of his skin against hers, everything would be better.

She could drag him away. Find a place where there weren't spies lurking inside the walls. A few minutes alone, that was all she needed to make things right. She could explain why she'd given Ronya a secret she'd never shared with him. Why the darkness of the bastards' island had made her too afraid to even think about the place until it became the only way she could protect his life.

She would find a way to earn absolution, even if he refused to condemn her.

The whispers in the hall swelled as Ronya appeared at the top of the steps. She paused, allowing the court a moment to behold her beauty.

She wore her hair loose, cascading around her shoulders. Her white gown sparkled as though covered in fresh snow, but the skirt had been spattered with red, the hem completely coated in it, as though she'd waded through a blood-soaked battlefield.

"People of Isfol, you must forgive my forgoing the normal formalities, but I'm afraid we do not have time to waste on revelry," Ronya said.

Kegan stepped out of the crowd to stand at the bottom of the steps right beside Mara, as though the Ilbreans were a united force.

"There are dark days ahead," Ronya said. "It is time for the Ice Walkers to choose between hiding, waiting for tragedy to trap and ruin us, or taking a stand and doing what is necessary to build a glorious future for our people. For some time now, the ice worm harvests have been dwindling. Our stores of their life-saving magic are dangerously low."

Panicked murmurs flew through the crowd.

Ronya held up a hand, silencing the court. "The Regent, in his desire to care for you as he would a child, hid this truth, prioritizing your comfort above the safety of our people. But we cannot hide from this danger. If we do not act now, it will be too late. We will lose our elders. We will lose the guards who dare to venture through the ice to protect our city. We will lose our children. But we mustn't give in to despair. I speak to you today with hope and purpose."

Footsteps hurried down the corridor at the top of the stairs. The Regent stormed into view, his blue robes billowing behind him.

"It's all right, father." Ronya's gentle tone echoed out over the crowd. "You don't have to worry anymore. You can go to your room and rest."

"Rest?" The Regent looked to the horde below, fear and rage filling his face.

"The Regent, in his wisdom, has begged me to lead the people of Isfol through the perils ahead. I have answered his cries for help and have taken my rightful place as Queen." Ronya nodded to her father. "The strength needed to face our enemies lies with magic. My dearest father has never been offered that gift."

Ronya scooped her hand through the air.

Four spikes of ice grew up from the floor, twisting together to form a chair beside the Regent.

"Please sit, father. You need to rest. There is no need for you to tire yourself." Ronya looked back to the crowd, ignoring her father standing resolutely beside the chair. "For too long, we have hidden inside this cavern, hoping the ice will continue to provide for us, ignoring the land south of the white mountains. Valuable land that waits for someone bold enough to seize it. Do not believe any villainous rumors that vanity has driven me to ask you to muster the bravery demanded as we venture outside the safe haven that has been our home for so long. There can be no question. We must expand our territory south if we want the next generation to thrive."

The soft sniffle of terrified tears filled the silence.

"I have spent months searching for another solution to our plight. I find no joy in the prospect of conquering any land or ending the lives of those who oppose us. I do not want to cause anyone pain. But, through my friendship with Mara Landil, I have learned of the horrors the Guilds inflict on their own children." Ronya looked down at Mara. "Ilbreans are not people we should feel any guilt in slaying. They are monsters that must be destroyed."

Mara tried to back away. Kegan gripped her shoulder, stopping her escape.

"Ilbrea's Guilded monsters torment their own, sending the babes they deem unwanted out to an island in the middle of the sea to suffer unimaginable torment. Precious children. Abandoned. Left to die. These are the demons we stand against. We will fight the monsters who so viciously abuse their own children. We will fight to save the lives of the Ice Walkers' babes. Our cause is just. Our fight is righteous.

"When you go out into the city, tell everyone you pass that Queen Ronya has taken her rightful place on the throne. Tell them your Queen will do whatever it takes to save her people from the ice worms' abandonment. Tell them the Queen of Isfol will ride against the monsters to the south, and when the battle is won, there will be none who can doubt that every sacrifice has been worthy."

Ronya turned and strode down the hall, the red train of her dress trailing behind her.

Chatter burst out in the entryway as half the horde headed straight for the doors while the rest searched for closer ears to endure their opinions.

"Do they really discard their children?"

Mara stumbled back as a woman squeezed in between her and the stairs.

"I asked"—the woman spoke louder—"do they really discard their children in Ilbrea?"

"They"—Mara's breath hitched in her chest—"the unwanted children are kept on Ian Ayres."

"It's true!" The woman gasped with delight. "The outside world is filled with such horrors. Do they literally torture the children? I bet they do. Do they use knives?"

A blessed weight wrapped around Mara's waist, guiding her away from the woman.

"Enough." Tham didn't shout, but the woman flinched as though he'd struck her. He kept his arm wrapped tight around Mara as he steered her through the remaining crowd toward the stairs that led to their room.

"Do not dare to run from me, Ilbreans," the Regent shouted.

Two guards cut in front of Mara and Tham, blocking their path.

Tham let go of Mara's waist and reached his arm in front of her, placing himself as a barrier between her and the Regent.

"Do you have any idea the damage you've done?" The Regent spoke in such a quiet tone, Mara had to lean closer to hear him. "The blood that is shed will be on your head."

"Mine?" Mara said. "I've tried to—"

"Do you think she'll choose a nice bit of land and be content to defend it?" the Regent said. "My daughter seeks glory and delights in pain. Declaring herself Queen—"

"You did that," Mara said.

"I did no such thing," the Regent said. "And now that she has declared herself the savior of our people, the righteous warrior the fools crave, I have no hope of fighting this coup without horrific bloodshed. If I so much as try to speak against her, I will be the demon who wishes to ignore the dangers to both Ice Walker and Ilbrean children. How much do you hate your own country that you would fill her head with tales of the Guilds slaughtering children?"

"I never said the children of Ian Ayres are killed." Tears stung Mara's eyes. "I don't know what happens to them."

"She will lead a storm of warriors out of the ice," the Regent said. "May you feel the death of her every victim."

"I didn't…" Mara swayed. Panic had numbed her limbs. She couldn't feel the floor.

The Regent strode away, his guards clearing Mara and Tham's path to the stairs.

Tham took her waist again, keeping her upright while they climbed the steps.

Ian Ayres. After all the things Ronya had said about the dangers to the people of Isfol, how could any of the Ice Walkers care about Ian Ayres?

Violence and tragedy are excellent entertainment, Allora whispered. *Especially when those horrors give you the chance to feel divinely superior.*

Andric remade the door to their room.

Elle darted out into the hall, knocking into Tham's knees.

Someone had taken her to their room. Gotten Elle out of the way for Ronya's grand announcement. Mara hadn't even noticed.

"Mara." Andric took her arm, guiding her away from the safety of Tham. "Please don't let the Regent upset you. He's not known for having a thoughtful temperament. I promise you, you've done nothing wrong. By helping Queen Ronya, you are saving innocent lives. The bravery it took to confess what you'd seen on the Guilds' island of horrors, the bravery you've shown by going into the ice to help a city you've only recently begun to call home, you are astounding, Mara. And I am grateful for everything you've done."

Mara didn't try to hide the tears that trailed down her cheeks. "Please don't call me brave. It only makes things worse."

She slipped free from his grip and went into the room she shared with Tham and Elle.

No one had carved *Coward* into the ice of the walls.

The bright light of Isfol poured in through the window, maddeningly consistent even as news of Queen Ronya's ascension spread through the city.

Mara leaned against the windowsill, letting the ice steady her.

Tham placed his hands on the windowsill, his pinky barely brushing against hers.

She closed her eyes, wishing the warmth from that slightest of touches could somehow envelop her, shutting out the world, making her feel whole and safe for even a moment.

"Keep breathing, Mara," Tham whispered. "That's all I ask."

15

NIKO

The maids didn't hurry through their afternoon work in Niko's room. Draining the tub, collecting the dishes, putting fresh sheets on the bed—the three women took their time, meticulously completing every task with plenty of pauses to glance in Niko's direction.

He sat in his chair by the window, looking out over the valley of the Brien stronghold.

Even on rainy days, the view from his room offered a balm to the wounds the Brien Elder had carved into his soul. Staring at the forest below dulled his fear, and rage, and pain just enough for him to take full breaths.

A cloud drifted in front of the sun, painting its silhouette on the valley floor.

One of the maids stopped beside his chair and held out her hands.

"Boots," Danu said.

She always stood at the front of the room while the maids worked. For the last few days, she'd started standing in the corner, out of the way of the windows, allowing Niko to have a fully clear view.

"Boots, Niko," Danu said.

"Sorry." Niko pulled off his boots and gave them to the maid.

She carried them away to be polished.

They always polished his boots even though he never left his room. A useless kindness offered by the Brien.

A maid carrying a bucket followed the boot maid out into the hall.

"I wish you didn't have to stand there." Niko pressed his sock-clad feet to the ground.

"Tired of my company already?" Danu said. "Wish I'd lock you in here all alone?"

"Not that." Niko looked toward her before he could stop himself.

Danu's lips slipped into a sly smile, as though she'd been able to see the burst of fear that shot through Niko's mind at the mere thought of being locked in with his nightmares as his only companions.

"I—I only meant there's little dignity a man can cling to after you've watched someone haul away his piss." Niko leaned back in his chair, pretending he couldn't hear the laughter in Danu's voice.

"If you're worried about losing your dignity, you have too much pride left to be a hopeless case."

"I'll cling to those words."

The cloud drifted beyond the stronghold, allowing the sun to bathe the valley in its brilliance once more.

Niko watched the leaves shift with the tides of the wind for a long while, not speaking as the maids replaced the bucket and returned his boots.

When they'd finally finished their work, a different woman entered Niko's room carrying a large tray of food.

She peeked at Niko as she settled his tray on the table. Moving around to the far side to arrange his frie and cup, giving herself a view of him without having to crane her neck.

Her eyes caught on Niko's, and she held his gaze, staring at him as though trying to discover some secret hidden deep within his mind.

Niko didn't allow himself to look away, not even as the woman moved on to studying the rest of him.

His pallor, the hollows in his cheeks that hadn't gone away in the days since he'd been moved out of his cell, the tension in his torso that never eased as he spent every moment waiting to be attacked.

The woman's gaze finally landed on his sock-clad feet. She huffed a laugh.

"Enough," Danu said. "Away with you."

The woman bowed to Danu and hurried out of the room, closing the door behind her.

Danu followed, pressing her fingers to the door to lock them in.

She leaned against the wall, almost as though the maids bustling around Niko's room had exhausted her as much as it had him.

"Eat." She nodded Niko toward the table.

He pulled on his freshly polished boots then sat for a moment, trying to convince himself to stand.

"You have to eat." Danu pushed away from the wall and sat in the second seat at Niko's table.

"I don't know if I can stomach it." Niko gripped his knees.

"You have to stomach it. Eat, Niko. Don't force me to make it an order."

"If I end up spewing sick all over the room, at least it'll give the maids something new to whisper about as they tell tales of the shoeless Ilbrean."

"Don't pay attention to the maids."

"A hard thing to do when they invade the room."

"You'd rather live in filth?"

"I'd rather leave the room while they work."

Danu planted her hands on the table, splaying her fingers and taking a breath before speaking. "You'll be allowed out of your room soon."

"Has your elder finally told you my purpose? Has the great mystery—"

"I can't let you leave the room until you've gotten your strength back." Danu spoke over him. "Which means you have to eat, or you'll stay stuck in here."

"Yes, guardian." Niko stood, gritting his teeth as he waited for pain to rip through him. A dull ache in his ribs and feet greeted him instead.

He sat at the table and started on his bowl of soup. There was more food on the tray than he'd be able to eat, the Brien's kitchen always sent him plenty of choices, but the soup had the least chance of making him violently ill.

Danu leaned back in her chair, crossing her arms as she watched him. "Are you going to tell me what's wrong?"

"I'm being held prisoner."

"You were yesterday as well," Danu said. "So why is your mood worse today? Nightmares again?"

"No." Niko pushed his empty soup bowl aside and reached for the bottle of frie. "It was a good dream, actually."

"Sounds awful."

"It was." Niko swigged straight from the bottle. "I woke up."

Danu pushed the bowl of fruit his way. "What was the dream about?"

"Why should my guardian care?" Niko popped four purple berries into his mouth, washing them down with more frie.

"Boredom. Curiosity. Wanting to be your friend."

"Friends don't lock friends up."

"They do when it's the order they've been given by the Elder of their clan."

Niko chose a few more berries, actually chewing this batch to let their earthy sweetness coat his tongue.

"I'm not your enemy, Niko. And I'm the only soul you've got to speak to. We're going to keep spending every day in each other's company, so just chivving tell me. What was the dream?"

"I got back to Ilara. Rode in through the southern gates and charged all the way to the Map Master's Palace. Allora was waiting there. I asked her to marry me."

"Did she say yes?"

"There was too much passionate kissing for her to say actual words, but I understood her answer. We were going to be married." He took another swig of frie. "The worst part is, she doesn't know where I am. The woman I love will be sick with worry. The Map Makers Guild will hold my funeral when the journey returns without me. Allora will grieve for me. She'll be shoved into mourning even as her heart waits for me to come home. I don't want her to endure that sort of pain."

"If she's strong enough for you to love her, she's strong enough to survive grief."

Niko pushed the bottle of frie toward Danu.

"It was sent up for you." She shook her head.

"I can't finish the whole bottle before they send a new one tomorrow. I tried it once. I'm amazed the maids came back after carrying those buckets away."

Danu wrinkled her nose and took a drink from the bottle.

"I just need to get home to her." Niko dragged his hands down his face. "I could go back to Ilara, marry Allora, and look for signs of Regan. I'll keep my promise to your elder. I'll spend every day searching for the Brien's lost trueborn. I'm of better use to your elder in Ilara than I am locked in this room."

"I'm not sure Bryana trusts you enough to send you out into Ilbrea." Danu took another drink and passed the bottle back to Niko. "You could disappear the moment you're through the city gates."

"I couldn't disappear. I have to go to Allora. She's waiting for me." Niko swigged the frie, pretending the tightness in his chest had come from the burning liquor.

"I'm not allowed to let you out of this room. I couldn't get you out of the Brien stronghold even if I were fool enough to try."

"I have to eat and wait for your elder to release me. I know." Niko tore a chunk from the loaf of bread.

"I do know a few people in Ilbrea." Danu stole berries from Niko's bowl. "I could send a message. See if they can get word to your Allora. Let her know you're alive."

"You could?" The feeling drained from Niko's hands. "You'd help me get a message to Allora?"

"I'm willing to try. I can't guarantee it'll work."

"Thank you, Danu." His whole body trembled. He set his bread down before it could tumble from his hand. "Allora knowing I'm alive, it would—it would be a great comfort to me."

"I understand."

"What about Amec? Could you send word to his family? Have you heard anything about him?"

"Not a peep." Danu stole the frie from Niko. "But there are whispers of another Ilbrean in the keep. Another live Ilbrean."

"Good. That's good."

Niko worked his way through the loaf of bread, imagining a hundred different ways Allora receiving word of his survival might unfold.

She might be on the cliffs at the Map Master's Palace, staring out over the city, the wind sweeping around her. A messenger would ride up and deliver the news. She would fall to her knees, weeping with joy as she thanked Dudia for protecting the man she loved.

Or, perhaps it couldn't be such a dramatic affair. Perhaps she'd have news of his survival whispered to her by a stranger while she was out in the city. The stranger would disappear into the crowd, leaving Allora standing alone, the world rushing by her as she tried to hide her tears of joy.

"Is that why you were chosen as my guardian?" Niko took a gulp of frie and moved on from bread to roasted meat.

"Is what why?"

"Were you chosen because you have friends in Ilbrea? Because you know about Ilbrea?"

"I was chosen because I am just enough." She cheersed Niko with the bottle and claimed another mouthful.

"Enough?"

"I have enough magic in me to close locks you can't pick, but not enough to be useful to the clan as a sorcerer. I'm a good enough fighter to be able to easily slit your throat if you're fool enough to try and attack me, but not a fierce enough warrior for them to grant my request to fight in the war. I'm close enough to Bryana for her to trust me as your guardian, but not well-liked enough to be given grander duties."

"I'm sorry."

"Don't be." She slid the bottle back to Niko. "Unless you wish someone else were your guardian."

"Would I have any chance of a different guardian helping me escape?"

"No Brien would disobey Bryana like that."

"Then I'm grateful you're just enough to be given the sad task of minding me."

"If you truly are grateful, then I need something from you. A favor in exchange for trying to get word to your girl."

"The message comes with a price." Niko choked on a large swig of frie. "And I thought you wanted to be friends."

"It's not a price. More a warning and a request." Danu planted her elbows on the table and leaned toward Niko. "Whatever role Bryana tells you to play, just do it. Gratefully accept whatever task she commands."

"Or I'll be tortured again." Niko let the burn of the frie dull the remembered pain shooting through his ribs.

"Maybe. She might find a more inventive way to make you her puppet. She might just kill you."

"Your elder has never offered me the mercy of greeting Death."

Danu snatched the bottle away before Niko could raise it to his mouth.

"At the best of times, Bryana is a fearsome ruler. After everything the Brien clan has suffered, I don't think there's anything she wouldn't do if she thought it had the smallest chance of helping her people."

"Including torturing innocent strangers. Do you know how many times her blade cut straight down to my bones?"

"I don't. And if you're wise, you'll forget those weeks ever happened."

Niko coughed a laugh and snatched the bottle back.

"I'm serious, Niko. Do as Bryana says, or there's no use in me trying to get word to your Allora that you're alive. Anger Bryana, and you will never see Allora again."

"What a fine guardian you are. Helpful and wise."

"Exactly."

"You should leave." Niko tipped the bottle up, draining the last of the frie. "I need rest if I'm going to recover enough strength to serve your beloved elder."

"Fine. But as you're wallowing and cursing me, remember I'm the only chivving Brien who cares about keeping you alive." Danu took the empty bottle. "Drink some water before you pass out. You won't put on weight if you spew out all the food my clan has graciously provided."

Niko kept his gaze fixed on the windows as she stormed out of the room and locked the door behind her.

16

KAI

The throbbing in Kai's feet did nothing to subdue the joy skittering through his heart.

The towering trees of the forest along the edge of the eastern mountains were the same sort that grew near Ilara. He'd spent the happier part of his childhood running through woods like these with the people he loved best.

And soon, tantalizingly soon, he would be home. He'd be back with his family.

Sleeping in a real bed. Drinking frie at his favorite pub.

Speaking against the Sorcerers Guild and hoping to survive.

Kai shoved the thought aside.

He'd go to Lord Karron.

He'd slip through the city gates, hurry up the cliff to the Map Master's Palace, and go right to Lord Karron. Tell the Lord Map Maker the whole awful tale of Sorcerer Roo's treachery and let him figure out how to tell the Guilds Council what had happened.

Allora would feed him, see that he had a bath and some chamb. Find him a fresh pair of boots and a comfortable place to tuck himself away until the sorcerers could be dealt with.

There is no dealing with the sorcerers. You'll be a target for magical vengeance from the moment you speak against the Sorcerers Guild.

Kai shook his head, trying to rattle the awful thought away.

Hating the truth doesn't make it less real.

He dug his knuckles into his temples.

"You all right?" Drew eyed Kai.

"Better than I've been in ages." Kai pressed a smile onto his face.

A wrinkle formed between Drew's eyebrows.

"Trying to decide which tavern I want to visit first." Kai clapped Drew on the shoulder, begging his friend to ignore his false smile. "There are so many choices, I keep giving myself a headache thinking of all the frie I'm determined to consume."

"I've only ever been to a few proper taverns." Piran spoke from behind them. "We don't really have them where I grew up with the Brien, and I've not had the chance to visit many in Ilbrea."

"Because it's an unnecessary risk," Arto said. "*I* can sit in a pub in Ilara. *You'd* be a fool to try it. You're better off staying well away from crowds."

"Afraid Piran will charm everyone and you'll have a mess of Ilbreans begging to join the Black Bloods?" Kai said.

"More afraid the Sorcerers Guild will catch the scent of magic they haven't claimed and drag Piran and Isla to their tower," Arto said.

"Ah," Kai said. "Best to avoid that. But there are decent taverns south of Ilara. I've been to some places in Frason's Glenn that would put the best spots in Ilara to shame."

"He shouldn't be going to a tavern in Frason's Glenn, either," Arto said.

"Quite right." Kai frowned. "Wouldn't want to start out with the best. You'd be ruined for every other pub you visited."

"Really?" Piran said.

"I try not to boast, but I'm a bit of an expert in debauchery," Kai said.

Drew coughed a laugh.

"Don't blame me for enjoying an area in which I excel." Kai gripped Drew's shoulder harder. "Since we're following alongside the mountain road, we're passing by towns. We could cut down to the edge of the trees and see what woeful village we're near."

"Nantic," Isla said. "We're passing by Nantic."

"Nantic?" Kai pictured a map of Ilbrea. "That's a bigger town than some of the pissant villages along the mountain road."

"It's got four taverns." Isla didn't look at Kai. She kept to the path she'd chosen—upslope from the rest of their party, always weaving through the trees, seeming to search for the most shadowed way forward. "Only two of them are decent, and there's not a chivving chance we're going out into the open to visit any of them."

"Not fond of taverns?" Kai dared to let go of Drew to jog up the slope to Isla. "We could skip the ale and just go for a decent meal. A bowl of stew and bit of bread would go a long way toward refreshing us from the hell this journey has been."

"We're not going to Nantic." Isla glanced sideways, not to the rest of their party walking below, but through the branches of the trees.

Kai stopped, peering through the leaves, searching for whatever she had seen.

In the distance, beyond the forest that covered the slopes of the eastern mountains, a town surrounded the path of the mountain road. The buildings were clustered tightly in the center, like shops and businesses all packed together. Then the buildings dwindled, spreading out until farmland took over the outskirts.

"Is that Nantic?" Kai pointed through the trees. "Can you tell that's Nantic from here? There are plenty of other towns along the mountain road that are built just the same."

"Leave it," Arto said.

"Leave what?" Kai said. "There's nothing remarkable about that town. So either it's sorcery or she's got the best chivving eyesight I've ever heard of."

"Neither," Isla said. "I can tell by the loathing twisting my gut. That's Nantic."

Kai looked down at the town for another long moment, letting Isla get ahead of him. When he started walking again, he matched her pace, careful not to catch up to her.

She kept glancing through the trees, as though wanting to make sure Nantic hadn't crept closer.

Their group stayed quiet for most of the afternoon, as though trying to postpone the moment Isla would explode.

Kai watched her, the slant of her shoulders, the way she fidgeted with her sleeve. They'd walked an hour past Nantic when she finally untied her red curls from the string that held them captive. The sun had begun to fade from the sky before her shoulders relaxed and she stopped tugging on her sleeve.

She didn't rage or say they had to press on when Arto decided they should find a place to camp before darkness claimed the mountains.

Piran chose a spot beside an outcropping of rocks.

Isla placed her half of the stones for the boundary that would protect their haven without arguing for a better place to rest.

Kai set his bag beside Drew's, lingering as he drank from his waterskin.

"We should grab wood," Drew said. "I don't fancy being without a fire tonight."

"I'll go." Kai corked his waterskin. "You've been dragging your feet today. Rest while you can. We're not to Ilara yet."

"We'll go find wood together," Drew said. "You're not wandering through the forest alone."

"I'll be fine." Kai looked from Kelsea setting out their slim rations, to Arto studying his chivving useless map. He frowned at Piran before looking to Isla. "Isla, will you come collect firewood with me? Protect me from whatever monsters lurk in the eastern mountains."

"There aren't monsters this far west in the eastern mountains," Piran said.

"Remind me to tell you the tale of an ill-fated picnic I took with my fellow wards. I promise there's good reason to fear monsters anywhere in Ilbrea. Please, Isla." Kai reached for her hand. "Take pity on a poor saelk?"

"I can go with you," Piran said.

"I'm afraid I might need your help," Drew said. "I didn't want to slow anyone down, but I think the blisters on my blisters may be infected."

"Perfect." Kai kept his hand out to Isla as he stood. "We should find some moss to toss into the fire as well. I like watching it crackle."

"Have you ever tried green berry buds?" Isla ignored Kai's hand as she stepped beyond the safety of the stones. "The scent is delicious."

"We'll have to look for some." Kai followed her into the trees, stifling his laugh at Drew's, "Careful, the skin's peeling off."

He followed Isla up the slope, then farther north, then down the slope, collecting wood in the deepening darkness while Isla collected nothing.

She stopped beside a boulder that jutted out from the mountain. She trailed her fingers along the stone before pressing her palm to the rock.

"Is it time for me to apologize yet?" Kai stayed carefully out of arm's reach as he leaned against the boulder to face her.

"I have no idea what you're talking about."

"If I'd known you were from Nantic, I never would have needled you about going down to find a tavern." Kai kept his voice low. "I'm ashamed to admit it, but I'd never wondered where in Ilbrea you might be from."

"I never said I was from Nantic."

"You didn't have to."

She pressed more of her weight against the boulder.

"Do you still have family there?" Kai asked.

"Even if I do, there's no one I'd be happy to see." She shut her eyes and pressed her other hand against the stone.

"Then I'm even more sorry."

"You don't have to be nice to me," Isla said. "You could cut down to the mountain road and walk back to Ilara with no help from us."

"The others would never let Drew and me leave." Kai tipped his head back, looking up at the sky. Clouds had begun rolling in from the west, blocking out the emerging stars. "He and I are pieces in a game we're not supposed to know is being played."

"Paranoia doesn't suit you."

"Lies don't suit you." Kai closed his eyes, scenting the storm on the breeze. "There is no benevolence in the Brien. There's not a chivving chance under all the stars that the others have risked their necks to keep Drew and me alive just so we could make it back to Ilara to tell a story of the Sorcerers Guild's treachery that will be silenced by the Lady Sorcerer before it's made a bit of difference."

"So, you wanted to collect firewood in case this evening is your last?"

"I don't care about the fire." Kai opened his eyes. Isla had drifted closer to him. "But if I'm going to be murdered by Kelsea or thrown to the mercy of the Brien hiding in Ilara by Arto, I don't want to die knowing I owe an apology to someone who's saved my life more than once."

"If you think we've dragged you through all this just to kill you, would I have ever actually saved your life?"

"Forget the life saving, then. You're an Ilbrean who's suffered at the hands of the Guilds. Even if I don't owe you my life, I don't want to add to your pain."

Isla pulled her hands away from the boulder. She looked

down at her palms, as though expecting to find some heart-breaking message written on her skin.

"I'm sorry, Isla. For all the damage the Guilds have done to you."

"When I met Adrial, he apologized for the sins of the Sorcerers Guild." She touched the center of her palm. "While he was risking his life to help me, Adrial Ayres begged me to forgive him for the pain the sorcerers had caused."

"That sounds right. Adrial was born on Ian Ayres. He understands pain and trauma that cut too deep to heal. My life on the ships as a child wasn't easy, I'd not wish it on anyone, but I've never heard of darkness and suffering to match what Adrial survived on that demon's island."

"And he apologized to me." She pressed her hands together as though locking away whatever she'd been studying on her palms.

"It's easy for a person with a good heart to feel responsible for the pain they encounter. Even if there's not a chivving way to blame them for it."

"I've caused so much pain, maybe I deserve the suffering the gods rain down on me."

"I doubt that's—"

"But you don't." Isla took Kai's shoulders, stepping close to him in what might have felt like an intimate way if the air around him hadn't chilled.

"You're being herded to Ilara to be sacrificed," she whispered in Kai's ear.

The chill of the air dripped into his veins.

"I don't know how, I don't know exactly what their plan is, but they're going to make it look like you and Drew have been fighting against the Guilds."

"We're going to speak against the Sorcerers Guild. That's why we've been trying to get back to Ilara."

"Not speaking against the Guilds. Fighting them. In the streets of the city as a part of the rebellion."

He pressed his hand to the boulder as fear threatened to buckle his knees.

"They want the Guilds to think you're one of the rebels who have killed so many paun. A Guilded sailor who happens to be one of Lord Karron's wards leading the fight in the city would do more damage to the sanctity of the Guilds than a battalion of Black Bloods with swords could ever manage."

"What about Drew?"

"Are you fool enough to think they could kill you without having to kill him too?"

"Do you know when they'll attack us?"

"No. But you need to get away from them before we pass through Ilara's gates."

"Help us." Kai looked into Isla's eyes. "Come with us when we run. If you want to blacken the reign of the Guilds, help us tell the truth about the sorcerers."

"I can't. The person I need to find is with the Brien. But I'll give you a chance to run when we reach Ilara. It's the best I can do. I'm sorry."

"Then Drew and I really will owe you our lives. Again."

"If you're half as good a man as Adrial, you're more use to this world alive than dead."

"I'll let Adrial know you hold him in such high regard."

17

ALLORA

The fire crackled merrily in the grate, fighting away the gloom of the evening. Rain pounded against the palace windows as though the end-of-summer storms wished to prove it was their time to seize Ilara.

"How many sorcerers are there to be at the wedding?" Allora looked up from the letter she'd been reading.

"More than have left the tower at once within my lifetime," Gillien said. "There have been thirty scouring the palace grounds for any threat for the last week. There will be more greeting everyone who enters the palace on the day of the wedding. We even have sorcerers in the kitchens as we speak."

"The cooks must be terrified," Allora said. "I'll have to thank them for their work after the wedding."

"They are servants, Lady Karron." Gillien gave Allora an indulgent smile and set her book in her lap. "It is their duty to work."

"But a word of thanks and a bit of kindness can win a world of loyalty. This palace is to be my home for the rest of my life. I would like the people who scamper through the halls to be happy in the palace, not grudgingly serving the royal family so they don't starve on the streets."

"You have a streak of kindness to you. I hope you find it to be a strength."

"It has served me well so far." Allora looked back to her letter.

Lady Karron,

It is my honor to congratulate you on your upcoming nuptials. All Ilbrea celebrates the marriage of King Brannon to a fine and worthy Lady of the Guilds.

Allora folded up the letter. It was the fifth that had arrived that day. All from members of the Guilds or rich merchants. All offering congratulations and praise. All of them preludes from those who would be seeking to bend her ear as soon as she married the King.

She shut her eyes, willing her heart to calm.

This is an opportunity, Allora Karron. The darkest of paths can lead to triumph if you are brave enough to stay the course.

Ilbrea needs you.

"Allora, are you all right?"

Allora took another breath before opening her eyes. "Of course. I'm getting married in two days. My home is protected by sorcerers. I am the most fortunate woman in all Ilbrea."

"Indeed, you are." Gillien leaned closer to Allora. "But that doesn't mean there can't be anything wrong."

Allora swallowed hard, forcing heat toward her eyes.

"There are spells a sorcerer can use to hear a racing heart, but I don't need magic to see that something is upsetting you. Scaring you even."

"Really, I'm fine." Allora brushed a tear from her eye before it could form.

"I am here to protect you, but I want to be your friend." Gillien took her hand. "Please, Allora. What's wrong?"

"It's all just so much." Allora let the pitch of her words rise. "Attending the first ceremony at the cathedral was intimidating. To marry the King, to become the Queen of Ilbrea, to be taken to the King's bed. It was all terrifying.

"But now, knowing we've been attacked before, and that the celebration will be in the palace, in the same place where my husband will take me to his bed—my father will still be in the Royal Palace when Brannon..." Allora shuddered. "I know what my duty as his wife will be. I know I must give my body to my husband. But the terror of letting him inside me for the first time while the elite of Ilara dance in the ballroom? How can I be a happy bride while trying to ignore the danger that has brought the might of the Sorcerers Guild to protect us and trying to pretend there is anything else on my mind but what will come after the ceremony?"

"My sweet Allora." Gillien knelt in front of her. "There is nothing to be afraid of. The King is a good man and an experienced lover. I'm sure he will make it a gentle and pleasurable wedding night."

Heat rose to Allora's cheeks. "You say that, but I won't know what lying with my husband will be like. Not until it's done."

"That's the beauty of the first time. Cherish learning the passion of the King." Gillien squeezed her hand. "It will be magnificent."

"I want to believe you. I just—I wish I could be done with it now. I know it's a crass and awful thing for the future Queen to say, but if I could just go to him, give myself to him now, then I wouldn't have to be afraid of it anymore. And the wedding could just be a beautiful ceremony, and there wouldn't be a horde of people lurking in the ballroom the first time I feel the King's skin against mine.

"And it's horrible to even consider, but if he were to slip a child into me now, it's so soon before the wedding, no one would ever know." Allora looked up to the ceiling, true tears brimming in her eyes. "Feeling his arms around me, knowing what our marriage bed will bring, it would make everything so much easier. I would feel so much safer."

"Sweet Allora, you'll worry yourself sick."

Allora met Gillien's gaze. "You must think I'm no better than a common petal whore."

"Not at all." Gillien stood and kissed Allora on the forehead. "I think you are a wise woman who understands where her needs lie. If discovering the bliss of your marital bed a bit early will bring joy to our future Queen, I don't think the King would argue with your desires."

"It doesn't matter if he would argue. It can't happen. If I were seen anywhere near his chambers, the entire palace would buzz with gossip."

"There's no need for you to be seen." Gillien pressed on the wall. Without a sound, a panel swung open. "I will leave you a trail to the King's bedroom and keep the servants away from your chambers for the rest of the night. Be back by morning, and no one will ever need know that you discovered the joy of the King's touch before your vows were exchanged."

"Do you mean it?" Allora stood, peering into the dark passage.

"A happy royal marriage bed benefits all Ilbrea." Gillien winked. "Go change into something easy for him to take off. And don't forget to breathe." The sorcerer stepped into the passage, closing the door behind her with a snap of her fingers.

Allora stared at the place the door had been, waiting for the room to start swimming, or for her legs to give out as fear and grief stole her strength.

This is the choice you have made. Your battle cannot be won with blades, Allora Karron.

She went into her bedroom, trying to ignore the other voices swirling through her mind.

You knew you would have to bed him when you agreed to become his wife, Mara said. *You are only facing the inevitable a bit early. Gain the advantage while you can. Trust and adoration are valuable weapons.*

It can't be me, Allora. Sadness filled Niko's voice. *Whatever might have been, I'm gone. You owe me nothing, my love.*

Tears trailed down Allora's cheeks.

There are other ways to fight the demons, Adrial whispered. *You deserve happiness. You don't have to do this. I found Ena. There is joy left for you in this world.*

Allora unfastened the buttons on the front of her green dress.

I am Allora Karron. Daughter of Marco Karron, Lord of the Map Makers Guild. I have risked my life to protect Ilbrea from the sorcerers. I will find a way to stand against the sorcerers again. I will free myself from them. I will free the palace of their vile rule, even if the only weapon I have is my body.

She dropped her dress on the floor and shrugged out of her shift.

She touched each of the clean shifts in her wardrobe, choosing the softest—made of thin material that easily showed the outline of her body.

She pulled the pins from her hair, draping her blond locks over her shoulders to cover the color at the peaks of her breasts. She studied her face in the mirror, pinching her cheeks, forging a rosy and supple offering for the King's desires.

Don't think.

She walked to the wall in the sitting room and pressed on the place Gillien had touched to open the door.

Don't think.

A trail of glimmering blue had been left on the wall, glowing just bright enough to light Allora's way.

Memorize the path.

Don't think about his skin against yours.

Straight down the passage. Passing two doors. Then a staircase that cut down into the darkness.

You are the Lord Map Maker's daughter. You were born to discover hidden secrets.

Another door, wider than the rest. A slot placed high up in the wall, pointing toward the main corridor that led along the second floor of the palace, offering a spy a perfect view of passersby.

A stairway leading up.

Two doors set close together, as though leading to opposite sides of the same perpendicular wall.

The trail ended with a seven-pointed star gleaming on a door that looked the same as so many of the others.

Don't think.

Allora raised her hand, ready to push the door open.

You can run. Tell Gillien you lost your nerve. Decided you wanted to wait.

She looked to the faint blue trail leading back to her room.

Gillien's trust is more valuable than two nights' sanctuary in your own bed.

Forgive me, sweet Niko. It should have been you.

She pushed on the door.

It swung open with barely a touch.

The glow from the chandelier shimmered off the golden decorations in the King's chamber, sparkling off the fourposter bed, and the gold inlaid in the fireplace, and the gold decorating each of the chairs.

I am another treasure for Ilbrea's King.

Brannon sat beside the fireplace, staring into the flames as though waiting for wisdom from Dudia to spark into being.

Allora stepped into the King's bedroom.

The passage door clicked closed behind her.

Brannon leapt to his feet, reaching for the dagger at his hip as he spun to face her.

He stared at Allora, blinking for a moment before loosening his hold on his weapon. "My love, what are you—"

"I don't want to wait." Allora stepped farther into his room, letting the light from the sconces on the wall behind her cast the curves of her body in silhouette. "The sorcerers have claimed control of our wedding. Chaos has seized the city. Our vows will be what royal tradition decrees. There is so much in my life that will be ruled by what Ilbrea demands of me. I want this to be my choice."

"Allora." His gaze devoured the outline of her body as he walked toward her like a man lured by a spell.

"Give me one night that's just ours." She reached for the ribbon at the top of her shift.

He gripped her hands, keeping the ribbon tied. "If anyone found out you were here, you would begin your life as Queen with whispers chasing you through the halls."

She leaned in, brushing her lips against his. "Let the first time be my choice, not because marriage laws demand I give myself to you. Let me want you." She let go of her shift's ribbon, tracing the line of his chin. "Please, Brannon."

He kissed her gently, as though daring her to run as he trailed his fingers down her neck.

She kissed him back, willing her feet to stay planted as he untied the ribbon, loosening the neck of her shift.

The fabric fell past her shoulders, exposing the tops of her breasts.

Brannon's lips left hers. He kissed down her throat, his mouth lingering on the skin her shift had revealed. He ran his hand up her thigh, lifting the fabric, exposing parts of her no man had ever seen.

She gasped as he pulled her shift lower, claiming her breast with his mouth.

She laced her fingers through his hair, anchoring herself to the man who would be her husband rather than give in to the voice in her head that begged her to flee.

He moved his lips back to hers as his hand took over the groping of her breasts.

He pressed himself to her, his wanting pulsing against her stomach, as though the beast of his desire had become its own living thing.

She shut her eyes tight, pulling herself against him, trying to match his strength as he clung to her.

She swayed as he let go, air whooshing into her lungs as for one slim moment she thought he might be done.

He yanked her shift down, letting it drop to the floor.

Wonder lit the King's eyes as he stared at her naked form. He reached out, brushing his thumb across her breasts. He trailed his fingers down her stomach.

Her breath caught in her throat as he pushed into the place their bodies would join.

"My wife." Brannon smiled, as though touching the inside of her brought him more joy than his kingdom could offer.

He kissed her as he lifted her, cradling her head as he laid her down on the bed they would share.

He tasted her breasts as he undressed himself.

She met him on the field of battle, arching into his touch, letting him gain ground as he parted her thighs.

He stood naked before her, displaying the weapon she would face, before plunging himself into her.

She took comfort in the pain that shocked through her as he filled a void she hadn't known existed.

I have won. This battle, I have won.

18

ADRIAL

He tried not to watch her as she drew kohl around her eyes and painted pink onto her cheeks, but there was something in the way her fingers moved as she wound her hair into delicate twists that made it impossible for Adrial to look away.

She wore nothing but her shift and black stone pendant as she groomed natural perfection to suit the taste of the Guilds.

My wife.

"There's nothing for you to gape at, scribe." Ena nestled her silver bird charm into her hair, matching it to the side that bore the bird marked on her ribs.

"I'm not gaping." Adrial tightened his hold on the book in his hands but couldn't make himself look away from her. "You're trying to make yourself mesmerizing. You can't blame me for falling victim to the trap of your beauty."

She turned to face him. A smile curved her lips. She'd painted them such a lush shade of pink, a band tightened around his lungs at the mere thought of being able to kiss her.

"You've discovered my secret." Ena stood. Her shift draped over the ever-growing roundness of her belly. "I suppose you'll be done with me now."

"Never." The band around his lungs tightened as she reached for his hand.

He set his book on his desk. He'd taken two steps before realizing he hadn't thought to hide his limp.

She took his hands, brushing her lips against his as she whispered, "Good. You made a vow, scribe, and I don't intend to let you go. You're mine."

"I love you, Ena." He rested his forehead against hers. "I am irrevocably yours."

"Then you're the largest fool of them all. Now help me get ready for this chivving wedding."

A fleeting hollowness tingled Adrial's fingers as she let go of him and turned to the scribe white dress she'd laid out on the bed.

"You don't have to come with me," Adrial said.

She picked up the padding she'd stitched, holding it up to the gap between her breasts and belly. "I'm the wife of the heir to the Lord Scribe and it's the King's wedding to the daughter of the Lord Map Maker. Lord Gareth made it very clear that he expects me to attend when he sent seamstresses to make me a new dress."

"We can tell him you're ill." Adrial tied the laces of the padding behind Ena's back.

"And risk suspicion that I'm pregnant flying through the library?" She lifted her dress off the bed.

"We've been married long enough it would be well within reason for you to know you're carrying a child conceived after the wedding."

Ena froze, staring at the dress in her hands. Delicate white lace trimmed the sleeves. She'd chosen a higher waist to better hide the child.

"Ena, I—"

"You have no idea how badly I wish that were true. Or that I'd claimed you as soon as I had a chance. I should've rolled you in the cave at the waterfall, or the night of the rebellion. I should've made you mine long before you gave up your future to protect me."

He lifted the dress from her hands.

"I could've convinced you, at the waterfall." Her gaze stayed fixed on the dress. "One kiss, and you would've crumbled. I could've taken you, and we would've conceived this child, and he wouldn't have an ounce of Cade's shadow haunting him. By the gods, I swear I can hear Cade laughing from the grave, giddy with all the pain he's caused."

"Hush, my love." Adrial wrapped his arms around her, waiting for her to accept his comfort. "Cade is dead and gone. He has no place in our child's life. That demon's shadow will not harm our baby. I swear to you. Our child is safe."

"Only if we protect him. We have to get to the wedding." She pulled away from Adrial. "There can be no rumors that the wife of the head scribe is ill." She lifted her dress over her head.

"There are storm clouds coming in from the Arion Sea."

"You think the Lord Scribe wouldn't mind me missing the King's wedding to keep my boots dry?" She turned her back to Adrial. "Lace me in."

"Or you could stay here." He dared to lay his hands on her hips. "Work on inks. Stay well away from the palace."

"You really don't want me to go with you?"

"The last time Allora tried to marry King Brannon, the dome of the cathedral was blown apart right over our heads."

"Which is another chivving wonderful reason I'm coming with you. Now lace me in or call a maid to do it."

"Ena—"

"Do the laces, scribe."

"Don't blame me for wanting to keep you safe." Adrial tightened the laces on the back of her dress. "If the wedding is attacked—"

"I will be standing beside my husband to defend him."

"You're pregnant. Your safety is more important than mine."

He tied the laces, letting his fingers linger on the back of her neck. "You shouldn't risk going anywhere there might be trouble."

She pulled away from his touch. "Just while I'm carrying this child, or will you try to confine me to the library every time I'm pregnant?"

"Every time you're pregnant?"

"Do you intend to abandon our marriage bed as soon as the baby is born?" Ena yanked on her boots.

"What?" Adrial sat on the bed, hiding the sudden weakness that buckled his knees.

"Do you intend to never touch me again? Are you going to deprive yourself the pleasure of entering your wife and letting yourself go while inside her?" She tucked a sheathed knife into the ankle of her boot.

"I…" Adrial gripped the sheets beneath him. "If that's what you want."

"It's not what I want, scribe. You're my husband, and I would be chivving well furious if you abandoned our bed." She tucked a two-inch-long blade along the side of her breast. "And if you intend to spend the rest of your life rolling me, you're doomed to father a flock of children. This will not be the last child I carry, and I won't allow you to tuck me safely in a box like a wounded animal every time I'm growing a new babe."

Adrial grabbed her hand before she could head for the door. "You really want more than one child?"

"I will bear you a horde of children. Our home will be filled with such chaos and noise, none of our brood will ever feel alone or abandoned. Your perfect robes will be covered in filthy hand-prints as our children cling to their father, demanding his atten-tion. My hair will go gray as I worry over the trouble they cause." She kissed the back of his hand. "We will never sleep a full night, and the rest of the scribes will whisper of the crumbling of order brought on by the head scribe's brood."

Heat burned in Adrial's eyes as he found the strength to stand. "We will be the bringers of the most beautiful chaos."

"Only if I can keep you safe." She kissed him, folding herself into his arms. "Never tell me to sit in safety while you face the demons of the world. I will walk by your side, scribe. We battle the storm hand-in-hand or not at all."

"Promise me you'll be careful at the wedding." He held her tight. "Lady Gwell will be there. I know she deserves whatever vengeance the common folk can rain down on her, but there will be sorcerers and soldiers guarding the wedding."

"This isn't the day to attack." She kissed the side of his neck just below his ear. "I promise, my knives are only to keep my family safe."

He tipped her chin up, kissing her. Giving in to the sheer, boundless bliss of knowing with perfect certainty that she wanted to be in his arms.

She laced her fingers through his as she backed toward the door. "We can't be late to the royal wedding. The new Queen would never forgive the impropriety."

Adrial held tightly to her hand as they cut through the sitting room and into the corridor that ran through the scribes' living quarters.

They would need more space once the baby came. Much more space if Ena got the brood of children she wanted.

She kept his hand in hers as they went down the stairs, lifting her arm just slightly, offering him support on the steps in a way the gaggle of apprentices waiting at the door to the courtyard would only see as affection.

Two white-trimmed carriages waited by the library gates.

Lord Gareth stood beside one, gesturing toward the library as he spoke to the sorcerer who would be his escort.

"Why are there two carriages?" Ena asked. "I thought it was only us and Lord Gareth going to the palace."

"We're taking two different carriages along two different

routes," Adrial said. "In case we're attacked on our way through the city."

Lord Gareth gave Adrial a nod before letting a scribes' guard help him into his carriage. His escorting sorcerer climbed up beside the driver.

"You really can stay behind," Adrial whispered as the sorcerer who had been assigned to protect him took her seat beside Adrial's driver.

She adjusted her purple robes, as though trying not to look at Adrial.

"Allora will understand," Adrial said. "I'll explain to Lord Gareth that I begged you to stay in—"

"I will not be parted from my husband. Not even by his own fear." Ena climbed into the carriage, pulling Adrial up behind her.

They sat side by side, neither of them speaking as the carriage rattled through the gates.

Dark clouds coated the sky, giving a grim, mournful look to the stone of the library.

Adrial had always thought of the home of the Scribes Guild as a shining bastion of knowledge and hope, but even the library could not stand up to the air of despair that coated Ilara.

Ena let go of Adrial, draping her hand across her breast in a way anyone who didn't know about her hidden blades might think an expression of shock as they left the Guilded portion of the city behind and cut through the destruction of the merchants' district.

The carriage slowed as the driver wound through the selective ruin.

The scent of ash and rot filled the air. Blocks of stone lay strewn across half the street, the cast-aside remnants of the front wall of what had been a fine home. Dried blood marred some of the stones, as though they'd been used as weapons.

Even without having been present to witness the violence, there was no mistaking the magical making of the wreckage.

The front wall appeared to have been sliced away in one solid sheet, leaving the rooms of the home open to the street, like the front of a child's dollhouse.

But the blood on the stones, Adrial wasn't sure if it had been shed by sorcerers or by a merchant defending their home, or by common folk trying to stop the monsters from terrorizing their city.

The selective destruction continued as they wound closer to the Sorcerers Tower.

One shop had been burnt badly enough, not even the walls still stood, but the shops on either side hadn't even been singed.

A gap of bare ground, too wide for Adrial not to have noticed before, stretched between a dress shop and a cobbler.

If the sorcerers have done this much damage here, how bad are the common sections of the city?

Adrial fought the urge to scream the question out the carriage window. The tally of deceased he'd been given couldn't be complete. Had anyone died in the shop that had burned? How many had died when a whole building had vanished? How many had fallen without leaving anyone behind to report their murder?

Not now. Do not rage now.

Be quiet. Be thankful for the sorcerers' protection.

He made himself look at a bakery that had crumbled in on itself.

Protecting Ena and the child is worth staying silent until they are safely back in the library.

"Perhaps the driver can give us a tour of different monuments of the sorcerers' destruction on the way back to the library," Ena said. "They plotted our path to the palace through such fine examples of their work in purging the city of danger, there must be other ruinous wonders for us to behold."

Adrial laid his hand palm up on her lap. "I'm sure they will take us by whatever route they deem safest."

"What kindness the Sorcerers Guild has bestowed upon us."

She kept her hand near her knife, ignoring his plea for an anchor beyond his anger.

The sound of the carriage's wheels changed as they crossed onto the bridge leading into the palace grounds.

A pair of sorcerers stood at the far side of the bridge, as though waiting to collapse the stone pathway their Guild had created, dropping whatever victims they chose into the water far below.

Adrial held his breath as they neared the sorcerers.

Ena can swim. She would survive the fall.

"Breathe, scribe," Ena whispered as they left the bridge and ventured beneath the walls that surrounded the palace grounds. "Enjoy the display of the sorcerers' might. There is so much to be learned from watching their power at work."

He forced himself to drag in air and willed his racing heart to slow as they joined the line of carriages at the front of the palace.

A den of horrors—that was where he'd brought his wife.

Murderers with a might he could not match surrounding them, trapping them.

Rain began pounding down as their carriage neared the palace steps. The merchants at the front of the line scampered inside. So did the Guilded who came next. All of them fleeing as though the rain were a threat they could not bear to face.

Ena didn't move her hand away from the knife hidden beside her breast until it was their turn to step out onto the palace steps. She leaned forward, taking Adrial's hand and placing it behind her waist as though they had ridden the whole way as a pair lost in each other's arms.

A soldier opened the door, taking a moment to check the shadows inside the carriage before speaking. "Head Scribe, welcome."

"Thank you." Adrial gave the soldier a nod. He kept his hand on the back of Ena's waist, as though he were helping her, as she ignored the soldier's offer of aid and stepped out into the storm.

She didn't scamper up the steps to dodge out of the rain as everyone else had. She reached for Adrial, a hint of something he knew to be deadly glinting in her eyes as a second soldier tried to take her arm to lead her inside. She sidestepped the soldier, dodging his grip without having seemed to notice him.

"Miss"—the soldier reached for her again—"the storm is getting worse—"

"Have you not heard? The head scribe married a common girl." Ena took Adrial's hand as he climbed down from the carriage. "There is no help I need from a Guilded soldier."

Adrial wrapped his arm around Ena's waist, as though anyone in Ilbrea might believe he was the one guarding her from the storm. "Come, my love. Allora will be angry if we're late to her wedding."

They stayed in step as they climbed the stairs.

"I thought you told me to breathe and stay calm," Adrial whispered.

"I will not suffer a paun soldier to touch me, not while I can defend myself."

"Ena—"

"There are some wounds even time can't heal, scribe."

He stopped beside the door, shifting her out of the path of the paun racing for the promise of shelter. "I'm sorry, Ena, for every wound you've had to survive, but there are good people trapped inside every Guild."

"A good person who allows the innocent to suffer at the hands of a monster is still an unforgivable beast."

"Ena—"

"He's not here." She brushed her sodden tendrils of hair over her shoulder. "Whoever's taken up the mantle of the Demon's Torch. The wedding won't be attacked."

"How do you know?" Adrial looked to the palace gates, a foolish part of him expecting flames to rise up from the bridge beyond.

"There's no way into the palace without facing the sorcerers. But with so many soldiers guarding the wedding, every other nest of the Guilds is open to attack. Something will burn tonight, but it won't be near the King's wedding."

"We should tell someone."

"They'd never believe you without you tossing them secrets that would put my neck in a noose." She took his arm, leading him toward the door. "It'll be something dangerous or valuable. Not something symbolic he'll want people to watch collapse. The library won't be touched."

He didn't have a chance to ask her how she could be so sure before they stepped into the entryway of the Royal Palace.

"Head Scribe." A sorcerer bustled toward them. "Welcome to the Royal Palace." The sorcerer gave them a nod, as though it truly were her place to welcome them into the home of the King.

"Thank you." Adrial eased in front of Ena as he bowed to the sorcerer. "I hope we're not late."

"Everyone's been a bit detained by the arrival of the storm. Don't worry. Lady Gwell ensured accommodations were made." The sorcerer twirled her finger through the air.

A heat that should have been delicious blossomed up from Adrial's toes, engulfing his body before he could decide if he should try and fight against the warmth.

"There you are." The sorcerer smiled. "Nice and dry."

Adrial looked down at his robes. The pure white was as dry and crisp as if it had come straight from the library's laundry.

The sorcerer ducked around Adrial to Ena.

"I'm fine." Ena stepped away, her hand moving to her chest as she placed Adrial between herself and the sorcerer. "I find the rain to be refreshing."

"Nonsense." The sorcerer twirled her finger again.

Ena gasped.

Adrial took her arm, holding on tight.

"That's better, isn't it?" The sorcerer looked from Ena to

Adrial. "We wouldn't want to risk you falling ill. Not when the future holds such bountiful joy for you both." She turned away from them, moving on to a man in healer red who dripped on the entryway floor.

Adrial placed his hand on the back of Ena's waist, propelling her forward, past the stairs to the royal quarters and into the corridor that led to the throne room.

Ena didn't flinch as they walked through the flock of soldiers flanking the entrance to the royal wedding. She stayed stone-faced and silent, as though the sorcerer's infliction of magic had driven her beyond normal rage to a place of dark stillness.

It's for the best. Let her anger distract her.

They joined Lord Karron toward the front of the crowd.

Best that Ena doesn't wonder what bountiful joy the Sorcerers Guild sees in our future.

19

—————

ALLORA

My Darling Niko,

It is selfish of me to drag your beloved memory through this day. But I am weak and terrified. I will not survive the hours ahead without you beside me.

I am strong enough to make myself smile for the women as they drape my wedding gown around me. They coo over the stitching that trims the fabric. The sorcerers themselves made the gown, twining more gold and silver through the white than the dress I wore the first time they sent me to marry the King.

I have to swallow my laugh as I look at myself in the mirror. There is so much metal glinting through the white, I look like a soldier riding into battle in full armor.

But I cannot let the women see me laugh. They would not under-stand as you could.

The sorcerers made me armor without realizing which battle I face.

I try to hear your voice whispering in my ear, promising I am strong enough to conquer any enemy. I am daring and brave. I am a warrior who will change the fate of Ilbrea without ever touching a sword.

I want to believe you.

I wish I could feel your hand brush against mine as you promise my victory will be worth the cost.

The wedding veil pulls against the braids woven into my hair, clawing at my scalp as it begs me to flee.

But this is the fate I chose when I accepted the King's hand. I must marry him. I must give my vow and join my fate to his.

There is no other path for me.

The entryway is filled with sorcerers. I don't know if they're protecting us from attack or simply using their magic to dry the puddles of water dragged in from the storm by the horde of guests who've come to watch the King claim his new bride.

I should have been your bride. I should have accepted your proposal the first time you asked and never wasted time worrying over what sort of life we might build. We would have had each other. You would have been mine, and that would have been enough.

As much as I try to push thoughts of what our wedding should have been from my mind, the image lingers.

A subtle affair on the grounds of my father's estate. Surrounded by our friends. Finding joy with those we love best and ignoring the presence of those propriety demanded we invite.

My sweet Niko, I do not want to drag you into this ceremony with me, but my body is filled with stones and I don't know how to keep walking without you beside me.

Illia beams as though it were her own wedding. Brannon looks at me as though wanting to devour me.

It will happen again. I will be back in his bed tonight. I will hide my hatred of his touch.

I would have longed to sleep in your arms and burned with an indescribable need to join my body with yours.

I hope he will be gentle with me. I hope he will believe that I crave him and ignore the darker benefits of my having moved into his chambers.

Fueling the King's lust will make my work easier. I must remember that.

The Lady Sorcerer's voice fills the throne room.

The merchants in the horde seem filled with awe, astounded at having been granted an invitation to a royal wedding.

The Guilded seem nervous. I don't know how many of them lost friends the first time Dudia tried to give me to the King.

Adrial stands beside my father right below the platform. My father's face is set in what any who don't know him might mistake for stoic sentimentalism. You would know it was worry, and grief.

Brannon is not so wise.

Adrial keeps his wife close beside him, his arm tight around her waist as though daring the stars to try and steal her from him. He loves her so. I believe he would battle Dudia himself to protect his wife.

You would have battled every god and saint this world has ever heard of to stay with me. I know that, Niko. I know you did not surrender easily to death.

I wish I could tell you how much comfort that certainty brings me.

You loved me. With everything you were, you loved Allora Karron.

The Lady Sorcerer looks to me, triumph glinting in her eyes as she tells me to recite my vow to the King. The words claw their way out of my throat.

Brannon's smile broadens.

He speaks, but I cannot hear him past the pounding in my ears.

If Dudia has ever been kind, you'll run into the room right now and whisk me away. We'll flee Ilara and never look back.

I'll spend my days basking in the joy of loving you and my nights wrapped safely in your arms.

The horde cheers as Brannon steps in to kiss me. He puts his hand behind my head, locking me close to him as though I do not understand the prison I cannot escape.

He takes a deep breath. I don't know what scent he's trying to memorize.

The horde cheers again as Brannon takes my hand and turns me to face them.

A weight settles on my head.

For a moment, I am grateful, thinking the world has decided to grind me into ash and ask no more of me.

But the Lady Sorcerer has placed a bitter covenant on my head, and the people roar their joy for their new Queen.

I wish I could write this to you. Send these words to whatever force claims the dead and wait for your words of comfort to fly back to me.

But this letter can only exist in my mind.

No one may know the disgust that sours my throat as the King kisses my hand. No one can guess how desperately close to breaking my soul has been pushed.

I cannot crumble. Not when there is work that can be done by my hand.

My father doesn't see it. He gives me a genuine smile before he kisses my forehead and tells the King to care for me.

Adrial smiles, too, as though he believes I might find the same joy he fought so hard to discover.

But the inker sees through me.

She holds my gaze. Her determination and worry and pain guiding mine. Welcoming me to some dark sisterhood I had never looked deep enough into the shadows to find.

Music begins to play. The people—my people—expect me to dance.

I shall let the music blur my pain. I won't make you walk any further down this wretched path, my sweet Niko. There are some things I cannot ask you to see.

Thank you for standing beside me even in death.

I will love you beyond my final breath,

Allora

20

NIKO

"There's no need to rush." Danu took Niko's arm, planting it firmly on hers as though ordering him to accept her support. "If you fall down these steps, I'm not calling for anyone to carry you. You'll be crawling back to your room with blood on your face."

Niko looked down the long flight of stairs that cut through the mountain.

A pull in his chest begged him to run down the steps, burst through the doors, and sprint into the emerald forest he'd spent weeks watching from above.

Danu gripped his arm with her free hand, shifting him to the side as three women with red-trimmed, purple bodices passed.

The women slowed to stare at Niko. The eldest leaned toward the other two, whispering something Niko couldn't hear.

The youngest gasped, her eyes widening before she averted her gaze from Niko's scowl.

"Midwives." Danu kept moving down the stairs at a maddeningly steady pace.

"And what would midwives have to whisper about me?" Niko said. "I promise there's no child of my blood being born in the stronghold."

"You're going to see a lot of whispering Brien today."

They passed a landing with a hall cutting out on either side. The guards nodded to Danu and studied Niko.

"Why will I be seeing whisperers?" Niko asked once they'd left the guards' earshot. "Are you leading me to my execution? Will your clan dance around my corpse?"

"They'd be devastated if you died."

"The Brien care that much for their prisoners?"

"You're not our prisoner."

"Should I just nip back to Ilara then?" Niko moved to ease his arm away from her.

"You trying to run would end badly for both of us." She tightened her grip.

"Ah, perhaps your confusion lies in the definition of *prisoner*. You see, I've been kept locked—"

"You and I understand the reality of your situation, but we cannot allow the people to know."

She shifted him to the side again, allowing two young boys to pass.

One punched the other and pointed to Niko. "It's him."

"He's not tall enough," the second boy said.

"Go. Both of you." Danu shooed them up the stairs.

The boys bolted away.

"He's too short," the second boy said.

"What were you expecting? A giant?" the first said.

The boys' argument followed Niko all the way to the next landing.

"What under the chivving stars is going on?" Niko whispered.

"You're aiding the war effort." Danu nodded to the guards as they passed another corridor.

"By not being tall enough to be a giant?"

"By becoming Solcha."

"Solcha." Niko let the word roll around in his mind. "I've no chivving clue what a Solcha is."

"It doesn't matter. You're going to walk on my arm and let people see you. That's all your role requires."

"I'm not sure I agree." Niko planted his feet, not allowing her to guide him onto the next step.

"Niko—"

"Ignorance and evil often walk together. I can't trust any purpose your elder would use me for."

"Walk." She pulled on Niko's arm.

He didn't budge.

"We can't talk here." She put her hand on his back, pushing him hard enough he either had to walk or fall.

"You could have told me in my room." Niko spoke through his teeth as they passed another landing.

"I was hoping you'd be too pleased to be out of your room to notice anyone staring."

The stairs ended in a grand atrium that led out onto a terrace.

Trees grew up the walls of the atrium, their roots twisting as they buried themselves beneath the stone floor. Their leaves held the same vibrant green as the forest in the valley, despite their being trapped beneath the stone ceiling and out of reach of the sun, leaving magic as the only explanation for their bountiful growth.

And beyond the doors, so close Niko could smell the blooms, a garden covered the terrace. The sweet scent of the flowers floated into the atrium, promising Niko that if he could only make it outside, the wounds on his soul might truly begin to mend.

"This way." Danu led him away from the terrace, cutting into a narrow corridor tucked behind the stairs.

"You said I could go outside." Panic tightened Niko's voice. "You promised. Danu, please."

"Stop begging. You're the one who wants answers." Danu cut into another hall.

The stone walls in this corridor hadn't been meticulously smoothed like the rest of the places Niko had seen since entering the stronghold. The stone had been left rugged and curved, as though the mountain itself had created the path.

Danu ducked out of the corridor, pulling Niko into a niche barely wide enough for two.

"When Paiman brought you to the Stronghold, did he tell you anything about the Black Bloods?" Danu leaned out, glancing up and down the corridor.

"Only that a trueborn Black Blood can use stone magic, which I'd never even heard of in Ilbrea."

"Chivving Paiman." Her chest brushed against Niko's as she tugged him farther into the niche, out of view of anyone passing by.

"He told me your trueborn Regan had been lost," Niko said. "And for some reason, your elder chose to torture me for information I didn't have a hope of giving her."

"But the mountain, our place in the eastern mountains, Paiman never explained?"

"I don't think so."

Danu sighed, looking up to the stone ceiling of their tiny hiding place. "The Black Bloods were born of the mountain. We have the mountain's stone in our blood."

"All right." Niko leaned against the wall, gaining an inch between them.

"There are different clans, but at the heart of it, all Black Bloods are the same. We are one people, separate from any of the mess out in Ilbrea. If the stars were kind, there would never be any cause for Black Bloods and Ilbreans to meet. But there are some threats growing in Ilbrea that can't be ignored. For years now, the Brien have been taking children with magic in their blood out of Ilbrea, hiding them beyond the reach of your Sorcerers Guild."

"What?"

Danu pressed her fingers over Niko's mouth. "Even that small interference was met with suspicion and anger by some of the Black Blood clans. Then, Solcha came. A girl born in Ilbrea who was protected and loved by the mountain. In all ways showered with more care than any Black Blood had been granted in a long time. Solcha brought proof to the elders that the Guilds aren't some far away nuisance to be ignored. We can't just save the sorcerer children and ignore every other threat, not when the mountain led an Ilbrean straight to our home.

"That's how the war began. It's been two years of fighting and sieges. Children born of the mountain should never spill each other's blood, but that's the pain we've been left with. And it's more than the Brien want to bear. The people need a reminder of why this war began. They need Solcha. Living proof that an Ilbrean was loved by the mountain, that Ilbrea is a danger to all Black Bloods, and that those two simple truths are worth every bit of misery and grief this war has forced our people to endure."

Niko lifted Danu's fingers away from his mouth. "If they need Solcha, why aren't you parading around the girl your mountains are so in love with?"

"Solcha disappeared with Regan. Both of them went into the darkness below the mountains to find a path to Ilbrea. In her absence, Solcha's story has grown into a legend the people cling to."

"If your elder ever lets me leave the stronghold, I'll look for Solcha while I hunt for Regan. Maybe I can find them both."

"We don't need to hunt for Solcha, not when we have you for the people to look to."

"But I'm not Solcha. I'm not even a girl."

"You're an Ilbrean, taken in by the mountain, shown wonders the mountain hadn't revealed to anyone else. Provided food and water. Delivered to safety when our people rescued you."

"Captured me. Your people captured me. The Brien imprisoned and tortured me."

"The people don't know that. To them, the mountain has sent you as proof that our war is just, that we must continue to fight the fools who would rather the Black Bloods be slaughtered by the Guilds than admit their zealot of a chivving leader has dragged them to their doom."

"How are the Guilds going to slaughter you? They don't even know you're here!"

"You found your way under the mountains. How long until an evil paun finds a path to our territory and leads the Soldiers Guild to our stronghold? We need to win the clan war. We need to prepare for the day we're forced to stand against the Guilds."

"You'd be preparing for a fight that may never come."

"You're not a good enough liar to convince me of that. If the Guilds find out the Black Bloods exist, they will do everything in their power to slaughter every last one of us."

Niko shut his eyes. For a moment, his mind carried him back to his room, as though his prison had somehow become his refuge.

"The work your elder is demanding I perform is to parade around letting the people whisper of how the mountain cares for me."

"You don't have to do anything but let them see you. A walk outside, it's what you've been asking for anyway."

"Why me? Why not Amec? He's the one that touched the chivving stone that made the mountain swallow us."

"You're taller? Have a handsomer face? Better airs? I don't know why Bryana chose you, only that she has. And your taking a simple walk with me on your arm will spread faith through the people in the stronghold. Word will move out to the soldiers, and you, Niko"—she took his face in her hands—"you could change the course of the war."

The shadows shifted across Danu's face as she furrowed her

brow. "Please, Niko. Do as Bryana asks. Make things better for both of us."

"I'll walk with you today."

"Thank—"

"In exchange for books on your peoples' history being brought to my room. If there is some story about the mountains I'm supposed to play a part in, I need to be sure I'm not serving the demons."

"Even if that service got you back to your girl?"

"If I end up with the blood of thousands of innocents on my hands, I won't be the man Allora loves anymore. Better to die than live with that stain on my soul."

Danu touched the worried creases by the corners of Niko's eyes, smoothing them with her thumbs. "I'll bring you the books." She took his hand, leading him out of the niche. "We should get back into view. We don't want the wrong sort of whispers spreading through the valley."

"What would the wrong sort be?" Niko laced her arm through his, not to keep himself steady as they walked, as a detail to strengthen the image of the new Solcha.

"An unattached man and an unmarried woman disappearing together. It's an interesting tale, but not the one Bryana wants us to tell."

They stepped back into the atrium.

A crowd had filled the space in the time Niko and Danu had hidden away.

Danu tensed on Niko's arm.

"Isn't this what you wanted?" Niko looked to her rather than at the horde.

"I didn't think it would be this many at once."

"Can I still go outside?"

Danu nodded, worrying her lips together as though unsure whether to shout or be ill.

"I've faced the masses before." Niko led Danu toward the

horde, only acknowledging the crowd enough to nod in thanks when the people cleared their path. "Silent dignity is often the best tactic."

"Solcha." A woman shoved her way in front of Niko. Tears sparkled on her reddened cheeks. "My daughter is coming of age. She'll be sent to fight. You have to end the war, Solcha. Please." She reached for Niko's hand.

"Step back." Danu let go of Niko's arm, planting herself between him and the crying woman. "No one is to touch him."

The crowd backed away, all except the woman.

"Please, Danu." The woman reached for her instead. "Bryana knows you. You have her ear. Beg your aunt to let my daughter stay in the stronghold."

Danu took the woman's hand and kissed it. "We all have our place in this fight. If your daughter wants to stay in the stronghold, she knows the path."

The woman's shoulders slumped. She nodded her defeat and stepped aside.

Niko took Danu's arm, guiding her toward the doors.

"You're the Elder's chivving niece?" Niko asked through a calm smile.

"Of course I am." Danu nodded to three young girls who giggled and blushed as they stared at Niko. "I'm also Paiman's sister. Why do you think I've been trusted with Solcha's care?"

"Trusted by your aunt who tortured me."

"Not here." Danu gave a kind smile to a teary-eyed man. "You cannot cause a scene here."

"We cannot risk your auntie's wrath."

Niko turned his gaze away from the people, ignoring their awed and tearful and elated reactions to Solcha gliding through their midst. The horde had packed in so tight, he'd made it ten feet past the door before realizing he'd reached the open air.

A breeze ruffled his hair. He tipped his face up to the sky, letting the sunlight warm his skin.

"What did the mountain show you, Solcha?"

"How did you find your way?"

"Does the mountain still want war?"

Niko ignored the pleas for his wisdom. Smiling as he played Solcha was a small price to pay for his first steps outdoors in months.

21

THAM

The rolling racket of the dogs' barking cascaded down the row as Elle tore through the royal kennels.

At the far end, she pranced in place, gave a howl, and then charged back to Tham.

Each pen in the kennels held a team of sled dogs. Some packs were given one open space to share. Some had a few dogs separated from the rest of the team. Some had stacked cages, not allowing any of the dogs to reach one another.

Elle jumped up, knocking her head into Tham's hand before going for another pass down the row.

"She does love to run," Lynn said. "She has that much in common with our dogs."

"She does," Tham said.

Elle turned again, bolting past Tham to the kennel door where the rest of his guards waited outside. She barked at them, as though asking the guards to come join in her fun, before doing another pass down the line.

"The trainers run the dogs every day." Lynn leapt out of Elle's path. "You should see if you could go with them. Learn how to properly run a sled."

"If Queen Ronya would allow it." Tham knelt, reaching between the ice-formed slats of a pen to pet the flank of a massive gray dog.

"It's worth asking," Lynn said. "It'll be a useful skill for you to have when the Ice Walkers go south."

Tham eased his hand away from the gray dog before the animal could sense his anger. "I'm a soldier, not a musher. If I'm to be of any use, I need a sword, not a sled team. Do you think your Queen would allow me that?"

Lynn laid her hand on the pummel of her sword. "You could ask, but I wouldn't be surprised if Queen Ronya says no."

"I'll be a soldier without a weapon on a battlefield I didn't choose."

"How many soldiers actually choose which battles they fight?"

Tham moved on to the next pen. A mother and six pups had been given the space. The pups crawled over their mother, testing their balance on her uneven terrain.

"Tham, I know how you feel." Lynn leaned against the pen's gate. "I fought to be given a weapon and I'd fight like a demon if anyone tried to take it from me. It took more than a year to convince the Regent to let me join the guards."

"I've been told they prefer women to do anything else."

Lynn tipped her head back and laughed.

She wore the blue uniform of a guard and kept her hair in a well-slicked bun, but everything else about her seemed like a woman in a tavern chatting with a friend.

"The Regent gave me a list of positions I had to try before he'd let me join the guards," Lynn said. "The week I spent working in a pastry shop was delightful for me, but the bakers were thrilled to be shod of me when I was finally allowed to leave. I never made a thing worth eating. But it wasn't any of my failures that finally convinced the Regent."

Tham waited, letting her take the time to place her words in order.

"In the end, he just listened and believed me when I said I'd sworn never to marry. I'd been betrothed to the boy I'd been in love with since I'd realized the beauty of men. The wedding was all set, and then his magic began. Most with ice magic receive the gift when they're young, before they've grown into fertility, but it does happen later for some. I've even heard of a grandmother gaining magic. Can you imagine being sixty and realizing you've suddenly got magic coursing through you?"

Elle stopped, peering through the gate to sniff the pups before taking off again.

The mother gave a tired growl and a huff.

"Did gaining magic change his feelings for you?" Tham kept his gaze fixed on the two pups trying to gnaw on each other's ears.

"He still loved me, and wanted to marry me, but he felt it was his duty to do everything he could to protect Isfol. He joined the ice guard. They gave him a post far beyond the reaches of our mountain to defend our city against anyone who might try to invade." Lynn leaned her weight against the gate. "He was going to do two months out in the blue then come back and marry me.

"He was only a week in when outliers attacked. He got pulled into the ice somehow, just swallowed by the blue. I still don't know if he's properly dead or if he clawed his way out of the ice and there's just not enough of his mind left for him to find his way home."

"I'm sorry."

"Me, too. He was a good man." Lynn took a deep breath and brushed away tears Tham hadn't noticed falling. "I don't think I could survive another loss like that, so I vowed never to marry. And I had to join the guards because I needed to learn to fight. If I ever face the outlier who killed my beloved, I'm going to avenge him myself."

"The Regent gained a good guard when he granted your request."

"Thanks." Lynn gave a sad laugh. "I suppose vengeance is as good a reason as any for picking up a sword. The Regent understood that. He really is a good man, Tham. You'd do well to get to know him."

Elle squirmed in between Lynn and Tham, barking at the mother dog before shoving past Lynn to make another lap of the pens.

Lynn tripped toward Tham. He caught her arm to steady her.

She tipped her chin down as she stepped away, as though she'd suddenly found a reason to be shy.

Tham went to the next pen down the row. "I didn't know there was anyone who could attack the Ice Walkers."

"There isn't really," Lynn said. "The only ones who attack Ice Walkers are other Ice Walkers. There are some little settlements outside Isfol who don't align themselves with the crown. There are outliers, nomads who wander the ice, too. Most of them were banished from Isfol."

"Banished?"

"The politics in Isfol go far beyond the palace," Lynn said. "The city is crowded, commerce is crowded. Every lord and lady spends every moment clawing at the ice to keep what they have."

Tham scratched a pup's ear as his mind ran through the streets of Isfol—to the homes built with high walls and turrets, as though their owners were waiting for attack. "Seizing land south of the white mountains will give the gentry parcels to claim."

"Holding the land won't be easy," Lynn said. "And more territory means more land for the guards to protect. But Queen Ronya is determined to lead the Ice Walkers south. I don't know if there's anything that could change her mind."

Tham patted his leg, calling Elle back to him.

Lynn took his arm. "Please don't tell anyone that I doubt the Queen's cause. I'd lose my place as a guard."

"You don't need to agree with her. We don't choose the battles we fight." He gave Lynn a nod and stepped away, letting Elle run ahead of him through the kennel doors.

He should have pushed harder. Asked more questions. Been kinder.

Chatted. Gained her trust. Dug for information that might set Mara free.

He stepped out of the kennels. The only people in sight were his guards. Elle grabbed a branch from a bush, whipping her head back and forth as she tried to claim her prize.

He could fix things. Try to lead the conversation toward what the Regent's desperation might allow him to do to stop his murderous daughter.

You're failing her.

Elle carried her newly won stick to the far corner of the courtyard and began barking through clenched teeth as she wagged her tail at shin-wounding speed.

"Come on, Elle," Tham said.

Elle dug at the ground.

"Maybe we should let her run on the palace grounds." Lynn laughed as Elle attacked the ice. "I'd hate to see what damage she'd do to your room with this much energy."

"That's not it." Tham balled his hands into fists as he walked over to Elle, taking each step carefully, waiting for danger to leap out of the sparkling ice and hurt the pup that brought Mara so much joy.

Elle's claws caught on a hard edge in the ice.

Tham pushed her away, ready to grab her and run, but the crack in the ice wasn't large enough for her to tumble through. She wouldn't have been able to fit her whole head inside it.

Elle dove around Tham to scratch at the hole again.

The crack widened, growing large enough to swallow Elle.

Tham grabbed the wriggling dog and backed away from the still-growing fissure in the ice. "Get Mara."

22

MARA

"Keep the dogs back. Keep them back!"

Thirty guards formed a blockade around the corner of the courtyard, hiding what lay beyond and keeping the mass of panicking dogs from charging to their doom.

"Keep the braidic dogs moving!" an older guard in a deep blue uniform shouted at the kennel hands.

Ronya shifted her path, walking into the guard's line of sight.

All the color drained from the man's face.

"You"—Ronya pointed to the guard beside the cursing culprit—"take over giving orders as the dogs are evacuated. I don't want to hear that one's voice again."

"Yes, Your Majesty." The guard bowed. He backed out of Ronya's path, bowing again as she stepped past him.

Mara kept close on Ronya's heels, not waiting for Andric's permission.

Tham and Lynn stood together, staring at a six-foot-wide crevasse in the ice. Tham kept Elle on a lead, tethering her close to his side.

Elle whimpered, straining against Tham's hold as though

unnaturally desperate to reach the light glowing from within the fissure.

"Someone explain why I have been called here." Ronya glowered at Tham.

He stepped back, allowing Lynn to speak.

"I beg your forgiveness, Your Majesty." Lynn bowed. "We'd only planned to call for Mara, but the chasm is growing at such an alarming rate, it seemed best for you to see the situation for yourself."

Ronya stepped past Lynn, stopping close enough to the edge of the crevasse to stare straight down. Mara kept her gaze fixed away from Tham and Lynn as she joined Ronya.

Light sparkled up from the bottom of the crevasse, the intensity of the gleam making it impossible for Mara to tell exactly how far down the fissure went.

"Is it ice worms?" Mara inched closer to the edge.

"I've never seen a harvest presented like this," Ronya said.

Elle howled. Tham grabbed Mara's arm, yanking her back as the crack in the ice widened.

"Your Majesty." Lynn reached for Ronya.

Ronya swatted her away, not moving as the fissure continued to spread.

The walls didn't crumble and fall. They simply shifted, the ice slowly vanishing as though it had never existed.

The edge of the fissure reached Ronya.

Mara held her breath, waiting for their captor to tumble into the depths and be gone forever.

But the ice around Ronya's feet stayed solid, creating an arc in the wall of the crevasse.

The fissure stopped growing as suddenly as it had started.

Tham kept his grip on Mara's wrist as she inched toward the edge of the now ten-foot-wide gap.

Though the light sparkling from below hadn't changed, the

expansion of the fissure allowed Mara to see more of its depths. But it was all the same. A solid sheet of light.

"I want this area barricaded." Ronya stayed on her arc of ice. "Make sure the dogs are cleared, then bar anyone else from coming this way."

"Yes, Your Majesty," Andric said.

"Why is this happening?" Mara asked. "I've never seen any cracks in the ice on the palace grounds."

Ronya stared down into the crevasse. "Take them back to the palace."

Mara studied the light at the bottom of the fissure, a familiar longing filling her chest.

If she didn't climb down into the ice, she would never know what wonders might be hidden just out of sight. And the not knowing would gnaw at her for the rest of her life.

"We need to get out of the way," Lynn said.

Mara kept her gaze fixed on the crevasse as Tham guided her toward the palace.

When the line of guards blocked her view, a pang of regret pierced Mara's longing.

23

ALLORA

"Am I not the Queen of Ilbrea, husband?" Allora lifted a diamond pendant from the case of jewels the maids had brought to her dressing room.

"You are the Queen of Ilbrea." Brannon paced beside the windows, his gaze flicking between Allora and the shadows where Gillien silently lurked. "You are also my wife."

"And is it your wife or your Queen you are forbidding from seeing her father off today?" Allora set the pendant down and picked up a thin diamond choker.

"I am not forbidding you from seeing your father," Brannon said.

Allora held the choker up to the sunlight, which had finally managed to return to the city after days of unrelenting rain. "When my father's departure with the journey to the southern islands was set, you agreed I would go and see him off as is the tradition of the Map Makers Guild."

"You're the Queen of Ilbrea now. Not the Lady Map Maker." Brannon slid the choker from her hand and stepped behind her, holding the precious piece up to her throat.

"My father is still the Lord Map Maker, and I still need to see him off." Allora met Brannon's gaze in the mirror. "I am the Queen of Ilbrea. The people need to see me as someone who cherishes the traditions of the Guilds."

"Things have changed, my love." Brannon kissed the side of her neck. "I'm sorry."

"How have things changed?" Allora lifted the choker out of his hands, thrusting the diamonds at the maids in a manner that should have made her blush. "Brannon?"

"If I may, Your Majesty?" Gillien stepped out of the corner to bow to Brannon.

"I don't want her upset," Brannon said.

"I'm afraid you're too late, husband," Allora said. "I'm already upset."

"I am sorry for that, Allora." Gillien looked at Allora in the mirror, speaking to her as though Brannon had disappeared. "I am only thinking of your safety."

"The world is an unsafe place," Allora said. "I won't be a prisoner in my own home."

"And I don't want you to be." Gillien took Allora's hand. "But there was some trouble in the city the day of your wedding."

"Trouble?" Allora stepped off her dressing pedestal. "I thought the sorcerers had promised to clear the city of rebels."

"The violence in the city holds much deeper roots than the Soldiers Guild led us to believe. The rot weaves through all the unguilded in Ilara. While we were celebrating your wedding, the soldiers' barracks were attacked," Gillien said. "There were very few casualties, but fires were set in several of the buildings. The extensive damage to the soldiers' supplies and weapons indicates the attack was carefully planned."

"Why wasn't I told?" Allora looked out the window toward the city, as though some miracle might allow her to see the burnt-out ruins.

"There was nothing you could do," Brannon said.

"That doesn't mean I shouldn't be informed." Allora rounded on him.

"There was no need for you to upset yourself," Gillien said. "Nothing should taint your wedding day. That sort of stress can be very unhealthy for a new bride."

Allora pinned her hands at her sides, not allowing them to shift to her stomach as fear and disgust rolled through her in equal measure.

"I am afraid you have both misjudged me." Allora turned to the case of jewels, lifted out the most intricate of the necklaces, and fastened it around her neck. "I am not a delicate flower that will break with the first gust of wind. I am a Karron. I was born to endure hardship and pain in the name of duty.

"If you want me to be a placid and *healthy* new bride, you will not hide things from me—not your intention to keep me locked in the palace and certainly not the happenings in the city. I cannot be a queen the people of Ilbrea will love if I don't know what pain they're suffering. Did either the sorcerers or my husband announce to the people that I would not be seeing my father's journey off as custom demands?" She looked over her shoulder in the mirror, allowing them both a chance to speak.

"Not to my knowledge," Gillien said.

"Then I suppose you should weigh the rumors that will sweep through the people if I do not venture to the docks against the effort my protection will require of the sorcerers if I do." Allora brushed off the front of her silver skirt, grounding herself with the texture of the pattern stitched into the fabric. "My father is leaving on a long and dangerous journey. Please do not deny me the chance to say goodbye."

"I will send word to Lady Gwell that you wish to attend the leaving ceremony." Gillien gave Allora a nod and swept out of the room.

Allora looked back to the case of jewels, taking her time examining each pair of earrings.

"Leave us," Brannon said.

Allora snatched a pair of droplet earrings from the case before the maids scurried away. She pushed them through her ears, careful not to muss the curls her maids had carefully woven into her hair.

"I am your husband." Brannon placed his hand on her waist. "It is my duty to protect you."

"And it is kind of you to consider my safety." She laid her hand over his. "But not all wives need the same things to thrive. Hiding inside the palace will not make me stronger. I will wilt. I hate to speak ill of the dead, but Sorcerer Clery wanted to lock me inside the palace and keep me here for the rest of my life, never to leave these walls. If she'd had her way, our home would have become a living tomb."

"Allora—"

"I am more afraid of being trapped in a box than of any danger the world beyond the palace walls might offer." She turned to him, tracing the line of his chin before laying her hand on his cheek. "Our children will rule Ilbrea. They will lead this country long after we're gone. I want to know what sort of country we're leaving them. Please don't hide things from me, Brannon. I can't stand to call myself *Queen* if I don't even know our own soldiers were attacked in the city where we live."

He lifted her hand and kissed her palm. "The trouble with marrying a wise woman is forcing yourself to listen to her reason."

"You think that troubles you now, husband, but I promise you it will get worse."

"Worse?" Brannon leaned away from her.

"I was a headstrong child with a taste for adventure and an angelic face few could say no to." Allora brushed her lips against his. "If our children are anything like me, you'll be gray before your time."

Brannon wrapped his arms around her, pulling her close as though he might undo all the maids' work with a fit of lust.

"Nothing could please me more." He kissed down the side of her neck, pausing to take in the scent the women had daubed on her skin. His hands drifted down to her legs as he backed her toward the windowsill. He stopped, leaning down to kiss the scant part of her chest her dress revealed before turning her around.

Bright sunlight poured over the sodden palace grounds, valiantly trying to dry the gardens that had come so near to drowning in the terrible storms.

He lifted the back of her dress.

"Brannon."

He kissed her neck as he gripped her breast, his other hand nestling between her legs. "Our son will inherit this palace."

She gasped as he pushed himself inside her. She fell forward, bracing herself against the window frame.

"He will rule Ilbrea in the Willoc name." He panted the words.

Allora shut her eyes, blocking out the view of the grounds and the road that led to the palace gates.

"You will be bountiful." He gripped her hips. "For the glory of the Guilds."

She dug her nails into the golden paint on the window frame, hoping the sob that hitched in her throat might be taken as a sound of joy.

Her knees banged against the windowsill as the King of Ilbrea grunted and stopped.

He kissed her neck again before stepping away and lowering her skirt. He took her hand, turning her around to face him, kissing her gently as though they had shared something exquisite.

"Asking you to marry me was the wisest thing I've ever done." He straightened her necklace. "Give your father my best wishes for a safe journey."

He strode out of the room, leaving her alone.

She looked around her empty dressing room, searching for something.

Someone should come and tell her what to do.

No savior appeared.

A bath. She needed a bath before she could go into the city. Before she could see her father.

But there wasn't time. Not without risking the ship leaving before she arrived at the docks.

She choked on the air that seemed too thick to draw into her lungs. Her hands shook. Gold paint had gotten stuck beneath her nails.

She could at least wash her hands. She had time for that much.

24

KAI

The afternoon sun glinted off the Arion Sea, as though the waves themselves wanted to welcome Kai home. More soldiers patrolled the top of the city wall than he was accustomed to seeing. While their presence was an inconvenience, he couldn't be surprised, not if Isla's warning about the Brien wanting to use him as a faux martyred leader in the rebellion was true.

At least, Kai hoped the threat of the rebellion was worth adding a few more soldiers to patrol the city if the Brien were willing to murder him just to drag the Karron name into the chaos.

Kai let his gaze drift from the sparkling of the sea to the soldiers on top of the city wall and back again, not allowing himself to stare at the back of Isla's head as he waited for whatever opportunity she might provide for him and Drew to escape.

"Always looks like they're watching us, doesn't it?" Drew pointed to the top of the Sorcerers Tower.

Kai looked up at the black stone tower he usually tried to pretend didn't loom over the city.

"The whole chivving thing is made of solid stone, but it still feels like the sorcerers are staring down, plotting ways to torture us," Drew said.

"They are," Isla said. "Not in the way you think, but they are watching and plotting."

"Lovely." Kai took Drew's sleeve, pulling him to walk closer, hoping it might just look like he wanted someone beside him if the sorcerers' gaze truly was upon them.

Drew didn't fight the closeness. He stayed near enough that his arm brushed against Kai's with every step as they approached the city gates.

The line to enter Ilara was longer than Kai would have liked, and soldiers flanked the people waiting for their turn to cross under the city wall.

"Everyone stay perfectly calm," Arto said in a cheerful voice. "We'll get past the soldiers without trouble and finally have a proper meal tonight."

Isla slowed her steps, falling behind Arto and Kelsea.

"What I'm looking forward to most is a bath." Kai draped his arm around Drew's shoulders. "Once we've scrubbed the weeks' worth of grit away, shall we toast with chamb or skip straight to frie?"

"I'll take whatever the Lord Map Maker has in his cupboard and be grateful for it," Drew said.

"That doesn't really narrow the choices." Kai tightened his grip on Drew, pinning him as close as he could while still walking. "Chamb, frie, ale, liquors that hit you so hard I can't even remember the name on the label—the Lord Map Maker has them all, and Allora will gladly open any bottle we like."

"Then I'll let you choose." Drew wrapped his arm behind Kai's pack. "I wouldn't know where to start."

The sounds of the city drifted up the road.

The harsh voice of a soldier ordering a man to empty everything from his cart. The stomping of a horse protesting being packed in with so many anxious people. The cracking of wood as soldiers ripped open crates to examine whatever was inside.

As they neared the back of the line, Kai slowed his pace, dragging out every last moment that might allow Isla to keep her word.

A chance to escape, that's what she promised.

Maybe she's learned something else about the Brien's plan. Maybe you need to slip away once you're inside the city.

Maybe she's decided your life is a worthy sacrifice.

Arto and Kelsea reached the back of the line, stopping behind a woman with a handcart of tubers.

Isla paused as though trying to convince herself she really did want to go into the city.

"You'll be all right." Piran patted her arm. "You're not alone this time."

He stepped around her to stand with Arto and Kelsea.

Kai held his breath, waiting for any hint of a sign that it was time for him to run.

"Step aside," a soldier shouted to the line. "You have to share the path. All of you move to the side."

A grumble of displeasure fluttered down the line as everyone tried to shift to one side.

Kai pulled his arm from around Drew's shoulders, gripping his wrist as they filed in behind Isla. "If you don't fancy staying in the city, there's plenty of space at the Map Master's Palace. You'd be farther away from the Sorcerers Tower than anywhere in the city would allow."

Isla fidgeted with the bottom of her sleeve.

The rumble of voices from inside the gates grew louder as two wagons joined the line behind them.

"After all you've done for me, Allora would be happy to fill you with the best frie, too," Kai said. "Calm your nerves. Help you *escape* from the world for a while. We'd be glad for you to join us."

Isla gave the tiniest shake of her head.

"Keep moving," a soldier shouted. "If you're going to take forever to get through the gate, then wait until tomorrow to leave the city. Less chatter about the new Queen, more walking."

"New Queen?" Kai kept his grip on Drew as he leaned sideways to catch a glimpse of the front of the line.

A stream of people erupted through the gates. All of them, from the poor common folk to the fancy merchants, seemed to be wearing their best clothes.

"What under the stars is going on?" Kai whispered.

Isla held her hand out to the side, blocking Kai from moving closer to the horde of approaching travelers.

"Did we somehow sleep through the cold months?" Drew said. "Why are all these people in the city? Is this Winter's End? When did Ilbrea get a new chivving Queen?"

"The Queen's beauty is greater than I dreamt it could be," a young girl cooed from her seat high on a horse. "She looked so happy, too. Imagine falling in love with a king! It's got to happen to me. It's just got to!"

"There's only one King," the woman riding beside her said. "And he's already married."

"But this is his second wife," the girl said. "Maybe he'll need a third."

"May the gods forgive you for saying such an awful thing." The woman reached over and smacked the girl's leg. "The Queen is Mother to all Ilbrea. I shiver to think what you'd wish upon me to get your way."

"Let folks in to ogle the Queen and can't let me in to sell the food the people in the city need to survive." The woman with the cart of tubers spat on the ground in front of the girl who'd wished the new Queen a short life.

"Keep your spittle in your mouth, you old hag," the girl sneered.

Isla flicked her hand as though tapping the air.

A terrible feeling, like winter had claimed his veins, filled Kai.

Isla glanced back, giving him a tiny nod.

"Pay no attention to the rotta, dear," the mother said. "I'm more concerned with your wishing ill on the Queen."

Kai yanked Drew across the road, pulling him in front of the girl and her mother.

"I never said I wanted anything to happen to Queen Allora," the girl said.

Kai ran along the line of people leaving Ilara, heading toward the soldiers at the city gate as though he longed to throw himself into the mouth of the beast.

A cluster of young folk meandered away from the city, packed close together as they chatted and laughed as though the soldiers they'd just passed were unworthy of their fear.

Kai stopped and turned to walk with the crowd, laughing along with some joke he hadn't heard. He squeezed Drew's wrist until he joined in the forced mirth.

"I'm still not sure it was worth it," one of the men said. "We're going to be walking well into the night."

"Have you gone soft?" One of the other men punched him in the arm. "It's our duty to see the girls stay safe on their sojourn to glimpse the new Queen."

Kai bent his knees, keeping his head below the rest of the crowd as they passed the Brien's place in line. Drew ducked his chin, searching for something in his empty pockets.

"It was absolutely worth the walk, Sweets," one of the girls whacked him on the arm that had just been punched. Sweets grimaced. "The Lord Map Maker's ship was gorgeous. That purple sail just fluttering in the breeze."

"And the new Queen is absolutely stunning," another girl said.

"Of course she is," a third said. "She's had every luxury coin can buy. If I grew up in the Map Master's Palace and didn't look perfect, I'd be disappointed in myself."

Kai's feet fumbled.

Drew took Kai's arm, holding him steady, making him keep pace with the rest of the group.

"It's not just that she's pretty," the first girl said. "Did you see the tears on her cheeks when she kissed her father goodbye. She truly loves him. Our Queen is caring and beautiful."

"I—" Kai swallowed the sour that had somehow flooded his throat.

"Sorry," Drew said, "we got distracted at a tavern so we're a bit confused about the whole thing. What's the new Queen got to do with a ship with a purple sail?"

"You're deep in the cups," Sweets laughed.

"The new Queen is the daughter of the Lord Map Maker and used to be the Lady of the Map Makers Guild." The words rushed from the first girl as though she'd been longing for someone to spew the tale upon. "She just married the King a few days ago because their first wedding was attacked and the cathedral collapsed and so many people in the Guilds died. Murdered. At the royal wedding!"

Kai's lungs pinched. He couldn't pull in enough air.

"I heard the floor of the cathedral turned red with Guilded blood," the second girl said. "And then—"

"It was terrible," the first girl said. "Everything in the city is so awful they had to have the royal wedding inside the palace so they could protect Queen Allora. She hadn't even been seen outside the palace since the attack on her first wedding.

"But the Scribes Guild announced the sailing of the Lord Map Maker's journey to the southern islands, and everyone knows no one returns from the southern islands, so I thought Queen Allora would have to come see Lord Karron off and say goodbye since that *is* tradition and he *is* doomed, and she was there! The Queen was actually there, and we saw her."

"Bet you're sorry you drifted into a tavern now," Sweets said.

"You really did miss a beautiful treat." The third girl punched

Sweets again. "The Queen is radiant, so much prettier than Queen Carys the living corpse."

"Do you think the Queen will grieve for her father now or wait until the end of winter to accept he's sailed to his death?" Sweets asked.

Kai broke free from Drew's grip, swung, and punched Sweets in the nose.

The girls screamed.

"That's what you deserve for wishing ill fate on our Queen." Drew grabbed Kai's arm, dragging him away from the group and toward the shore of the Arion Sea.

25

KAI

He needed to speak to Allora. He needed to find out what had gone so horribly wrong in his time away that she had married the King. He needed to beg for her help in finding a way to stand against the Sorcerers Guild. With Lord Karron on a ship bound for the southern islands, she was the best hope he had.

Kai spent the hours he and Drew hid deep between the boulders along the shoreline plotting a way to speak to Allora without anyone but her knowing he was in Ilara.

He couldn't build a plan that didn't end with Death.

He wasn't sure it mattered.

Allora wasn't his Allora anymore. She wasn't the girl he'd considered his sister for so long he'd forgotten some people might not understand their bond.

Allora was the Queen of Ilbrea. Married to the King of Ilbrea, the man who stood by, letting the sorcerers chip away at the Guilds bit by bit.

Darkness swallowed the sea, and Kai still couldn't think of an answer.

Drew coaxed him from their hiding place, and they swam out,

cutting far into the sea to pass around the city walls without being seen.

The chill of the water did nothing to rattle his thoughts into working order. Even after his time away from the waves, the act of swimming didn't burn his muscles enough to jar his mind back into reason.

He'd swum the path too many times before. Most of the sailors had. When they wanted to get to the docks without risking anyone knowing of the debauchery they'd found beyond the city walls.

Niko.

If he couldn't get near enough Allora to speak to her, he could go to Niko. Ask what had broken between him and Allora that she'd agreed to marry the King.

But Niko wouldn't be back for weeks. His journey to the eastern mountains was meant to last until well after the end of summer.

The lights on the docks were too bright. There were too many ships, too many torches. Whatever madness had claimed Allora seemed to have struck the docks as well.

Kai and Drew pulled themselves up onto the stone-built strip of shore where the wealthiest of the merchants kept the boats they used to sail out onto the Arion Sea to take in the beauty of the waves.

The boats were all chained to the wharf. There were no locks on the chains, just solid, sorcerer-forged metal, forbidding the merchants from taking their pleasure boats out to sea.

Kai led the way to the nearest of the roofs that could easily be climbed onto.

They needed someplace safe to rest, but their haven couldn't be the Map Master's Palace. That would be the first place the Brien would search for their runaway prisoners.

Adrial would know what had happened between Allora and Niko. Adrial would be at the scribes' shop. Kai could slip through his window, and Adrial would explain everything. Adrial would help them find a safe haven.

The first few roofs were solid, just as Kai remembered them. But the weavers' shop had burned, so they had to turn back to find a way around.

Ruins blocked their path again. A house had collapsed in on itself, almost as though it had been stomped on by a giant.

Kai looked out over the city, searching for a path through the pattern of destruction.

He couldn't see anything in the darkness.

No taverns with their lights burning bright. No lanterns swinging on the front of carriages as wealthy merchants made their way home.

Drew took his hand, leading him back toward the water.

They left the roofs, daring to walk the abandoned streets as they made their way toward the shabbiest part of the city.

Kai kept waiting to hear screams echoing through the night. Or see flames leaping into the sky.

But there was nothing.

Desperate, derelict nothing.

Drew stopped at a sad building where poor slitches rented rooms. Brody had paid by the year for a room in the glorified two-story shack. Brody had coveted his secret place where he could hide from his wife when he'd earned her rage.

Brody had either visited the room since returning to Ilara with the captain or he had not.

Brody was dead. Or he was not.

Those were easy answers to learn.

Kai didn't want to know.

Drew reached under the board on the outside of the building where Brody had hidden his key. Spider webs covered his fingers when he finally found it.

None of the tenants peeked out to see who was climbing the steps to Brody's hideaway.

Drew had to work to turn the key. The dark room smelled of must and damp. Drew tossed the dust-covered blankets on the ground and made Kai curl up on the bed.

And even as the demons finally dragged him into sleep, Kai still couldn't understand how his home had vanished.

26

NIKO

Bright beams of afternoon sun bathed the trees and peered down through the leaves, scattering spots of light across the ground. Birds darted between branches, feasting on the brightly colored fruit that hung in tempting bunches. The rustling of the leaves in the breeze valiantly strove to carry over the chatter of children and hushing of parents that trailed behind Niko and Danu as they strolled through the forest.

The path turned, leading them to another cluster of houses—built of stone with wide windows and thatched roofs, just the same as all the homes Niko had seen in the valley of the Brien stronghold. The size of the houses, the gardens planted out front, and the people who ran out to catch a glimpse of Solcha marked the only differences between each batch of homes hidden in the forest.

"It's Solcha!" A little boy sprinted down the path, knocking into Danu as he shouted the glorious news. "You're going to miss Solcha."

Danu tightened her grip on Niko's arm as the doors of the houses began bursting open so their occupants could stare at Niko.

Solcha.

The whisper wound through the trees.

The Ilbrean who had been protected and guided by the mountain. Chosen to find a path to the Black Bloods so the children of the mountain might understand the perils posed by the Guilds lurking to the west.

Niko gave subtle nods to the people, carefully keeping his smile somewhere between honored and meek.

A man dropped to his knees beside the path, pressing his palms to the dirt as he wept. "We are grateful for the wisdom of the mountain. We are blessed as her children for the bounty she provides."

The man reached out. His fingers grazed Niko's boot.

Danu yanked Niko away. "There is nothing to be gained by pawing at Solcha."

"It's all right." Niko knelt to look into the man's eyes. "I'm sorry I'm not a saint or a god. If I could bless you with a touch, I would."

"The mountain sent you to us." The man grasped Niko's hand.

"The magic that burns at the heart of the mountains has always protected her children," Niko said. "I don't know why the mountain kept me alive. But there is meaning in her mercy, and I will do everything I can to fulfill the purpose she has chosen for me."

"Thank you, Solcha." The man wiped the tears from his cheeks, leaving streaks of dirt on his face.

Niko gave the man a solemn nod before standing and continuing down the path, letting the Brien stare at the one who'd been saved by their beloved mountain.

As they reached the last house in that cluster of homes, the path curved and branched. One way led back to the cliffs and the room that was Niko's cage. The other way cut deeper into the forest, farther away from his prison than Niko had ventured in the few days since he'd donned the role of Solcha in exchange for a façade of freedom.

Niko took Danu's hand, dragging her deeper into the trees.

Danu dug her heels into the soft earth, yanking Niko back. "We've gone far enough for one day."

"But there are more paths to explore. More people to parade past with dignity and compassion."

"If I didn't know how much you loathe Bryana, I'd think you were starting to enjoy your role as Solcha."

Niko let go of Danu's hand to stroll through the forest alone.

"Niko." Danu grabbed his arm, softening into a friendly stance as a woman bustled up the path.

The woman's eyes widened as they flicked from Danu to Niko and back again before landing on Danu holding Niko's arm. The woman's cheeks flushed as she dashed past, heading toward the batch of houses they'd just left.

"Why are you playing into something you don't believe?" Danu didn't fight as Niko continued down his chosen path.

"Would you rather I shout that I'm a prisoner who would like nothing more than to peel your elder's skin from her bones before escaping and running right back to Ilara?"

"Of course not. If you said something that chivving foolish I'd have to stab you. And I've gotten to know you a bit too well to not tear up as I slice out your guts."

"I'll take that as a compliment." Niko tipped his face up, letting the beams of light bursting through the leaves flicker across his face.

"I wish I could trust you to be wise, Niko. But it's my duty to make sure you follow Bryana's orders, and letting the people bask in the presence of Solcha reeks of a plot. Are you aiming for escape or vengeance?"

"Both, always."

"Either will end your life!"

Niko dragged Danu off the path, cutting behind a thick stand of trees that would hide them from any passersby.

"Do you want to know the plot I'm working on? Survival." Niko took Danu's hands, keeping them away from her blades. "Your elder believes the people need a reminder of their valiant purpose in going to war. They need Solcha to rally them enough to keep fighting. But what would happen if Solcha died? Or was locked up where the people couldn't see him? All that hope and purpose would vanish, leaving a darker void than the despair that filled the Brien before news of my arrival swept through your precious stronghold.

"I read the books you brought to my room, pored over them, and do you know what I learned? The Black Bloods are nothing without the mountain to bind them as a people. You must be the beloved children of the mountain, or you're nothing. Your war means nothing."

"If you had anyone else as your guardian, they would slit your throat right now." Danu wrenched her hands from Niko's grip and grabbed the hilts of her blades.

"But you won't slit my throat, because I am Solcha." Niko tipped his chin up, offering Danu the perfect chance to end his life. "I am your living proof that the mountain has not abandoned the Brien. You are the mountain's chosen victors in the Black Bloods' war. And the more the people love me, the safer my life becomes.

"How great a crime would I have to commit for your elder to order Solcha's execution, or torture, or imprisonment, or whatever other horror your chivving slitch of an elder can dream up? Every person I smile at is another layer in the armor that will keep me alive until I find my way home."

"You're a fool."

"No, I'm Solcha, and the Brien are starving for a glimpse of me."

He cut back around the cluster of trees and onto the path,

nearly crashing into a pack of men with baskets of fruit strapped to their backs.

"Niko, I—" Danu stopped with her hand on Niko's back.

The men all froze, their expressions drifting from startled to knowing as Danu's cheeks tinted with a sudden blush.

"Sorry about that." Niko wrapped his arm behind Danu, placing his hand on the small of her back as he gave the men a grin.

The men silently carried on, saving their tongue wagging for a grander audience.

"Why did you do that?" Danu rounded on Niko.

"To confirm their suspicions that we were in the trees so Solcha could twist you into the throws of passion and roll you on the forest floor."

"You chivving—"

"Is that a problem?" Niko frowned. "Do you have a husband you haven't told me about?"

"There is nothing romantic between us." Danu spoke through gritted teeth.

"And there never will be. I'm going to marry Allora as soon as I escape this paradise of a prison. But Solcha taking a Brien lover, the Elder's niece and trueborn heir's sister no less, it only builds up the story that the mountain destined this Ilbrean to become one with the Brien as they follow the path that will lead to Black Blood glory."

"You're a fool."

"I've rolled women before. I can assure you that was an accurate performance of being caught in a post-coital escape."

"I don't care if the whole chivving clan thinks I've spread my legs to gather Ilbrean seed." Danu stepped close to Niko, glaring up at him. "But you are meddling in things you do not understand. Do not pretend you are my lover. Do not mock willingness to join our clan. You tempt the mountain to mold your fate when you speak such things into the wind."

"If speaking into the wind will change my fate, then I will scream for all to hear that the only thing I desire is escape."

Boots thumped up the path.

Danu jumped away from Niko as though burned by the judgment of strangers.

Niko nodded, giving a wink to the man who passed.

"Jumping away like that was a nice touch," Niko whispered as the man rounded the corner and disappeared through the trees. "Definitely confirmed you shouldn't have been standing so close to me."

"Word of this will reach Bryana." Danu grabbed Niko's arm, steering him back toward the cliffs. "If she decides I'm not fit to be your guardian, whatever pain you receive from the next fool to hold my position will be on your own chivving head."

"She sliced notches into my ribs. I am exquisitely aware of the pain your elder might cause. And I will wrap myself in whatever lure it takes to not be strapped to her table again."

"A Guilded Ilbrean consorting with an enemy, playing beloved hero for his vile captors."

"The Black Bloods are not my enemy." Niko spun Danu toward him, taking her shoulders. "Your elder is my enemy. Her henchmen who tortured me are my enemies. But I hold no ill will for the Brien. Because you're right. If the Sorcerers Guild ever found out there were people with magic hiding in the eastern mountains, they would use their might to murder every last one of you. You do need to fear them.

"There are innocents and children in the stronghold. I would grab a sword and stand against the Sorcerers Guild myself if it meant protecting even one Brien babe from being slaughtered. But the only lives in danger right now are mine and Amec's. The fiend I face is your elder. So I will let every whisper of the mountain's protection of me, and rumor of my nestling in your bed, flood the valley. My battle is a game of strategy. I am dragging myself to higher ground, and I will not let go of that advantage."

A gaggle of women peered through the trees, wide-eyed and blushing.

Niko grabbed Danu's hand and placed it over his heart. "Come, sweet lover. The weight of Solcha lies heavy on my soul. Let us return to bed and remind ourselves of the pleasures that make life worth living."

"You should be murdered for this." Danu turned her reddened face away from the women.

"Fine. Slice me open and let your mountain drink my blood. I'd love to see what your precious people would do to the fool who murdered Solcha."

Niko wrapped his arm around Danu's waist, keeping her close to his side as they strolled through the forest, a storm of whispers following in their wake.

27

KAI

The pounding in his head just wouldn't stop. No matter how still he lay, a fist banged against the inside of his skull as a visceral reminder of the chivving mess of his life.

Kai rolled over, pulling the blanket up to his chin. The blanket was warm, despite its musty stench. And the roof of the shack where Brody had rented a room only leaked in two places, despite being a good decade past needing repairs.

Plink. Plop. Plink. Plop.

No one had come to murder him, despite there being at least two groups in Ilara that wanted him and Drew dead.

Plink. Plop. Plink. Plop.

The bowl and the bucket Drew had set out took turns catching drops of water as the rain kept pounding down.

Kai dragged the blanket over his head.

The pounding in his skull still didn't stop. And the pounding of the rain didn't stop. And the chivving plink plop didn't stop.

He lay very still, trying desperately not to think, until sleep finally took him.

A new sound dragged him back out of the blissful black. A thumping that wasn't coming from inside his head.

Heavy footsteps as someone walked up the creaking stairs.

He thought of reaching for the knives beneath his pillow.

But if the Sorcerers Guild, or Brien, or whoever else wanted him dead in this godsforsaken city had come to kill him, he didn't fancy dragging out the process by trying to defend himself.

Better to just let it happen.

A key scraped into the lock, and the bolt turned with a heavy thunk.

The footsteps came into the room, the door closed, and the lock thunked again.

Kai took a deep breath, steeling himself for attack, instantly regretting asking his body to work so hard as the throbbing in his head doubled.

"You'd better not be dead under those blankets," Drew said. "I just trapsed through a downpour to find something for the hangover you're so determined to wallow in."

Kai shut his eyes, willing himself to fall back asleep.

"I've got a stewed herb brew and heavy biscuits. It's the last food we'll be able to buy before we start selling Brody's belongings off, so enjoy it." Drew kicked the bedframe. "Don't make me rip the covers off you."

"I'll punch you if you try it." Kai tightened his grip on the blanket. His knuckles ached.

"I'll gladly take the hit, if punching me will get you moving."

"Moving where? Where exactly do you want me to be going, Drew?"

"I'd settle for you sitting up and drinking some of the brew I brought you." Drew sat on the creaky chair beside the bed. "Sit up. Drink the brew. Eat a biscuit, and I'll let you go back to sleeping in peace."

"Or I could sleep now, and you could eat the chivving biscuits yourself."

"Really? I thought you'd be interested in the news I heard about the head scribe."

"You heard more about Adrial?" Kai pushed the blanket back and sat up, his brain bashing against his skull as payment for the effort. "Oh gods and stars." He dug his knuckles into his temples. It didn't help the pain.

"Drink the brew and I'll tell you what I heard." Drew held an open jar in front of Kai.

"It's cruel to bargain with a man who's fallen so low." Kai took the jar and sipped the grayish-brown liquid.

"The folk I chatted to couldn't confirm if the head scribe had been injured at the cathedral when the first royal wedding was doomed by the gods," Drew said. "But everyone seemed quite sure he's alive and married."

"Married." Kai gagged down another gulp, trying to convince himself the sour in his throat had been born of the putrid stench and gritty texture of the brew.

"He married a common girl. An inker from what most are saying."

"An inker?" Kai kicked the blanket away. "Not the inker he met at Winter's End?"

"I've no idea."

"Adrial Ayres went and married a common girl." Kai snatched a biscuit out of Drew's hand. "Of all the chivving low things for him to do."

"You're right. Forget the evils of the Sorcerers Guild. We should rail at the Guilded scribe who dared to marry below his station."

"He got married while we were chivving lost at sea!" Kai got to his feet, letting the ache in his legs distract him from deeper pains. "He should have been mourning us. Or looking for us. He should have chivving well waited for me to get home."

He tore a chunk from the biscuit and paced the grit-covered floor. "Allora, I can almost forgive. I don't know what turned her against Niko, and I don't know what under the stars she was thinking when she agreed to marry the King, but I can understand her not waiting for me to get home. Royal weddings are all politics, I'm sure Allora didn't get to choose her wedding day. But Adrial"—he gulped down brew—"that chivving rat could have waited."

"And I would love to see you say all that to his face, but the scribes aren't leaving the library."

"And we can't go near the library without risking someone recognizing us." Kai's pacing slowed. "Can't tell Allora we're here without risking the sorcerers coming to kill us. Can't go up to the Map Master's Palace for frie that doesn't murder your head without risking the Brien coming to kill us so they can stage our corpses in the middle of whatever mess they want to cause."

Kai sank down onto the bed, holding the rest of the brew out for Drew.

"You finish it," Drew said. "It wasn't Brody's cheap frie that downed you, it was the amount you downed."

"And it still wasn't enough to forget. Always works that way, doesn't it? Our ship got taken over by a chivving sorcerer. We're shipwrecked. Locked in a warehouse. Abandoned our crew to try and protect our Guild. Walked across a chivving country to be almost killed by a madman roaming the southern mountains. Then used by Black Bloods—who happen to be real.

"Finally make it home to find my family's carried on with life like I was never chivving gone, and no one's heard from the survivors of our crew, and the city's in ruins because the sorcerers have been raiding everything and a bottle of chivving frie can't let me forget for one chivving night." Kai leaned against the damp wall. "You were right. We should've stayed in Pamerane and left Ilbrea behind for good."

"And risked the Sailors Guild never finding out what happened to our ship?"

"With what the sorcerers have done to this city, I doubt anyone would give a chivving sodden shaft about the fate of one lost ship. The Sorcerers Guild is too powerful for anyone to stand against. They rule Ilbrea, and there's nothing we can do about it."

"I thought you'd cling to hope as long as the Lady Sorcerer didn't sit on the throne?"

"Don't throw a hungover man's words back in his face."

"Don't let yourself dive deeper into the darkness when the Guild you say you love is in danger."

"Drew—"

"The docks are surrounded by sorcerers and soldiers." Drew stood, taking his turn to pace. "They're putting magic-made sails on more ships. We need to make sure Lord Nevon knows how dangerous the sorcerers' purple sails are. How are we going to do it?"

"It won't matter what we tell Lord Nevon. The sorcerers will force the ships to stay under their chivving magic sails."

"If that's what you believe, fine. Sell Brody's old boots and buy another bottle of frie. I'm going to find a way onto the docks to tell Lord Nevon what happened to our ship."

"What?" Kai pushed away from the wall as Drew headed toward the door. "You can't go to the docks. You'll get yourself killed."

"No, I won't. I know enough about ships that the soldiers and sorcerers won't question that I'm a common sailor, and they'll have no reason to guess I'm supposed to be dead."

"You can't be sure no one will recognize you."

"I'm going."

Kai shoved his biscuit into his pocket and grabbed Drew's arm. "If you're determined to go on this death wish of an errand, you'll have to stick to the roofs. As long as the sorcerers haven't destroyed any of the warehouses, you can make it to the docks without being seen."

"And then what, just hop down off a roof and stroll into Lord Nevon's office?"

"There's a window into his chambers on the floor above his

office. Crawl in there and make your way to him inside. With how things are going, I'm sure he's sleeping at the docks."

"Which warehouse should I climb up from?"

"At the—" Kai let go of Drew's arm. "No. I can't tell you that."

"Then I'll just hope I can find a warehouse to scramble up."

"You're not going to the warehouses." Kai gulped down the rest of the brew.

"We have to tell Lord Nevon about Sorcerer Roo. I didn't trek through hell to drink in this moldy room."

"One of us has to stay behind, and it's going to be you." Kai stomped his feet into his boots.

"What, now you're going to the docks?"

"I'm the better climber. Lord Nevon knows me better."

"Then let's go to the docks together."

"We can't." Kai pulled on his coat. "One of us needs to stay here. We can't risk both of us getting caught and killed before we tell anyone else the truth about Sorcerer Roo murdering our crew."

"If one of us is going, it's me." Drew stepped in front of the door, blocking Kai's path. "Tell me where to climb up onto the warehouses and—"

"No, old friend, it's got to be me." Kai took Drew's shoulders. "If I get caught, you'll find a way to tell the truth."

"No one would listen to a rotta."

Kai pressed his forehead to Drew's, shutting his eyes, stealing one glorious moment to imagine that the stars had let them find their way to a different room in a different city that wasn't haunted by sorcerers. A secluded place where they could wait out the storm in peace. "The sorcerers killing you would be my fatal wound. You'd be fine without me."

"Kai." Drew's hands grazed his hips.

Kai pulled away, stepping behind Drew. "Don't forget to empty the drip buckets."

He unlocked the door and stepped into the shabby hall, pulling the door closed behind him without looking back. He went down the steps, ignoring the whisper in his chest that promised the fate of the Guilds could wait a little while longer, he could chance a few more minutes in the quiet of the shabby room.

He shoved the rest of his biscuit into his mouth and stepped out into the storm.

The brew had done its job. The rain pounding on the top of his head didn't make him wish for a swift death. His stomach didn't fight against the weight of the biscuit, either.

Keeping his shoulders hunched and head down, he started toward the docks. It was still early in the evening. He could easily be a man coming home from work. Weary, angry at having to walk in the storm.

The people he passed all seemed too busy trying to keep the rain out of their eyes to worry about the other common folk around them.

They had no reason to suspect Kai had anything on his mind but a hot supper and warm bed.

It wasn't until he neared the warehouses that the common folks' demeanor changed. Walking quickly, but not so quickly as could be taken for running. Not so slowly it might look as though they were loitering to search for something, either.

He only had to make it to the first warehouse to spot the reason for their unease.

A sorcerer in a perfect purple robe stood in a shimmering cocoon. She watched the common folk passing by from her haven of dryness, ignoring the ten sopping-wet soldiers standing behind her.

There was another sorcerer and flock of soldiers at the next corner. This one was a man who grinned as though enjoying watching the people around him suffer through the rain.

The sorcerer at the third corner had extended the shelter of her spell to protect her soldiers as well. Her kindness offered no aid in getting Kai up onto the roofs.

"Chivving cact of a chivving sopping demon spawn." Kai studied the puddles on the street as he passed the low-fronted warehouse that had been the favored start of his climb.

He matched the pace of the people around him until he made it to the last of the warehouses, then followed the common folk for a few minutes more before looping back around to retrace his steps.

He'd have to take the path over the lower roofs. Closer to the soldiers' heads, farther jumps in between. Not at all a thing he longed to try in the rain.

Better me than Drew.

He hadn't said thank you for the brew and biscuits.

I'm a miserable slitch who doesn't deserve to be taken care of. I dragged him through hell and couldn't even thank him for a meal.

Guilt turned his stomach as he cut down an alley toward the fish mucking stalls that stank up the streets just north of the warehouses. Getting on top of the gutting stands was easy—just hop up on the counter then climb up onto the roof.

He leapt to the next roof over, gritting his teeth and tensing his stomach as his boots slid against the shingles. He twisted his feet to the left, stopping his momentum three feet before he would have shot out over the street and crashed to the ground.

"At least it's not thatch." Kai climbed up to the peak of the roof, sat, and pulled off his boots.

He reached into his left boot, peeling up the leather inside and pulling out the few coins he still had stashed in the hollowed-out heel. He put the coins in his pocket and tucked his boots into the crevice between the chimney and the ridge of the roof. "There are worse things to lose than a pair of old boots."

He swiped the rain from his eyes. "Like your mind, Kai Saso. Stop talking to yourself and leap to your doom."

He stood, testing the feel of his bare feet against the roof before making the next jump.

Splinters of pain digging into his soles was the price for not skidding as he landed. He didn't stop to check the damage to his feet. He kept to a run, bolting across the roof, picking up speed to make it onto the next, taller building.

That was the game. Keep the speed up. Don't look down to see if anyone's spotted you.

Momentum was necessary. Hesitation, deadly.

The docks came into view. Lanterns lined the wharfs as sailors kept to their work even in the unforgiving rain.

He jumped for the side of a warehouse, catching the top of a shutter.

The shutter swung open, pivoting him out over the street.

He hoisted himself up, looping one leg over the shutter then grabbing the lip of the roof to drag himself on top of the warehouse. He rolled to his feet and sprinted across the shingles, leaping onto the roof of the building where the sailors ate all their meals, wishing he could slip through a window and join the men of his Guild below. Sneak back into his life and pretend nothing horrible had happened.

"Hey!"

The shout from below broke his stride as he jumped to the next building over.

He tipped forward, landing hard, and skidded down the roof. He clawed at the wooden shingles, trying to grab hold of anything that might stop his slide toward the open air.

He dug his nails into the wood and jammed his bare toes against the lip of the roof.

"Get those crates into the warehouse before everything inside them is ruined by the rain," the voice from below continued. "I don't fancy having another round of angry merchants storming the docks."

"Let them rage," a second voice called back. "Maybe if the rich slitches make enough fuss, we can be done with this chivving nonsense."

"All of you keep moving," a third voice ordered. "Or have you forgotten your duty to Ilbrea?"

Kai pushed himself onto his hands and knees, crawling carefully up the roof.

"Of course not, sorcerer," the second voice said. "Just wishing for a return to simpler days."

"Best not to dwell on wishes that won't come true," the sorcerer said.

How I'd love to toss you into the sea, you chivving purple paun.

He reached the ridge of the roof, not letting himself look down to see which sorcerer he wished to drown. He grabbed hold of the chimney, using it to leverage himself around to the far side.

Plastering himself against the warm stone, he waited for someone to scream they'd seen a man leaping through the air.

But if any of the sailors had spotted a shape in the darkness, none of them cared to tell the sorcerer.

Keeping low, Kai crept down the roof on the side away from the docks.

Hello, Lord Nevon, it's been a bit. Did you know my crew is dead?

Kai lay on his stomach at the edge of the roof, peering down at the back of the building. The window in the eaves was dark, as he'd expected. The Lord Sailor wasn't the type to lurk in the private chamber his station afforded him.

Hello, Lord Nevon, I've got something to tell you that may end up getting both of us killed.

The Lord Sailor had another house in town where his wife and children lived. Telling him what the sorcerers had done meant putting the Lord Sailor's life at risk. Putting the Lord Sailor's family's lives at risk, too.

He's the Lord Sailor. You have to tell him.

Kai slid the window up, then twisted around to drop in through the window feet first.

If the sorcerers murder the Nevons, it'll be my fault.

It'll be the sorcerers' fault, Mara whispered. *You can't take the blame for someone else's evil.*

He turned to slide the window shut. Bloody fingerprints marred the perfect, white paint. He wiped them away with his wet sleeve.

His feet left damp, bloody footprints on the floor as he crept across the room.

"Of all the chivving things."

There are worse problems to be dealt with than a few unfortunate footprints, Mara whispered.

Get to the Lord Sailor, explain the fate of his ship. If he lived that long, he could clean up the mess on his way back out.

He kept to the wooden floor, avoiding stepping on the rug as he made his way to the far side of the Lord Sailor's bedroom. He listened for a moment before opening the door a crack.

No rumble of voices. No swish of maids bustling about.

He stepped out onto the landing in the hall, finally grateful for the inequity among the Guilds.

He'd never have been able to creep down the stairs in Lord Karron's home without being spotted by a flock of servants.

But the sailors were not as grand as the map makers.

The Lord Sailor may have moved his family away from the docks, but even that home was modest and could easily be broken into if Lord Nevon wasn't in his office and Kai had to take the risk of talking to him in the place where his children slept.

He reached the bottom of the stairs. Lamps had been lit, but there were still no servants in sight.

Kai hurried down the hall to listen at the door of the Lord Sailor's office.

Silence.

Too easy, Tham whispered. *Go back upstairs. Get out while you can.*

The gods owe me a bit of easy, Kai whispered back.

He opened the door and slipped into Lord Nevon's office.

"What do you think you're doing?" The Lord Sailor leapt to his feet, grabbing a knife from his desk.

"Good evening, Lord Nevon." Kai bowed. "I hope I didn't miss my own funeral."

28

KAI

"Of all the sodden spirits to show up in my office"—Lord Nevon kept his grip on his knife—"I never thought Kai Saso would be the one to haunt me."

"I never thought I'd have to crawl across rooftops in the pouring rain to reach the docks, but this is where the gods have dropped us." Kai stepped closer to Lord Nevon's desk.

"You're a ghost." Lord Nevon raised his knife.

"I'm not." Kai reached for him. Blood dripped from his fingertips. "I promise I'm not." He wiped the blood on his coat. "I slipped on a roof in the rain and ripped my fingers open. I tore my feet up, too, so there are bloody footprints going up your stairs, but I had to leave my boots behind. They were too slick in all the wet."

"You're alive." Lord Nevon's hand shook as he set down his knife. "You're actually alive."

"Yes, sir. I snuck in to see you because I'd like to keep it that way."

Lord Nevon sank into his chair. "Your ship wasn't lost. After all that searching—"

"Our ship was lost, sir." Kai dared to step right up in front of the desk. "She went down in the southern storms. Most of our crew never made it out. Eleven of us reached the shores of Pamerane, Captain Devlin included."

"Devlin is alive?" A flash of something dark flickered through Lord Nevon's eyes. "Where is he?"

"I've no idea, sir. Last I saw him, he was about to get on a Pameranian ship sailing for Ilara. Drew and I made our way here by land. If the captain hasn't made it back yet, I'm afraid I have to believe he and the other men are dead."

Lord Nevon buried his face in his hands.

"It was Sorcerer Roo who forced us into the southern storms. She took control of the ship and refused to listen to reason. The blood of every sailor lost is on her hands. The captain sent letters ahead of him from Pamerane, telling you and the King what Sorcerer Roo had done."

"I never received any such letter."

"I didn't think you would." Grief and anger pressed against Kai's lungs. "Roo told us the Lady Sorcerer wants to take control of the Sailors Guild, of all the Guilds. With the sorcerers grabbing for power, I knew there wasn't a chance of the captain's letter making it to you or the King without the sorcerers interfering. I knew they'd never let the survivors back into Ilara to tell the truth of what happened on our ship. That's why Drew and I left the rest of the crew.

"We dared to cross through the southern mountains so that if the captain didn't reach Ilara, the truth wouldn't die with him. And now I'm here and you know the truth and the city has fallen further than I ever thought it could and I don't know what else to say."

"Sit." The captain pointed to the chair in front of his desk.

"But—"

"A ruined chair is the least of our worries. Sit, Sailor Saso."

"Yes, sir." Kai sat on the finely upholstered chair.

Lord Nevon pulled a bottle of frie and two glasses from his desk. "Was it the sorcerers' magic-made sail that sank the ship?"

"It was the southern storms," Kai said. "But Sorcerer Roo could make the magic-made sail shrink to no wider than a rope. That's how her mutiny began. A threat to strand us in the middle of the Arion Sea."

Lord Nevon poured two glasses of frie.

"I shouldn't, sir." Kai held up his still-bloody hands. "I just managed to sober up. Went on a bit of a tear when I realized how much had happened in Ilara while I was gone."

"I doubt you know the half of it." Lord Nevon pushed the glass to Kai. "If you really made it from Pamerane by land, you deserve a dozen barrels of frie."

"Thank you, sir." Kai sipped the liquor, letting it burn away the chill that had sunk into his gut.

"The sorcerers have made a mess of everything. Lady Gwell is clawing her way into the King's seat on the Guilds Council, and her chivving purple-robed minions patrol the docks and the city. And now I find a sorcerer sank one of my ships and killed her crew." Lord Nevon shot back his frie. "They've pushed too far in the past, but this is a play for power beyond what even I thought they'd dare. All because a few fools thought they'd show their bravery by attacking the Guilds."

"What attacks have happened, sir? I was here for the first bit of trouble when the late Queen died, and I heard about the cathedral—"

"The cathedral, poisonings at the head scribe's wedding, the soldiers' barracks were set on fire during the latest royal wedding." Lord Nevon passed Kai his handkerchief.

"Thank you, sir." Kai wiped the blood from his hands.

"It's not only the sorcerers who've been destroying the city. Some of the rebels have been burning buildings. Merchants' shops, the homes of anyone they decide is collaborating with the

Guilds. Their violence gives the sorcerers more power. The fools are destroying their own city."

"It's not only Ilarans, sir." Kai leaned forward in his seat. "Or even Ilbreans that have been causing so much trouble."

"How do you mean?"

"When we were in Pamerane, we met a girl. She was from—" Kai froze.

Are all the Brien guilty? Adrial whispered. *If the children they rescued from the Sorcerers Guild are found—*

"She was born in Ilbrea but lived in an encampment at the edge of the southern mountains," Kai said. "She and a few others from her group helped Drew and me make it back to Ilara. Turns out they wanted to murder me and use my corpse to make it look like one of Lord Karron's wards had a hand in the violence here. Her people are trying to tear the city apart from the inside out."

Lord Nevon poured himself another frie. "Did you congratulate this girl on a job well done?"

"We have to push the sorcerers back. Rip the magic-made sails off the ships and drive the sorcerers away from the docks."

"I'm the Lord of the Sailors Guild." Lord Nevon stood. "Do you think I don't know my Guild needs to be defended?"

"I'm sure you know, sir." Kai stood and set his empty glass on the desk. "And I want to help. If I can spread word of what happened to our ship, people will see how dangerous the sorcerers are. I could go in front of the Guilds Council or speak out in the cathedral square."

"You'd be putting a noose around your neck."

"It would be worth it to free the Sailors Guild from the sorcerers!" Kai's voice pounded around the room. He swallowed, wishing he could take back his shout. "We have to fight."

"King Brannon rarely attends the Guilds Council's meetings anymore. If you're going to throw yourself to the demons, he needs to be there to hear your story himself."

"Then we'll find a way to get him there. If Allora truly is the

Queen now, and if I can get word to her that I'm home, maybe she can convince him to show up."

"She doesn't know you're alive?" Lord Nevon sank back into his seat. "She's been pressing the King to—"

Knock, knock, knock.

Kai grabbed the knife in his belt as he whipped around to face the door.

"Lord Nevon," a man called from the hall. "I heard shouting from outside."

"You're attempting to eavesdrop on the Lord Sailor?" Lord Nevon said. "I assure you there's no—"

The doorknob turned.

Kai leapt behind the door, plastering himself to the wall as it swung open.

"It is my duty to protect the Lord Sailor." A man with white-blond hair and a purple robe stepped into Lord Nevon's office. "Surely, you didn't expect me to ignore my duty despite your banishing me from your home."

"I assure you I am quite safe." Lord Nevon stepped around to the front of his desk. "Lady Gwell will be pleased to hear of your diligence."

"But I have not been diligent enough, Lord Nevon. I've been standing guard outside and somehow didn't know you had company." He pointed to Kai's empty frie glass on the desk.

Kai tightened his grip on his knife, waiting for the sorcerer to cast a spell to end his life.

"I've had no company, sorcerer," Lord Nevon said. "I'm simply a man who tends to misplace his glass when drinking frie."

"But surely you're not the one who left bloody footprints down the stairs. If you had been injured, you would have allowed me to heal you. Tell me who is here so these unpleasant lies may—"

Kai felt his arm rise. Felt his legs tense as he leapt forward.

But there were no thoughts in his mind as he sank his blade into the sorcerer's back. Not fear. Not vengeance.

The sorcerer staggered forward.

Kai grabbed the sorcerer, wrapping his arm around the man's shoulders as he slit his throat.

Blood sprayed from the sorcerer's neck. He got heavier as his legs gave out.

Kai stepped back and let go.

The sorcerer crumpled to the floor.

He lay still. Blood pooled around him. The same blood that was on Kai's hands and knife.

"We..." Kai swallowed, but there was no sour in his throat. His heart hadn't started racing in fear. "We should make sure the blood doesn't spread."

He grabbed a clean bit of the sorcerer's robe, wiped the blood from his knife, and slid it back into its sheath.

"Do you know if your servants keep a bucket and rags here?" Kai looked to Lord Nevon.

"You stabbed a sorcerer." Lord Nevon stared down at the man.

"Yes. Yes, sir I did. If he had found me here, the sorcerers would have murdered me. I didn't have a choice."

"Is he dead?"

Kai rolled the sorcerer onto his back. He felt the man's bloody neck for signs of life. Not a single thump of a heartbeat pulsed through his skin.

Kai had never wondered if his knife was sharp enough to slice a throat so easily.

"Yes, sir." He wiped his fingers clean. "He's dead."

"You killed a chivving sorcerer in my office." Lord Nevon poured another frie.

"We have to clean up the blood and get rid of the body." Kai stepped off the rug. "Do you like this rug? Could we roll him in it? Or maybe there's a crate. We could put him in a crate. If we can hide the body—"

"Hide the body?" Lord Nevon leaned against his desk. "You just killed a chivving sorcerer!"

"I know, sir. And I'm sure I'll feel terrible for killing a person later. But I'm a bit numb right now and I'd like to clean this up before I come back to my senses."

"I don't care about the rug." Lord Nevon wiped his mouth with the back of his hand. "Roll him up. I'll find a bucket."

"I am sorry, sir."

"You just killed a chivving sorcerer, Kai. When I saw you alive, a horrible part of me believed the Lady Sorcerer must have twisted you into a spy. And your tale of meeting a girl in the southern mountains—"

"I met her in Pamerane, sir."

"I don't think I ever could have trusted a man whose sister by home had married the King." Lord Nevon gripped Kai's shoulders. "But you slit a sorcerer's throat. You haven't become a traitor to your Guild. I've never known a more noble reason to ruin a rug."

Lord Nevon ran out of the room.

Kai looked down at the corpse he'd just created.

The man's eyes were still open. He had brown eyes.

Kai was careful not to look into the man's eyes as he moved the chairs and desk off the rug. An odd sense of relief eased the tension in his chest as he flopped the edge of the rug over the man's face. He rolled him up tight, hoping the thickness of the material would keep any more blood from leaking out.

A red stain had already seeped through onto the polished wooden floor.

Lord Nevon hurried back in with a bucket, rags, and scrub brush. "Is Drew here with you?"

"He's back at the shack where we've been staying," Kai said.

"We'll move you both." Lord Nevon threw Kai a rag. "There are some of us who've been trying to find a way to stop the sorcerers' bid for power. I won't lie and say things are going well, but I'll be glad to have you and Drew join us."

"Thank you, sir."

Kai scrubbed the blood from the floor while Lord Nevon cleaned the spatter from his desk.

"Did you really think the sorcerers might have turned me?" Kai asked.

"When a person shows up months after their ship's vanished, what's more believable—Dudia protected them and Saint Farrin led them home, or the sorcerers took them and played with their mind?"

"These are the desperate questions the sorcerers have driven into our heads."

"We'll weigh the body down and dump it off the deepest part of the dock." Lord Nevon tossed his rag back into the bucket. "There's a break in the soldiers' patrols. I can have one of my people help me get the body through."

"I can help you, sir."

"You can't be seen." Lord Nevon met his gaze. "If you want to help me, Kai Saso has to stay dead."

29

MARA

Mara lay beneath a tree, her ear pressed to the ground.

The steady thumping of striking axes had stopped resonating through the ice, though she had yet to decide if the silence should bring her comfort.

She opened her eyes, staring at the recently formed wall of ice surrounding the crevasse that had devoured the royal kennels. The massive wall shifted from day to day, expanding as the rift grew, creeping ever closer to the palace.

The servants who delivered Mara and Tham's food had no whispers to share of why the crevasse had been hidden behind the high wall, and the only other people Mara had seen were her guards.

The elite of Isfol had been banished from the palace grounds, the gates locked tight against any intruders.

"Has listening to the ground revealed any secrets?" Andric asked.

"Has the Queen given her permission for me to see what's eaten so much of the palace grounds?" Mara rolled onto her back.

"No." Andric stepped into Mara's view. "My orders remain the same."

"Keep Tham and me safely trapped within the grounds." Mara shut her eyes, listening for any sounds from the rift. Shouts of workers. Screams of terror. Anything that might offer a hint of the mysteries the wall concealed.

"I wish there was more I could do for you." Andric sat beside Mara. "I want to make you happy, Mara."

"Happiness requires freedom. Will you set me free?" Mara sat up to face Andric.

He glanced to the other four guards, all standing thirty feet away as though Andric had requested privacy. "I can't go against Queen Ronya's orders. But staying inside the palace walls is only temporary."

"And what about staying in Isfol?" Mara said. "Will I be asked to ride south with the Ice Walkers' army? Once the Queen claims land south of the white mountains, will I be allowed to go home?"

"Why would you want to go back to Ilbrea?" Andric asked. "Why put yourself back in the clutches of the people who sent you to suffer on Ian Ayres?"

Mara planted her hands on the soft, pale moss that covered the ground, picturing Tham sitting beside her, comforting, strong. A steady presence that tamed the worst of her temper.

"My family is in Ilbrea." Mara let the anger in her chest sharpen, twisting into the pain of missing the Karron clan. "Tham and I belong with our family."

Andric furrowed his brow, fixing his gaze on Mara's hand as though he were too shy to meet her eyes. "Have you considered that maybe you and Tham don't belong together at all? Not here. Not in Ilbrea."

"Tham and I have been together for years." Mara fought the new flame of anger that flared in her chest.

"That doesn't mean anything." The wrinkles on Andric's brow deepened. "Time changes people. Living in a new place changes people. Getting pulled through the blue profoundly changes people. Maybe Tham isn't the person he was before you came to Isfol."

"You can't judge that. You never met him before the Ice Walkers captured us."

"Fine, maybe he hasn't changed. Maybe he was always this angry and sullen."

"That's not fair."

"Holding on to something that isn't right is just putting your-self in a prison of your own making." Andric finally looked up. "Isfol could be your home. You could be happy with the Ice Walk-ers. If you'd only give us a chance."

Andric inched his hand forward, letting his fingers brush against Mara's.

"Let yourself be happy, Mara. I want to see you happy."

Slow, Mara, Allora whispered. *Slow and calm.*

Mara let Andric's fingers linger on hers for a moment before sliding her hand away.

"You're a very dedicated guard if you care about my happi-ness," Mara said.

"I could be more than a guard if you'd let me. You need to have friends."

"Did the decree that I should have friends come from Queen Ronya? Did she prowl through a line of guards and choose you to befriend me?"

"It sounds awful when you say it like that."

Mara coughed a laugh.

"Her Majesty worries about you," Andric said. "She wants you to feel at home in Isfol, to have friends here."

"Friends she's chosen for me. I'm sorry you were given such a taxing duty."

"I enjoy my time with you, Mara. I look forward to it every day. And you need someone to rely on." He offered her his hand.

Mara gripped the moss beneath her. "I have Tham."

"Queen Ronya doesn't believe that, and neither do I. She

knows things haven't been right between you and Tham since he found out you'd been hiding the truth of Ian Ayres."

"Of course your Queen knows things haven't been right, she has spies in the walls of our room."

"And you don't wonder if what you and Tham had has been broken forever? A man like Tham can't be quick to forgive."

"Tham and I will be fine as soon as we can talk without every word we say being reported to Ronya!" She stood, brushing the moss off her pants.

"Maybe you're right. But if you're wrong, just know that you could find joy without clinging to a broken thing because it's what you're used to."

"If Ronya is so concerned with her prisoners finding joy, I'm sure she won't mind my seeing what she's hiding behind that wall."

"*Queen* Ronya has given clear orders as to who is allowed to go beyond the wall." Andric stood, gripping the pommel of his sword. "You are not on that list."

"But has *Queen* Ronya forbidden me from asking her permission to see how large the crevasse has grown? Gaping holes in the ground bring me immense joy." Mara strode away, letting the soft clanks and thumps of her guards chasing behind her dull the sound of the blood pounding in her ears.

"If you wish to request an audience with Her Majesty—"

Mara whistled. "Elle! Come here, Elle!"

"I can submit a request for an audience," Andric said.

Elle bounded into view, Tham, Lynn, and the rest of Tham's guards running behind her.

Mara bit the corners of her mouth, wishing she felt the urge to smile as Tham raced toward her.

Elle crashed into Mara's legs, wriggling madly as she demanded affection.

"I'm going to ask to see the crevasse." Mara knelt, letting Elle cover her face in kisses. "I thought you'd like to come."

"If you'd like." Tham gave a formal nod, keeping his hands tucked behind his back as though he were just another one of her guards.

"Is there a gate to get through the wall?" Mara looked to Lynn.

"It's completely solid as far as I know," Lynn said. "If you'd like to request a tour—"

"Do you know, I've never gotten a single thing from Queen Ronya with a simple request. I find demands and dramatic shows to be the tactics that gain a favored response." Mara cut through the trees, heading toward the point in the wall that had shifted the least during the past several days.

In a few hurried steps, Tham was by her side, matching her stride as she headed toward madness.

She waited for him to give her some sign that he wanted her to stop, not daring to begin shouting until she stood five feet from the wall.

"Queen Ronya!" Mara took a breath to shout again. "Queen Ronya, it's Mara. I'd like to see the crevasse! Queen Ronya?"

Mara rocked back on her heels, unsure if she should be waiting for the ice to melt away or an arrow to pierce her heart.

"Queen Ronya!" She dug her nails into her palms. "I would very much like the chance to be useful. Queen Ronya!"

"We should go." Andric took her arm.

"Has Kegan given you all the help you need, then?" Mara shouted. "Am I no longer your favorite pet Ilbrean?"

Tham tensed, easing himself in front of Mara.

"Very well," Mara shouted. "Best of luck to you. I hope no one falls into the crevasse from a badly tied knot."

"If you're angry at what I said, I'll bear it. Please don't put yourself in danger." Andric kept his grip on Mara's arm. "I'm taking you back to your room."

"Wait for it," Mara whispered. "Just give her a moment longer."

The wall in front of them dissolved, opening into an ornate archway.

Ronya stood under the center of the arch, dressed in a robe made of pure white fur, a silver crown perched in her pale curls.

"Your Majesty." Mara stepped past Tham, giving Ronya a deep, reverent bow.

"Do you dare to holler at me as though I am a common peddler?" The ice in front of Ronya grew, twisting up into spikes like demon's teeth.

"I'm sorry, Your Majesty." Mara bowed again. "If you hadn't been on the other side of a wall, I would have spoken much more quietly."

"Sweet Mara, do I need to remind you that I am your Queen? Don't force me to spill the blood of a friend." Ronya smiled as though imagining all the ways she might damage Mara.

"Then I hope you'll forgive my impertinence, Your Majesty, but I'd like the opportunity to examine the crevasse." Mara stepped closer to Ronya. "You made it my duty to explore any breaks in the ice. Those were your orders. There wouldn't be a wall around the crevasse if it weren't large, dangerous, or something you didn't want people to see. Don't blame me for being unable to control my curiosity, Your Majesty. You made delving into the ice my obsession."

The spikes around Ronya twisted and swayed, like snakes tasting the air.

"I suppose it would do you good to see my discovery. We must further your education," Ronya said. "Leave your guards behind."

Mara faltered on the verge of taking Tham's hand and insisting he go with her.

"With your permission, I would like to see the crevasse as well." Tham bowed. "I was the one who discovered the break in the ice. I feel…" Tham tucked his chin. A familiar line formed between his eyebrows. "I feel drawn to it, Your Majesty. I would like to know why."

"Drawn to it, you say?" The spikes around Ronya froze. "In the way you're drawn to animals? *Were* drawn to Mara?"

Mara flinched as loathing urged her to scream.

"Mara and Tham may come. The pup may not," Ronya said.

"Stay with me, Elle." Lynn knelt beside Elle.

"This way." Ronya stepped back. The spikes in front of her disappeared.

Mara's heart raced as she walked toward the wall, despite her having begged to do just that.

She didn't allow herself to leap over the place where Ronya's spikes had grown but couldn't hide her sigh of relief as she reached the far side of the wall without having been skewered.

She glanced back, needing to be sure Tham had made it safely past the wall, too. He met Mara's gaze just as Elle began howling and the wall regrew, trapping them with Ronya.

"Thank you for allowing…" Mara's ability to speak faded as her gaze caught on the ground behind Ronya.

The crevasse had grown into a chasm far larger than the royal kennels it had devoured. Large enough to swallow several manor-sized homes.

Steps had been carved into the ice of the chasm's walls, allowing workmen to climb into the ground. But the horde of miners Mara had expected weren't bustling around the pit.

She crept closer to the edge.

Fifty feet below the surface, the base of the chasm became an almost level floor, with large mounds rising up from the ground in straight rows.

Five men clustered around the far side of the cavern, all of them holding pickaxes or shovels, all of them staring at a stone door set into the wall of ice.

The door had been carved with an image of a wide path reaching toward a horizon rived by mountain peaks, their jagged summits' shapes familiar enough that a less-trained eye might insist it was the silhouette of the white mountains as seen from Whitend.

"A wonder, isn't it?" Ronya stepped closer to the edge than Mara had dared. "A miracle granted to us by the ice."

One of the workers charged toward the door, slamming his pickaxe against the stone with bone-breaking force.

The man fell backward and slid across the ice.

"No!" Another worker snatched for the man's foot but missed.

The man skidded into one of the mounds that rose up from the ground. But the mound didn't stop his slide. He sank into the blue as though the ice were sucking him in. He started to scream just before he disappeared from view.

The other workers froze, as though trapped between the instinct to help their friend and the horrible certainty there was nothing they could do.

"Like children. You give them a simple warning and they can't manage to heed it." Ronya walked around the rim of the chasm to the staircase carved into the near wall.

The men by the door had clustered closer together, staring at the icy mound that had eaten their comrade as though it might spring forward and attack.

"Why aren't there more miners here?" Mara asked. "If you've accomplished this much excavation, there must have been hundreds of people working."

"We've not dug anything up. Everything you see has been revealed by the ice." Ronya started down the stairs.

For one foolish moment, Mara thought of shoving Ronya off the side of the steps. There was no railing to break her fall, no guards to catch her, and fifty feet might be enough to kill her.

And I could celebrate all the way to my execution.

"Don't touch anything. Not even the walls," Ronya said. "I'd hate for you to be sucked into the blue after all the heartbreak you've managed to endure."

"I appreciate your concern." Mara tested every step as she walked down the stairs.

"Of course," Ronya said. "I have the utmost concern for my sweet Mara's comfort. Which reminds me, wouldn't you two be happier if I placed you in separate chambers?"

Mara's balance wavered as rage slammed through her.

"We're happy together," Tham said.

"Really?" Ronya stopped on the bottom stair and turned to face them. "Are you sure you wouldn't prefer to spend a bit of time apart? The distance between you grows every day. Why suffer the chill of sharing a bed?"

Heat raced to Mara's face.

"We'll stay together," Tham said. "Thank you for the offer."

"Let me know when you change your mind." Ronya winked at Mara before stepping off the bottom stair, clearing their path. She beckoned them toward the center of the chasm, stopping between two of the mounds. "Now take a moment and truly look around. I want to watch your faces."

The mounds flanking them were nearly eight feet tall and longer than they'd looked from up above. All the mounds in the chasm stood in straight rows, though not all of them were the same size.

Mara stepped closer to the mound on her right, squinting into the ice.

It wasn't a solid blue. But there weren't any dazzling, wriggling points of light either.

Instead, darker lines sliced through the ice, like the outline of some massive figure.

She walked along the side of the mound, studying the figure's silhouette.

A nose—no, a snout—with a massive jaw that could crunch through bone. Long legs and wide feet, perfect for running on snow. A powerful body and bristled tail.

"That's the confusion," Ronya said.

Mara moved to the next mound down. Another dark figure waited within.

"They're wolves," Mara whispered.

"And the realization," Ronya said.

"Mara." Tham pointed to the chasm wall.

More dark shapes filled the ice.

Some narrow and long, as though swords had been stored deep underground.

"And the worry," Ronya said.

The sword-like shapes surrounded other figures.

People.

People had been stored in the ice.

People and weapons and wolves.

"And the terror," Ronya whispered over Mara's shoulder. "It's an army. My army."

"An army created by who?" Mara backed away from the wall.

Tham put a hand behind her, steadying her, protecting her.

"The one who gave the Ice Walkers their home. For generations, she has waited for a worthy heir. She swore vengeance on the demons to the south, and I have offered her a noble and righteous cause." Ronya took Mara's hand. "Give in, my sweet Mara. Accept my friendship and your honored place in my kingdom. For I have been granted a mighty legion. I will cover the land in my enemies' blood, and none who stand against me will survive."

30

MARA

Mara couldn't feel herself moving as she climbed up out of the chasm. She couldn't feel the ice beneath her feet or the pressure of Tham's hand on her back as he herded her toward the wall that hid Ronya's horrible treasure.

Rows upon rows of mounds bulging up from the ground.

If they were all wolves, with jaws large enough to snap a man's spine…

It'll be a massacre.

Everyone in Whitend would be slaughtered in an hour. Less. Maybe only a few minutes.

"Let us out," Tham shouted over the wall. "We're to be taken back to the palace."

"The people locked in the ice." Mara swayed as she tried to turn back to the chasm. "Are they alive? We have to help them."

"They're beyond our help."

The wall in front of them shifted, forming a less grand arch than the one Ronya had created.

Tham pushed Mara through the opening, as though he could feel the ice-shrouded wolves waiting to attack.

Andric caught Mara as she stumbled into the palace gardens.

"Are you hurt?" He eased her to the ground.

"Close the wall," Tham said.

No one moved.

"Close it now," Tham shouted.

Andric let go of Mara and pressed his palm to the ice, returning to her side as soon as the wall had resealed. "Are you ill?"

"I need to sit." Mara pulled her knees to her chest, battling the panic that threatened her reason.

"Take a breath." Andric put his hand on her back where Tham's had been just a minute before. "What happened?"

"Nothing." Mara shut her eyes, dragging her mind back to a place of comfort and calm.

Pale light flickered in the pink and white marble tomb. She leaned against the wall, working her way through the books Adrial had snuck out of the library.

Adrial, Niko, Allora—they all sat with her. Combing through fairy stories and histories alike, searching the books for hints of wild magic still hiding in the world.

The chance to discover something wonderful, that was what had started her dream of becoming a map maker.

A discovery, that's all the chasm was. A discovery of something wrought by magic.

Simple. Nothing she hadn't faced before.

"Mara?" Andric said.

"I'd like to speak to the Regent." Mara opened her eyes and stood, carefully brushing off her pants to avoid looking at Tham.

"Isfol no longer has a Regent," Andric said. "Queen Ronya is our ruler."

"Right, sorry." Mara squared her shoulders. "I'd like to speak to Ture Kian who was formerly the Regent. Do you know where he is?"

"He's been keeping to his study," Lynn said.

"Perfect." Mara started toward the palace, taking a path through the gardens that would allow Tham to walk beside her.

Andric dodged between Tham and Mara. "Are you sure paying Ture Kian a visit is in your best interest?"

"Of course," Mara said. "My ignorance of Isfol's history has become intolerable. Ture Kian once encouraged me to learn more about the Ice Walkers. I'm going to ask him where I should begin."

Elle dove between Mara and Andric, knocking into Andric's leg.

Andric stumbled back and Elle took his place, trotting along between Mara and Tham.

The absence of the usual gossiping elite left the path to the palace doors feeling longer than usual, as though the ice were dragging the palace away, keeping the prize just out of Mara's reach.

Panic can't protect you, Mara.

Twenty guards flanked the palace doors, all of them well-armed and stoic.

Do they know what beasts lurk so close by?

How deep would a sword have to slice to kill such a monstrous wolf?

When they finally reached the palace steps, the guards opened the doors without question.

The clacking of Elle's claws and thumping of the guards' boots echoed through the empty entryway.

"Mara. Please, take a moment to consider—" Andric began.

"Ture Kian was a scholar," Mara said. "I only want to ask him about your people's history."

"Do you know where his study is?" Lynn asked.

"Could you please show me the way?" Mara didn't slow her steps.

Lynn cut in front of Mara to lead their group.

"We could summon another scholar," Andric said. "Someone who specializes in the history of the Ice Walkers."

"But Ture Kian seemed so eager to teach me," Mara said.

Lynn led them up the stairs to the royals' private wing of the palace.

A tiny bit of Mara was shocked Ronya hadn't thrown her father out. Or, more fitting of Ronya's temperament, allowed the ice to take him.

"If Ture Kian doesn't want to see you," Andric said, "or if you find his grasp on what you're asking to be lacking, I'm happy to petition to bring in a competent scholar to teach you."

Lynn stopped in front of an ornately carved, ice-made door.

An inscription Mara couldn't read looped around the pages of an open book. A man stood behind the book, his face tipped up as though he sought wisdom far greater than himself.

"Ture Kian spent years enduring the rigors of playing the part of Regent. His mind isn't what it used to be," Andric said. "It would be cruel to push him."

"I've always found him to be incredibly alert and relentlessly determined to share his knowledge." Mara hesitated, unsure of how to request entry.

Andric slid past Mara, facing her, brushing the muscles of his chest against her arm. He raised his hand and knocked.

"Thank you," Mara murmured.

"Of course." A flicker of humor lifted the corners of Andric's eyes. "When you need to escape the old man's blathering, I'll be waiting here to rescue you."

The ice-made door swung open without the need for any magic.

Ture Kian's lips thinned to a narrow strip as he glared at the group in the hall.

"I hope I'm not interrupting." Mara stepped around Andric and into the doorway, planting her feet to keep Ture from slamming the door shut. "You once mentioned the importance of learning the history of Isfol. Things are changing so quickly here, only a fool wouldn't feel a desperate need to understand the Ice Walkers."

Mara held Ture's gaze, trying to convey her fear without seeming to slip into madness.

"Very few people have visited since my tenure as Regent ended." Ture bowed Mara through the door. "It'll be nice to have company."

"Thank you." Mara entered the study.

Tham's boot caught her heel as he followed.

"Gratitude for company does not imply the wish to entertain a crowd." Ture shooed Tham back toward the hall.

"Tham actually had some questions of his own," Mara said.

"I didn't think of how long the palace kennels had been on the grounds until the chasm took the building," Tham said. "I don't even know how the Ice Walkers managed to tame mountain wolves."

Ture's eyes went blank. "The history of sled travel within the Ice Walkers is fascinating." He spoke in a jovial tone that didn't match the expressionless void in his eyes. "You guards prowl the hall, or whatever you like. But be sure to have someone send up a tea tray. My throat gets dry when I do too much talking."

Ture closed the door. He leaned against the ice for a moment before rounding on Tham and Mara.

"What madness has brought you to my door?" Anger filled Ture's eyes, as though he'd tossed aside whatever veil he'd used to hide his ire from the guards.

"Can they hear us?" Mara whispered.

"Not in this sanctuary. At least not for now. A gift from my late wife. I don't know how much longer her protection will last now that Ronya has seized the throne." Ture settled himself in a seat by the fireplace.

The flames glinted off the perfectly polished ice, sending spots of light dancing across the fur-covered furniture and book-case-lined walls.

"If you dared to come to me, I assume there's a reason why." Ture pointed to two of the smaller chairs beside his.

"I need to know if there's a legend about a hidden army." Mara took Tham's hand, leading him to their seats. "Or a woman who might have left something buried deep in the ice. If there's a story about warriors and wolves, that might be helpful, too."

"You're only interested in legends?" Ture said. "The history of the Ice Walkers isn't important enough for you?"

"Of course it is." Mara leaned forward, making herself forgo the comfort of clinging to Tham's hand. "If the Ice Walkers have a history of massive, battle-worthy wolves, I need to know."

"Why?" Ture studied the ring on his right hand. "Why should one of my daughter's playthings come to me for tales of our peoples' past?"

"You were right about Ronya," Mara said. "She's more dangerous than I ever imagined. Ture Kian, I need your help."

"What a wonderful thing to hear," Ture said. "But if you've come seeking easy answers, you'll be disappointed. It's not as simple as reciting a grand historic tale. There are grave differences between the legend my people cling to and the facts scholars have carefully teased out of our records. Separating the two versions is not an easy task, nor is it one my daughter has ever looked upon with any kindness. Queen Ronya believes there is power in the legend and thinks it best not to confuse the people of Isfol."

"We're not from Isfol," Mara said. "I have no attachments to your legend. I'm only trying to understand what I saw today. You'll have to forgive me, Ture Kian. I have seen many magnificent and magical things in my life. Very few have managed to frighten me."

"If all you are is afraid, then I fear for your sanity. The path Ronya has chosen should be met with pure terror." Ture stood.

Tham mirrored the movement.

Ture gave a tired laugh as he walked to the bookshelf nearest the fireplace. "It's probably best to begin with the legend. If I began with the history, you'd find it to be completely unbelievable."

He pressed his right hand to the wall beside the shelf.

The ice shifted, melting away to reveal a stack of books.

"Several centuries ago, just before the seven Guilds seized control of the land south of the white mountains, Ilbrea was a violent place." Ture pulled a worn, red book from the cubby. The stone in the ring on his right hand shimmered as he ran his fingers along the place the wall had been, regrowing the ice to hide his cache of books. "The constant battle for rule over Ilbrea drove many to desperation. Fighting for scraps of food. Murdering for land. Murdering for lust. Murdering for power.

"One fateful day, a village just south of the white was raided. After watching a bandit fell her mate, a woman took her infant child and fled north into the snow. The bandits followed her." Ture sat beside Mara and opened the red book, carefully turning the pages until he reached an image of a woman wrapped in a red cloak carrying a screaming, terrified babe.

"The woman ran all the way to the white mountains, fleeing the murderous bandits. When she reached the base of the cliffs at the edge of the mountains, the bandits surrounded her. The woman begged for aid, calling upon the sky and the gods and the ice and the mountains, pleading for safety for herself and her child."

Ture flipped to the next page. The woman stood on the peak of an ice-covered mountain.

"A mighty wind whipped through the snow, lifting the woman, carrying her and the child to the summit of a mountain, far out of reach of the bandits' blades. The bandits raged at the wind for stealing their prey. The wind laughed at the men's folly and grew into a storm so fierce it swallowed the bandits. And all those who fought to rule Ilbrea saw the power of the great storm and abandoned any hope of ever claiming the white."

He turned the page again, revealing the woman kneeling on a mountaintop, presenting her child to the sky as a terrible storm consumed the land beneath her.

"As the storm faded, the woman begged the ice for shelter for her babe. In its mercy, the ice formed tunnels, leading the woman to the cavern where Isfol now stands. The ice brought her its precious worms to eat, making her and the child who still suckled from her breast immune to the cold. The ice protected them from the great beasts that roamed the mountains. The ice cared for the two as best it could, but the ice did not understand that the hearts of people are fickle and fragile. The woman grew desperate. Driven to madness by her seclusion, she began to hate the protection the ice provided."

On the next page, the woman knelt, holding an ice-made blade overhead, aiming the tip of her weapon at her child's heart.

"The woman murdered the child. The babe's warm blood befouled the ice. The ice grieved. Realizing too late the horror of what she had done, the woman wailed, begging the ice to restore the child's life. The ice in its mercy revived the babe, filling her veins with magic."

Blue light glowed from the babe's body. The woman shrank back in fear.

"Revolted by the unnatural thing her child had become, the woman picked up her blade to murder her child for a second time. But the ice could not let the child it had filled with magic be slain. The ice opened and swallowed the woman, saving the babe for a third time."

The babe sat alone on the ice, surrounded by a pool of her own blood.

Ture turned the page.

The child had grown. She stood on a tower of ice, her arms spread wide as though wishing she could embrace the magic that protected her.

"The ice raised the child as well as it could. Sheltered her.

Taught her. The ice tamed the beasts that roamed the mountains, training them to calm the child and bend to her will. The ice named the girl Kalene."

The girl slept nestled against an enormous wolf's flank, with a white mountain cat curled up at her feet and a massive bird soaring overhead.

"As the child came of age, she asked the ice how it had come to be that she was so different from the beasts that were her friends. The ice told her of the violence and bloodshed that tortured Ilbrea. The ice told her how her mother had fled from Ilbrea and how, in her madness and desperation, the mother had tried to end the girl's life."

The girl looked closer to a woman than a child as she knelt on the ice, weeping. The beasts that loved her stayed close to her side, comforting her in her grief.

"The girl stayed quiet for a long time, refusing to speak to the ice. The ice feared it had lost the girl's love, so the ice offered the girl a gift. The ability to control the magic the ice had pushed through her veins to restore her life. As Kalene felt the power the ice had granted her, she claimed the titles of woman and warrior."

Kalene sat astride the wolf, a spear made of ice in her hand.

"Kalene used the magic the ice had granted her to carve a path to Ilbrea. The ice grieved, thinking she would abandon the white forever. But the woman the ice had raised was not running from her home. Kalene rode south seeking vengeance on those who had killed her father and driven her mother to madness."

Kalene rode the wolf, charging down from the mountains, blood dripping from her spear, her bird soaring overhead.

"Kalene found the village where she had been born and slaughtered those guilty of harming the innocent, staining the snow red with blood. But her thirst for vengeance was not slaked."

The snow of the mountains traveled with her, forming a path of ice that worked her will in battle.

"She continued south, slaying every murderer and brute she found. Then Kalene came upon a great city, ruled by murderers and filled with vile thieves. She mourned, for she knew the city was beyond her aid. She vowed vengeance on the monsters to the south, swearing to the ice and wind that she would use her power to save the innocent and torment the guilty."

Blood covered both woman and wolf, dripping down the spire of ice where she stood cursing the dark and twisted city below.

"Kalene rode north, ready to return to the solitude of her home in the white. Along the way, she met the innocents she had freed. They bowed to her, called her savior, and begged to stay under her protection. Unwilling to abandon them, she led them into the white, giving them shelter in this very cavern. She fed them ice worms and taught them to survive in the cold. She built them homes made of ice and created a village where they could live in peace. She dubbed them the Ice Walkers and called them her children."

Kalene had aged. She lay on a bed, her face gaunt, her arms feeble. But her eyes held great love as she looked upon the people who knelt around her.

"As Kalene lay dying, she bade her people drink her blood so they might take in the magic of the ice that filled her veins. In drinking, those who received the magic vowed to protect the Ice Walkers. In return, she promised them that one day the ice would choose her true heir—a woman with a righteous heart and a warrior's power. Kalene's heir would ride south, soaking the ground in blood as she cleansed the land of evil."

Ture closed the book.

"Is that what Ronya thinks she's doing?" Mara gripped the fur of her seat. "She's going to ride south to keep some centuries-old promise of vengeance?"

"It doesn't matter what Ronya thinks," Ture said. "If the people believe she is Kalene's true heir, their fervor will cause more bloodshed than the Ice Walkers have endured in generations."

"You said you knew the Ice Walkers' real history," Mara said. "Could anything in the truth of your people stop Ronya from going south?"

Ture drummed his fingers on the binding of the book before going back to his hidden cubby. "We know the first leader of the Ice Walkers was a woman. We know the early Ice Walkers tamed the great beasts of the mountains and used them for hunting and other domestic purposes. We know at least some of the Ice Walkers came north from Ilbrea, bringing their traditions of architecture and hierarchy with them.

"We know the ice has sentience of some form and has, at several points in history, pushed the fate of the Ice Walkers through its changes. Unfortunately, even if I could convince everyone in Isfol to toss away the legend and cling only to the facts, Ronya riding south to free the children of Ian Ayres would be justified. Heroic and righteous. Fitting both the legend of Kalene's heir and the need for the Ice Walkers to view attacking Ilbrea as the right thing to do. By giving my daughter the secrets of an Ilbrean heart, you handed her an invaluable weapon."

"I'm sorry," Mara said. "I didn't have a choice."

"Yes," Ture said, "you did."

"Not one I could survive," Mara said.

"If you cannot harden your heart, you've no hope of enduring the coming chaos." Ture sighed and placed the book back in the cubby. The blue stone in his ring glinted as the wall grew back into place. "Ronya seeks power, and the ice has given her an army to bring into battle."

"But that can't mean everyone agrees with her riding south," Mara said. "She'll be exposing the Ice Walkers to the world. Once

Ilbrea knows you've been living in the ice, you'll never be allowed to hide in peace again."

"I am painfully aware of that," Ture said. "My daughter will bring death and destruction to us all."

"Not if you retake control," Mara said.

"Those are deadly words." Anger flared in Ture's eyes. "Do not give my daughter another reason to execute me."

"Do you think silence will protect you?" Tham asked.

Ture's lips narrowed back into a thin line. "I will not have my actions questioned by the fools who delivered my daughter the gift of Ian Ayres. Now get out of my study and don't come back unless the ice grants you a vision of our path to salvation."

31

ALLORA

The single candle she carried did little to fight the darkness of the passages hidden inside the palace walls. But, even if she could have snuck a brighter lantern from her room, Allora preferred the faint glow of the light she carried.

The gently flickering flame seemed to understand the secrecy of her work. Better to be small, unassuming. Harder to discover. Easier to mask in a simple lie.

Allora closed her eyes and held her breath, listening for any faint sounds in the black.

Nothing.

She peered into the darkness behind her one more time before daring to venture down the stairs.

The stone of the steps hadn't been worn into grooves by whoever usually trekked up and down them. The walls themselves held none of the dust or grit one might expect in a secret passage hidden inside the King's home.

Allora had seen servants pop out of the palace walls before, bearing trays of food or wood for the hearths, but they'd never carried a light with them or entered through any of the doors she had discovered.

Since the servants didn't carry lanterns, the passages they used had to have sconces or torches—or some more magical lighting—mounted on the walls.

Why build passages servants can't use to bring you cakes and chamb?

The possible answers were both easy and obvious, and made it worth the risk of exploring the passages in the dead of night.

She stopped and looked up to the top of the stairs. She should have already reached the ground floor, but there were no corridors branching away from the steps allowing secret access to the public rooms of the palace, just more stairs leading down.

She listened for the swishing of sorcerer's robes before continuing down the steps.

These passages could have been built as an easy means for escape should the royal family ever be attacked. Or as a means to creep between rooms to indulge in lust that was best kept below the notice of gossips, both servant and Guilded.

Or, the passages could have been built as a way to spy on the happenings in the Royal Palace.

Allora stopped another sixteen stairs down. She needed to ask to see the kitchens in the palace. Meet the staff of her new home. See how far below the palace the kitchens extended.

Another dozen steps and a landing broke the monotony of the staircase. Wooden doors with heavy metal locks led to the right and left.

She held her breath as she tried the door on the left and again as she tried the door on the right. Neither budged. She peered into the locks. They seemed like normal pieces made by a smith rather than anything forged by nefarious magic.

Something with which to pick a lock—possible to find, but tricky to reason away should she be caught and questioned.

Allora peered down the stairs leading deeper into the darkness. She pressed her hand to the door on the right, feeling for... she didn't know what, before continuing down.

How often would the servants have to scrub the stone walls to keep the dust and spiders at bay? They would have to haul buckets through the darkness to wash every step.

Or a sorcerer could clean it all with a bit of magic.

She would have preferred spiderwebs clinging to her hair above knowing that sorcerers prowled through the walls of her home.

Another twenty steps down, the stairs ended at another locked door.

She'd gone too far underground, below the depth any normal part of the palace could reach. Not a wine cellar, root cellar, or ice cellar. There was no logical reason to dig this deep into the earth.

"Why?" She whispered to the door. "What could be worth the trouble of burrowing so far down?"

A tiny glistening in the door caught her eye. A latticework of swirls and symbols had been inlaid into the wood.

She held her candle closer to the door. The pattern wasn't made of metal. It looked more like glistening black stone. The archway around the door had been built of black stone, too. So had the threshold below.

The need to break through the door no matter the cost tugged at Allora's chest.

She backed away, climbing the stairs with reckless speed, running toward the doors on the landing above.

They'd been built of plain wood and surrounded by the same plain, gray stone as the rest of the passages.

Why?

The question rattled around in Allora's mind as she kept climbing the steps.

Why? Why? Why?

Why black stone? Why go through the trouble of digging so deep?

She cut down the passage that led past the room where Brannon had slept as a child, then past the chambers where Illia still lived, not bothering to peer out through the peephole that would give her a view of the backs of Illia's guards' heads.

She turned down the next passage, stopping at the panel that led to the room she and Brannon shared.

Letting out a long breath, she replaced the worry on her face with childish intrigue. She had gone on an adventure. Such a daring lark for a clever little wife.

Blowing out her candle, she pressed on the panel, and stepped into her room.

Brannon slept soundly in bed. Mouth open and arms splayed out as though Allora didn't need any space to sleep.

She shut the panel behind her and froze for a moment, waiting for Gillien to jump out of the shadows and curse her for having prowled through the walls of the palace at night.

But no one leapt out of the shadows in her room, just as no one had leapt out of the darkness on the stone steps.

In the few nights she had crept through the walls, she had never met another person in the well-scrubbed passages.

You are not that skilled, Allora Karron.

She set the candle and extra matches she had tucked into the pocket of her robe on her bedside table.

Monsters plague this place, even if you can't see them.

She crept to the bathroom, using the faint light from the high window to check for anyone lurking in the shadows before shutting the door.

The maids had been sure to make the King's new bride comfortable, leaving her a basket of cloths should, Dudia forbid, she not be pregnant before her time to bleed came again.

She reached deep into the basket and pulled out one of the cloths. Her heart gave an extra thump as she unrolled it to find her treasures—a tiny pencil and a few well-folded pieces of paper.

Poor tools for the Lady Map Maker.

She sat in the square of moonlight on the chill stone floor, carefully adding the staircase leading to the locked doors.

"What is worth locking up? And who wants me to find it?"

Allora studied the map for a few minutes more, postponing the moment she would have to climb back into bed with her husband. She'd try to sleep until the sun rose and try to seem eager when the monster of his lust woke her in the morning.

32

NIKO

The rhythm of the fiddle playing pounded into Niko's head, blurring the words of the men around him. Someone had pressed a new mug of ale into his hand. At least, he thought someone had given him a new mug of ale. He'd most likely, to the best of his remembrance, been given a new mug of ale by a mysterious benefactor. Or, possibly, a Black Blood ghost who longed to see him drunk.

But no.

No, if he really tried to work it out, he had definitely been drinking long enough his mug shouldn't have been full, and it was almost full, though he had no idea how or when the mountain had blessed him with more of the spiced brew the Black Bloods liked to call ale.

But where had the ale come from?

Niko sat on top of the table, pressing his free hand to the wood beneath him to keep the room from spinning, and hoping that whatever kind spirit had brought him ale might bring him something for his headache in the morning.

"The chivving Hayes, they don't know what war is meant to be." The man sitting to Niko's right leaned into the crowd that had gathered around Solcha. "They hide behind their walls, letting their people starve so they don't have to come out and face the wrath of the Brien on the battlefield." He raised his mug to his lips and sloshed ale down his front. "Chivving hand, can't even manage ale."

Niko began reaching to help the man before turning his attention back to his own ale as the man shifted his grip, using his left hand to angle the mug of ale to his mouth with less than perfect aim.

It was a sight Niko had become accustomed to in the nights he'd been allowed to visit the common hall of the stronghold. Men and women who'd returned from the Black Bloods' war. Some missing arms, like the man with ale dribbling from his chin. Others missing legs or eyes, or with magic-wrought burns the healers hadn't managed to erase, or with a pained and empty look in their eyes Niko recognized.

The empty Brien, he could connect with best.

Bryana had made sure Niko knew what it was to be stripped of his spirit and wrapped in so much pain he forgot what life beyond the horror was meant to look like.

"If the Hayes knew how to face a proper battle, we'd have been celebrating victory a full year ago." A woman who'd lost most of her left leg slid closer to Niko, sitting on the bench where he rested his feet. "The mountain has set our course. Victory is inevitable. If only the Hayes were wise enough to accept it."

The people cheered, looking to Niko, needing him to join in the call, offering affirmation of their certain victory.

He shouted with the crowd and downed the rest of his mug, hating himself for letting his thoughts drift to worrying about the consequences of filling his head with so much ale.

If the warriors around him could cling to hope and cheer for the Brien's eventual victory, how could he argue? How could the man who'd been declared Solcha steal the hope of those who'd lost limbs, and minds, and friends to the fight against the Hayes.

The Hayes Clan was evil. They had to be stopped, no matter the cost.

At least, that was the story Niko had been told. But he'd also been called chosen and beloved of the mountain. Those things couldn't be true. A mountain couldn't love a map maker. That wasn't how sediment worked.

The mug in his hand grew heavy again as some imp refilled his ale.

"What we need is the aid of mountain stone," one of the men, Shay, said. "Use the might of the mountain herself to save her children."

The warriors' gazes drifted to Niko.

"I'm not a soldier," Niko said. "I don't know what's needed to win a war."

"But if we could use weapons forged of mountain stone—" Shay said.

"It's against the Black Bloods' treaty," the woman who'd lost her leg said. "If we break the treaty, we'll have fallen as far as the Hayes. Better to keep fighting an honest war than pervert the mountain's stone and win before winter."

"Did you see anything when the mountain led you here?" A boy who looked too young to have been marched off to war limped forward, his eyes filled with hope as he stared at Niko. "Any signs of what's to come? Or what we should be doing to win?"

Niko took a long drink of his ale, letting himself choke on the brew to buy another moment to think. "I won't lie and say I know anything about signs, or how to read the mountain's will. When I was in the darkness, I saw things I can't explain. I told your elder everything. She'll have to decide what to make of it."

Niko gripped his mug, waiting for the crowd to disperse in disappointment, or give him a solid punch in the face because they'd finally figured out he was a rat who'd fallen down a hole and gotten himself trapped, not a person who'd been favored by the mountain in a chivving meaningful way.

But the boy's eyes brightened, and the hardened warriors nodded their approval.

"Bryana has always kept her own counsel," an older man with burn scars on his neck and face said. "The mountain allowed Solcha to deliver the wisdom Bryana needed. Our elder will lead us to victory."

Another round of cheers rang through the hall.

Niko's mug disappeared from his hand, but a new one didn't take its place.

Someone gripped his arm.

Danu stood on the other side of the table, her face an odd type of calm as she pulled on Niko's arm.

"Being packed off to bed so soon?" Niko let his voice carry over the crowd.

"You'll thank me when you're not ill on the floor later." Danu kept her hold on his arm.

Niko lifted his feet off the bench and twisted around, setting his feet on the far side of the table in a movement that might have been impressive if he hadn't stumbled into Danu's arms as he stood.

"Sorry 'bout that." Niko stepped away from Danu, brushed off her shoulders, and realized everyone was still watching him.

He draped his arm around her shoulders and gave her a grin. "Please lead the way. I promise I'll apologize for being a sloppy mess when I wake up in the morning."

"Chivving well better." Danu wrapped her arm around Niko's waist and hauled him toward the door.

"Though I would like to say I only poured myself the first ale. The rest of it, it just happened."

"Of course it did." Danu nodded as she passed a man who used his crutches in an uncertain way as he fumbled down the hall.

"Someone's going to need to help him home," Niko whispered. "The floor's a bit tipped as it is. With crutches, *pfft*, pure doom."

"He'll be taken care of. You focus on your own walking." Danu tightened her grip on Niko as he sagged into a laugh.

"You're mad at me." Niko tempered his humor. "Are you angry I'm drunk? Do you not approve of what I said about your elder? I don't think I have it in me to be any nicer about that chivving slitch of an evil vermin."

"Watch your words." Danu angled Niko toward the stairs. "For what it's worth, I thought you handled them well. Sometimes, it seems the wounded need more assurance that the war is necessary than the ones who are still fighting."

"They need someone to tell them their sacrifices were worth it," Niko said. "It would be awful to lose a leg in a battle that should never have been fought."

"Whatever the reason, you're good with them."

"Then why am I being hauled off to bed like a naughty child?"

"I'm not hauling you anywhere."

"I beg to differ."

Niko didn't bother fighting as Danu led him up the stairs, down a long hall, up another flight of stairs, and to his bedroom door.

She touched her fingers to the door, unlocking it even though she'd had no prisoner to trap when she'd let Niko out so Solcha might mingle with the people…two hours ago. No, five hours.

How long until the sun was supposed to come up?

Only Dudia would ever know.

Niko leaned on Danu, taking off his boots before letting her flop him into his chair.

"I'll make you some tea."

"Water's fine." Niko reached for the pitcher. "A few glasses, and I'll be ready for morning."

"Things would go better if you were sober." Danu bit her lips together, looking toward the locked door.

Niko took her hand, urging her toward his other chair. "If you're going to tell me I'm to be executed or sent back to your elder for more torture, I'd rather have frie than tea."

"It's not"—Danu sat, easing her hand from Niko's—"it's not to do with Bryana." She straightened the leftover dinner plates on the table, as though order might change the impact of her words.

"Is it Amec? Has that fiend of a chivving elder killed him?" Niko sprang to his feet, gripping the table as the room swayed. "I'll tear her throat out with my thumbs."

"It's not Amec." Danu grabbed his arm as he whipped around to charge for the door. "I still don't know where Amec is."

Niko sank back into his seat, his limbs heavier after the surge of energy popped and faded.

"I told you I would try to contact your girl in Ilbrea." Danu shifted her grip on Niko, holding his wrist. "I kept my word. I sent a message to my friend in Ilara."

"And?" Pressure dug into the front of Niko's throat. "What did Allora say? Has her father arranged ransom to buy me back?"

"My friend couldn't get word to Allora."

The comforting warmth of the ale syphoned from his body. "Is she ill? Did something happen to Allora?"

Danu let out a shaky breath, her gaze locked on the table.

"Danu, tell me!"

"She's married." Tears glinted in the corners of her eyes as she met Niko's gaze. "I'm so sorry, Niko."

Niko leaned back in his seat, dragging his free hand over his face as a laugh cracked through his panic. "Your friend found the wrong Allora. My Allora is Allora Karron. The Lord Map Maker's daughter."

"Who is now Queen Allora Willoc. Your girl got married, Niko. She married the King."

"No." Niko yanked his wrist from Danu's grip. "Ilbrea already has a queen."

"Queen Carys Willoc died months ago. I'm not sure why the King remarried so quickly, but he did. King Brannon married Allora Karron."

Niko leapt to his feet, knocking over his chair. The clatter of wood striking stone burst through his words. "Why are you saying this? Has your elder decided I deserve more torture? Has she sent you to tell me lies about Allora? Since she couldn't break my mind, she'll shatter my heart?"

"Bryana doesn't know. She knows I sent a message to Ilara, but I haven't told her about the letter I got back. I wanted you to hear it first."

"Hear your lies first? No, Danu, I may be a prisoner, but I don't have to listen to this. Get out of my room." Niko pointed at the door, glaring at Danu, waiting for her to use her magic to punish his temper.

"I wish it was a lie." She reached into her pocket and pulled out a little bird carved of black stone. She set the bird on the table, then ran her finger down the bird's back.

The bird ruffled to life, shaking out its stone wings, hopping from foot to foot.

Danu touched the bird's back again. The stone-made creature tipped its head up. A scroll pushed out of the front of the bird's neck.

Danu pulled out the scroll and held it up, offering it to Niko.

"I don't—" A weight crushed Niko's chest. His breath hitched as he forced himself to speak. "I've already heard your lies. I don't need to read them."

Danu unrolled the scroll and shook her head, as though banishing her tears. "Danu, this of all things is what you write me for? You've wounded me beyond measure. At least send some gossip from the stronghold next time instead of diving right into asking me to run a fool's errand that'll end with a broken heart."

She looked up at Niko, watching him for a moment before reading on. "If this man Niko really is in love with Allora Karron, give the slitch my sympathy. Allora Karron has married the King of the Paun and now sits as the Queen of Ilbrea.

"Tell your sorry slitch that she didn't marry the demon King by accident, either. Her first wedding to the King was interrupted. The paun did the whole chivving wedding pomp a second time, so Allora must have been determined to lay her claim on the King. I suppose the Royal Palace is the only place for a girl raised in the Map Master's Palace to go that wouldn't seem like a pissing rat's hole.

"I can't get to Queen Allora to tell her Niko's alive. Even if I could, I don't think it would be safe for the Brien or kind to the fool, Niko. I hope it was only lust between them. Chivving awful if he really was in love with the Queen. You still owe me a favor even though this was a waste of parchment. Down an ale for me. Peadar"

Stillness filled the room. The floor stopped tilting. Niko's lungs stopped taking in air.

Danu managed to move first. "I'm so sorry, Niko." She brushed the tears from her cheeks and rolled the scroll back up as though its pain could be tucked away. She pushed the paper into the bird's neck and slipped the stone bird back into her pocket.

"I know it's not the message you'd hoped to receive," Danu said. "But Allora is alive and well and—"

"And a captive." Niko doubled over, bracing his hands against the table. "The King is holding her captive."

"The King is her husband."

"No. He made Allora marry him. He must have threatened her. Now he's got her locked up. I have to save her." Niko pushed away from the table. His heartbeat raged in his ears as he grabbed his boots from the floor. "I have to get back to Ilara. I have to go now. I'll find some way out of here. I ha—I have to rescue Allora."

"She married a king."

"She's supposed to marry me!" Niko jammed his feet into his boots. "Allora Karron loves me. She's waiting for me. It's in the letter she wrote me. Your elder stole it when she tortured me, but the letter is proof that Allora's waiting for me."

"But did she know she'd have a chance with a king?" Danu stayed at the table, not stopping Niko as he stormed to the wardrobe.

"Allora doesn't want a king." Niko pulled out his coat and yanked it on.

"She doesn't want to be a queen? Doesn't want to live in the Royal Palace? Queen Allora Willoc is now the wealthiest woman in all Ilbrea. Is it so hard to believe she chose that over marrying a map maker?"

"You don't know her." Niko grabbed food from the table, shoving it into his coat pockets.

"I'm not sure you do either. Did you share a bed with her? Did you plan a life with her? From what you've said, she never actually accepted your proposal, even though you'd been asking for her hand for ages."

"I wasn't proposing well enough. I need to do it properly."

"And if the King proposed properly while you were away?" Danu pulled the bowl of cut fruit out of Niko's reach. "Would she really turn down the chance to be Queen?"

"Of course she would!" Even as he shouted, pain clawed deep into Niko's memories.

Allora not wanting to be left alone while Niko adventured on map making journeys. Allora not wanting to leave her father's palace for modest rooms in Ilara. Allora treating his love as a children's game over and over again.

"I have to be sure." Niko patted his pockets, trying to remember what he'd been so desperate to pack, as a heavy, drowning shroud replaced his panic. "The Guilds have done far worse than forcing a woman into marriage. I have...Danu, if there's even a small chance it's not the marriage Allora wanted, I have to go. I have to make sure she's safe."

"You can't leave, Niko. I'm so sorry."

"Sorry?" Niko smacked the bowl of fruit from her hand. Brightly colored debris rained down onto the gray stone floor. "You can free me from the stronghold. You're a sorcerer."

"Barely. The kind of magic I've been given—"

"Is magic!" Niko grabbed her arms. "You can manipulate locks. That's all I need, just let me out."

"I can't!" Danu stood, knocking Niko away. "I don't have stone magic. I can't open the paths that lead out of the stronghold. And even if I'd been born with that magic, I still couldn't help you!"

"Why not? Because the Brien need to watch Solcha roam through the woods and drink ale? Give someone else the title. I don't care about offering your people comfort. The only thing that matters is Allora."

"I can't help you." Danu tore at the knot at the top of her bodice. "I wish I could. I wish I had the power to set you free, but I don't."

"Then find me someone who does."

Danu shimmied out of her bodice and tossed it onto the floor.

"If you think your tits will keep me from fighting my way to Allora—"

Danu pulled up the bottom of her shirt. A mark covered the side of her ribs. A tightly tied knot, placed like a stone in the center of a stream, had been carefully drawn in black.

"I am sworn to Bryana," Danu said. "She drew this mark herself. I am bound to her. When you give a trueborn your vow and they give you their mark, you are handing them your life. To disobey is to die."

"Your aunt drew that on you?" Niko reached for the mark.

"It's not so different from the mark your Guilds put on your wrist. But Black Blood marks are drawn with mountain stone.

The stone in my side is joined with Bryana in a way you and I could never hope to understand."

Niko trailed his fingertips across the knot in the center of the stream, waiting for a flare of magic to burn him.

"Tiny bits of stone wait beneath my skin. If I disobey Bryana, it wouldn't take more than a glance from her to rip the stone through my body. Thousands of fragments tearing through my heart and lungs before I could shout for help."

"It would kill you." Niko pressed his palm to the mark. He couldn't feel a trace of magic from the weapon lodged beneath her skin. "Why would your aunt do this to you?"

"It's Brien tradition. Those who serve are marked. Brien aren't even allowed to leave the stronghold without giving their vow and taking the mark of a trueborn."

"Why would you agree to be bound to your chivving monster of an elder?" He looked into Danu's eyes, searching for a hint of betrayal or pleading. He didn't know which would slice deeper.

"I'm the niece of the Elder. There was never any question of my swearing loyalty to Bryana." She lifted his hand away from her ribs to hold it in both of hers. "Every trueborn Brien who can open the passages into the mountain is sworn to Bryana. Every Brien who's traveled the paths out of the stronghold is sworn to a trueborn. There isn't a person in this valley who could help you escape without causing their own execution.

"Whatever you think of the Brien and Bryana, I hope you can believe I didn't want to break your heart." She kissed his hand. "Allora is married, Niko. It's over. There's nothing you can do."

A sob punched through Niko's throat, wrenching the air from his lungs.

His legs gave out. His knees crashed against the floor as the stone walls of his cage closed in around him.

Panic and grief clawed all reasonable thought from his mind, stealing the bit of himself he'd managed to salvage through the months of darkness and torture.

"I—there's no—" Tears swallowed his words.

"I'm sorry." Danu held him up, letting him wrap his arms around her, burying his face in her stomach to mute his sobs. "I'm so sorry."

She didn't let go until sleep finally stilled his tears.

33

ALLORA

"Isn't she just the most gorgeous thing you've ever seen?" Illia cooed her excitement, her gaze riveted on her new puppy.

The pup slipped on the marble floor of the veranda, tripped over her paws, and skidded nose first into the side of the sorcerer-made pen.

"Oh, my poor, sweet babe." Illia scooped the pup out of the pen.

"The barrier won't hurt the dog, Princess," Sorcerer Terin said. "It's just to keep her…"

The pup leapt off Illia's lap and ran straight for the rain pouring down around the veranda.

Allora sipped her tea, biting back her laughter as the pup leapt into the deepest puddle in sight.

Terin sighed as a faint shimmer blossomed around her. She stepped out into the rain, picked up the dripping dog, and set it back in the pen.

She hovered a hand over the pup as it rolled on the marble. The mud from the dog's gray and white fur syphoned up into Terin's hand, forming a sphere of muck, which she promptly tossed back out into the rain.

The pup whined and barked as though horrified at having its well-earned filth stolen by the sorcerer. Her paws slipped out from under her again as she bolted for the side of her pen, determined to get back out into the mud.

"She does have quite the adventurous spirit," Allora said.

"That's why I chose her," Illia said. "Of all the pups brought for me to meet, she was the one who looked most eager to explore the palace. If she likes poking around here, I'm sure she'll like exploring Wyrain with me as well."

The pup rolled onto her back, displaying the spots on her stomach as she gazed at Illia with ardent devotion.

"I think she'd be happy to go wherever you do." Allora poured Illia another cup of tea. "Have you chosen a name for her yet?"

"No. I want it to be perfect." Illia furrowed her brow even as she grinned at the dog. "Something playful, but worthy of living in a palace. Respectable, but not so primped and pampered it would be absurd for her to be running through the gardens with mud on her paws. She loves to be outside."

Terin shifted her stance, as though she would have very much preferred guarding a princess whose dog despised filth.

"Perhaps you should write to the head scribe," Allora said. "He's still working on the vellum for you. He could create a list of names for you to choose from."

"That's a wonderful idea. Isn't it, my little love?" Illia giggled as the pup tried to climb out of the sorcerer-made pen, her paws sliding down the translucent barrier. "Oh you just want a scratch, don't you?"

She lifted the dog out of the pen and set it on her lap.

With a bark of triumph, the pup leapt out of her lap and charged for the mud.

"Your Majesty."

Allora spun toward the male voice.

A palace guard stood at the door to the veranda. He bowed to Allora, bravely ignoring Gillien prowling closer to him.

"I beg your forgiveness for the interruption, Your Majesty, but I've been sent to bring you to the council chamber." The soldier kept his gaze straight front as the now-muddy pup charged him, immediately sinking her teeth into the guard's boot.

"Why have I been summoned to the council chamber?" Allora stood, brushing the pup's fur from the front of her skirt.

"I don't know, Your Majesty." The guard bowed again. "But it was the King who asked me to fetch you."

"How intriguing." Allora stepped around the guard and through the veranda doors. "No need to escort me, I know where the council chamber is, and the royal pup seems quite happy chewing your feet."

She made it ten steps before a trickle of guilt crept into her stomach. She needn't have sacrificed the guard to the pup. It was a petty, petulant distraction from her instincts as they screamed she should run from the palace and never return. The guard had delivered the message, not forged her fear.

Gillien's footsteps followed her down the gilded hall, past the portraits and vases that decorated the public portion of the palace.

There could be dozens of reasons Brannon might want her to go to the council chamber. It could be something silly. A trivial request from her doting husband.

Her mind couldn't convince her panic there was a single reason to be called to the chamber that wasn't dire.

A veritable battalion of guards and soldiers had been stationed outside the council chamber's doors.

Their presence locked cold dread around Allora's lungs.

Scribes' guards with white around their cuffs stood beside the guards of the Map Makers Guild, whose sleeves were marked with green. Four purple-robed sorcerers stood within the pack as well. Representatives of every Guild stood in the battalion of guards outside the council chamber, which had to mean the full council was inside, and the might of the Guilds wanted to see her.

You're the Queen, Allora, Kai's voice laughed in her mind. *You're perched at the center of it all now.*

A soldier opened the door for her before she'd had time to take a breath to compose herself. She stepped into the chamber, graciously accepting her doom.

The gray of the storm filled the room, giving the meeting of the thirteen leaders of Ilbrea a foreboding air.

Brannon stood from his seat on the far side of the table, reaching for Allora's hand as soon as he caught sight of her. "My darling."

The other twelve around the table all stood.

Adrial stepped away from his chair behind Lord Gareth, giving himself a clear view of Allora. He bowed with the rest, then held her gaze with a furrowed brow, as though asking her why she'd been called to the chamber.

Allora cocked her head to the side, giving him a passing smile, hoping he might take the look as *I've no chivving clue.*

She swept around the table, careful not to look at Map Maker Traim standing beside what should have been her father's seat.

But Traim couldn't be blamed for taking her father's place on the council while Lord Karron journeyed to the southern islands. That was how things were done in the Map Makers Guild. Traim had taken her father's seat before. He'd give it right back when the Lord Map Maker returned.

"Thank you for joining us." Brannon kissed the back of Allora's hand.

"Of course, husband." Allora let jewels of playful delight sparkle in her eyes. "I'm honored to have been called to the council chamber. Though I must admit, I don't know what business I have with the council."

"I requested you be brought into the meeting." Lady Gwell stepped toward the King.

Allora pictured the sorcerer shoving Brannon away from his seat, demanding the place at the head of the table remain under her control. "Then I must heighten my admission to being bemused."

"I understand," Lady Gwell said. "You haven't been called here as the Queen of Ilbrea, but rather as the former Lady of the Map Makers Guild."

Allora shifted closer to Brannon, letting go of his hand in a way that urged him to touch the back of her waist, joining the King and Queen of Ilbrea in a singular unit as they stood before the Lady Sorcerer.

"A delegation from Wyrain will soon be visiting Ilara, to be sure the city is suitable for the Princess's wedding," Lady Gwell said. "In preparation for their arrival, the decision has been made that Map Maker Traim shall take over residence of the Map Master's Palace."

Allora dug her nails into her palms, burying the rage that burned in her chest.

"With the palace on the cliffs as his home, he will be well suited to entertain the delegation from Wyrain," Lady Gwell said. "The change will benefit—"

"Lady Gwell, you seem to be the victim of misinformation." Allora kept her words steady, ensuring everyone in the room would understand her. "The Map Master's Palace is my father's private residence and is not the property of the Map Makers Guild. The home granted him by his position as Lord Map Maker is within the Guilded section of Ilara. And my father, in his great generosity, has already allowed Map Maker Traim to take up residence in that home."

"Your father is at sea on a journey from which he shall not return for quite some time, if at all," Lady Gwell said.

Brannon wrapped his arm behind Allora, pulling her closer.

"You live in the Royal Palace, Your Majesty. There is no reason but greed that Map Maker Traim shouldn't take up residence at the Map Master's Palace," Lady Gwell said. "Our decision is final."

"The decision is not yours to make, Lady Gwell," Allora said. "My father will return from his journey, and I assure you, in no uncertain terms, he will resume living in his *private* estate on the cliffs."

"The southern islands—"

"And should Saint Aximander decide this is my father's final journey, the Map Master's Palace would still not be the Sorcerers Guild's, nor any other Guild's, to claim. I may live in the Royal Palace, but I am not my father's only heir. Should I be unable to inherit his estate, and have no heirs of my own, his former wards will take joint ownership of the property and all his assets. But as long as I am alive, the palace will go to me, and then to my children.

"If Dudia blesses us, the King and I will have more than one child, but Ilbrea can only have one ruler." Allora looked up to Brannon. "Our secondborn will inherit my father's estate and wealth. Surely you are not planning on illegally commandeering any property that rightfully belongs to a future prince or princess of Ilbrea."

Brannon beamed down at her, tears glinting in the corners of his eyes.

"The line of inheritance for the Map Master's Palace is muddy at best," Lady Gwell said.

"I'm afraid not." Lord Gareth tapped on the table as though pointing to a document only he could see. "I helped Lord Karron draw up the papers myself. The Map Master's Palace is a private residence, with a very clear, very legal line of inheritance in the event of his passing."

"One man's wishes for his estate cannot be placed above the good of Ilbrea." Lady Gwell planted her palms on the table, leaning toward Lord Gareth with fire gleaming in her eyes.

"If you seize the Lord Map Maker's property without legal

cause, what will you take next? Will you start stealing the property of other Guild members? Will you come after my house?" Lord Nevon asked.

"Nothing you own could be of use to the Guilds," Lady Gwell said. "The value of the Map Master's Palace cannot be underestimated."

"Laws of inheritance must be respected," Lord Gareth said. "If we don't obey our own laws, then what have we become? We can't ask our Guild members to dedicate their lives to Ilbrea if they believe the bounty of their labor could be stolen from them on a whim."

"Ensuring the Wyrainian delegation's safety and comfort is not a whim," Lady Gwell said.

"If you want a place to house the Wyrainians, put them in the Sorcerers Tower," Lord Nevon said.

"Outsiders will not be permitted in the Sorcerers Tower," Lady Gwell said.

"Even if you could legally put them in the Map Master's Palace, it would be a terrible idea," Lord Kearney said. "The destruction of the city looks worse from above than it does riding through the streets. Why would the people of Wyrain want their prince to marry a princess from a country whose own sorcerers have reduced its capital to ruins?"

"The Sorcerers Guild is protecting the people of Ilara," Lady Gwell said.

"If the sorcerers carry on *protecting* Ilara much longer, there won't be a city left," Lord Kearney said.

"And what would you have us do? Ignore the dissidents infesting the city?" Lady Gwell said. "Your soldiers can't even protect their own barracks."

"Do not accuse my men—" Lord Kearney began.

"Something has to be done to stop the violence once and for all." Lord Gareth jabbed his finger onto the table.

"It's the common rabble that endanger us all," Lady Byrd

shouted over him. "Purge Ilara of the rats. Keep them outside the city walls."

"Would that include your bevy of servants, or will you keep the common folk who scrub your floors?" Lord Nevon rounded on Lady Byrd.

"Enough!" Lady Gwell clapped her hands.

A crackle of sparks swept around the room.

"The sorcerers will continue their hunt for the dissidents that threaten our city," Lady Gwell said. "The delegation from Wyrain—"

"Will not be housed at the Map Master's Palace," Brannon said. "We cannot seize the property of loyal Guild members."

"Thank you, husband." Allora touched Brannon's cheek.

"You should go. Leave us to the filthy work of keeping Ilbrea safe." He kissed her forehead.

"I'm sorry, Your Majesties, but if I may," Lord Nevon said. "I hadn't meant to deliver this news now, but as Queen Allora and the head scribe are both here, I don't think there's a point in waiting for a kinder time."

"What sort of news would require kindness?" Allora gripped the back of Brannon's chair, waiting for the floor to drop out from under her.

Adrial took a step toward Allora before rooting himself in place, maintaining the distance she had demanded.

I have to keep you safe.

"The time has come to stop looking for Kai Saso's ship," Lord Nevon said.

Allora's hands throbbed as she clung to the chair.

"We've searched for reports of the crew and any sign of the ship," Lord Nevon said. "Short of having a boat row along the coastline looking for wreckage, there's nothing else to be done."

"Yes, there is," Allora said. "You just said so. Have boats row along the coastline of the whole continent. Have men search on foot."

"It would take too long," Lord Nevon said.

"Why does it matter how long it would take?" Allora shouted.

Brannon wrapped his arm around her waist, holding her steady.

"You can't"—she forced air into her lungs—"you cannot abandon your own people."

"The sailors would want me to." There was no anger in Lord Nevon's tone, only a gentle sorrow that made it even harder to breathe. "If Dudia spared them, they've been surviving on their own. There isn't a rescue to be performed. But as long as we're searching for them, they can't be declared dead. I can't pay their families the death benefits owed by the Sailors Guild."

Tears streamed down Allora's cheeks.

"The families need the coin, especially with the destruction that's drowning the city," Lord Nevon said. "Those men would rather see their families fed than given false hope."

"The families must be looked after." Adrial's face had gone pale. He didn't bother wiping the tears from his cheeks. "It's time they receive their payment."

Allora wanted to run to him, to cling to the only family she had left in Ilara.

You can't put him in danger. He has a family, too. Protect him. Protect his child.

"Will there be a ceremony?" Adrial asked.

Lord Gareth took Adrial's arm, offering comfort to his heir.

"Of course," Lord Nevon said. "I would be honored if you would attend."

"Kai isn't dead." Allora's voice sounded too low. Too far away to truly be her speaking. "I've already lost Niko. I can't lose Kai, too."

"I'm so sorry, darling." Brannon reached to brush the tears from her cheeks.

"No." Allora backed away from him. "Kai is coming home. He'll burst into Ilara with a black eye and some tale of adventure.

Have your ceremony if you want. It'll be an amusing story to tell him when he returns."

"Allora." Adrial barely whispered her name. There was pain in his eyes. Horrible, soul-tearing grief. "We can't wish him home."

Tears tightened her throat. "How will we tell Mara and Tham?"

"Tell them your friends knew their duty to the Guilds and Ilbrea," Lady Gwell said. "Tell them Nikolas Endur and Kai Saso sacrificed their lives for Ilbrea while some refuse to yield unused property."

"Whatever I tell them, I will do it in my father's home," Allora said. "And I will tell them how the sorcerers tried to steal it."

Allora strode out of the council chamber, abandoning Adrial to the serpent sorcerer and battling lords and ladies.

Fighting for the good of a city they'd already destroyed.

Trying to take her father's home, his sanctuary on the cliffs away from the chaos, the place they'd hidden the secrets that could condemn her whole family to be hanged.

"Allora." Gillien stepped out of the pack of guards.

"Do not trail behind me," Allora snapped. "I am not in the mood to be stalked by a minion of the Lady Sorcerer."

Stupid girl. Stupid, stupid girl.

She couldn't make herself turn back to beg Gillien's forgiveness.

She needed to be kind to the sorcerers. She had to protect Adrial from their wrath and his child from their wrath and her father from their wrath and Mara and Tham from their wrath.

A sob pummeled her chest.

She lifted her skirt, running up the steps to the private wing of the palace, not caring that the merchants and Guilded lingering in the entryway would be whispering about the mad Queen for weeks.

How could she have lost so much so quickly?

The sobs kept crashing against her ribs.

Kai.

He should be here, laughing at the news of his death. Planning a toast to give to all who showed up to mourn him.

She'd never hear her sweet Kai laugh again. Never see him grin as he called her Miss, knowing he'd get away with anything in exchange for that impish smile.

A guard opened the door to her chambers.

The guards would protect her from having to open a door but couldn't save her shattered family.

Her tears blurred the room.

The sorcerers wanted to steal her home. The place where they'd all been together and happy.

Where her father had hidden proof of wild magic the Sorcerers Guild would gladly murder to destroy. All the true maps Niko, Mara, and her father had risked their lives to create. Hidden in her mother's tomb.

If they stole the Map Master's Palace, the sorcerers could freely search the estate. They'd find the maps.

The throbbing in Allora's chest stopped as a chill born of reckless rage swept through her.

"Is that why you wanted me here?" She spoke to the empty sitting room. "Did you want me to marry the King so you could steal my father's home? It wasn't anything to do with who I am, you just needed to clear the line of inheritance for the Map Master's Palace."

She couldn't feel her feet touching the ground as she strode to the desk. She took the gold-inlaid letter opener and tucked it into her pocket.

"I'm impressed you planned so far in advance." She went into her dressing room and pulled the box of hairpins from inside the vanity. "Knowing you wanted Father's home for so long you managed to convince the King to marry me."

She tucked a handful of pins into her pocket.

"Will you keep this going for as long as I'm alive? Hiding your plans as you herd me through your maze of wicked plots?"

She stopped in the doorway to the bedroom, waiting for a sorcerer to appear from the walls to punish her for her brazen defiance.

"I will not be a blind pawn any longer."

The walls stayed solid, without any murderer jumping out to slay her.

"I am the daughter of the Lord Map Maker." She took the candle and matches from her bedside table. "I will not abide secrets lurking in my home."

She wrenched the wall open and stepped into the darkness of the passage.

34

ALLORA

The match sizzled to life, hissing as though the darkness itself taunted her.

"Ghouls and demons and darkness surround, but fear isn't all to be found." Allora lit her candle and dropped the match on the floor. "What hides in the shadows is waiting for me. I search for the truth, and I shall set it free."

She closed her eyes, listening for laughter carrying through the dark passage hidden within the palace walls.

Cowards.

"My father used to say that rhyme to me when I was little." Allora crept down the corridor. "I'm not even sure where it came from. Maybe he made it up. A father's attempt to soothe a little girl's nightmares. He'd never admit it, but I think raising a daughter on his own has been the most terrifying adventure he's ever faced.

"There's so much society expects from a well-bred woman of the Guilds, and to know I would be the Lady of the Map Makers Guild? How could a man who felt most comfortable in the wilds be expected to raise a woman fit to stand at the very pinnacle of Ilbrean elite?"

She paused at the top of the steps, staring down into the darkness. A monster could lurk below, waiting to devour her.

She would have welcomed the beast's jaws.

"My father did the best he could." Allora climbed down the stairs. "Nursemaids, and tutors, every ounce of education needed to embody the perfection expected of me. But my father is a mortal man, not a saint. He didn't manage to forge me into a perfect lady. Bits of his wild nature crept into my soul."

She paused as she reached the landing with two doors, but still, no one leapt out of the darkness.

"For a while, I thought you understood my father's failings." She knelt in front of the left-hand door. "I thought maybe you'd pushed the King toward me because you knew I wasn't a frail creature like his first Queen."

She set her candle down and pulled the hairpins from her pocket.

"But if you just wanted to steal the Map Master's Palace, maybe you only saw me as a daughter with an inheritance and not as a person." She pushed the pins into the keyhole, closing her eyes as she felt for the teeth within the lock.

A void. A ridge.

There.

A bit of pressure.

She clicked the lock open.

"Did you underestimate me? Or have you been entirely certain I would pick this lock?" She tucked the pins back into her pocket and stood, holding her candle to the latch as she pushed the door open.

A stale scent engulfed her as she stepped into the room.

Racks surrounded the space, which was so small she couldn't have spread her arms without touching the walls.

Spears took up the area closest to the door. Each of them had a tip made of carved black stone.

A double row of knives came next. The blades had been made

of metal but edged with black stone, as though the ore were too precious to be wasted forging whole knives.

A rack of swords took up the back wall. Only the tips of those blades had been made of black stone.

Allora reached out, daring to trace her finger along the edge of a blade.

The stone was smooth, well-sharpened. No pain shocked through her body as flesh met weapon.

But there was something about the stone.

Something alluring and terrifying all at the same time.

"Whose throats are you planning to slit with these blades?" She stepped back out onto the landing, using the pins to lock the door behind her.

"My father taught me to throw a punch when I was little. I hated hitting his palm, I didn't want him to think I was mad at him." She dug the pins into the lock on the righthand door. "It took me a long time to understand he wasn't teaching me to hit out of anger."

Her poor excuse for picks stuck in the lock. She shimmied the pins out and pushed them back into position, finding the weight inside the mechanism and flipping the lock.

"My father understood the dangers that waited for me in the world. He wanted me to be prepared." She pushed the door open.

The light of her candle filled the tiny space beyond.

A second door waited just past the first, leaving barely enough room for one to swing open without hitting the other.

Allora braced her foot against the first door, propping it open as she examined the second.

It had been made of wood with metal brackets to strengthen it. But there was no keyhole, no latch, no knob. No hint of how to pry the door open.

She trailed her fingers along the wood, searching for the faint feeling of something…other. Something her mind could not meld with the normal world.

Magic.

There. Along the seams. In the wood.

The door had been carved by magic, designed to be opened by magic.

"Does your King know what you've hidden in his palace?" Allora backed out of the tiny space, closing the outer door and locking it behind her. "I doubt Brannon would like you building doors he can't open. But he doesn't know, does he? You want me to see things you've kept hidden from your King."

The flame on her candle wavered.

"A breeding mare. A pretty face for the people to love. A way to steal from my father. I am so many things to the demons who lurk just out of sight."

She reached into her pocket, gripping the handle of the letter opener as she walked down the stairs, heading deeper into the darkness.

"Did you want me to be all those things, or only one? Are you truly too cowardly to tell me?"

The swishing of her skirt offered the only answer.

Nothing. Nothing. Nothing.

All your family will come to nothing.

Allora stopped, leaning against the wall, begging her lungs to drag in air.

The overwhelming desire to crumple onto the steps and sob tore at her anger.

"You're all giving up on Kai." She looked up the stairs into the darkness, hoping whatever evil stared back could feel even a shred of her pain. "You're abandoning all the men who were on his ship. I know I have proven myself to be a selfish creature, I only care so much because I love Kai, but the other sailors on his ship were loved, too. Either they died for the reckless pride of the sorcerers testing their magic-made sail, or you've abandoned them. Those are the only two options. Both leave you as the villain."

A tingle flickered across the back of her neck as she kept climbing down.

"Perhaps I've made a fundamental error. Perhaps it's not as simple as the Sorcerers Guild being willing to do any desperate thing to lord over us as the strength and light that guides Ilbrea. Perhaps you long to be the villains. You crave our fear and hatred. You want us to wish you would burn because you know you control the fire. You don't want to be saints. You want to be demons."

The light of her candle found the door at the bottom of the steps. Stone swirls marked the wood as something exceptional, but the lock screamed of something meant to be accessed by those who had no magic of their own.

Allora knelt in front of the door, relinquishing the comfort of gripping the letter opener to pick the lock.

"When you tell Lady Gwell the story of your stalking me through hidden passages, be sure to tell her I knew you were watching, and I didn't care."

The lock clicked open.

Allora stood, smoothed out the front of her skirt, and opened the door.

A tingling chill like cold sparks danced across her skin.

She inched forward, easing her candle into the room.

Hundreds of faint glimmers reflected back from the walls, their mesmerizing beauty dancing around the room as the candle's flame flickered.

The tingling on Allora's flesh heightened as she stepped beyond the threshold.

Black stones lined the walls of the room. Not in the perfect pattern of a mosaic, but as though the stones had been left in their original size and shape and pressed into the wall wherever an open spot could be found. The ceiling had been covered in stone as well, creating a solid layer of black.

A wooden table sat at the center of the space. Metal dishes

held more black stones, as though they'd been abandoned when the maker had run out of room.

"Why?" Allora grazed her fingers against the wall. A sharp buzz, as though an energy trapped within the stone longed to break free, shot up her arm. She didn't mind the feeling. There was something magnificent in the pain. "What purpose could make this room worth all the work required for its creation?"

She set her candle on the table, studying the stones that hadn't been melded to the walls. The black stones glimmered the same as the rest, with no flaws she could see. Her breath hitched in her throat, and a flare of energy rampaged into her chest as she picked up a stone and held it close to the flame.

"Why are rocks worth hiding beneath the palace?" Allora whispered.

"Protection." A familiar voice spoke from the darkness. "Protection for Ilbrea, for the Sorcerers Guild."

Allora set the stone back on the table. "And who would the Sorcerers Guild need to protect themselves from?"

"Everyone." Gillien stepped out of the darkness at the bottom of the stairs. "It's a sad truth all sorcerers learn. We are not like everyone else in Ilbrea. And being different is very dangerous. Even when your difference makes you powerful."

"So you hoard stone-edged weapons." Allora slipped her hand into her pocket. "Do the sorcerers plan on leaping out of the walls to murder the King?"

"Of course not. Those weapons are here to protect us against intruders and interlopers. If the danger to our kind crept as high as the King, this room would be our salvation." Gillien trailed her fingers along the wall. "The magic within these stones would bring the entire palace crumbling down. No King, no Willocs—Ilbrea's royal family would disappear in a heartbeat."

"How?"

"That's not for you to understand. All you, Queen Allora of

Ilbrea, need to know is that we can destroy it all. The Sorcerers Guild holds that power."

"And what do the mighty sorcerers want from me?" Allora pulled the letter opener from her pocket, aiming the tip at Gillien's stomach.

"I don't want anything from you." Gillien didn't even glance at Allora's poor weapon.

"Only a fool would attempt to intimidate a queen."

"I'm not trying to scare you, Allora. I'm not Ciara Clery. I'm not going to bully you or threaten your family. Such menacing tactics help no one. You are a wise woman. You are strong and brave. I believe we can work together to make Ilbrea a better, safer place. I want us to be allies."

"Allies? You just told me you could destroy my home!"

"You're right." Gillien stepped into the room and closed the door behind her. "But I did not force you into this room. I did not press a blade to your back and make you march into the darkness. I let you discover this place all on your own."

"So I can spend every day I'm trapped in this palace knowing you could kill me on a whim?"

"So you can appreciate the danger and restraint of the Sorcerers Guild. We could destroy the palace at any moment. But this room has been here for years, and the palace still stands. It's not a thing to be afraid of. It's a triumph to appreciate."

"I don't tend to appreciate things that could kill me."

"I've heard you speak fondly of sailing. The Arion Sea could easily kill you. But you don't back away in fright or scream that the waves are evil. You appreciate the power within the beauty.

"Think of yourself as living on an island in the center of the sea. Waves lap at the shore, but you stay safe. You understand the danger of the water and are careful not to swim out too far. You protect yourself when storms come.

"You would teach your children to respect the sea, even as they played in the shallows. You wouldn't fall asleep at night dreading a terrible, deadly storm that may never come. You'd appreciate the moonlight glimmering on the water as the sound of the waves sings you to sleep. Peaceful coexistence with something more powerful than you will ever be. This is what I want for us, Allora."

"And if I displease the sorcerers? Will the sea swallow me? Will it be you who murders me?"

"If you swim out further than you can swim back, you can't blame the sea when you drown." Gillien circled her finger.

The letter opener flew from Allora's grip and settled itself on the table.

"Let us have a truce." Gillien reached for Allora's hand. "Allow yourself to live a life where you can be happy."

"Brannon may be happy to bring a child into a home that could be destroyed on a whim, but—"

"It's best for all if the King doesn't know what's in this room." Gillien stepped closer to Allora. "He's not like you. This kind of reason doesn't appeal to him."

"He knows this passage exists. What does he think is down here?" Allora tucked her hands behind her back, inching as far from Gillien as the room would allow.

"A path to safety should the worst ever come."

"I'll tell Brannon everything I've found."

"If that's what you believe is best." Gillien took Allora's shoulders. "But think it through first. Make sure that's really the path you want for your husband and Ilbrea. You're a good queen, Allora. You want what's best for your people. I have faith in you. I know you'll do the right thing."

The door swung open.

"Let's get you back upstairs before anyone misses you." Gillien guided Allora to the door. "They've just acknowledged the loss of Sailor Saso. The King will be worried sick over his grieving bride."

35

MARA

A fire crackled in the grate. The flames did nothing to offer Mara comfort. The blaze danced across the ice. The ice remained unharmed by the fire.

Useless. Helpless. Flames trapped in a place they did not belong.

Still, Mara kept the fire lit as she watched Tham sleep, waiting for him to sink deep enough into the darkness that her tossing and turning wouldn't bother him.

If she woke him up, she'd see the pain in his eyes when he remembered the secrets she'd hidden from him and the silence she'd forced between them.

She'd tried to convince herself that maybe Ronya had been lying, that there weren't spies lurking in the walls. But the eerie feeling of being constantly watched kept her silent.

If she could have even a few minutes alone with Tham, she could try to break through the disastrous detachment the endless intrusion on their lives had wrought.

She could finally explain that it hadn't been a lack of trust or love that kept her from telling him the truth of her memories of

Ian Ayres. It was her shame, her fear that the demons from that awful place would grab her and drag her back to the shadows.

And she'd only told Ronya about Ian Ayres to protect him. To keep him safe.

But she couldn't risk baring her heart and pain. Not with Ronya's spies in the walls. They'd carry Mara's weakness straight back to Ronya, where every word would be fashioned into a weapon.

Keep him safe.

He'll understand that you had to keep him safe.

She closed her eyes and leaned back in her chair, letting herself imagine Tham sleeping beside her in her bed in the Map Master's Palace. His warmth surrounding her. His shoulder as her pillow.

A faint rumble came from the place that became their door.

"Tham." Mara stood, spinning toward the door, grabbing the sharpest object in their room—her pen—from the table.

Elle leapt off the bed, growling at the emerging door as she planted herself in front of Mara. Tham stood shirtless beside her, his muscles tense and ready to fight.

"Calm down, Elle," Lynn said, keeping the door open only a crack. "It's me, Elle. You know me."

Elle barked and sat, settling herself on Mara's toes.

"What's going on?" Tham asked.

"Trouble at the gates," Lynn said. "Get dressed. We're going to move you."

"Why?" Mara ran to the wardrobe, yanking out pants and a shirt for Tham before grabbing clothes for herself.

"Everyone in the palace knows where the Ilbreans sleep," Lynn said. "If anyone blames Mara for convincing Queen Ronya to lead us out of hiding, I don't fancy standing in the hall waiting for them to come charging in to attack you."

"Thank you." Mara buttoned her pants and yanked on her

boots, tucking the pen in her coat pocket and checking for her light before heading toward the door. "Where are you taking us?"

"There are unused quarters in the royals' wing," Lynn said. "We'll stay there until the trouble's sorted."

Mara followed Lynn into the hall, Tham, Elle, and four guards right behind them.

Shouts carried from the corridor leading down to the entryway.

"What sort of trouble is at the gates?" Tham asked.

Lynn quickened her pace as a woman's scream rang through the hall. "A mob has gathered. That's all I've heard."

"Lynn." The shout came from a narrow hall leading off to the right. "Lynn, stop." Andric ran toward them, sword in hand. "Where do you think you're going?"

"Taking them somewhere they'll—"

"You were given orders." Andric aimed the tip of his sword at Lynn's throat. "Defiance will not be tolerated."

"Hers is the path of madness," Lynn said.

"Take her to the cells. Lock her in," Andric said.

"To stop me from keeping more people alive?" Lynn said.

Mara backed away as the guards stepped around her, pinning Lynn between them and Andric.

"I'm trying to keep Tham and Mara safe," Lynn said. "How is that wrong?"

"Go peacefully, or I'll cut your throat right here," Andric said.

"You're a braidic fool." Lynn held her arms out to her sides, letting the other guards grab her. "I hope you live long enough to realize I'm right."

The guards dragged Lynn back the way they'd come.

"What did she do?" Tham asked.

"Disobeyed an order from the Queen and sought counsel from Ture Kian," Andric said.

"And for that, you'll lock her up?" Mara asked.

"The Queen will do worse if I can prove Lynn planned to help

Ture Kian seize power. We need to move." Andric beckoned them back the way he'd come.

"You just arrested Lynn for taking us out of our room." Mara glanced over her shoulder, making sure Elle and Tham really were behind her as she followed Andric. "Shouldn't we go back?"

"Queen Ronya has ordered your presence at the palace gates," Andric said.

"Then give me a weapon," Tham said. "Give Mara a weapon, too. If there's a mob at the gates, we need to be able to defend ourselves."

"You'll be protected," Andric said.

Six guards stood between the bottom of the stairs and the door that led out to the side of the palace gardens.

"Clear a path," Andric ordered.

The guards stepped aside, not questioning why the Ilbreans were being herded toward the mob.

Andric pressed his palm to the door, allowing the ice to move freely.

Mara had never before appreciated how much sound the walls kept from seeping into the palace.

The steady rhythm of the mob's chanting thundered from the front gardens by the gates. The closer chaos of shouted orders and panicked men filled the grounds.

Andric strode through the mayhem without hesitation.

Elle kept her flank pressed to Mara's leg, whimpering as the gates came into view.

Hundreds of Ice Walkers had gathered, barely obscured by the twists and swirls of the ice-wrought gates. The horde wore masks of patchwork colors, as though they didn't want hiding their faces to bring suspicion on their households' banners.

Guards in blue uniforms lined the inside of the wall that surrounded the palace, leaving a gap in front of the gates large enough for the mob to charge through.

Tham brushed his hand against the small of Mara's back, then took her arm, shifting her to walk behind him.

"What does the Queen want from us?" Tham asked. "Handing us to the mob won't make her people—"

Andric rounded on Tham. "Queen Ronya has never raised a finger to hurt you. I have never hurt you. Learn which side you're on before the Queen begins to doubt your loyalty."

"We are loyal to the Queen," Mara said. "That doesn't make being led toward a mob less frightening."

"I'm sorry." Andric cut around Tham to take Mara's hand. He kissed it before tightening his grip. "This way. You're to wait in front of the fountain."

Andric kept Mara's hand in his, trailing her behind him as though planning to fight with one hand and cling to Mara with the other.

The thunder of the crowd's chanting pounded into Mara's ears, but she couldn't make out what they were saying.

Chank!

Chank!

Something had changed at the gates. The crowd at the center had shifted, clearing a space for a metal-tipped battering ram.

"Can the guards keep them out?" Mara asked.

Chank!

Elle leapt up onto the lip of the fountain, raising her hackles as she growled at the horde.

Chank!

The guards on either side of the gates began to stir as though battling against whatever orders kept them from facing the mob.

"Let Mara go back inside," Tham said. "I'll stay to represent both of us."

"I'm not leaving you," Mara said.

A guard on the northern side of the line shouted, pointing to something in the trees.

Elle whimpered, cowering behind Mara.

Another guard shouted and punched the air with glee.

The one beside him fled, running south. An arrow struck that guard in the neck before he'd managed to cross in front of the gates.

The pure white leaves of the trees shifted, the branches cracking as they were shoved aside by a massive beast.

Taller than a bear, with white fur stained dark with blood, and sharp teeth bared in a snarl—a wolf stalked into view.

Ronya rode on the monster's back, a crown of red flowers in her hair and a sword in her hand.

The mob beyond the gates screamed as the monstrous wolf stepped onto the path. The beast stopped, as though enjoying the chaos of the people trying to push back through the horde in a hopeless attempt to flee.

The wolf stalked closer to the gates.

Ronya raised a hand, sending a blast of painfully frozen air whipping through the cavern of Isfol.

The wolf tipped its head back and howled.

The crowd fell silent, even as some of them still tried to run.

"Fools of Isfol, if you dare stand against me, you stand against the power Kalene has given me. She has named me her true heir. I am the righteous warrior who will face the demons to the south," Ronya said. "Flee and live. Defy me and die."

The gates opened, pushing into the crowd.

The wolf swayed his head as he scented his prey.

The moment the gates were wide enough, the beast leapt into the mob.

"No." Mara tried to wrench free of Andric's grip.

Screams echoed through the grounds as the wolf tossed a woman into the air. The wolf caught her in its massive teeth. The woman's screaming stopped.

Mara couldn't see what happened after that. The guards filed in behind the wolf, moving out onto the street, ready to murder anyone who escaped the wolf's jaws.

"Those are her own people!" Mara tore her hand away from Andric.

"They're traitors," Andric said. "They have lost their right to survive in Isfol."

"Seek shelter!" a voice bellowed from the path leading back to the palace. Four guards hurried toward them with Ture Kian bustling in the middle. "Everyone who is not a guard has been ordered to seek shelter!"

"Ordered by who?" Andric raised his sword, pinning his glare on Ture. "My orders to bring the Ilbreans here came from my Queen. They are to witness her glorious victory."

"The mob will come through the gates," Ture Kian said. "If Ronya ordered you to stand here, it's because she wants you dead."

Chank. Bang!

Someone had lodged the battering ram through the gates, keeping them from swinging closed.

"I am taking them." Ture walked right up to Andric, stepping around the tip of his sword to stop a foot in front of him. "May you always regret the choices you've made."

A flicker of silver glinted in Ture's hand the moment before he jerked his arm back and plunged it forward.

Andric stumbled away, gasping, his eyes wide. "Traitor."

Ture grabbed Andric's sword arm then slashed his knife across Andric's throat. He shoved Andric back, wrinkling his nose at the spray of Andric's blood spattering his robes.

"Regent, you aren't safe in the open." One of the guards bowed to Ture as Andric collapsed, ignoring the dying man as though nothing odd or terrible had happened.

Andric's fingers twitched, curling on the ice of the walkway.

"Follow me." Ture beckoned them toward the trees to the north.

"You just murdered him." Mara kept her feet planted though

her fingers shook as she pulled her pen from her pocket, aiming the tip at Ture.

"And now I'm helping you," Ture said. "The people will swarm through the gates. I would hate for them to kill you before they realize you haven't been tainted by my daughter's evil."

"If you think what she's doing is wrong, then stop her." Mara stepped closer to Ture, avoiding the growing pool of Andric's blood. "How many people is she going to kill tonight?"

"There is nothing I can do to save those people from my daughter's rampage," Ture said. "But if I survive the night, there may be something I can do to help them in the morning. I am of no use to anyone dead, and neither are you."

Roars of rage came from the gates as a cluster of rebels broke through.

"Regent, we have to move," one of the guards said.

"We'll go with you." Tham grabbed Andric's sword and took Mara's arm, steering her to follow Ture north.

Mara made herself run, matching the pace set by the guards as they cut into the trees. "This is wrong."

"It doesn't matter," Tham said.

Once the trees had swallowed the fountain behind them, the guards headed east, keeping to paths that couldn't be seen from the palace windows, not slowing until they neared the wall that surrounded the chasm.

"Two of you keep running, lead anyone who might have followed us to the far side of the palace. The other two, wait here." Ture pressed his palm to the ice wall as two of the guards obediently sprinted away through the trees.

The ice shifted, opening into an archway.

"Once we're sealed in, run back to the front of the palace." Ture looked to the two remaining guards. "Don't tell anyone where we've hidden."

"Yes, Regent." The guards bowed.

Ture dodged through the archway, waving for Mara and Tham to hurry in behind him.

It was Mara's turn to drag Tham, yanking him inside the wall. "Elle, come." Mara kept one foot planted in the archway until Elle had made it through.

Ture touched the wall again, his ring glimmering as the wall regrew, sealing them in.

"If any of the other wolves are awake, they'll kill us before you can reopen the archway," Mara said.

"They aren't. If more than one of the beasts were awake, more than one would be rampaging through the city." Ture bustled toward a sled loaded with picks, rope, and shovels that had been left on the far side of the chasm.

He dragged two picks off the sled. "There is a certain benefit to having people wish you would murder your daughter. You can push them for information and provisions. Help an old man."

Mara let go of Tham to pull shovels off the pile.

Elle grabbed the handle of a pick, trying to kill it with her teeth, while Tham cleared the rest of the tools.

Three packs had been tucked under the pile.

"Good." Ture nodded as though convincing himself of his success. "One for each of us, though I can't say how long I'll be able to carry my own."

"Why do we have packs?" Mara asked, even as she grabbed a bag and pulled it on over her coat. "Ture Kian?"

"After tonight, my daughter will see how dangerous it is to keep me alive." Ture struggled to put on his own pack. "Ever since Ronya claimed the crown, my execution has been inevitable. I would like to survive long enough to plot against my daughter. You would like to escape. We seem to be fitting companions."

"We have one more in our party," Tham said. "Another Ilbrean soldier is still in the care of the healers. We can't abandon him."

"Either come with me now or stay and hope Ronya doesn't

murder you for being seen with me right before my escape." Ture shoved the last pack into Tham's arms.

Tham looked to Mara.

"Don't even suggest I go without you," Mara said.

"Bicker while we walk." Ture headed to the northern-most point of the wall that surrounded the chasm, farthest away from the palace. "We're going to take a longer route than I'd like, but every passage leading south will be swarming with Ronya's guards."

"We have to go, Tham." Mara took his hand. "I hate it. But there are too many lives at stake to risk waiting for Elver. We have to warn Ilbrea before Ronya attacks. I'm sorry."

He nodded. Pain creased his brow as he kissed Mara's hand.

He stayed close to her as Ture pressed his palm to the far wall.

Another archway appeared, leading out onto a row of houses that had barely been spared by the chasm's growth.

Ture looked back toward Mara and Tham as he stepped through the wall.

A figure dressed in a white robe leapt into view, skidding to a stop as he drove his sword through Ture's stomach.

36

MARA

Tham shoved Mara aside as the figure dressed in white ripped his blade from Ture's gut.

Ture screamed, stumbling back through the archway, sagging under the weight of his pack.

Tham dodged around him, Andric's sword held ready for attack.

Mara leapt forward, catching Ture before he crumpled to the ground. The old man's hands trembled as he touched the blood leaking through his blue robes.

"Tham."

The perfectly calm word shocked Mara's attention away from the growing stain on Ture's stomach.

Elver stepped through the archway, bloody sword in hand. "I wasn't sure I'd found the right place in the wall." He edged around Tham. "Hello, Mara. Could you lay him on his front so we can get his pack off?"

"But he's—" Mara looked back down at Ture. The light had already left his eyes.

"We really don't have time to waste." Elver set down his sword and grabbed Ture's wrist. He yanked hard, twisting Ture out of Mara's arms to fall face first onto the ice. "The pack, Tham."

Tham glanced to Mara before kneeling to drag the pack off Ture's back.

"How did you get here?" Mara blocked Elle from licking Ture's spilt blood. "Why did you kill him?"

"I escaped." Elver picked his sword back up and knelt beside Ture, staining the knees of the white matron's robe he wore with blood. "And this one had to go. He's not invited to come with us." He raised his sword and hacked into Ture's right wrist.

"Elver stop!" Mara shouted.

Elver raised his sword and swung again, severing Ture's hand. "Harder than it looks." He set his sword down and grabbed Ture's pack, ignoring the stain and slice in the fabric his murdering Ture had left behind.

"Elver." Tham planted his foot on Elver's blade, pinning it to the ice. "I need you to stop and tell us what's going on."

"We're escaping." Elver ignored his sword, instead grabbing Ture's severed hand before running to the stairs. "Come on. The Queen will get bored with killing people soon."

Mara looked from Ture's corpse to Tham, before letting go of Elle to chase after Elver.

"Elver, be careful," she called. "You can't touch anything. Not even the walls. It's not safe!"

"I know," Elver called back. "It warned me."

"What warned you?" Mara paused at the top of the steps, making sure Tham was following before going down the ice-made stairs as quickly as she dared.

The mounds of ice had changed since she'd last seen the chasm. The ice had shrunk, revealing the details of the wolves' monstrous forms.

But it was more than wolves. Great white cats and birds as large as people had joined the wolves' ranks.

No ruler should command such a monstrous army.

Fear ripped down Mara's spine as she reached the bottom of the steps.

Elver. She'd lost sight of Elver. She'd been too busy looking at the monsters.

"Stop dawdling," Elver called from near the stone door. "It's almost time!"

Elle took off toward Elver.

"Elle!" Mara chased after her, gasping as the pup skidded near one of the mounds. "Elle, no!"

Elle's claws scraped on the ice as she scampered sideways and righted herself just before the tip of her tail would have struck the wolf-filled mound. She skidded twice more as she ran up to paw at the stone door, her gaze fixed on Ture's hand, begging for a taste of the bloody treat as though she hadn't nearly been lost to them forever.

"It's not for you." Elver dragged the stump of Ture's hand across the stone of the door, leaving a smear of blood behind. "That should be enough." He looked to Mara. "I guess we could go back for the other hand."

"We're not cutting off that poor man's other hand," Mara said.

"All right." Elver tossed something silver to Mara before dropping Ture's hand.

Elle lunged toward the hand.

"No, Elle." Mara grabbed the dog, wrestling her away from the macabre snack.

Elver knelt in front of the door. "I have followed the path you showed me." He pressed his palms to the stone and dipped his chin as though in prayer. "Please allow us to begin the next part of our journey."

Mara stared at the door, waiting for something worth ending a man's life to happen.

The blood Elver had spread on the stone hadn't been smeared in a random streak. He'd followed the path that led toward the mountains silhouetted at the top of the carved image, then sliced a line across the middle of the range.

"Do not make me have suffered these stories for nothing. You clawed through my mind," Elver whispered. "I have to continue this journey."

The door stayed silent and unmoving.

"Please." Elver pressed his forehead to the stone. "This is the only way. I've done everything you've asked of me. It's time."

With a sharp crack, the edges of the door shifted, gaining depth.

Elver leapt to his feet, digging his fingers into the side of the door.

Tham rammed Elver's bloody sword into the crack, risking the weapon in favor of leverage.

Mara let go of Elle, tucked the silver Elver had tossed her into her pocket, and joined the others to pull on the door. Her heart shot into her throat as the stone moved.

Elle pawed at the wall beside the door, barking encouragement, as the door began to creep open.

Tham tossed the ruined sword aside, digging his fingers into the gap as a slice of blue light cut through the stone.

"Keep going," Elver grunted. "It's this or die."

Mara shoved her arm through the gap, pressing her palm against the doorframe, leveraging her body to push the stone.

"I should go first," Tham said.

"Mara first," Elver said.

The door ground open enough for Mara to slip through. She twisted, pulling her pack in with her, then rammed her weight against the door to push it farther open.

The carvings on the inside of the door cut into Mara's hands. She pushed harder.

The door slid open another inch.

"Call Elle," Tham said.

"Come here, Elle." Mara fought to keep her voice cheerful and calm. "Come on."

Elle burst through the crack and crashed into Mara's legs.

"Go!" Tham shouted.

Elver dodged through the crack and slammed himself against the door beside Mara.

"Tham!" Mara gritted her teeth, pushing against the door with the last bit of strength she had.

Two swords slid through the gap, skidding on the floor. Tham's pack flew through next, landing behind Mara.

Finally, Tham shoved himself sideways through the gap, his chest scraping against the door as he squeezed through.

The moment he was free, Elver stepped away from the door.

The door pressed Mara back, sliding her boots across the ice, before she finally let go.

"You're bleeding." Tham took Mara's hands, holding them palm up as he checked the slices the door had left in her skin.

"Tham," Mara whispered.

"I don't know what's in our packs. We'll find something to use as a bandage."

"Tham."

He looked up, meeting her gaze.

She brushed her finger along his cheek, savoring the warmth of his skin.

"Do you have the ring?" Elver took Mara's arm, spinning her toward him.

"What ring?" Mara asked.

"The one I threw at you," Elver said. "I was supposed to make sure you had it."

Mara dug into her pocket, trying not to get the filth from her coat in the cuts on her hands. Her fingers found something hard between the tip of her pen and stone of her light. The metal chilled her fingers as she pulled it out.

Ture Kian's ring glistened in the blue light of the tunnels.

Whether it was his blood staining the silver or Mara's, she didn't know.

"Good," Elver sighed. "You're definitely supposed to have that." He picked up the ruined sword. "Let's go."

"No, Elver," Mara said. "You have to tell us what's going on. Ture Kian is dead."

"Yes. I stabbed him and cut off his hand. I needed it for the door." Elver pointed to the door.

The inside had been carved of jagged ice. Mara's blood tainted the image of a woman riding a wolf as she charged down the mountains.

"We need to follow the tunnel." Elver pointed the other way, where the blue glow of an ice-carved tunnel reached as far as Mara could see. "I don't think they'll be allowed through the door, but I can't be certain. I'm also not certain how long the tunnel is, so we should start walking, because I'm also not certain what the former Regent put in our packs."

"Who told you how to get through the door?" Tham took Elver's shoulders. "Take a breath. Start there."

"The blue." Elver shook his head. "No, the ice. Maybe not the ice, but the stories in my mind that have happened since I was stuck in the ice. But not really stories. Visions. Not all of them, but some are visions. I thought the pain of the ice had driven me mad and the stories were just another torment.

"But some of them came true. Like escaping from the matrons, and killing the Regent, and opening the door. And I know walking down this tunnel is true, too. We're supposed to go, fast. We have to. I've seen that part too many times for it not to be important. This tunnel is the way to make Death stop."

Mara stepped past the men to look down the tunnel.

Blue. Endless blue, leading to a fate she couldn't see.

She pushed up the right sleeve of her coat, smearing her wrist with blood.

She pressed her finger to the compass mark the sorcerers had etched into her skin the day she'd joined the Map Makers Guild. The arrow on the compass spun to face north, to the door behind them.

"The tunnel goes south," Mara said. "Southbound and free is better than executed in Isfol."

Tham tucked his sword through his belt and picked up his pack. "I'll search for bandages while we move."

"Thanks." Mara ignored the knot in her chest born of excitement, longing, and fear in equal measure. "Come on."

Elle scampered toward Mara, Ture's hand clenched between her teeth.

"Oh, Elle, no." Mara flinched as she reached down to pull the hand from Elle's mouth.

Elver got there first. "We don't need this anymore." He tugged the hand from Elle and tossed it behind him.

The hand hit the door with a strangely light thud.

Elle barked and ran back to get it.

"Let's go then." Elver strode down the tunnel.

Elle chased after him, Ture's hand dangling from her mouth.

37

NIKO

The morning sun sliced through Niko's eyelids, jabbing at his headache with sharp vengeance.

The rustle of ill-concealed whispers came from the left.

"We can still get closer."

"We'll get in trouble."

Niko kept his eyes closed, pretending he didn't hear the swishing of the tall grass as the whisperers crept closer.

If the ones approaching were armed and ready to kill him, good on them for giving him a swift end.

If it was only another batch of children come to gape at Solcha, he'd rather deal with the sunlight jabbing at his headache than the endless rattle of childish questions slicing into his skull.

"He's handsome."

"I thought he'd be taller."

"You don't know how tall he is. He's lying down, you fool."

"Don't call me a fool."

The footsteps scuffled, stopped, scuffled again.

"You don't have to be so mean to everyone."

Smack!

Niko bit the corners of his lips, refusing to betray a hint of shock or humor as the children went completely silent for a moment before one screamed like a demon.

The painful intrusion of the sound was quick, fading as the demon ran away and the rest of the children followed behind, restoring the quiet of Niko's resting place.

After a few blissful moments, in which Niko's biggest bother was whether or not to raise his arm to cover his eyes or if it would be better to simply let the sunlight bore through his head, a rolling rustle came from the right.

The footsteps were steady, moving back and forth in a consistent pattern.

Niko didn't have to open his eyes to know it was Danu who paced, maintaining a respectable distance as she watched over Solcha.

A fleeting desire to rage at her and demand to be left alone rumbled through Niko's thoughts. But speaking would require an impossible amount of effort.

A cloud drifted in front of the sun, giving his eyes a reprieve.

The soil around him was soft, malleable. Perhaps if the clouds let loose a terrible storm, he might sink into the ground, be swallowed by the dirt and never have to worry about sunlight, or whispers, or shattered hearts ever again.

The cloud drifted past the sun, and light once again bored into Niko's eyes.

An uneven rustling came from the right.

"Danu," a man called. "How are you this fine morning?"

"Well enough." Danu's pacing stopped. "What's brought you so far from home, Shay?"

Niko opened his eyes, summoning the will to roll onto his side to watch Shay's approach.

Shay used a crutch to aid the ruined leg that had seen him sent home from the fight against the Hayes Clan. He had a bag over his shoulder that bounced against his hip with every step, making his gait less steady than after he'd had a few cups of ale.

"Is Solcha with you?" Shay asked. "I was told at the cliff he'd come out this way."

Danu pointed at Niko's hiding place in the tall grass.

"Solcha!" Shay raised a hand in greeting, his smile almost hiding the pain the walk across the valley had cost him.

Niko pushed himself out of the dirt, sitting up in a poor attempt to match Shay's hardy perseverance.

"I brought you something, Solcha." Shay fought against the tall grass that wrapped around his crutch with every step as he made his way to Niko. "After our chat last night. I think it might be just what you need."

"Now you have me curious," Niko said.

Shay dropped to the ground to sit beside Niko. "It's an old family recipe." He tossed his crutch aside and pulled a bottle from his bag. "Mostly like normal frie, but it's got a healthier spice to it."

"Niko," Danu said.

He glanced up to meet her gaze, catching enough worry and pity in her eyes for him to look back to Shay before she could say anything more.

"Start with a little sip." Shay pulled the cork from the bottle. "Breathe in through your nose and mouth with the frie still on your tongue. It'll give you a better taste of the spices."

Niko took a swig from the bottle, letting the frie burn on his tongue so he could catch a hint of wood and something like spiced cake. "It's good," Niko coughed as he finally swallowed. "Deeper taste than I'm used to."

"This is an easy recipe," Shay said. "Now that I'm home again, I'll be distilling batches that'll make you swear the mountain herself wanted the Black Bloods to behold the beauty of frie."

"I look forward to it." Niko took another drink, trying to decide if he actually liked Shay's frie better than what the Black Bloods continuously sent to his room. It definitely had a more demanding flavor.

"I've heard whispers drifting through the shadows, Solcha. I know you've been asking about someone." Shay kept his voice low. "A friend the mountain carried with you through the darkness. One Ilbrean finding his way to the stronghold is a miracle, but two? I'm not sure if I should celebrate or cower before whatever plans the mountain has laid out for us. Whatever the end, I don't think there's a fool alive who wouldn't agree that Solcha and his companion being delivered to the Brien is a sign of tremendous changes brewing in the mountain's stone."

"Wouldn't it be wonderful if anything in this wretched world ever sent signs of peace and happiness to loom over us poor mortals?"

"Ha!" Shay smacked Niko on the back. "Have some more frie. It'll bring you cheer."

"Thanks." The frie didn't burn as much on Niko's third taste.

"I have more comfort to offer than drink," Shay whispered. "I used to be one of Bryana's guards before the war sent me north. Poked around through the rosters and asked a few questions. The other Ilbrean is being kept in Paiman's quarters. Minded by Paiman, too, from the look of it."

"Amec is with Paiman?" Niko gripped the glass bottle.

"Don't know why, only that that's where your friend is. People who've never served the clan outside the stronghold, they don't understand. If you're going to face a danger you've no hope of defeating with a single sword, you should have an old friend fighting beside you. It was true on the front, and I can't imagine it's any different when fighting through a fate chosen for you by the mountain."

"Thank you, Shay."

"No thanks required. Just keep my name out of it." Shay grabbed his crutch and pushed himself to his feet.

Niko reached up to hand him the bottle.

"Keep it." Shay waved the frie away. "A decent drink is almost as needed as a good friend when the path grows dark."

Shay limped back toward the cliffs, tearing his crutch through the tall grass with every step.

Danu didn't speak until Shay had gone far past hearing distance. "Are you going to tell me what the whispering was about, or am I going to have to pay Shay's home a visit tonight?"

"Your honored Brien soldier was giving me advice for dealing with the headache his homemade brew is bound to leave." Niko took a long drink, washing down his desire to scream.

"I thought we agreed not to lie, Niko." Danu cut through the grass, stepping into the sanctity of Niko's hiding place to sit in front of him. "I thought we were friends."

"And that means I'm not allowed to have other friends? I'd have thought you'd be pleased I'm bonding with other Brien."

"I am." Danu lifted the bottle from Niko's grip, sniffed the frie, and winced. "But whatever Shay dragged himself all the way out here to tell you won't lead to anything good."

"And if I'm not aiming for good?"

Danu took the cork from the ground and rammed it into the top of the frie bottle. "Niko, I'm sorry Allora is a two-faced slitch who married a king rather than wait for you. I'm sorry I can't help you leave the stronghold. I'm sorry you've had the weight of *Solcha* tossed upon you. But none of that is my fault. I'm the best ally you've got, and I can only help you if you're honest with me."

"You want honesty? I'm done playing Solcha."

"What?"

Niko stood, brushing the grass off his pants. "No more comforting wounded soldiers. No more letting children gawk. No more Solcha."

"You can't just decide to toss the title away, Niko."

"Sure I can." Niko snatched the bottle back. "If your elder wants to murder me, I welcome her blade."

"You don't mean that."

"I do."

"The mountain doesn't take kindly to people ignoring the paths she's laid out." Danu stood.

"The mountain can tickle my mast and gems." Niko yanked the cork from the bottle and hurled it far off into the grass. "Your love of stone has nothing to do with me."

"Don't you think it's just a bit of a miracle you were kept fed and alive during the months you spent underground?"

"A miracle I was led here to be tortured by your chivving elder? I must offer the mountain my gratitude." Niko stormed away from Danu, cutting back toward the cliffs.

"The mountain didn't make Bryana hurt you." Danu matched his stride. "That was the act of a terrified and grieving mother."

"Hadn't thought of it that way. Should I simply forgive the chivving demon who drove her knives into me?" Niko gulped down frie.

"I'm not asking you to forgive Bryana. I'm begging you to take a moment to think about what you're doing before you destroy the fragile bits of a life you've built here just because you're heartbroken and drunk."

"Not drunk yet, still working on it." Niko raised the bottle to the sky.

"The mountain's protection of you. Her guiding you through the darkness so Paiman could—"

"Don't you mention that chivving bastard's name to me." Niko stopped, rounding on Danu.

"What?" Danu held her ground even as wrinkles pinched between her eyebrows. "What have you got against Paiman?"

"Don't play innocent with me. You've known this whole chivving time, haven't you?"

"Known what?" She grabbed his arm, holding him in place. "Niko, what under the stars did Shay say to you?"

"Has everything you've said been a lie? Was the letter about Allora real?"

"Of course the—"

"Did you truly want to comfort me after lying to me, or did you laugh while I sobbed like a chivving, heartbroken babe?"

"Why would you ask that?"

"Where's Amec, Danu?" Niko jerked his arm away from her. "Where is he?"

"Amec? The other Ilbrean?"

"Do not play the fool with me! I'm already a chivving prisoner. I've already lost everything. Why bother lying, you heartless, chivving beast?"

Danu stepped away from Niko, the worry on her face shifting to anger. "Tell me what Shay said."

"So you can send him to your elder to be punished? Sod a chivving hole." Niko cheersed the air and downed another gulp of frie.

"Judging by the heartless, thoughtless slitch you've dissolved into, I can promise you I have as much right to know Shay's gossip as you do."

"What a line." Niko managed to take one step before Danu grabbed his arm, whipping him back around.

"I don't know where Amec is, Niko. I've never gotten anything but vague assurances he's still alive. If Shay's come up with better information than what I've been given while I play nursemaid to the drunken, angry Solcha, then there are a good many people who deserve a fist to their jaw."

"I'm not going to rat out Shay."

"Tell me."

"No."

"Tell me where Amec is, and I'll take you to him!"

"I don't think your precious brother would like us breaking into his quarters!" Niko shouted.

Two birds burst out of the grass, fleeing Niko's rage.

"Paiman?" Danu tightened her hold on Niko's arm. "Shay told you Amec is with Paiman?"

"Your chivving brother has been hiding Amec in the cliffs

while your chivving aunt parades me around as some blessed sign of the mountain. So what's your role in all this, Danu? Are you the best liar in your family? Is that why you were sent to mind drunken Solcha?"

"I'm the chivving fool of the family. That's my gift." Danu grabbed the bottle from Niko and downed a bigger gulp than he'd dared. "Chivving Paiman." She thrust the bottle into Niko's chest and stormed toward the cliffs.

"What are you doing?" Niko called.

"Going to pay a visit to my brother. Keep up if you want to watch me pummel the slitch."

Niko took another swig and chased after her.

"The low-lying, dirt-gobbling, ass on a fire spit slitch." Danu cursed through gritted teeth.

"Paiman?" Niko trotted alongside her. "You are talking about Paiman, right?"

"Who else would I be ranting about?"

"I don't know how you define an *ass on a fire spit slitch*, so you could be talking about anyone."

"I've asked him." Danu charged onto the path beyond the grass, sending a gaggle of women scattering out of her way. "Only the mountain knows how many times I've asked my chivving brother where your friend is being held, and every chivving time that cacting, slitching, fool of an ass told me he didn't know."

Frie sloshed out of the bottle as Niko ducked under a tree branch to keep up with Danu.

"Been going to him for advice on how to handle your drunken tear since the letter came from Ilara. Asked him a dozen times what he thought the Brien might do to comfort you. If that slitch had your chivving friend in his chivving room the whole chivving time, I'll owe him a stab to the chivving gut!"

"I'll happily watch your glorious wrath smite your elder's heir"—Niko dodged around a pack of children—"but keep Shay's name out of it. I don't want a trueborn tearing stone through his heart for outing your brother's lies."

"My brother's lies?" Danu stopped short, bracing her hand against the center of Niko's chest as he bumped into her. "A little tantrum, and you're willing to believe I'm not a liar?"

"I—" Niko looked up through the leaves shading the path, wishing someone with finer words were there to guide him. "I don't know if you've been playing me as the paun fool in the weeks you've been my guardian. But my choices are to believe either Paiman's been hiding something from you, or the only Brien I've come close to trusting has tormented me as badly as the demon elder who won't set me free. Paiman being a slitch, I can manage. If you've been lying to me, Danu…I don't think I can keep trying to survive in the stronghold without you."

The tension in her shoulders eased. "When we get to my brother's rooms, I will do the talking. I will do the punching if it comes to it. He's Bryana's heir. If Paiman's guards see you as a threat, I won't be able to protect you."

"What if I don't want to be protected?" Niko's voice caught in his throat. "What if I would welcome a swift slice to the neck? Let his guards have me."

Danu stepped closer to Niko. She placed her hand on his shoulder and brushed her lips against his cheek. "Don't let pain defeat you, Solcha."

"I'm not Solcha."

"You are. *Solcha* is the name given to an Ilbrean who survived the darkness below the mountain. That's you, Niko. It's another title like map maker or friend. You may not be a Brien, but Shay counts you as a friend and so do I. And so do the horde of wounded you slosh down ale with every night. You've lost so much, Niko. But I hope you can believe you've gained a few things, too."

"You didn't have to drive quite so deep to order me to keep my mouth shut."

"I'd rather convince you than order you." She kissed his cheek again. "And if you won't behave for the sake of the Brien who'd like you to keep breathing, think of Amec. He might need you alive."

She turned away from him and strode down the path.

Niko sighed and took one last swig from the bottle before handing it to a passing woman wearing a midwife's bodice.

Running on Danu's heels meant every door opened before Niko reached it. There was never a guard who questioned where Danu wanted to go, just a long series of bows as the Brien guards let the sister of their elder's heir pass from one staircase to the next, climbing higher in the cliff face than Niko had ever been allowed.

By the time they reached the top of the ninth staircase, Niko's lungs had begun to protest being asked to work so hard. Especially with the amount of frie still seeping into his blood.

He tried to keep his ragged breathing even as they cut through a gallery filled with mosaic portraits he could only assume were previous elders of the Brien Clan. The few people in the gallery all bowed as Danu passed, offering her more respect than Niko had noticed on any of their other outings.

It wasn't until Danu had made it to the far side of the gallery and the people still stayed bent in their bows that a dreadful realization wormed into Niko's mind. They were bowing to him. The people all the way up the cliffs where their elder and her heir dwelled were bowing to Solcha.

I am not loved by your mountain!

Niko wished he hadn't passed the bottle off.

I am not loved by anyone.

He followed Danu into a wide corridor with guards stationed every few feet. Instead of the usual blue lae stones set into the ceiling, chandeliers dripping with tiny orange lae stones filled the hall with their golden light.

Danu stopped at a wide, wooden door, pounding on it with the side of her fist before Niko reached her.

"Are you all right?" One of the guards looked to Danu with a furrowed brow. "Are you in danger?"

"My chivving brother is the one you should worry about." Danu banged on the door again. "Open the door, you coward!"

Niko stood behind Danu, catching his breath while enjoying watching the guards squirm with uncertainty.

"Of—all—the—low—things!" Danu punctuated each word with a slam against the door. "I am your sister, Paiman. Not your servant and not your fool!"

"Maybe he's not here." Niko rocked back on his heels as Danu shot a glare his way.

"Open—this—door—Paiman." Danu kicked the door. "Open it now, or I'll take my grievance to grandmother!"

The door to Paiman's room swung open just far enough for Paiman to stand in the gap. "What are you screaming about, sister?"

"Would you like to confess to your chivving lies now, or shall we go into your rooms so the guards aren't forced to witness your shame?" Danu said.

"What are you prattling on about?" Paiman looked beyond Danu. The set of his jaw tightened as his gaze landed on Niko.

"Hello, Paiman." Niko bowed. "I haven't seen you since you handed me over to your aunt to be tortured."

Paiman stayed silent.

"Did you drop by to watch her slice into my skin and tear through my mind?" Niko asked. "Honestly, I was a bit preoccupied with the unbelievable pain, so I might not have noticed you there."

"Where is he, Paiman?" Danu said.

Paiman worked his lips together, as though forcing his teeth to unclench, before stepping back, opening the door wide enough to allow them entry.

"Someone send for frie and food." Paiman spoke in the general direction of the guards.

"Have a few bandages brought up, too," Danu said. "My darling brother will need them."

Niko followed Danu, dodging into the room just before Paiman slammed the door shut.

"You are wise enough to understand that causing a scene is the foolish act of a petulant child." Paiman strode over to the fireplace and leaned against the mantle, which was decorated with carvings of sharp-clawed wildcats.

"A petulant child?" Danu laughed. "You're lucky I didn't challenge you to come to the training field with a sharpened sword."

Niko stepped farther into the room, wondering at the beauty of the massive windows looking out over a white-stone balcony. And the polished wooden table, still set with the remains of an afternoon meal and scattered with books and maps.

"You would challenge your elder's current heir?" Paiman said.

"You would lie to your own chivving sister?" Danu said. "And for what? Does Bryana have some plan only you're allowed to know? Have you come up with your own clever scheme to use Solcha to gain power?"

"I don't want power."

"Then why are you hiding Amec?"

Paiman didn't shout back. He pursed his lips and looked up to the ceiling.

"Do you have him chained up in your wardrobe? Have you been torturing him?" Danu said.

"Amec knows nothing worth torturing him for!" Niko shouted.

"How many times have I asked you where he is, and you've been hiding him in your rooms?" Danu jabbed her finger into her brother's chest. "Don't break the trust I have in you, Paiman. It's the only thing you and I can hold on to."

Paiman looked down at his sister and lifted her finger away

from his ribs. "I've never hurt Amec. He's been well cared for and seems quite happy to be living the pampered life."

"Why have you kept him here?" Danu asked.

"Can I see him?" Niko stepped closer to Paiman, stopping at the right distance to swing a fist for his jaw.

"Niko and Amec are supposed to be kept apart," Paiman said. "Bryana's orders."

"Why?" Danu shifted, sliding between Niko and Paiman.

"In case Niko fails in his role as Solcha." Paiman sighed and stepped past them, heading toward a door on the far side of the room.

"I am a chivving disaster at playing Solcha." Niko followed Paiman.

"You're not. The people love you." Danu took his arm, gripping just hard enough to remind Niko she could yank him back and throttle him.

"And, should the mountain will it, Niko will continue to bring hope to the Brien by reminding the clan that the cause we fight for is just and necessary. The mountain has not forsaken her children." Paiman cut through his bedroom.

The bed stood on a platform at the center of the space and was wide enough for three people to sleep side-by-side without ever touching. Four wardrobes stood along the back wall, all of them built of well-polished wood. Another fireplace, carved with the same images of wildcats, was large enough to provide warmth even during the worst of the winter.

"Bryana couldn't promise people the hope Solcha brings and tear it away from them when she had to execute Solcha for crimes against the Brien Clan," Paiman said.

"What crimes have I committed?" Niko asked.

"None." Paiman stopped in front of a door on the far side of his room. "But Bryana couldn't risk the future of her clan on the back of one Ilbrean who was ill-disposed to help her."

"Because she tortured me! For weeks, that chivving demon tortured me!"

"I'm aware." Paiman frowned, the slant of his lips accentuating the long scar on his chin. "I don't agree with Bryana's methods during your questioning, but keeping Amec out of view as an option should the Brien need a new hope to look to—"

"You've been saving him as a spare Solcha?" Danu said. "Keeping that Ilbrean tucked away like an extra pair of boots?"

"A well cared for pair of boots." Paiman raised a hand, silencing Niko's shout. "Amec had the weaker constitution for questioning. He was placed in my care to find out any information he was hiding about Regan and to keep him out of sight in case a new Solcha was needed. I assure you, he has no reason to complain of his treatment."

Paiman touched the stone-carved lock, clicking the latch open in the same way Danu opened the lock to Niko's room.

A lock you can't open makes you a prisoner.

Niko swallowed the words as a familiar voice came from the next room.

"Paiman, I didn't think I'd see you this afternoon," Amec said, his voice bright with genuine pleasure.

"I've brought some guests. They couldn't wait any longer for a visit."

"Visit?" Amec said.

Niko stepped into Amec's prison.

A room three times the size of Niko's led out onto a balcony like Paiman's. A massive bed stood on a raised platform. A bookshelf took up most of one of the walls.

Amec sat at a table, playing a game of dice with a maid, using buttons and nuts as betting pieces.

"Niko?" Amec stood. "Niko!" He ran to Niko, yanking him into a hug and clapping him on the back. "I was hoping you'd find time for a visit soon."

"Find time? I didn't even know you were here." Niko stepped

back, gripping Amec's shoulders as he studied his face, trying to convince himself this really was the soldier who'd walked beside him through the endless darkness.

"You didn't?" Amec looked to Paiman.

"It was better for him not to know," Paiman said. "It's hard enough to accept a weighty fate, but taking on the burden when you know the mountain has provided someone else who might carry the load..."

"You're right." Amec nodded solemnly. "I can't imagine what you've been going through out there, Niko."

"Is this Solcha?" The girl at the table stood, gaping at Niko with a look of absolute awe.

"It is." Amec patted Niko's back again and guided him toward the table. "Glyn, this is Niko, who is Solcha."

"I'm honored." Glyn curtsied.

"That's completely unnecessary," Niko said.

"Glyn, would you mind fetching some frie for Solcha?" Amec planted Niko in a seat at the table. "We often missed frie in our time underground."

"Niko's had enough for one day," Danu said.

Glyn ignored her as she scurried through the door to Paiman's room and out of sight.

"Isn't she breathtaking?" Amec said. "And such a mind, too. She loves to talk about books. I have to read each one twice just to make sure I can keep up with her in conversation."

"Glad you've found a way to pass the time while you've been locked in here," Niko said.

"It's not bad at all." Amec laughed. "I get a bit stir-crazy sometimes, but Paiman's been kind enough to sneak me out for a few walks. There're a couple of sorcerers who pop by from time to time as well. They do little spells to entertain me. That makes for an excellent evening. The food's lovely, I have a soft bed, Glyn keeps my mind sharp. A chance to practice with my sword and I'd have all a man could want!"

"But you're locked in, Amec," Niko said. "Trapped. Just like we were in the dark."

"This is nothing like being in the dark." Amec leaned closer to Niko. "And the women here aren't like Ilbrean women. A girl can spend the night in your bed, and no one rages about it. There's just a blush and a titter, and life goes on."

Niko grabbed Amec's wrist. "Did they hurt you when we got here? Did they torture you for information?"

"Of course not. I was in a cell for a bit, and Paiman spent a few weeks asking me the same questions over and over, but once we'd settled that I don't know anything about poor Bryana's missing heir, I moved right up here," Amec said. "They haven't treated me poorly just because I'm not Solcha."

"I'm not Solcha either!" Niko said. "There's no such thing as Solcha."

Amec peered around Niko to Paiman.

"It's not an easy thing to accept," Paiman said.

"What?" Niko looked between Paiman and Amec. "That demon elder decided to call me Solcha to make people feel better, but it's a chivving lie. There is nothing blessed about being trapped in the darkness for months!"

"Niko." Amec clapped his hand on Niko's shoulder. "Take a breath, friend."

"Amec, don't—"

"Do you remember all the tales you told me? The different legends and fairy stories about things happening in and below the eastern mountains? You told me there was truth to every legend, and you were right." Amec pointed to the window and the view of the valley beyond. "We are in the middle of a legend filled with beauty and magic. It might not be exactly how the story would be told around the fire, but we are in a place most Ilbreans can't even dream of."

"We're prisoners!" Niko knocked Amec's hand away.

"Barely," Amec said. "We're guests with locks on the doors.

Guests who are given everything a person could want in exchange for staying safely where the Brien tell them to be."

"You've lost your mind."

"You've lost sight of where we are!" Amec stood, grabbed Niko's arm, and yanked him to his feet. "You are a map maker, an explorer, who has found a place filled with more wonders than you could ever have hoped to find trudging through the eastern mountains searching for a path to Wyrain." He dragged Niko to the window. "The stronghold is incredible, Niko. Let yourself appreciate it."

"We have to get back to Ilbrea, Amec." A flock of birds soared up from the trees deep within the forest. "I'm not Solcha."

"Solcha is a legend, Niko. Legends are based on truths. Don't shy away from your part in the story."

38

KAI

Dust puffed up from the bottom of the crate as they laid down the carefully tied sail, coiling the heavy fabric in a tight swirl that made the sailor in Kai's heart scream.

"It's still too bulky." Merial stood on her toes, frowning as she peered down into the crate. "You'd have to be a getch of a fool not to notice there was something below the legal goods."

"Then we'll have to be sure fools load the crates onto the ships," Drew said. "The bulk of a sail is the bulk of a sail."

"I'll be sure to mention that to the sorcerers as they place a rope around my neck for smuggling a bulky chivving sail onto the docks," Merial said.

"If you're as good a smuggler as you think, I'm sure they'll never catch you." Kai heaved the false bottom of the crate off the floor.

"I'm the best smuggler in Ilara *because* I worry about little things like the bulk of the less than legal items I'm moving." Merial stepped back. "The surest way to not get caught is to not do stupid things."

"If there were a way to make the sail smaller, we'd do it," Kai grunted as the lip of the crate dug into his gut while he and Drew lowered the wooden slats into place, covering the coiled-up sail. "We can't use a smaller or lighter sail."

"And we can't let the ships leave the docks with only a sorcerer-made sail." Merial passed Kai a mallet. "Yes. I am aware of why I am so nobly risking my life."

"And we are grateful." Kai tapped down his two corners of the crate before passing the mallet to Drew.

He stood up, taking a deep breath as blood rushed back into his head.

"Gratitude." Merial looked up at the lamp hanging from the arch of the stone ceiling. "If gratitude could buy horses, I'd've stopped selling frie and started gifting sweeties to babes a long time ago."

"Then the gods have my gratitude you've stuck to smuggling frie." Kai bowed.

"How many more sails have we got to do?" Drew tossed the mallet back to Merial.

"Three." She pulled a little book from her pocket. "I might be able to get another two sails onto ships sometime next week. But none of my other legal goods going out over the next few days will be packed in crates large enough to mask sails."

"Four is better than none." Kai tucked his hands into his pockets, stilling his urge to tear the crate apart.

Four sails.

Four sails hidden on ships to give the sailors on board a chance of overthrowing whatever sorcerer might seize their vessel.

If the sailors could control the sorcerer long enough to replace the magic-made sail.

And keep her contained until they got the ship to shore.

Which would mean killing the sorcerer.

But a sail stashed on board might've saved my crew.

Kai dragged his fingers through his beard.

"Come on." Drew beckoned Kai to the next sail.

"Wait a tick." The clunk of metal on metal carried over Landon's voice as he ran down the stairs into the dim stone room.

"Wait for what?" Merial shoved her little book back into her pocket.

"I just got word from Lord Nevon." Landon set the crate he'd been carrying down with a heavy thunk. "He's agreed to us stashing a few spare weapons in with each of the sails."

Landon looked from Merial to Drew to Kai, as though waiting for one of them to say something gleeful and congratulatory.

"We have spare weapons?" Merial ran her tongue over her teeth. "Why have I never been told we have spare weapons?"

Landon rocked back on his heels. "Because they aren't anything I'd be willing to place in a person's hand if I was sending them to fight aboveground. But a poor weapon is better than no weapon at all."

Kai knelt beside Landon's crate.

Two knives with nicked blades seemed to be the pick of the stash, with a handful of spiked clubs and sling shots as the lesser of the options.

"Just tuck a few in with each of the sails," Landon said.

Merial pinched the bridge of her nose. "A sling shot and a sail—this is what we hope saves Ilbrea's ships."

"If a sorcerer were to steal all the sailors' weapons before they could rebel, I bet you they'd be grateful for a knife even if the blade wasn't the best," Landon said. "Kai killed a sorcerer with a knife."

"Just because the brave and heroic Kai Saso managed to kill a sorcerer with a chivving decent knife, you want me to go from smuggling sails to weapons?" Merial said.

"If you're going to be hanged for a sail, you might as well add a blade to the reasons the Guilds want you dead," Landon said. "It's not as though they can hang you twice."

Kai stood, brushed the dirt off his knees and grabbed a prybar from the corner.

"They could torture me before they hang me," Merial said. "Have you thought of that, you chivving fool?"

Kai dug the prybar between the slats of wood and pulled the false bottom up.

"And what happens when we run out of weapons for our people fighting in the city?" Merial said.

Drew tucked a knife, a club, and a sling shot on top of the sail.

"We find more weapons," Landon said. "You can smuggle some in from outside the city."

Kai and Drew passed the mallet back and forth to pound the false bottom back into place.

Landon and Merial kept fighting as Drew and Kai loaded the second and third sails into crates.

Kai let Drew choose the weapons for each stash. He didn't want the responsibility of choosing the wrong weapon and having a fellow sailor die because they'd attacked a sorcerer with a chivving slingshot they didn't know how to use.

He hoped Drew wouldn't think of the weight the selection of each weapon bore. Even if he did, Drew was stronger than Kai. It was a burden he'd be able to carry.

By the time they tucked the fourth sail into the fourth crate, two more people had arrived in the stone chamber below the streets of Ilara.

Kai didn't know the names of the two young men. But from the way they kept glancing at Kai as they trekked crates of glass bottles down the stairs, adding them to the growing stacks of supplies in the corner, they both knew who Kai was. Or, at the very least, had some idea he was the one who'd slit a sorcerer's throat in the Lord Sailor's office.

Drew nestled a knife and a club into the fourth crate and lowered the false bottom over them.

"It's not as though I don't want to be doing more." Landon

grabbed his empty crate from the ground. "If you have a better idea of how to steal our city back from the sorcerers, take it to Lord Nevon. In the meantime, I'll keep doing what I can with the weapons I've been given. Now if you'll excuse me, I'm going to try and fashion a few more shields from barrel sides rather than stand around moaning like a slitch because I don't like how our rebellion is going."

Landon stomped up the stairs.

"I didn't like that getch before I joined the underground, and I like him even less now." Merial glared at the stairs as Landon's shadow disappeared.

"But he's not wrong." Kai put the mallet in the corner with the other tools. "We're doing what we can. It may not feel like much, but if a single ship needs to use one of these sails, that could be as many as seventy sailors we'll have saved working in this glorified cellar."

"Stop sounding noble." Merial shifted her glare to Kai. "I don't like it when you tamp down my anger."

"My apologies, Miss." Kai bowed. "Anything else you need done before we rats scurry back into our hole?"

"Not unless you can grow new faces so you can work aboveground," Merial said.

Kai dragged his fingers through his beard again. "I'm trying."

"Useless for you." Merial said. "A young, handsome, dark-skinned man sticks out too much in an Ilaran crowd. But, with the right hat, Drew might be able to scoot aboveground soon."

"I breathlessly await the day." Drew headed toward the stone steps without waiting for Kai.

"He's being sarcastic," Kai said. "I promise I'll make him take at least two big breaths."

Drew stopped on the fifth stair up, hugging the left wall to make room for Kai beside him.

"Seeing a bit of sun might do you good." Kai bent over, pushing all his weight against the eighth stone step.

"I'm sure it would. Men aren't meant to live in tunnels." Drew joined him, both of them shoving the step in what for a moment seemed a useless endeavor.

With a dull thunk, the stone shifted, pushing the eighth and ninth stairs in, opening a tunnel that led into the darkness.

Drew climbed down into the gap and disappeared into the black.

Kai shook out his shoulders, banishing the frightened voice in his mind that promised something terrifying would trap him in the darkness forever. He lowered himself through the gap. The stones that lined the tunnel offered an odd sense of familiarity as they snagged his clothes.

Once he'd gotten his head below the level of the stairs, he mashed himself against the wall. "Come on."

Drew crawled up, jamming himself into the space beside Kai.

Kai braced the toes of his boots against the rocks and pushed on the stairs as hard as he could while in such an awkward position.

The steps slid back into place, sealing Kai and Drew into the perfect black of the tunnel.

"I miss doors." Kai rested his forehead on the stone. "Opening doors. Closing doors. Walking through doors. I never appreciated the beauty of doors. When we retake Ilara, I'm going to go up to the Map Master's Palace and kiss every door in the whole chivving place."

"I'm sure it'll set all the maids to swooning." Drew's back pressed against Kai as he twisted to ease himself down the tunnel.

"We'll make the maids swoon together." Kai gripped Drew's arm. "You're coming with me. We're going to get brutally drunk on fine frie, kiss every door in the palace, and have the best feast you've ever seen to sober ourselves back up. Then we'll get drunk again on chamb for good measure."

"It's a nice dream."

"It's not a dream at all. I'm going to drag you up to the cliffs whether you like it or not. We're fighting this thing together. We'll celebrate our victory together."

"I'm not sure this is a battle we can win." Drew lifted Kai's hand from his arm and slid farther into the darkness.

"Any battle can be won if it's fought properly." Kai waited for the sound of Drew's boots hitting stone before he eased himself down the slant of the tunnel.

His gut tightened as he reached the end of the tunnel and the ridges of the rocks disappeared, leaving his feet dangling in the darkness. He shut his eyes, banishing his instinctive fear, and pushed himself farther down.

When everything below his chest hung over the open air, he shoved himself out of the tunnel, forcing himself to exhale as he fell the five feet before his boots hit solid ground.

"I really want to know what sort of a slitch designed these passages." Kai fumbled to the right, searching for a gap in the wall.

"A slitch who wanted to slow down anyone who might try to chase them from one warren to another," Drew said. "But clever places to hide won't help our cause."

"We're working—"

"We've got three separate groups fighting in Ilara besides the Sorcerers Guild. We've got the Brien, who've got sorcerers on their side so we're chivving out of luck if they storm into the warrens trying to kill us. We've got whatever rebels started this mess months ago. And we've got the underground we've joined, who, other than a very accurate name, don't have much going for them. And then we've got the Sorcerers Guild who could slaughter us all before we could scream if they penned us in."

Kai stepped into the passage, trailing his fingers along both walls as he walked through the black. "It's a bit of a messy fight we've found ourselves in, but at least we're fighting."

"Of course you're happy to be fighting. You're Kai Saso, the hero who slit a sorcerer's throat."

"I hate it when people talk about that like I did something wonderful."

The tunnel took a sharp turn, doubling back on itself.

"I'm sorry, Kai. I shouldn't have said it like that. I know you'd never be glad to end a life."

"It's not a weight I ever wanted to carry." Kai held his right hand out in front of him. "It still doesn't feel like it was actually me who spilt all that blood in Lord Nevon's office. It's more like an odd nightmare that won't go away."

"It'll get better."

"I'm not sure that's comforting. And it's not just the killing someone part that bothers me. Everyone should be cooing over you, not me. You sent Sorcerer Roo into the sea with a chivving board as a weapon. You're the hero. I want to tell them you're the one who deserves praise, but if anyone who knew was captured and told the sorcerers—"

"They'd torture me for killing one of their own before they hanged me for being in the underground."

Kai's right hand found a wall. He dug his nails into the dirt packed between the stones, funneling his panic into the rocks.

Drew's hand brushed against Kai's back before fumbling up to grip his shoulder. "I don't need praise. And if they're going to point to anyone as a hero for killing a sorcerer, you'll do much better at playing the handsome savior than I ever could."

"Come now, even the fine beard you've been growing can't hide the devilish cut of your chin. Every soul in Ilara would swoon over you if you'd give them a chance." Kai let go of the wall and reached overhead, groping through the darkness until his fingers found the cold metal ring.

"You don't have to protect my pride."

"I'm not." Kai pulled on the ring.

With a creak that set his teeth on edge, the trapdoor lowered.

Kai blinked against the light spilling down from above. "You've got the sort of face that's easy to overlook at first glance, but once a person takes the time to actually see you, you steal their breath away. Then you cruelly notch out a slice of their lungs right beside their heart, so even when they've looked at you a thousand times, their breath still hitches a bit when they look into your eyes, like the gods themselves have doomed anyone who's gazed upon you to judge every other face as lacking for the rest of their life."

"Kai—"

"You're right, though." Kai reached up into the light to pull the ladder down. "Better to have everyone keep their eyes fixed on me as the sailor who killed a sorcerer. Save a horde of poor slitches from tumbling into the madness of an adoration they can't escape."

He stomped on the lowest rung of the ladder, testing it was steady before beginning to climb. The warm light from the room above brushed away a bit of the gnawing fatigue that always plagued Kai in the tunnels and cellars of the underground's warrens.

The room wasn't large, the ceiling barely allowed him to stand upright, but some kind soul had painted the stone walls a light, cheery color and placed mirrors behind the two lamps to brighten their glow.

Kai leaned against the wall, waiting for Drew to climb up.

"If it makes you feel any better, there will be plenty more who can rightfully claim to have killed a sorcerer before this bloody thing is done," Kai said.

Drew knelt beside the trapdoor, carefully pulling the ladder back up before closing the hatch. "How many of us, do you think?"

"I don't know. I suppose it depends on how many more you and I have to end, then there are the scary lads at the far end of the tunnels. I bet they'll go for blood every chance they get once Lord Nevon sets them loose."

"But how many sorcerer corpses will it take to win our freedom?" Drew brushed off his hands. "I've no guess for how many sorcerers there are in Ilara."

"I suppose I don't, either. It was always the same pack in the cathedral when the Guilds were called together, but that can't be all the beasts they have hidden in their tower."

"No, it can't."

"If the Brien hadn't been so set on murdering us, we might've been able to ask Isla."

Kai tipped the panel in the wall open just a slit, taking a moment to listen before peeking out into the room beyond.

Three people sat around the table, two lurked near the fireplace, a few more lay on their bunks. None of them were covered in blood or seemed bent on murder.

He pushed the panel all the way open and stepped into the bunk room.

The three at the table all sprang to their feet, brandishing their knives.

"It's only us." Kai raised his hands. "Please tell me you've saved us a bit of food."

The three from the table sank back into their seats without bothering to answer.

"Lovely." Kai waited while Drew pressed the panel closed, checking to be sure the façade of rocks lined up with the wall before stepping away to squint at the cracks between the stones, making absolutely certain nothing looked out of place.

Drew finally gave Kai a nod, and they headed to the fireplace at the far end of the space.

The room had been built of stone, same as the supply cellar they'd been working in as they hid the sails, but the former occupants of this chamber had done their best to make the place more cheerful, coating the walls and ceiling with the same bright paint as the tiny room Kai and Drew had just left behind.

While the dirt and mortar packed between the stones had eaten through the paint, that dull feature had been made up for by a mural of the Arion Sea on the southern wall. The image was not well painted, the few birds flying over the splotchy blue waves looked like bats with orange beaks, but the color of the mess made the place seem less like a prison and more like an underground nursery.

The bunks where the members of the underground rotated sleeping were stacked three high and made of woven ropes covered with an odd assortment of blankets. The close sleeping quarters felt nearly like being on a ship to Kai, which helped him pretend he was free to climb up and walk the streets whenever he chivving well pleased.

The pair near the fireplace shifted aside, letting Kai and Drew reach the pot hanging over the hearth.

Stew still bubbled in the pot, and rolls sat in a basket nearby. As long as Kai didn't let himself wonder what was in the stew, he'd be in for a fine dinner. Or lunch.

He had no idea what time of day it was.

It's not going to be like this forever. It's worth living in a cellar for a chance to fight the chivving sorcerers.

Kai took the ladle from the hook beside the fire. "We should ask Lord Nevon if he knows how many sorcerers live in the tower." He dished stew into a bowl and passed it to Drew. "If he doesn't know, maybe he can ask Lord Gareth to check the records."

"I'm not sure if anyone besides the Lady Sorcerer really knows how many demons she has hidden."

"The answers don't get any easier." Kai sank to the ground, letting the warmth from his bowl seep into his hands. "Next time we end up in a fight, let's make sure our enemies are closer to normal folks than chivving gods."

"If you figure out how to arrange that, I'll let you keep the token forever." Drew sat next to Kai, staring into the fire.

Kai tried to focus on eating his stew. He may not have known what time it was, but he was certainly hungry. The stew was hearty and spicy. A nice meal to banish the underground chill.

Wrinkles creased the corners of Drew's eyes, as though he were trying to reason through some question the flames had whispered in his ear. He stirred his stew without taking a bite.

Kai looked back down at his own bowl. The stem of his spoon was crooked. The lip of his bowl was cracked.

One of the rocks beside the fireplace had fallen out of the wall, leaving a dark scar in the bright paint.

There were plenty of interesting things to look at that weren't Drew.

Drew shifted, setting his bowl aside and lacing his fingers together under his chin. He worried his lips together.

Not many men were capable of truly beautiful brooding. If Kai could only—

Don't even think of it, fool. There are some friendships too valuable to risk.

"Would it be the worst idea to try and find a way to ask Isla about the sorcerers?" Drew said. "She knows more about what's hiding in the Sorcerers Tower than anyone else we could hope to question. And she'd have no qualms with us wanting to fight against them."

"If we could find her and speak to her without us ending up dead." Kai grabbed a roll from the basket. "She'd be as valuable to our cause as she is to the Brien's chaos."

"Don't suppose she gave you a hint as to where in Ilara the Brien hide."

"Not a peep."

A flicker of movement caught the corner of Kai's eye.

He leapt to his feet, dropping his roll and grabbing the knife in his belt as a panel beside the fireplace swung open.

A boy stepped into the chamber, not seeming to notice everyone around him gripping their weapons, or at the very least not caring that he was outnumbered.

"Good, you're here." The boy brushed his sweaty hair from his forehead as he stepped toward Kai. "I was sent to fetch you and someone named Drew. You're to go through the tunnel to the docks."

Kai's heart throttled up into his throat. "What's happened at the docks?"

"They're having the ceremony for your lost shipmates," the boy said. "Lord Nevon told Fenn to have someone fetch you and this Drew so you've a chance to attend the funeral."

Kai stepped around the boy, walking into the passage before allowing himself time to think.

"Fenn said Lord Nevon said you have to stay out of sight!" the boy called after him. "And—"

The light in the tunnel faded as the panel closed behind him, blocking out whatever else the boy wanted to shout.

Kai glanced back, making sure Drew had followed, before striding down the passage.

The way had been dug straight and wide enough for large crates to be hauled through.

Lamps had been set into the stone walls so far apart, a dim gap stretched between the final glow of one light and the beginning of the next. The pools of water dotting the ground reflected the flames' feeble gleam.

As they neared the western end of the tunnel, the scent of the air shifted from stale stone to the tang of dead fish mixed with the fresh salt of the sea.

Cold seeped into Kai's boots as the pools of water joined and deepened, rising up to his ankles as the tunnel curved and daylight bathed the path forward.

The sloshing of Drew's steps changed as he hurried to reach Kai. He took Kai's hand, walking beside him until they reached the end of the passage and stepped out into the closest thing to the open air either of them had seen in days.

A waist-high wall separated the Arion Sea from the passage, but the waves were right there, close enough for Kai to touch. The wood of the docks stretched out over their heads, but sunlight trickled through the cracks, a beauty to behold even though thick gray clouds tainted the sky.

A bell clanged up above. Footsteps thumped on the dock.

Kai gripped Drew's hand as he watched the shadows shifting through the slats, wondering if any of his family stood above him, saying their final goodbyes to the brother they hadn't bothered to mourn.

39

ADRIAL

"Saint Farrin guides sailors on all their voyages. Even the voyage that took these brave sailors to a shore we cannot yet reach." Lord Nevon looked up to the sky as though unwilling to accept that his voice had to carry them through the ceremony.

No one spoke up to save him.

Even the rain had gone quiet, shifting to a gentle mist that made no sound as it settled on the canvas shelters that protected the mourners.

But the waves still lapped against the docks. A solemn apology from the Arion Sea, begging forgiveness for having stolen so many beloved sailors.

"Though we cannot follow the sailors we have lost," Lord Nevon pressed on, "it is our duty to remember them."

A bell clanged on the dock, the sound jarring and obscene.

A line of sailors filed in front of the mourners, each of them carrying a sheet of bark with a candle stuck in the middle.

Wood and wax. That was their goodbye.

Rage filled Adrial's gut as a sailor stopped in front of him.

He needed to blow the candle out. To rip the pathetic memorial from the stranger's grip and smash it on the dock. Scream to

Dudia and all the saints that they had torn too many good people from the world. The ones who'd been left behind could not be expected to keep fighting the army of demons Dudia allowed to live.

Ena squeezed his hand, dragging him out of his anger and back to the dreary morning.

Adrial looked away from the candle, seeking solace in his wife's face.

Pain furrowed her brow. Not for her own grief—she'd never known Kai. She hurt because her husband did.

"You would have loved him," Adrial said. "He would've tried to steal you from me."

"It wouldn't have worked," Ena said. "But it might've been a fun game."

The candle bearers on either side of them left their mourners and walked to the far end of the dock.

"I'm supposed to say something." Adrial looked toward the royal platform where Allora stood with the King, tears streaming down her cheeks as she stood away from the family she should have been grieving beside.

"You don't have to say anything, Head Scribe," the candle bearer said. "It's entirely up to you."

"I…" For a slim moment, embarrassment overwhelmed Adrial's grief. "I will always be grateful for the time we had together. I hope you've found peace, brother. Or maybe joyful chaos would be a better end for you. I don't know. But I'll miss you. I'm sorry that's—I've nothing else to say."

The candle bearer nodded and joined the procession heading to the end of the dock where a boat lined with oars waited to row the candles out to sea.

"I'm so sorry," Ena whispered.

"I was always jealous of Kai." Adrial eased his hand from Ena's and wrapped his arm around her waist, binding himself to her in a vain attempt to match his wife's strength. "Kai would climb the trees on Lord Karron's estate like he was meant to live in the branches. He would charm everyone he met. If we were to group together everyone who'd ever fallen in love with Kai, we'd have a battleworthy battalion. But I couldn't hate him for it. He was too kind. He never taunted me for being less than he was."

"Maybe he was wise enough to know you've never been less than any man." Ena tucked herself closer to him.

Lord Nevon stepped forward as the last of the candle bearers reached the boat.

"May Dudia ease the burden of your grief, and may we all meet again on brighter shores." Lord Nevon turned toward the sea.

The bell rang again.

The mourners stayed quiet through all seven clangs.

As the bell fell silent, a woman began to sob.

Allora pressed her hand to her mouth, fighting her own tears. The King bundled her into his arms, holding her close.

"We should go." Ena twisted away from Adrial.

For one horrible moment, he thought she might abandon him on the dock, but she stepped in front of him, laying her head on his shoulder. "You're a valuable target, scribe. The longer you stay on the dock, the longer you put the other mourners in danger."

"You're right." He kissed the side of her head. She'd twisted her hair back for the ceremony, nestling the bird charm near her temple. "Kai would never forgive me if one of his shipmates' families suffered because of me."

"It wouldn't be because of you." Ena took his hand, leading him back to their white-trimmed carriage.

"Then who should we blame it on? The Arion Sea seems to be the culprit in Kai's death." Saying the words sent a fresh round of pain to claw at his lungs.

"If you don't know who the monster is, I haven't taught you half as well as I thought," Ena said.

"Head Scribe."

Adrial turned toward the call without thinking, instantly despising his instinct as Travers Gend strode toward him, his white robe a vivid contrast against the purple-robed pair trailing in his wake.

"Head Scribe." Travers bowed to Adrial and offered a nod to Ena. "I didn't know one of Lord Karron's other wards was among those lost to the sea. You have my condolences."

"Thank you, Scribe Gend," Adrial said. "It's not an easy loss to bear."

"I'm sure." Travers bowed again. "That's why I wanted to offer my assistance. If you need time to mourn the death of Sailor Saso, I would be happy to take on whatever work you can't manage."

"I will manage just fine." Adrial reached behind, searching for Ena's hand, desperate to anchor himself to something stronger than his need to punch Travers Gend in his falsely sympathetic face.

Ena slipped her hand into Adrial's as she stepped forward to stand beside him.

The anger in his chest ebbed. "I've found work to be my best comfort in times of sorrow. But I am grateful for the offer."

He switched his hold on Ena's hand, turning toward the carriage.

"It's not only grief that might distract you from your work," Travers said. "A baby will certainly steal time from the vellum."

Ena pulled her hand from Adrial's, easing it toward the blade hidden beside her breast.

Adrial shifted in front of her, blocking her path to Travers. "Sailor Saso had no children to leave in my care."

"Of course not." Travers bowed. "And I apologize if I've spoken out of turn. I was referring to the child your wife is carrying."

A terrifying hollow dug into Adrial's chest.

"You *have* spoken out of turn," Ena said. "Perhaps your life has been too privileged, but where I come from, we don't cheerfully greet a babe so early. Only a fool tempts the gods' wrath. Come, husband, I don't fancy lingering in the mist."

She led Adrial toward the carriage.

"How did he know?" Adrial whispered. "I promise you I've been careful."

"My tits are massive, and there's only so much belly I can hide." Ena clung to his hand. "I knew this was coming, I just didn't think it would come from Travers chivving Gend."

"Head Scribe." Allora's voice stopped Adrial just outside the safety of his carriage.

"Get in the carriage." He opened the door for Ena. "I don't want you to catch a chill."

"Head Scribe." Allora bustled toward him, a horde of soldiers and sorcerers trailing in her wake. "I was afraid you'd left already."

"There should be a blanket in the corner." Adrial pressed on Ena's back, urging her into the carriage.

"Of course, husband." Ena let him whisk her out of sight.

"I'm sorry I couldn't stand with you today." Allora extended her hand, graciously allowing Adrial to reach for the solace of touching an old friend. "I know this has been a terrible time for us both."

"It has." Adrial took her hand. The distant, shallow feel of the formal touch when they should have been weeping in each other's arms rolled another comforting wave of rage through Adrial's gut.

"When Mara and Tham come home, we should have a dinner, just the four of us," Allora said. "We can tell stories of the way things were when we all lived in my father's house. Remember all the playful adventures we used to imagine with Kai."

"I would be honored, Your Majesty." Adrial bowed.

"I look forward to it." Allora applied a strange pressure before releasing his hand. "We all shared so much. Those bonds shouldn't be forgotten."

She turned, cutting through the throng of her guards and back toward the King.

Adrial waited for the soldiers and sorcerers to file in behind her before daring to clench his hand into a fist, crinkling the paper Allora had pressed into his palm.

"Shall we go, scribe?" Ena leaned out of the carriage. "The clouds are darkening over the sea. We should get back to the library before the proper storm breaks."

"Of course." Adrial tucked the paper into his pocket and climbed into the carriage. "Kai wouldn't approve of such public grief."

40

MARA

If Mara hadn't been trapped in the constant glow of Isfol for so long, the unending blue light of the tunnel might have driven her mad.

The curves of the passage were so slight that, even with a sorcerer-made scroll, she would have been hard-pressed to properly map their route. The walls hadn't changed—always flat ice. Not perfectly smooth and polished, but she hadn't spotted a single rough patch, either.

Only the travelers had changed in the days they'd been walking. Mara had gone through three sets of bandages for the slices on her palms. Tham had fashioned a lead for Elle to stop her from running back to collect Ture's decaying hand.

Elver had started whispering to himself, furrowing his brow and tipping his head as he spoke, as though he were listening to someone who whispered back.

The Healers Guild would help him. That was the lie Mara kept telling herself. They would get to Ilara, and the Healers Guild would put Elver's mind to right.

She pressed her palms together, testing the stinging of her wounds.

"Don't," Elver said. "Can't risk your fingers swelling. You'll need them soon."

"Sorry." Mara dropped her hands to her sides.

She glanced back to Tham walking with Elle right beside him.

If Elver could take Elle, walk a bit ahead of them, she and Tham could finally have a moment to talk.

It could be days, weeks before we get out of this tunnel. If we ever make it out at all.

He deserves better than a vague apology.

You've already waited too long, Mara.

"I…" Mara chewed her lips. "It's my fault we're in this tunnel. It's my fault Ronya's riding to Ilbrea. I told her about Ian Ayres. I let myself be her puppet. I deserve all the anger anyone can throw at me. I accept the blame."

"You have no blame to carry," Tham said.

"Ronya always wanted to murder people," Elver said. "If it wasn't Ian Ayres, it would have been Ilbrea's lack of ice that drove her to violence. Or the way they belittle women. Or hide magic. Or taxes. Ilbrean soldiers kill lots of people over taxes."

"Please," Mara said. "I just need you to know I'm sorry. I helped a monster. I don't deserve to be forgiven, but I am so sorry."

"I'm sorry, too. I killed the matron who was gentle when she cut my hair," Elver said. "She was nice. But it had to be done."

"Right." Mara stepped back to walk beside Tham. "I hope I can be forgiven for the secrets I gave Ronya. I never wanted to hurt anyone."

"You kept me alive," Tham said. "I can't be anything but grateful."

She let the back of her hand brush against his.

"But what's to be done if we get back to Ilbrea?" Tham said. "Carry on lying? Hiding in the shadows, pretending we're only friends?"

"Tham—"

"The Guilds' rules won't have changed. It'll be back to climbing in your window at night. After everything we've survived, I won't be able to sleep with you in my arms. In Ilbrea, I'm the thing you hide, Mara. I'm your terrible secret. I can't go on pretending I don't love you."

"No more pretending. No more lies, I promise." Mara laced her fingers through his, not caring about the pain in her palm, as long as she could claim Tham Karron as her own. "We'll go to the Guilds Council, beg for an exemption. Plead until they let me stay in the Map Makers Guild and be with you."

"Don't fuss about being chucked from the Guilds." Elver walked backward in front of them. "You have to warn people about an army of wolves charging down from the north. Even the stories in my head don't know if that will end with us being hanged. Noose first. Then sex. Put the worries in order."

"They won't hang us," Mara said.

"They might," Elver said.

"Not if we take what we know straight to the Sorcerers Guild." Mara kept her gaze fixed on Elver, ignoring the burning of Tham staring at her. "If we go to the Guilds Council, we'll be standing against the sorcerers, revealing the presence of magic outside their control, undermining the power of the Sorcerers Tower. If the Sorcerers Guild thinks we're plotting against them, the best we can hope for is a swift death. But if we go to the Lady Sorcerer herself, tell her exactly what happened and how catastrophic an attack from Isfol would be, maybe we could convince her to see us as useful allies."

Tham's hand turned to stone in her grip. The relief that had begun to trickle through her drifted away.

"I have no love for the sorcerers, but it's the best I've been able to think of," Mara said. "If someone knows a way to stop Ronya that doesn't involve the Sorcerers Guild, I'm all for it."

Elle growled and flattened her neck.

"If Ronya's wolves reach the villages north of Ilara, there

won't be any survivors," Mara said. "We have to stop her, whatever the risks."

Tham kept his gaze pinned front.

Mara gripped his hand even tighter, letting the wounds on her palm crack. "I don't know what else to do."

A hollow pain sank in her throat as Tham stayed silent.

Elle pulled at her lead, barking and growling as her paws slipped on the ice.

"You're all right, Elle." Mara let go of Tham, stepping ahead of him to peer down the tunnel.

Farther south, the blue shifted, darkening as the tunnel curved out of sight.

"Thank the gods," Mara breathed.

"What is it?" Elver tipped his head, squinting down their path.

"I've no idea," Mara said. "But it's different, and that's as good a place to start as any."

Elle kept yanking on her lead, paws scampering as she tried to bolt down the tunnel.

Mara quickened her pace, striding ahead of the men until she reached the dark spots tainting the blue of the ice.

Gray, blissfully normal stone dotted the ice, breaking through the perfection of the tunnel as though whoever had carved the passage had run out of ice and used rocks to fill in the gaps.

A hundred feet farther down, the stone and ice had been packed together in equal portions. The light within the ice shone in a strange, mottled pattern, as though protesting having been contaminated by stone.

Mara dug into her coat pocket, reaching beneath her fabric-wrapped portion of stale bread and the pen she still carried. Her fingers grazed the cold metal of Ture's ring before closing around her light and flint.

"Let me." Tham reached for the stones.

Mara opened her mouth to speak before swallowing the words she knew she'd regret.

Hurt flickered through Tham's eyes. "Your hands are bleeding."

"Thanks." Mara passed him the stones.

Keeping Elle's lead in his hand, he struck the flint and a tiny flame hissed to life.

The flame wavered on the walls as he passed the light back to Mara.

"Thank you." She caught his hand for a moment. "Truly."

He nodded and stepped behind, letting her lead the way.

Soon, stone took over the walls of the tunnel. The few spots of ice that managed to break through glowed in a feeble way, as though they'd been too separated from whatever magic fed light into the ice.

The sounds of their footsteps changed as a layer of moisture clung to the ground.

Open air. Sunlight.

Freedom.

You sell your freedom the moment you bargain with the sorcerers. Lord Karron's warning echoed through Mara's mind.

We don't have a choice, Mara whispered back. *There are degrees of evil. Ronya is a demon we cannot survive.*

The edge of her light reached a layer of texture scattered over the ground. Rocks—some larger than her head, others barely the size of her fist—had been strewn across the tunnel.

Mara knelt to examine the rocks, feeling their texture and squinting to see their color in the dim light. "They don't belong."

"Of course not," Elver said. "Tunnels are meant to have smooth floors."

"I mean the rocks didn't all come from here." Mara held up a rounded stone. "If this were from a cave-in, the rock would have jagged edges. They're different types of minerals, too. Someone brought these rocks here."

Mara replaced the stone and stood, picking her way down the tunnel, holding her light by her side to give the men behind her a chance of keeping their footing as the layer of rocks grew dense enough she had to walk on the stones.

Elle growled, snarling at something Mara couldn't see.

"You're all right," Tham said.

Mara absorbed all the comfort she could from the calm, steady tone of his voice as the rocks piled higher, sweeping all the way up to the ceiling, blocking their path.

"This isn't right." Elver cut past Mara to glare at the wall of rocks. "We were supposed to come down this tunnel, and we did. There has to be a way out."

He dug into the pile of stones, dragging handfuls out of their way. Before he had made a dent, more rocks poured down from above, filling in the hole Elver had made, widening the wall as they crashed down onto his feet.

"Chivving nightmares!" Elver's scream echoed north. "This is the way out! You terrorize me. You break me. Don't betray me!" He ripped more stones from the pile.

"Elver, no!" Mara grabbed his arm, dragging him back as rocks cascaded from the ceiling.

"But this is the path." Elver clawed at his head, trying to grip his too-short hair. "It's the way to battle. It's supposed to lead us out of the mountains. Kalene prepared the path."

"The path for Kareen." Mara dragged Elver farther away from the looming mound of rocks.

"No *Kalene*. This is her path to battle." Elver shook free from Mara's grip.

"In Whitend, they don't call the woman from the white mountains Kalene," Mara said. "They call her Kareen. They built that massive mound of rocks in the center of their village to block Kareen's path, to keep her from charging down from the mountains to slaughter them all."

"She will still come." Elver lunged toward the wall of rocks. "They're all going to die."

Tham let go of Elle's lead and caught Elver around the middle, hauling him back.

"Death will find a way!" Elver screamed.

"If I'm right, we're beneath that massive mound of stones," Mara shouted over his wails. "If we pull at those rocks, more will keep falling on us. We'll be smothered in a wave of stone before we ever come near reaching the surface."

Elver sagged in Tham's arms, sobbing as Tham lowered him to the ground.

"I can't go back." Elver spoke between gasps. "I can't let them put the chain back on."

"We're not going back." Mara sat beside Elver, rubbing his back as she studied the mountain of stones that stood between them and freedom. "We'll find a way out. I won't let anyone chain you up."

"I went to the wall, I killed the Regent, I cut off his hand, I opened the door." Elver banged his fist against the side of his head. "I did everything right."

"You did." Mara tried to keep his hands away from his head, but Elver twisted out of her reach.

"Why would it want me trapped here?" Elver whispered. Tears streamed down his face, catching in his badly chopped beard. "Why make me watch the stories in my head if I was just going to die?"

Mara reached into her pocket, unwrapping the bit of cloth around the stale bread that would be her next meal. Her fingers grazed the still-cold metal of the Regent's ring.

"Dry your face." Mara passed the cloth to Elver. "We can find a way out of here if we don't panic."

Elver toppled sideways and curled in on himself, scrubbing his face with the crumb-covered cloth.

Mara reached back into her pocket and fished out the Regent's ring. She held it close to the light, trying not to think of how easily Ture's magic might have saved them if Elver hadn't stabbed him in the stomach and chopped off his hand.

Even near the flame, the metal of the ring stayed cold.

"We have the swords," Tham said. "We could go back to where the rock and ice mix. Use the swords to try and pry a section free. See if we can dig our way out with our hands from there."

"That's what I forgot." Elver sat up, all traces of fear and worry gone. "I had to cut off a hand and not a foot because the hand had his ring and Mara needs the Regent's ring."

"How could it be useful to me?" Mara held the ring out to Elver.

"The ice. The ice!" Elver scrambled to his feet.

"The Regent could control ice. I can't," Mara said.

"Not the Regent, the ring." Elver grabbed Mara's wrist, yanking her to her feet and dragging her back up the tunnel. "The ring controls the ice. The old Queen gave it to the Regent so Ronya couldn't lock him up. But he's dead, and you have the ring, so you control the magic. Make the ice open, and we can go up to the sky and breathe."

Elle bolted past them, carrying her lead in her teeth.

"Even if Ture used the ring to control the ice, that doesn't mean I can." Mara tripped on a rock, barely keeping her footing as Elver dragged her north.

"You can. You've already done it," Elver said. "I've seen the story in my head."

"The stories in your mind may have been true enough to lead us here, but I promise I've never used magic."

Elver skidded to a halt right below the place where rocks stopped contaminating the ice of the tunnel walls. "Put it on."

"Elver—"

"Put it on." He snatched the ring from her and shoved it onto her finger.

The cold of the ring spread through her hand, dulling the ache of the cuts on her palm.

"Now make the magic go." Elver beamed at her.

"I can't," Mara said. "I'm sorry. I don't know how to use magic."

"Don't lie." Elver's joy vanished. "You promised no more lies. I've seen you use magic. I've seen it. You carry the tube with the scrolls. You make the magic in the scrolls go with your mind to make the maps." He flicked Mara on the forehead. "Now make it go."

"He's right." A wrinkle of worry pinched between Tham's eyebrows. "It's using a magically forged tool."

"Make it go." Elver jabbed his finger into Mara's forehead. "Do it."

"I'll try." Mara swatted Elver's hand away and shut her eyes, sweating like a fool as she felt the others staring at her.

She focused on the cold in her hand. It didn't bite. It soothed. The cold wanted to be liked, welcomed even.

She pushed away the hint of fear that tainted the pleasure the cold offered.

A tingle—subtle, painless—longed to surround more than her hand.

Magic.

The magic wrapped around her, cradling her as a mother would a newborn babe. Gentle. Protective.

She pulled her thoughts away from the ebbing of the aches in her body as the ring soothed the fatigue born of traveling through the tunnel for days.

There, in the back of her mind, a different kind of tingle, as though her thoughts were reaching out of her body, blending with something much larger than herself.

She sank into the sensation, letting her mind mingle with the magic.

They needed a way out. That's all. Simple. Easy.

The ice in the ceiling should shift, forming a staircase.

The ice just below the surface above them should tilt up like a trapdoor, pushing away any dirt or snow that might block their path.

The stairs didn't have to be anything fancy, just steps that would allow them to climb.

She reached for the wall, keeping her eyes closed as she pressed her fingertips to the ice.

Cold flowed up her arm to her neck, then climbed higher, encircling the part of her mind where magic met thought.

As she pictured the stairs unfurling from the ceiling, the cold sank into her chest, filling her lungs with a strange vibrancy she didn't understand.

She imagined the top layer of ice pushing up, opening their path.

A sharp crack sounded from above.

Mara gasped, opening her eyes as Tham grabbed her, pressing her to the wall, sheltering her head with his chest.

But the cascade of falling debris only lasted a few seconds.

Tham kept her pinned for a breath before pulling away just enough to be able to look at her. He stared into her eyes, searching for something, as he brushed a curl away from her forehead. "Are you hurt?"

"I'm fine." Mara pressed her palm to his cheek. "I promise."

Tham leaned into her touch.

"Did I make something happen?" Mara asked. "Did I make it worse?"

He stepped aside, letting Mara see past his broad chest.

A staircase reached up from the ground, cutting through the ceiling of the tunnel.

"I told you you knew how," Elver called from up above.

"It actually worked." Mara touched the side of the steps, trailing her fingers along the ice. The cold of it tingled up her arm as though the magic within the ice were greeting her.

"Come on!" Elver shouted.

Elle shook the dirt from her fur and raced up the stairs, barking like mad.

"You next." Tham put his hand on the back of her waist, making sure she knew he was there, making sure she felt safe even though she'd just done the impossible.

Mara pulled off the ring. The magnificent cold faded away.

"Not yet," Tham said. "You have to seal the path behind us."

"Of course." Mara climbed the stairs, ignoring the fear gnawing at the edges of her wonder.

The steps cut up through a thick layer of ice, but even when the ground gave way to dirt, the ice of the stairs reached higher, leading all the way to the open air.

Stars gleamed in the moonless night sky. A chill wind whipped over the snow-covered ground. To the south, the faint lights of a village peered through the darkness.

"I'm free." Elver sat in the snow, tears streaming down his cheeks. "I don't have to go back. It's gone. It's all gone. It's quiet. I'd forgotten it could be so quiet."

Tham climbed out of the ground, looking to Mara before turning his gaze up to the stars.

Mara slipped the ring back on and knelt beside the stairs, willing the ice to close the path behind them.

The stairs rose up, folding in on themselves to create a solid sheet of ice. The ground beside Mara tipped, dropping a pile of dirt onto the ice that had been the stairs, before melding with the snow-covered ground.

The dark scar of rogue dirt marring the snow left the only trace of the magic wrought by Mara Landil.

41

ADRIAL

Though the mines in the south bore precious jewels, there were none that seemed to please the sorcerers who oversaw our enterprise.

We continued to dig through the rains of the early fall, counting on the milder clime to keep us comfortable through the winter months. The miners brought many complaints to my desk, but none of the men were bold enough to decline the opportunity to work when the sorcerers presented their case.

Sorcerers and mines.

Sorcerers and black stones.

Adrial dug his knuckles into his eyes, picturing a map of the southernmost region of Ilbrea.

So much had changed in the seventy years since the account was written. Now, the southern lands were plagued by drought. They had been for years.

Most of the documents he'd handled for that territory involved farmers either begging for aid or failing to pay their taxes. Never once had he filed papers for mining.

In fact, the only account of the southern mines he'd found

was in the journal that lay open on his desk. And, if the writer was to be considered reliable, the mining operation was not successful enough to be worth continuing.

Unfortunately, the journal was also the only reference he'd been able to find that tied the Sorcerers Guild to mining of any kind.

Chivving cact of a chivving demon spawn. A silent laugh shook his chest. *My wife is a bad influence.*

Adrial opened his eyes, blinking in the dim glow of the light above his desk.

"There's got to be something here," he whispered to the book.

Room filled with black stone. Sorcerers can destroy the palace.

Those were the only clues Allora had written on the map she'd slipped into his hand at Kai's funeral. There had been a horde of sorcerers and soldiers watching her. If she'd taken the risk of pressing a paper into his palm, the information had to mean something.

He returned to the old scribe's journal.

A sorcerer rode down from Ilara, calling a halt to all mining. The men and I were confined to the drab tents we call home, forbidden from even peeking outside for two days' time.

My station has always granted me a tent of my own. Never in my life have I been so grateful for solitude.

Through the canvas of my poor dwelling, I could hear the troubles of the other men, some of whom were clustered three or even five to a tent as small as my own. The crude daily business of a living body should not be shared in such close quarters. I do not think the men will forgive the sorcerers for their lack of compassion, even if the new location they've chosen for us to dig proves to be as profitable as they believe it will be.

Shit. Adrial Ayres, the Head Scribe of Ilara, heir to the Lord Scribe, had resorted to sneaking out of bed to read about shit.

He shut the book and leaned back in his chair, waiting for a sudden stroke of inspiration or perseverance to strike.

Neither came.

Tucking the journal under his arm, he turned off the lamp and crept toward the bedroom.

Ena lay in bed, her hair splayed out behind her, her shoulder peeking out of her shift.

He could curl up with her and grab a few hours' sleep before morning.

No one could fault him for a wanting to lie in bed beside his wife. Kai would want him to. Allora herself would needle him to, telling him a mind couldn't work well without rest.

He knelt beside the wardrobe, reaching beneath to tuck the book up onto the lip of the wood where neither maid nor spy would find it. He pushed himself back to his feet and slipped into bed, his mind spiraling into dreams of dark magic before he'd settled his head on his pillow.

The covers shifted, leaving his torso cold as Ena threw them back.

"I'm sorry." Adrial pushed himself up on his elbows. "I didn't mean to wake you."

"I gathered that from your creeping through the darkness." She cut around the bed and knelt beside the wardrobe.

"Ena, what are you doing?" Adrial kicked the covers away.

"Finding out what has my husband sneaking out of bed." She reached up under the wardrobe.

"It's nothing. Truly, I swear."

"You're a good scribe and a wonderful man, but you're a terrible liar."

"Please don't, Ena." He knelt beside her, the pain in his hip adding to his panic.

Ena stopped fumbling under the wardrobe. She met his gaze as she pulled out the journal. "A book. Such a strange thing for a scribe to hide."

"Please, give me the book and go back to bed. I'm trying to protect you." He held out his hand. "It's safer for you and the baby if you're not involved."

"Safer for *us* means whatever's in this book is dangerous for *you*." She clutched the journal to her chest. "My safety means nothing without you, scribe. Whatever danger you find, we face it together."

"Ena." He reached for the book.

"Do not push me, scribe." She stood, backing out of his reach. "Losing you is a wound I will not bear. Tell me what is in this book."

"I'm begging you—"

"I'll read it myself." She stormed past him, heading toward the sitting room.

"Allora slipped me a map at Kai's ceremony." He sat, leaning against the wardrobe, burying his face in his hands.

"A map of what?"

"From what I can tell, it's a section of hidden passages leading through the palace."

"I'm not surprised that place has tunnels for vermin built into the walls."

"The more worrying part is the warning she wrote on the map. I can't understand what she's talking about. I've been trying to research as best I can, but the whole thing's a mess." He looked up at Ena. "It's something to do with the sorcerers. You and the baby need to stay well away from anything to do with those monsters."

"What was the warning?" Ena loosened her hold on the book as though daring Adrial to try and snatch it from her.

"The map is tucked in the front of the journal. Turn the light on and have a look. I don't want to keep secrets from you. I only want to protect my family."

"No one in Ilara is safe with the sorcerers rampaging through the city every other night." She lit the lamp next to the bed and sat beside Adrial on the floor.

He'd tucked the folded and wrinkled map inside the book so he could take it out and stare at it as he tried to muddle through the miseries of a scribe assigned to minding mining operations.

Ena smoothed out the map on the cover of the journal. She trailed her finger along the corridors on the first page before flipping to the second.

She froze, her finger hovering over Allora's scrawled words.

Room filled with black stone. Sorcerers can destroy the palace.

"I've been trying to figure out what black stone she might be talking about." Adrial scrubbed his palm over the stubble on his chin. "It's not black mining powder, or Allora would have just written that. This journal mentions black stone, but not what it is or why the sorcerers were looking for it, or if they ever found it."

"Mountain stone." Ena folded the map and tucked it back in the cover of the book. "She's saying there's mountain stone under the palace. At least, that's the name I've always known it by."

"Mountain stone?" Adrial dug through his memory, trying to find a time he'd ever heard of it.

"It's not common in Ilbrea. Really, it shouldn't be in Ilbrea at all. It belongs to the Black Bloods."

"Black Bloods?"

"From the stories of bandits and ghosts that haunt the eastern mountains. The Black Bloods are real, living people, and they're connected to the eastern mountains by more than simple magic. Mountain stone being outside the eastern mountains is nothing but a curse for everyone it touches." Her fingers shook as she clasped the stone pendant around her neck.

"Ena, is that—are you wearing mountain stone?"

"If the sorcerers truly have a room filled with mountain stone, they could easily bring the whole palace down, most of the city, too, if they aren't careful. The sorcerers are chivving fools."

"How could they bring the palace down?" Adrial twisted to kneel in front of her. "It's just stone."

"It's not. Mountain stone can be infused with magic. Most of it's good magic. It can protect you from horrible things, give light in the darkest of places. But if mountain stone is twisted into a weapon, the damage it can do…I promise you, you can't imagine how deadly mountain stone can be."

"Then why are you wearing it?"

Ena didn't stop him when he moved her hand to examine her pendant.

"There's no magic in this stone. Not anymore. It's nothing but a shiny rock." She held his gaze. There was no fear or secrecy in her eyes. "I still can't make myself take it off."

"The sorcerers couldn't use it to hurt you?"

"The Sorcerers Guild would have to steal it and work their vile spells on it to make it dangerous. But even this bit of stone could kill dozens of people if it got into the wrong sorcerer's hands."

"And Allora is living above a cache of it."

"Murderous brilliance on the sorcerers' part." Ena looked up at the ceiling. "I don't think there's a chivving thing we could do to get the stone away from them. Even if Allora could sneak it out bit by bit, she'd be caught before she stole enough to make a difference. And if they put that much below the palace, where else have they hidden their weapons ready to destroy the city? How much have they stored in their tower?"

"The tower." Cold terror encased Adrial's lungs. "The Sorcerers Tower is made of black stone."

"It's not mountain stone. It doesn't burn with the same seductive power. There's a purple hint to it when the sun strikes it from the right angle." Ena reached for his hand. "I don't know if they built their tower in a sad mimicry of mountain stone, or if its stone making holds some power in its own right. Either way, the gods showed a hint of mercy when they didn't give the sorcerers enough mountain stone to build their lair. I can't even make myself imagine how much damage a tower of mountain stone could do."

Adrial laced his fingers through hers. "The Black Bloods and mountain stone, how do you know so much about them? Ena, did you come from the eastern mountains?" His arm pressed against hers as she pulled him to sit right by her side.

"I'm from Ilbrea." She laid her free hand on her belly, as though trying to protect the child from whatever secrets she still couldn't share. "I went into the mountains searching for someone. I stayed for a while. The girl I was when I lived with the myths hiding in the east died a long time ago. But I can't forget the things that girl saw. The gods should never have allowed such magic to exist.

"With mountain stone, the sorcerers could bring down the palace or library or anything they please in a blast that lights the sky with fire that burns your eyes. We wouldn't see it coming, and there's not a chivving thing we could do to stop them."

"Ena—"

"Don't you even for a moment suggest I leave the city without you. Whatever weapons the paun sorcerers have, my place is with you, and I will not leave your side."

An odd armor grew around the fear in Adrial's chest. He kissed the back of her hand. "If you won't leave Ilara, then we'll find a way to protect the city from the sorcerers' weapons."

"I've never heard of anything that could stand up to a mountain stone-made weapon."

"Then we stand up to the sorcerers themselves." He kissed her hand again.

"Slay the demons." She leaned her head on his shoulder.

"I'd tear down the stars to protect my family. Stopping the

sorcerers only sounds a bit more difficult than ripping apart the sky."

42

KAI

The scent of foul liquor only the most desperate of slitches would dare to drink stung Kai's nose as it filled the air trapped beneath the thick, black blanket that was his poor hope of safety.

He reached to his right, feeling for his line of glass bottles even though their stench promised they hadn't disappeared.

One, two, three, four, five, six. All lined up in the sling, filled with liquor, topped with a cloth, and ready for whatever nightmare might come. He checked the flint and liquor-soaked candle he'd nestled between the roof's shingles before easing his hand to his pocket, making sure he hadn't lost the spare flint he'd tucked away.

He sighed and rested his cheek against the damp roof, wishing he had listened to Allora on one of the hundred occasions she'd told him to practice being patient.

The blanket shifted as Drew reached over, letting his fingers drape across Kai's left hand.

Kai's gratitude at not being alone under the blanket, suffocating on the fumes of cheap liquor, could not outweigh his worry.

He lifted his hand just enough to weave his fingers through Drew's.

They had agreed to the plan. It was the best plan the underground had.

There was nothing for them to do but lie on the roof, choking on the awful stench, and wait.

You're not a soldier, Kai, Tham whispered. *There is no shame in running from this fight.*

Someone has to stand up to the sorcerers, Kai whispered back. *There's no reason it shouldn't be me. I've got decent aim. I've already taken a life.*

This will be different, Kai. You and I both know it.

The clomping of hooves carried through the darkness.

Drew squeezed Kai's hand before slipping his away.

Kai held his breath, willing his heart to stay silent.

The clomping reached the street hidden behind the peak of the roof where Kai and Drew lay.

The clomping stopped.

One of the horses stomped his hooves. There was definitely more than one horse, but Kai couldn't tell how many from the clacking of metal on stone.

Kai slipped his flint from between the shingles and reached his hands over his head.

A rumble of voices came from below. Then a lilting laugh.

Kai dug the toes of his boots into the roof.

His heartbeat pounded in his ears, muddying the sounds from the street.

Patience, sweet Kai, Allora whispered. *Patience.*

Sweat slicked Kai's hands, threatening his grip on the flint.

Patience.

Bang!

The sound ripped through the night.

Kai sprang up onto his knees, striking his flint as he tossed the blanket behind him.

The scent of sulfur and smoke tainted his first breath of fresh air.

He couldn't see what damage the explosion below had managed as he lit the liquor-soaked candle and pulled himself to the peak of the roof.

He grabbed the first of his bottles.

The fabric tucked into the top of the glass caught fire. He looked down onto the street to take aim and gained his first glimpse of the scene below.

The front wall of the shop across the street had exploded, crumbling out onto the sorcerers who had come to raid the milliner.

An arrow flew from the left, striking a sorcerer in the back.

The man nearest the shot sorcerer spun toward the archer.

Kai took aim, tossing his bottle at the man's feet.

The bottle exploded in flames, setting fire to the hem of the man's purple robes.

Kai ducked down, lit his second bottle, then yanked himself back up to the peak of the roof. In the moment Kai had lost sight of the sorcerer, the man had extinguished the flames on his robes, but he was too busy aiming a spell at the archer to notice the blaze growing on the street.

All the gods should bless Merial for spending her day planting liquor and black mining powder on the street as she paced in front of the milliner's while dozens of unwitting passersby hid her preparations for the evening's violence.

One of the sorcerers lay on the ground, separated from the flames by the rubble from the milliner's front wall. Kai threw his second bottle at her, willing the fire to consume her before any of her fellows could offer aid.

A horrible scream came from the left.

Kai lit his third bottle.

The flames on the street had grown bright enough to give him a decent view of the fight.

Four sorcerers standing. Two on the ground, one covered in flames.

Kai threw his bottle at the base of the building to the right of the milliner's.

One of the sorcerers looked toward the crash of the smashing glass.

Kai ducked below the peak of the roof as she spun toward him.

He lit his fourth bottle.

Bang!

Flames leapt up into the night.

Kai raised his arm to take aim. The corner of the building where he'd thrown his third bottle had exploded. The sorcerer who'd looked his way had been tossed aside by the blast.

Kai thew his bottle at her head. The glass shattered against her skull, catching her hair on fire.

He felt no pity as she screamed.

He lit his fifth bottle.

A sorcerer stood in the middle of the chaos, untouched by the flames that roared around her. She looked up at the bottle in Kai's hand and grinned.

Kai threw the bottle at the building to the left of the milliner's.

"We have to go!" He grabbed Drew's arm instead of his last bottle, dragging Drew away from the fight and toward the lip of the roof.

The world tilted as the roof rocked, sinking before pulsing out in a silent explosion, shooting Kai and Drew into the air in a storm of splintered wood.

Kai exhaled, relaxing his limbs and begging the gods for mercy as he flew over a roof and plummeted toward the next street over.

He rolled as he hit the ground, losing his grip on Drew as he tumbled over the stones of the street and crashed into a building.

He gasped in a breath only to hack it back out again as the pain in his ribs sent stars dancing through his vision.

Bang!

The third explosion shot a burst of flames into the sky. The beauty of the underground's work sent shadows dancing across the destruction on the street.

Splintered wood. Broken shingles. A body lying in the center of it all.

"Drew!"

He lay on his back, his arms splayed at his sides.

Kai lurched to his feet, fighting against the swaying of the street as his brain sloshed in his head. "Drew!"

Drew coughed, gasping as he tried to move.

"We have to go." Kai stumbled as he bent over to help Drew up.

Drew turned his head and spat blood onto the ground, stealing the bit of relief Kai had dared to feel.

"Get up. We've got to run." Kai spread his feet wide, steadying himself as he bent over, looping an arm behind Drew and hauling him to his feet.

Drew screamed and spat another round of blood onto the wreckage strewn around him.

"Yes, I know it's very painful, but we have to go." Kai braced Drew against his side, ignoring the pain raging through his own body as he dragged Drew down the street.

A high, wailing scream sliced through the night.

Drew got his feet under him, managing a few steps before tipping forward.

"Don't do this, Drew." Kai dragged him around the corner. "You're not allowed to chivving die on me. You know that."

"Sorry." Drew turned his head to hack out more blood. "I'll do my best." He wrapped his arm around Kai's shoulder, bracing his weight against him as he limped forward.

"Your best isn't good enough." Kai looked back, paying for the movement with a pain that shot from his ear to his ass. The street behind them was clear. "If you die on me, I'll live the rest of my days as a heartbroken shell of a man. You can't do that to me."

"You'll find someone to comfort you." Drew panted the words. "They'll line up to offer you a distraction. It's always the way of it."

"I could roll every willing getch in Ilbrea, and I'd still be heartbroken." Kai cut across the street, aiming for an alley between two houses. "The gods have never created a soul that could replace you."

"You don't have to lie to try and keep me alive, old friend."

"It's not a lie." Kai sidled into the alley, dragging Drew along beside him. "I'd be yours in an instant if you were ever fool enough to want me."

"You flit around flirting with everyone who gives you a glance and end up in bed with half of them." Drew coughed. Flecks of blood speckled the wall in front of him.

"So you don't want me because I enjoy a good roll? I'd have thought my expertise would be an asset." Kai stopped in the center of the alley, peeking around Drew to make sure the street was clear before stomping five times on the widest of the stones in the ground.

"Wanting you has never been the problem." Drew sagged against the wall. "It's sharing you I couldn't stand. A few nights of fun wouldn't be enough for me, and a lifetime sharing a bed with the same person doesn't interest you."

"I never said that."

The wide stone shifted, lifting up before sliding over, leaving a hole just wide enough to climb into.

"I need help getting him down." Kai leaned against the wall, squeezing Drew in front of him toward the hole.

Blood covered the back of Drew's head.

"Chivving demon's spawn." Landon reached out of the hole,

taking Drew's waist, while Kai held him under the arms, both of them barely managing to lower Drew into the ground.

"He needs a healer," Kai said.

"I figured that." Landon reached for Kai.

Kai took his hand, forgetting any pretense of pride as Landon steadied him while he turned onto the slanted ladder that led below the alley.

"Someone needs to check aboveground for blood. The sorcerers will know we fled this way. We can't risk them looking too closely at the alley." Kai gripped the ladder rails, carefully moving his hands and feet down one step at a time, trying to decide which of the pains in his body came from injured bones and which from torn flesh.

"I'll send one of the lads up."

"Thank you." Kai's feet reached level ground. He kept his gaze fixed on the ladder, too afraid of turning to find Drew crumpled on the ground, wounded beyond any healer's aid.

"I've been worse off before." Drew coughed.

A wave of relief rolled through Kai, somehow tripling the pain in his limbs.

"That doesn't make it much better," a man said. "Get his shirt off and get him on a cot. I don't like that cough."

Kai turned, watching as the girl cut away the bloody remnants of Drew's shirt.

"You're bleeding." The man rounded on Kai. "Don't linger. Get on the other cot. The sooner I get through taking care of you two, the better off we'll be if any more wounded crawl through my ceiling."

Kai sat on the second cot.

"He's got a lot of blood on the back of his head," the girl said.

"Still more worried about the coughing blood," the man snapped. "Do as I say, girl."

"Yes, Papa."

"I'll be fine," Drew groaned as the girl helped him lie down.

"I've been told I'm not allowed to die or I'll break the only man I've ever cared for."

"And I've been told my flitting days are through." Kai winced as he unbuttoned his shirt. "Can't bounce from bed to bed if it'll break my love's heart."

Drew looked to Kai. A smile flickered through his pain before the doctor stepped between them, stealing Kai's view of the most beautiful face in all Ilbrea.

43

ADRIAL

"There's got to be more to it, Taddy." Adrial added another jar of blue ink to the collection that stretched the length of his work-table. He squinted at the hues, trying to choose the exact right shade for the bright edge of the sky the storm hadn't managed to consume.

"I've gone down to pester the guards at the gates twice, sir." Taddy bounced on his toes.

"You aren't pestering them," Adrial said. "You are doing your work as my apprentice."

"Yes, sir." Taddy cut around the table to face Adrial. "I've gone down to ask them for new reports twice this morning. There was a sorcerer-led raid in the city last night. But, as far as I can tell, no one was wounded, and no buildings were destroyed."

Adrial held a jar of sparkling, pale blue up to the lantern, wishing the sun were out so he could better see the color. "It's not right. There was a fire in the merchants' section of the city, I saw the flames from my window."

"That's what I told the guards, sir. I said there was a raid last night, so *something* bad had to have happened to *something* in the city. It's how the sorcerers have been doing business for weeks. But the guards promised me twice that their account was right."

"Thank you for double checking, Taddy." Adrial held a slightly brighter blue up to the lantern. The hue had a cheerfulness blended into the color that brought a smile to his lips, despite the worry gnawing at his gut.

"I could, sir"—Taddy bounced more quickly—"I could go out into the city and check for you. See if there really weren't any buildings brought down. The wounded would be harder to check on, but I could—"

"Under no circumstances are you going out into the city, Taddy."

"But if we know the reports are lies, we have to—"

"—send an adult to scour the city for information." Adrial held a third ink up to the light. The painfully beautiful hue whisked the air from his lungs, as though his wife had embodied the color of mourning. "You've already been bloodied up on my account once, Taddy. I'll not have you put in danger again. Wait two hours. Go back to the gates and ask for a third report. If nothing's changed, I'll find a scribes' guard who's willing to go out into the city."

"Yes, sir." Taddy bowed.

"Go work on your papers for a bit. I don't want the troubles in the city to put you behind in your studies."

"Helping you track the damage in the city is more important than my transcriptions, sir." Pink flooded the boy's cheeks. "I'm sorry if it's out of line, but I'd take being set back a year as an apprentice if it meant getting more work done for you."

"Thank you, Taddy." Adrial set the jar of mournful blue ink beside his pens. "Let's make sure it doesn't come to that."

"He's in his office." Tammin's voice carried through the door. "But he's working now. If there's something I could help you with."

A sharp knock rapped on the door right before it flung open.

Taddy planted himself in front of Adrial as a Guilded soldier stepped through the door.

"The head scribe's office should not be barged into," Tammin shouted.

The soldier ignored her as he bowed to Adrial. "Head Scribe, your immediate presence is required in the scribes' gallery."

A sorcerer stepped into view behind the soldier.

"May I inquire as to who has sent you to barge into my office?" Adrial asked.

"Lady Gwell, Map Maker Traim, Lady Byrd, Lord Gareth, and the King himself." The soldier stepped aside, bowing Adrial through the door. "It would be wise for you to come with me, Head Scribe."

The sorcerer shifted out of Adrial's path.

"Of course." A cold calm stilled Adrial's racing heart. He pushed a placid smile onto his face. "One does not deny a summons from their King."

He kept his gait even as he walked out of his office and into the work room beyond. Three of his scribes' desks were empty.

Tammin stepped out from behind the sorcerer, her usual color drained from her face.

Taddy bounced from foot to foot on Adrial's heels, as though intending to follow him all the way to the scribes' gallery.

"Tammin, oversee Taddy's work." Adrial held her gaze. "I don't want him falling behind on today's assignments."

"Yes, Head Scribe." Tammin cut around Adrial, grabbing Taddy's arm and holding him in place.

"But, Head Scribe—"

"Get to your work, Taddy. I'll be back to check it soon," Adrial said.

The sorcerer pursed her lips.

Adrial fixed his gaze on the door to the hall. That was the first step—make himself walk to the hall.

Whatever fate Dudia had waiting for him, he could walk to the hall as a brave, free man.

It was the reports he'd been giving in the council meetings. He'd intentionally caused a stir, forcing the Guild leaders to face the casualties of the sorcerers' wave of violence. The council had grown tired of his rabblerousing and decided to banish him from the Scribes Guild.

Unless the sorcerers had found out he'd been researching the danger of the black stone hidden beneath the palace. If they'd found out Allora had sent him the map, they'd both be punished by the Sorcerers Guild.

Would the King have come to the scribes' gallery to tell Adrial he would hang beside Allora in the cathedral square?

Would they be hanged side by side?

Or, worst of all, had the sorcerers managed to find the true maps hidden in Lord Karron's estate?

The sorcerers would seek vengeance on the whole Karron clan.

Would they hang him and Allora now? Or wait for Mara, Tham, and Lord Karron to come home so they could all swing together?

Panic overwhelmed his façade of calm, amplifying the pain in his leg to a gut-slicing throb as he approached the scribes' gallery.

Ena. The baby.

They needed to be safe. He needed to protect them.

Ena could defend herself.

Not that she should need to. There was no reason for her to be implicated in any of the trouble Adrial had wrapped around his own neck.

He'd been careful. Never told a soul what Ena knew of the black stone or Black Bloods or fighting sorcerers.

But the book hidden under the wardrobe. If the sorcerers thought it was hers…

He would confess to having hidden the book. Make sure they

understood that *he* had been reading the old journal. Ena had nothing to do with it.

As long as Ena and the baby were safe, he could bravely face his doom.

Six soldiers flanked the entrance to the Scribes' Hall. Two sorcerers stood in front of the platform where Ena had agreed to be Adrial's wife just a few short months before.

He should have been more grateful for his time with her.

He should run. Flee whatever doom waited for him in the gallery.

He wouldn't make it twenty feet.

Better to face his fate bravely. Be sure he had a chance to protect Ena from any suspicion.

The five Guild leaders who had summoned him waited on the platform.

Lord Gareth sat behind the rest. His shoulders rounded. His weathered face dripping with tears.

Adrial truly had been summoned to his slaughter.

One other person wearing scribe white lurked beside the platform.

Scribe Travers Gend smiled as he bowed to Adrial.

Adrial straightened his spine, staring at the place where he and Ena had exchanged their vows.

"Scribe Adrial Ayres." King Brannon's voice thundered around the gallery.

The doors shut behind Adrial with a dull thump.

"It has come to the attention of the Guilds Council that a most egregious error in justice has taken place within the Guilds." The King kept his gaze fixed over Adrial's head, as though he'd forbidden himself from looking at his wife's truest friend. "It is our duty as leaders of the Guilds to address this error."

You are not a coward like your King.

Adrial's uneven footsteps echoed around the room as he walked closer to the platform. "I am sorry to display my ignorance, Your Majesty, but I'm afraid I don't know what injustice has occurred."

"It has come to the council's attention that you have broken the law of paternity sans matrimony," the King said.

"What?" Slow tendrils of terror seeped into Adrial's mind, muddying his thoughts.

"The laws of Ilbrea provide punishment for a man who waits to marry a woman until after she is with child," the King said. "The laws of Ilbrea apply to Guild members as much as to common men."

"Your Majesty, whatever rumors have reached you—"

"There are no rumors." Lady Gwell stepped forward to stand beside the King. "Healers have already examined your wife. They have confirmed she became pregnant well before you were married."

"They had no right to touch her!" Adrial looked back toward the door.

The sorcerer and soldier who'd come to his office blocked his path to escape. To her.

"The laws of Ilbrea demand forty-two lashes for men found guilty of impregnating a woman outside wedlock," Lady Gwell said.

"That law has not been used in years," Adrial said. "The practical use of the law was found to contradict its original intent years ago."

"Shameful for a scribe to be ignorant of the state of our laws. The lashes are regularly given to rotta in Ilbrea." Lady Gwell looked to Map Maker Traim.

"Members of the Guilds do not deserve different justice than common folk," Traim said. "Neither your station within the Scribes Guild nor any relation to Lord Karron can excuse your actions."

"Do you seek vengeance for being denied the Map Master's Palace, Traim?" Adrial said. "Is that why you're standing with the

Lady Sorcerer?"

Traim stepped behind Lady Gwell, his gaze nailed to the floor of the platform.

"Your marrying a pregnant bride is a disgusting misuse of power. The Guilded cannot be allowed to place themselves above the law," Lady Byrd said.

"Adrial Ayres, you have been sentenced to forty-two lashes for the offense of paternity sans matrimony." Lady Gwell stepped to the edge of the platform. "By a majority vote of the Guilds Council, in the unlikely event you survive your lashings, you will be stripped of your position within the Scribes Guild."

"You can't do this. You can't punish me for getting married!" Adrial's shout echoed around the gallery.

One of the sorcerers in front of the platform waved her hand.

Heat wrapped around Adrial's wrists as a bright band of light locked them together. He stared at his trapped hands.

Bound. Useless.

Even free, he hadn't a hope of fighting his way through sorcerers and soldiers.

"For the sake of your dignity, accept your punishment with grace," Lady Gwell said.

"Leave the boy alone." Lord Gareth pushed himself to his feet. "This is barbaric. You cannot commit murder in my library."

"No one has mentioned murder. Our only aim is justice. If the former head scribe is too weak to survive the penalty for his crime, none of us can be blamed. The law is the law." Lady Gwell nodded to a soldier on the side of the gallery.

He strode toward Adrial, dragging a whip behind him. Three-inch-long spikes stuck out of the leather. The metal clawed through the wooden floor with an ear-splitting screech.

Sweat slicked Adrial's skin. His heart raced, flying through as many beats as it could before the spikes of the whip ripped through his flesh.

The sorcerers in front of the platform grinned, bloodlust

dancing in their eyes. Travers kept his hands tucked behind his back, a solemnity hanging about him as though he were attending a dignified funeral.

"You cannot do this!" Lord Gareth shouted. "This is murder. Outright murder!"

"Lord Gareth." An eerie calm stilled Adrial's heart. "Promise me you'll take care of her. Whatever happens, take care of Ena."

A heavy blow struck Adrial behind the knees. His legs buckled. An invisible force kept his chest upright as his knees struck the ground.

"No. No, you cannot do this!" Lord Gareth reached for Lady Gwell. He screamed as his arms plastered themselves to his sides.

"See that Ena is cared for." Adrial kept his gaze fixed on the Lord Scribe. "Nothing else matters."

"How sweet," Lady Byrd said. "If only you'd put such care into protecting the rotta before you slipped a child into her."

"Please, Lord Gareth," Adrial whispered.

"She shall be my own daughter." Lord Gareth spoke through his tears. "I swear to you."

The whip shrieked across the floor as the soldier drew his hand back.

"Thank you," Adrial said.

White hot pain crashed across his back. The force of the blow knocked him forward. His forehead struck the ground.

An invisible force lifted him, shoving him back onto his knees as the soldier drew his whip back for another blow.

The second lash knocked the air from his lungs. A chill band tightened around his neck, keeping him from falling forward.

It was worth it.

Letting them beat him and kill him would be worth it.

He tried to picture it. Ena holding the baby. Safe and healthy.

A scream tore from his throat as the third lash struck.

Pain sent sparks bursting through his mind, stealing the beautiful image of his wife and child.

His pulse thundered in his ears as his heart tried again to prove its worth.

A bang echoed over the fourth lash.

"Shut the door." The command pierced the pain. "These proceedings are not to be interrupted."

"Stop!" The shout carried over Adrial's scream as the whip tore his flesh again.

"It has come to my attention that the head scribe has been falsely accused," a familiar voice shouted. "Forgive me if I am speaking out of turn, Lady Sorcerer, but I am sure the Guilds Council would not want to punish an innocent member of the Guilds, especially the head scribe."

"I promise you the head scribe is guilty of the crime for which he is receiving his due punishment."

"No, he's not." Ena's voice rang through Adrial's mind.

The band around his throat loosened. He tipped forward, falling face first onto the ground.

"I assure you my healers can tell how far along a woman is."

Adrial blinked past the spots dancing in his eyes as Lady Byrd stepped to the front of the platform.

"Head Scribe Adrial Ayres knowingly married a woman with a child already growing in her womb," Lady Byrd said.

"He didn't," Ena said.

Pain radiated through Adrial's back as he twisted to see her standing beside Tammin.

"Ena." He choked on her name, coughing blood onto the perfectly polished floor.

She didn't look at him.

"The head scribe didn't know I was carrying a child when he married me," Ena said. "I never told him. He's innocent."

"You poor thing. I'm afraid ignorance does not equal innocence," Lady Gwell said. "Adrial Ayres impregnated an unmarried woman. For that, he shall be punished."

Ena's gaze flicked down to Adrial for a moment so quick, it seemed impossible that it could fill him with such painful terror.

"I'm afraid you're mistaken again, Lady Sorcerer." Ena curtsied.

"Ena, run." Adrial gagged on his own blood. A weight clapped around his mouth, stealing his shout.

"Whoever has been whispering in your ear is a fool." Ena stepped in front of Adrial. He couldn't see her face. "If you're looking for a villain, blame the head scribe's common whore of a wife. You should let my husband go before you embarrass yourselves."

Lord Gareth swayed. Map Maker Traim caught him before he hit the ground.

"Cheeky little rotta. I admire your attempt to protect your husband," Lady Gwell said, "but you have no business—"

"I didn't share a bed with my husband until our wedding night," Ena said. "The child isn't his."

The gag shoved Adrial's scream back down his throat. He banged his fists on the floor, begging her to look at him.

"You already killed this child's father." Ena strolled closer to the platform. "One of the rebels that started all your trouble in Ilara. He was bent on blood. It was either lift my skirt for him or wait for his knife to slit an innocent throat. I chose the path that didn't end in death. But I'm sure that doesn't matter to you."

Adrial banged on the floor again and again. A sharp shock shoved him back to his knees. Invisible talons pierced his arms, pinning him in place.

"Adrial Ayres married a woman he'd never touched. He didn't father a bastard. He didn't wait too long to marry a woman he'd shoved a child into." Ena spread her arms wide. "I'm a whore who rolled a man on the back of a cart. The only one you can punish is me."

"You knowingly married an innocent man who was not the father of your child?" Lady Byrd sneered.

"There it is. The hatred you long to spit on filthy rotta like me." Ena tipped her head. The rainbow of her hair cascaded over her shoulder. "Your precious scribe is innocent, and you get to punish his common wife. What a beautiful day for Ilbrea's glorious Guilds."

No. Please no. Adrial fought to scream.

"If what you say is true, then you leave the Guilds Council no choice." Lady Gwell clasped her hands in front of her. "You have allowed us to punish an innocent man for your crimes. You are the basest of liars and criminals. We cannot show you mercy."

"Don't do this," Lord Gareth wheezed. "You've no cause."

"Lady Gwell, if we could consider—"

"Ena Ayres will be sent to Ian Ayres." Lady Gwell flicked her finger, silencing Map Maker Traim. "Such a fitting end for the wife of a man born on the bastards' island."

The two sorcerers at the front of the platform stepped toward Ena.

Blood pounded in Adrial's ears as he tried to scream.

"I won't fight you. I wouldn't dream of robbing the Guilds Council of the joy of punishing a lowly commoner." Ena turned and strode toward the door. A flicker of silver fell from her hand as she passed Adrial.

Please. Don't. Please!

The magic that bound him twisted him around, making him watch his wife walk away without glancing back.

The gallery door flung open.

A cluster of scribes lurked in the hall.

"When you whisper rumors of the head scribe's wife, make it a tale of soul-tearing romance." Ena's voice carried back into the gallery. "A scribe who loved a girl with everything he had, and a common inker who cared for the scribe too much to let him sacrifice himself to protect her. It's the closest you'll come to the truth."

She disappeared down the hall, the flicker of her white skirt devoured by the purple robes of the sorcerers that stalked behind her.

The doors banged shut, blocking out the storm of whispers flying through the scribes beyond the gallery.

"Our business here is done. The Guilds justice has been granted." Lady Gwell snapped her fingers.

"You're sending a married woman to Ian Ayres," Map Maker Traim shouted over Lord Gareth's wheezing cry of, "This is not justice!"

Adrial tipped forward, his chest shaking with sobs before he knew he could breathe.

"I hope you are not foolish enough to blame us for your pain, Head Scribe." Lady Gwell's voice carried above the chaos. "Your wife demanded her own fate. Be grateful for her sacrifice and our forgiveness."

"Ena." He dragged himself to his knees, crawling for the door. Something hard pressed into his palm.

A silver charm lay on the floor. A bird with its wings spread wide, ready to fly far away from his reach.

"Ena!" Pain raked down Adrial's spine, blurring his vision as he scrambled to his feet, Ena's bird charm clutched in his hand. "Come back! Ena!"

Light wrapped around him, binding him from his feet to his shoulders, leaving him helpless as he screamed.

44

NIKO

If the fine clothing and note from a woman had been delivered to him in Ilara, Niko would have dressed with a thrill of delight in his heart as he pictured the pleasures the evening might offer.

But in the stronghold, a hastily scrawled note from Danu telling him to put on the clothes and be ready before dusk…that raised a different sort of awareness.

He held up the pants. Made of normal fabric with a normal cut, there didn't seem to be any danger in putting them on. He examined the boots, even shoving his hand inside, checking the heel for a secret compartment of the sort Kai favored.

He couldn't find a hint of malice hidden in the boots.

The shirt was larger than normal, made of soft white fabric that would billow in a magnificently romantic fashion if he were in the right weather with a woman he wanted to impress.

By the time Niko managed to finish dressing, two voices had begun arguing in his mind.

One sounded rather like Adrial. *Not everything is a trap. There is kindness in the world if only you allow yourself to see it.*

The other was definitely Mara. *If a snake has bitten you once, don't let its pretty colors convince you it's not a threat. A snake that's struck once will strike again.*

Doubting everyone around you is no way to live, Adrial said.

Niko stared into the mirror, running his fingers through his hair, trying to arrange himself in a way that befitted his clothes.

Wise of you, Mara said. *Don't let them see your suspicion. Hide your worry.*

A steady rapping came from the door.

Danu stepped into his room before Niko could tell her to come in. "All dressed?"

"No, I'm standing around naked." Niko planted his hands on his clearly clothed hips.

"Right, sorry." Danu shook her head, blinking for a moment before seeming to actually see Niko.

"Everything all right?"

"Sure. I'm sure it is." Danu gave him a too-bright smile.

"Could you come look at this with me?" Niko waved Danu toward the corner of the windows, as far from the door as his room would allow.

"We can't be late," Danu said.

"It'll only take a moment." Niko widened his eyes, hoping the Black Bloods knew that to be a sign of *don't be a slitch, just do as I say.*

"A quick moment." Danu hurried to join him in the corner.

"What's that bare patch in the forest." Niko pointed out the window, speaking in a loud enough voice for the guards in the hall to hear, before whispering, "What's going on, why are you nervous?"

"I'm not nervous," Danu whispered, then raised her voice to say, "It's the sorcerers' compound. They like to train their students far away from non-magical saelk like you."

"You're flustered. I've never seen you flustered. Am I being led to slaughter?" Niko cleared his throat. "Saelk, what an interesting word. I don't think I've heard the term before."

"It's not usually used in non-magical company." Danu squeezed Niko's hand. "I have no idea what's going on. I was told to bring you to the atrium, and there're extra guards to accompany us. I'm sorry, Niko. There's no choice but to follow Bryana's orders."

"If your elder's decided to torture me again, find a way to slip me a blade. If you've ever for a moment considered me your friend, let me end my life."

"We have to go."

"Danu, please." He gripped her hand with both of his. "Please."

She held his gaze. "You have my word."

She led Niko toward the door, not shaking free of him as they stepped out into the hall.

Eight guards waited to trail behind them, making sure Solcha didn't escape whatever doom Bryana had planned.

The corridors and stairs leading away from Niko's room were all empty, leaving the steady thumping of his guards' boots against the stone floor as the only sound Niko could hear over the rumble of his heartbeat pounding in his ears, until a hum of voices carried up from the atrium.

Danu held tighter to Niko's hand as the crowd in the atrium came into view.

Hundreds of Black Bloods had packed into the space with more spilling through the massive doors and onto the veranda beyond.

Niko leaned close to Danu's ear. "Do the Brien prefer public executions?"

"Depending on the crime, yes."

In a rolling shift like a wave reaching up onto the sand, the horde looked toward Niko. The murmurs of the people grew. There was an excitement in the chatter Niko couldn't quite convince himself wasn't the people's joy at getting to watch an Ilbrean bleed.

A line of guards waited at the bottom of the steps, keeping a path to the back of the atrium clear.

Niko smiled for the people, giving good natured nods in a poor attempt to ensure the Brien felt at least a little bad for showing up to watch his execution.

Maybe it will be a swift death. A blade across my throat. I won't have to fear torture ever again.

You have to fight back, Mara said. *Even if you know you can't win. You owe it to the people who love you to try and survive.*

No one loves me, Niko whispered.

Don't be a moping fool, Mara snapped.

Her words shocked fear back into Niko's body. The sounds of the horde gained distinction. Voices grew out of the all-encompassing hum.

Solcha. Mountain. Elder. Blood.

The peoples' words didn't join together.

Sweat beaded on the back of his neck. His muscles tensed, preparing to fight or flee.

Mara would be furious if he willingly surrendered to death. So would Tham and Kai for that matter. Adrial would grieve for him in a quiet, sincere way few could match. Even Lord Karron would mourn the loss of his former apprentice.

Niko pressed his shoulders back and lifted his chin, taking in the line of guards keeping the path open to the platform that had been erected at the back of the atrium. The tunnel Danu had led him down once before was tucked right behind the stage with only two guards blocking that exit.

Bryana stepped up onto the platform.

Niko lunged forward as rage swallowed sense.

Danu grabbed his arm, yanking him back, pinning him to her side.

"Breathe, Niko," Danu hushed. "Don't give her a reason to hurt you."

"I'll tear out her eyes," Niko whispered.

"The guards will kill you before you can scratch her."

The air caught in Niko's throat, dragging into his lungs in ragged gasps. A heavy darkness pressed in around the edges of his mind, blurring all reasonable thought.

"Do whatever she says, Niko. Whatever it takes to stay alive." Danu stopped at the edge of the stage. She leaned in, brushing a kiss on his cheek. "Don't make me mourn you."

One of the guards took Niko's elbow, propelling him up onto the platform.

Niko fixed his gaze on the demon elder's dress.

The guard placed him five feet away from Bryana. Practically within arm's reach.

"My people." The demon spoke to the mob. "I have invited you here today to witness a moment of great importance and solemn joy."

He couldn't hate a dress. He couldn't want to kill a dress. It was only fabric stitched together.

"The mountain has asked her children for many sacrifices in the last two years," the demon said. "We have been led into battle. Forced to do unthinkable things."

Niko's heart raced. All his muscles burned, screaming for him to attack.

The dress. He needed to focus on the dress.

"But in all things, the mountain grants us mercy," the demon said.

The purple gown had been decorated with streaks of beads that glinted in the light.

"As we mourn those we have lost, the mountain has led hope to our stronghold," the demon said.

Someone had spent hours stitching those beads. In a quiet, safe place. Stitching the beads, one by one.

"Solcha traveled to us from Ilbrea. Protected on his journey by the benevolence of the mountain and delivered to the Brien with great purpose."

If he could wrap himself in the purple cloth, be protected by a thick shroud so the horde couldn't stare at him as the demon spread lies about Solcha—

"Solcha has proven that the war we fight against the Hayes is necessary. Ilbrea is just beyond the western border of our mountains. We cannot hide and pretend the outside world will never reach us. The Ilbrean sorcerers are a threat to our home!"

A guttural roar rose up from the crowd.

The noise stabbed into Niko's ears, pummeling the thin shred of his mind that was still trying to keep him from screaming.

The beads.

Every bead had to have been made by someone. He didn't know what sort of person would have the job of making beads.

"But Solcha's presence offers more than the mountain's assurance that we have chosen the right path," the demon said. "Solcha has given me his sacred vow that he will spend every moment his god grants him searching for what was lost. Solcha has promised to find our Regan."

The throng's shouts battered Niko. He staggered back, as though the weight of the people's hope might crush him.

You will not be crushed by cheers, Mara said.

Someone had made the beads. Someone had sewn the beads. Both of those people might be in the cheering horde. Neither of those people had ever done anything to harm him.

He shifted his gaze to the crowd.

An old man stood at the front of the platform, tears streaming down his cheeks. He had the weathered look of someone who worked in the sun. A farmer, perhaps. A farmer who provided the food Niko ate.

The shouts of the crowd stopped all at once.

"Whether the search leads him into the darkness below the mountain or out into the horrific dangers that fill Ilbrea, Solcha will find my daughter. His devotion to our cause runs so deep, Solcha has asked to be marked as a servant of our clan."

A flutter of whispers whipped through the atrium.

Panic joined Niko's rage. He glanced to the side of the platform. Danu stood not even ten feet from him.

She widened her fear-filled eyes, mouthing, *Don't fight it.*

"Though the Brien have never allowed an outsider the honor of being marked as a servant of our clan, we must trust the mountain's wisdom. The mountain delivered Solcha to us. The mountain will guide Solcha on his journey as he serves the Brien Clan."

The horde cheered, clapping and stomping as though Niko had already found the lost heir.

Two guards carried something up onto the platform. They set it between the Elder and Niko.

Large and made of wood—fear clawed at Niko's mind as he tried to make sense of it.

"I can take your shirt, Solcha." One of the guards held out his hands.

"My shirt?" Niko backed away.

"Of course." A cold hand grabbed Niko's wrist. "Thirteen trueborn Brien will place their marks on your flesh tonight. They can't do their work with your shirt on."

Niko wrenched his wrist free, daring to look at Bryana's face.

A furious wave of loathing rolled through his gut.

The Brien Elder smiled.

"I'm not taking anyone's mark." Niko kept his words below the cheering of the crowd. "I'm not going to let you worm your stone into my flesh so you can use it to murder me with a glance."

"Choose your words wisely, Ilbrean." Bryana's smile didn't falter. "If you make a scene in front of the crowd, Amec will become Solcha."

"Let him have your sham of a title."

"I would have to teach him the ways of the Brien first. Make sure he has no secrets to hide, that he fully understands the consequences of stoking my anger. Do you remember the weeks we spent together? Do you think Amec will survive such an education?" Bryana stepped back, presenting the thing the guards had brought to Niko.

Niko looked out over the atrium. If he dove straight into the crowd, he might make it ten maybe thirty feet before the guards got him.

Thirty feet of freedom.

Defiance as his final act.

Pain radiated through Niko's chest as though his body was imagining what having tiny fragments of rock torn through his heart and lungs might actually feel like.

Danu shoved her way through the crowd, stopping right in front of Niko. A strange glimmer caught in the corners of her eyes as she held Niko's gaze.

Stay alive. Her words broke through the rest of his thoughts. *Stay alive.*

A tear rolled down her cheek as Niko nodded.

He pulled off the billowing white shirt, tossed it to the soldier, and turned to face the thing.

Wooden. Shaped like an X.

The thing dragged terror from the edges of Niko's memory.

They'd strapped him to an X like that. Bound his hands and feet so the Elder could slice into him. So she could burn him.

This X was different. There weren't any blood stains or straps to bind him.

"You can grip right here." A guard patted the top of the X. "It'll help steady you."

Niko didn't know how many times the Elder had strapped him to the blood-stained X. His mind didn't want him to remember.

"Face the back, if you would." The guard bowed Niko toward the stand.

Stay alive, Niko, Danu whispered.

Niko stepped up onto the base of the stand. He forced his

arms up, fighting against their weight as his limbs begged him to flee.

Stay alive.

He gripped the top of the X.

Stay alive.

Could Danu truly be placing words in his mind? He'd never thought to ask. Never even questioned how much magic she possessed.

Stay alive.

The horde fell silent.

"As Elder of the Brien Clan, it is my honor to give Solcha his first mark. By taking this mark, Solcha swears his loyalty to the Brien Clan. He vows to serve the clan, to work until his dying breath to bring the trueborn Regan home."

Niko dug his nails into the wood, shutting his eyes, trying to picture somewhere far away from the Brien.

"And should Solcha betray our clan or abandon his work, he willingly surrenders his life to right the wrongs of his betrayal." The Elder spoke close to Niko's ear. "Don't scream. The people can't see weakness in Solcha."

Sharp heat jabbed into Niko's back. He gasped as the pain dragged down, slicing a line beside his spine.

The gardens at the Map Master's Palace. The sun beaming down. Allora sitting beside him.

The pain pulled away from his spine, looping toward his right shoulder.

Allora flickered, then vanished, leaving a void beside him.

The void inhaled, dragging the sunlight into its terrible darkness.

Another line cut across Niko's back.

A scream pressed up into his throat.

He couldn't let the Elder make him scream. Never again. The demon didn't deserve that power.

The sunlight blossomed back into being, warming Niko's

face. He sat in a field, the tall grass blocking out the rest of the world. Danu took a drink from a bottle, wrinkling her nose against the burn of the frie, raising her eyebrows as Niko tried not to laugh.

The pain carved down to the base of his spine.

Niko took a drink, coughing as the frie caught in his throat.

The rustling of the grass blurred every sound but Danu's laugh.

Nothing else existed. Not pain. Not regret.

The sunlight glinting in Danu's hair was the only thing left in the world.

45

ADRIAL

Rain pattered against the bedroom windows. If Dudia had been kinder, he would have sent a flood to drown Ilara. Wash the whole wretched place away.

Or at least send a surge that could sweep Adrial from his room and carry him out to sea.

Let him sink into the darkness where the grief that gripped him might finally fade.

He sat between the bed and wardrobe, leaning against the wall, letting pain spark through the bandaged wounds on his back. He kept his gaze on the floor in front of him as he tried to find the right words to scream at a god as he begged for mercy.

Fatigue weighed heavy in his lungs. He hadn't slept. Not since they'd stolen her.

Maybe *stolen* wasn't the right word.

No, it was.

They had taken her. Forced her to leave.

They had stolen Ena.

His failing to protect his wife did not free the Guilds of their guilt.

But they hadn't dragged Ena away. She'd walked willingly out of the scribes' gallery. Told the paun the secret she'd sworn to Adrial she would hide even from the gods…and then walked away.

Adrial wasn't the child's father. Those words should never have been spoken. That was the one promise he'd asked her to make, and she'd broken it.

He was willing to die to protect *his* wife, *his* child.

Adrial gripped the pain in his chest, willing his heart to explode.

How the child had been conceived didn't matter. He, Adrial Ayres, was the father of that baby.

It was his right to protect his family, and she'd stolen that from him.

Ena had betrayed him. Abandoned him with more grief than his heart could bear.

But his heart kept beating. Another betrayal.

The floor grayed in and out of view as sleep tried to claim him.

He dug his fingers into his hair, yanking at the roots.

The pain didn't clear his mind.

He wouldn't be able to keep sleep at bay much longer.

But he couldn't even look at the bed.

Her pillow still lay beside his, waiting for her to come home. The pillow would hold her scent.

If he fell asleep in the bed, his mind might trick him into thinking she was home.

Waking up to find she truly was gone was a wound not even a useless fool who couldn't protect his family deserved.

He curled up on the floor. Pain shot from his hip to his shoulder. The ache did nothing to dull the grief.

He stared into the shadows beneath the wardrobe, wishing the depth of the void could swallow his mind.

He'd never get to hold the baby. He'd never hold Ena again.

A corner of white marred the welcoming shadows. A bit of

paper stuck out from the ledge below the wardrobe where he hid his books.

The books he'd been reading to try and stand against the sorcerers.

Had they found out what he'd been researching? Was that why he'd lost everything? Or was it daring to speak against the Sorcerers Guild in the council meetings?

Whatever his offense, he'd done something to spark their revenge.

It's my fault she's gone. If I'd been quiet. If I'd had the sense to leave the sorcerers alone.

They took her. They stole my wife.

Our child.

My son will be born on Ian Ayres.

Grief and rage battled in his chest. Perhaps the two would crack through his ribs and his soul would dissolve, freeing him from his pain.

You deserve the pain.

Black surrounded his vision as sleep tried to take hold. The white of the paper still sliced through the shadows.

It wasn't right. Loose parchment didn't belong under the wardrobe.

He grabbed the paper before realizing he'd reached for it.

The single piece of parchment had been folded in half. Black spots of spattered ink bled through the page.

Adrial's lungs froze, incapable of pulling in air as he recognized Ena's script.

The words had been scrawled with an unusual slant, the spatter on the page born of her haste.

He closed his eyes, blocking out whatever message she had left.

Her words would only bring more pain, he was sure of it.

But he had failed her. He deserved every ounce of suffering Dudia could offer.

His hands trembled as he read the page.

Scribe,

I won't ask you to forgive me. I know that's not possible.

But I cannot survive losing you. I'm not strong enough. It would destroy me.

This is the only choice I have.

Please keep fighting, scribe. Ilbrea needs you.

You of all people could finally change our fate.

I will never regret a moment I spent beside you, only that we didn't have more time.

Ena

The page slipped from his hand as pain stabbed into his chest, tearing through his heart, stealing the world from him.

46

ENA

The storm swallowed the horizon to the north, devouring the sea and land without care for the bitter mess the paun had made of the world.

The sailors didn't seem bothered by the storm as they guided the ship south along the coast of Ilbrea, carrying their prisoners to Ian Ayres, where we would suffer the wrath of the Guilds.

I tipped my head back, letting the chill of the wind play across my cheeks.

If I had been a different person, who'd lived a different life, I might've been curled up, crying with the rest of the pregnant girls the Guilds had captured.

But I had no urge to shed tears. Crying would waste the precious time I had left. And tears, no matter how justified, wouldn't save the child or me from the demon's island that was our fate.

The sailors kept away from the cluster of weeping girls, staying out of reach of their pleading hands. They ignored me entirely. I don't know if it was out of respect for the scribe's position or fear of my silence.

Whatever the reason, their distance suited me. I didn't need their hovering, only the promise of the waves pounding against the ship.

Sea mist filled my lungs with every breath, the cold of it sweeping into my chest as though trying to prove the beauty of simply breathing.

I gripped the ship's rail, digging my nails into the damp wood.

One swift move. That was all I had to manage. Such an easy thing.

"Careful now." A sailor stepped up to the rail beside me. "If a wrong lurch of the ship tosses you overboard, there's no guarantee we could save you."

He waited as though expecting me to speak.

"The currents along this part of the coast are nasty." The sailor pointed to the low, rocky shore. "Ships can't even sail along here in the dark. It's too dangerous."

He leaned forward, resting his forearms on the rail. He didn't wear the blue of a Guilded sailor. The man was a tilk who'd chosen to work on a paun ship.

Collaborator.

I tightened my grip on the rail, wishing the sailors hadn't found the knife tucked in my boot when they'd brought me on board.

"We wouldn't be sailing this close to shore at all if we'd been allowed to wait at the docks until the storm passed. But the sorcerers wanted us gone," the sailor said. "The waters get worse just a bit farther south from here. Sandbars and rocks lurking just below the surface. It's a tense bit of travel for the crew. The captain'll ring the bell, and it's all hands to watch south, keeping an eye out for anything that might sink our ship.

"Now, if a person were to fall overboard there, they might survive long enough to be pulled back onto the ship. The currents are far kinder. And, if a person could swim, they might even make it to shore. But the sea meets a cliff there. So, I suppose anyone who managed to swim to safety would just die of cold anyway. Soaked and shivering at the base of a rock wall. In that case, drowning might be a kinder death."

He rapped his knuckles against the rail.

I fought the urge to grab the man and pitch him overboard. Let ending a collaborator be my legacy.

He rapped his knuckles on the rail again.

"I knew a girl once," he said, "or knew of her, more like, could climb any chivving thing she set her mind to. Could fight as well. Like a dark princess forged in legends, bound to a trueborn prince, standing against the demons with flames of vengeance dancing in her raven hair."

I let go of the rail and curled my hands into fists.

"She disappeared after she went off to fight. Most say she died. Pity, really. From what I know, there aren't many born with the courage that one held. If she were to come back from the dead, she'd be welcomed with open arms. But Death is a cruel beast. He doesn't give people back just because they're needed." He rapped his knuckles on the rail a third time. "I'd better go. The captain will be ringing the bell in a moment. Best of luck to you, Solcha. However your journey ends."

He walked away, leaving a chill creeping across my skin as though a ghost had wrapped his arms around me.

I looked down at my hands, willing them not to shake as I pressed my knuckles to the rail just to keep on my feet.

A glimmer caught my eye.

A black stone rested on the rail where the sailor had knocked.

I snatched up the stone, hiding it in my palm.

Warmth traveled up my arm, banishing the cold fear that had surrounded me.

I have been so many things. An orphan. A Black Blood. A killer. A wife.

None of those names have ever led to my salvation. None of them have helped me save Ilbrea from the Guilds. None of them have let me protect the people I love.

I was not made to live in a world of beautiful peace.

My story is written in blood and pain.

If becoming a ghost of vengeance was the path the gods demanded, I would see my blade slicked with paun blood.

Cliffs grew up the shore, cutting jagged lines against the graying sky. The shadows of the cracks and imperfections in the high rock wall called to me, begging me to come and climb.

I tucked the little black stone into my pocket.

The bell rang.

The sailors ran to their positions, watching the southern path of the ship.

The second clang covered the splash as I jumped into the water, letting the Arion Sea wash away the wife the Guilds had condemned.

The Guilds of Ilbrea series continues with Tower and Grave.

Uncover the mysterious past of Ena Ayres, the first Solcha, in the *Ena of Ilbrea* series. Turn the page for a sneak peek of book one, *Ember and Stone*.

1

The crack of the whip sent the birds scattering into the sky. They cawed their displeasure at the violence of the men below as they flew over the village and to the mountains beyond.

The whip cracked again.

Aaron did well. He didn't start to moan until the fourth lash. By the seventh, he screamed in earnest.

No one had given him a belt to bite down on. There hadn't been time when the soldiers hauled him from his house and tied him to the post in the square.

I clutched the little wooden box of salve hidden in my pocket, letting the corners bite deep into my palm.

The soldier passed forty lashes, not caring that Aaron's back had already turned to pulp.

I squeezed my way to the back of the crowd, unwilling to watch Aaron's blood stain the packed dirt.

Behind the rest of the villagers, children cowered in their mother's skirts, hiding from the horrors the Guilds' soldiers brought with them.

I didn't know how many strokes Aaron had been sentenced

to. I didn't want to know. I made myself stop counting how many times the whip sliced his back.

Bida, Aaron's wife, wept on the edge of the crowd. When his screams stopped, hers grew louder.

The women around Bida held her back, keeping her out of reach of the soldiers.

My stomach stung with the urge to offer comfort as she watched her husband being beaten by the men in black uniforms. But, with the salve tucked in my pocket, hiding in the back was safest.

I couldn't give Bida the box unless Aaron survived. Spring hadn't fully arrived, and the plants Lily needed to make more salves still hadn't bloomed. The tiny portion of the stuff hidden in my pocket was worth more than someone's life, especially if that person wasn't going to survive even with Lily's help.

Lily's orders had been clear—wait and see if Aaron made it through. Give Bida the salve if he did. If he didn't, come back home and hide the wooden box under the floorboards for the next poor soul who might need it.

Aaron fell to the ground. Blood leaked from a gash under his arm.

The soldier raised his whip again.

I sank farther into the shadows, trying to comfort myself with the beautiful lie that I could never be tied to the post in the village square, though I knew the salve clutched in my hand would see me whipped at the post as quickly as whatever offense the soldiers had decided Aaron had committed.

When my fingers had gone numb from gripping the box, the soldier stopped brandishing his whip and turned to face the crowd.

"We did not come here to torment you," the soldier said. "We came here to protect Ilbrea. We came here to protect the Guilds. We are here to provide peace to all the people of this great country.

This man committed a crime, and he has been punished. Do not think me cruel for upholding the law." He wrapped the bloody whip around his hand and led the other nine soldiers out of the square.

Ten soldiers. It had only taken ten of them to walk into our village and drag Aaron from his home. Ten men to tie him to the post and leave us all helpless as they beat a man who'd lived among us all his life.

The soldiers disappeared, and the crowd shifted in toward Aaron. I couldn't hear him crying or moaning over the angry mutters of the crowd.

His wife knelt by his side, wailing.

I wound my way forward, ignoring the stench of fear that surrounded the villagers.

Aaron lay on the ground, his hands still tied around the post. His back had been flayed open by the whip. His flesh looked more like something for a butcher to deal with than an illegal healer like me.

I knelt by his side, pressing my fingers to his neck to feel for a pulse.

Nothing.

I wiped my fingers on the cleanest part of Aaron's shirt I could find and weaved my way back out of the crowd, still clutching the box of salve in my hand.

Carrion birds gathered on the rooftops near the square, scenting the fresh blood in the air. They didn't know Aaron wouldn't be food for them. The villagers of Harane had yet to fall so low as to leave our own out as a feast for the birds.

There was no joy in the spring sun as I walked toward Lily's house on the eastern edge of the village.

I passed by the tavern, which had already filled with men who didn't mind we hadn't reached midday. I didn't blame them for hiding in there. If they could find somewhere away from the torment of the soldiers, better on them for seizing it. I only hoped there weren't any soldiers laughing inside the tavern's walls.

I followed the familiar path home. Along our one, wide dirt road, past the few shops Harane had to offer, to the edge of the village where only fields and pastures stood between us and the forest that reached up the eastern mountains' slopes.

It didn't take long to reach the worn wooden house with the one giant tree towering out front. It didn't take long to reach anywhere in the tiny village of Harane.

Part of me hated knowing every person who lived nearby. Part of me wished the village were smaller. Then maybe we'd fall off the Guilds' maps entirely.

As it was, the Guilds only came when they wanted to collect our taxes, to steal our men to fight their wars, or to find some other sick pleasure in inflicting agony on people who wanted nothing more than to survive. Or if their business brought them far enough south on the mountain road they had to pass through our home on their way to torment someone else.

I allowed myself a moment to breathe before facing Lily. I blinked away the images of Aaron covered in blood and shoved them into a dark corner with the rest of the wretched things it was better not to ponder.

Lily barely glanced up as I swung open the gate and stepped into the back garden. Dirt covered her hands and skirt. Her shoulders were hunched from the hours spent planting our summer garden. She never allowed me to help with the task. Everything had to be carefully planned, keeping the vegetables toward the outermost edges. Hiding the plants she could be hanged for in the center, where soldiers were less likely to spot the things she grew to protect the people of our village. The people the soldiers were so eager to hurt.

"Did he make it?" Lily stretched her shoulders back and brushed the dirt off her weathered hands.

I held the wooden box out as my response. Blood stained the

corners. It wasn't Aaron's blood. It was mine. Cuts marked my hand where I'd squeezed the box too tightly.

Lily glared at my palm. "You'd better go in and wrap your hand. If you let it get infected, I'll have to treat you with the salve, and you know we're running out."

I tucked the box back into my pocket and went inside, not bothering to argue that I could heal from a tiny cut. I didn't want to look into Lily's wrinkled face and see the glimmer of pity in her eyes.

The inside of the house smelled of herbs and dried flowers. Their familiar scent did nothing to drive the stench of blood and fear from my nose.

A pot hung over the stove, waiting with whatever Lily had made for breakfast.

My stomach churned at the thought of eating. I needed to get out. Out of the village, away from the soldiers.

I pulled up the loose floorboard by the stove and tucked the salve in between the other boxes, tins, and vials. I grabbed my bag off the long, wooden table and shoved a piece of bread and a waterskin into it for later. I didn't bother grabbing a coat or shawl. I didn't care about getting cold.

I have to get out.

I was back through the door and in the garden a minute later. Lily didn't even look up from her work. "If you're running into the forest, you had better come back with something good."

"I will," I said. "I'll bring you back all sorts of wonderful things. Just make sure you save some dinner for me."

I didn't need to ask her to save me food. In all the years I'd lived with her, Lily had never let me go hungry. But she was afraid I would run away into the forest and never return. Or maybe it was me that feared I might disappear into the trees and never come back. Either way, I felt myself relax as I stepped out of the garden and turned my feet toward the forest.

2

The mountains rose up beyond the edge of the trees, fierce towers I could never hope to climb. No one else from the village would ever even dream of trying such a thing.

The soldiers wouldn't enter the woods. The villagers rarely dared to go near them. The forest was where darkness and solitude lay. A quiet place where the violence of the village couldn't follow me.

I skirted farmers' fields and picked my way through the pastures. No one bothered me as I climbed over the fences they built to keep in their scarce amounts of sheep and cows.

No one kept much livestock. They couldn't afford it in the first place. And besides, if the soldiers saw that one farmer had too many animals, they would take the beasts as taxes. Safer to be poor. Better for your belly to go empty than for the soldiers to think you had something to give.

I moved faster as I got past the last of the farmhouses and beyond the reach of the stench of animal dung.

When I was a very little girl, my brother had told me that the woods were ruled by ghosts. That none of the villagers dared to cut down the trees or venture into their shelter for fear of being taken by the dead and given a worse fate than even the Guilds could provide.

I'd never been afraid of ghosts, and I'd wandered through the woods often enough to be certain that no spirits roamed the eastern mountains.

When I first started going into the forest, I convinced myself I was braver than everyone else in Harane. I was an adventurer, and they were cowards.

Maybe I just knew better. Maybe I knew that no matter what ghosts did, they could never match the horrors men inflict on each other. What I'd seen them do to each other.

By the time I was a hundred feet into the trees, I could no longer see the village behind me. I couldn't smell anything but the fresh scent of damp earth as the little plants fought for survival in the fertile spring ground. I knew my way through the woods well enough I didn't need to bother worrying about which direction to go. It was more a question of which direction I wanted to chase the gentle wind.

I could go and find fungi for Lily to make into something useful, or I could climb. If I went quickly, I would have time to climb and still be able to find something worth Lily getting herself hanged for.

Smiling to myself, I headed due east toward the steepest part of the mountains near our village. Dirt soon covered the hem of my skirt, and mud squelched beneath my shoes, creeping in through the cracked leather of the soles. I didn't mind so much. What the cold could do to me was nothing more than a refreshing chance to prove I was still alive. Life existed outside the village, and there was beauty beyond our battered walls.

Bits of green peeked through the brown of the trees as new buds forced their way out of the branches.

I stopped, staring up at the sky, marveling at the beauty hidden within our woods.

Birds chirped overhead. Not the angry cawing of birds of

death, but the beautiful songs of lovebirds who had nothing more to worry about than tipping their wings up toward the sky.

A gray and blue bird burst from a tree, carrying his song deeper into the forest.

A stream gurgled to one side of me. The snap of breaking branches came from the other. I didn't change my pace as the crackling came closer.

I headed south to a steeper slope where I had to use my hands to pull myself up the rocks.

I moved faster, outpacing the one who lumbered through the trees behind me. A rock face cut through the forest, blocking my path. I dug my fingers into the cracks in the stone, pulling myself up. Careful to keep my legs from being tangled in my skirt, I found purchase on the rock with the soft toes of my boots. In a few quick movements, I pushed myself up over the top of the ledge. I leapt to my feet and ran to the nearest tree, climbing up to the highest thick branch.

I sat silently on my perch, waiting to see what sounds would come from below.

A rustle came from the base of the rock, followed by a long string of inventive curses.

I bit my lips together, not allowing myself to call out.

The cursing came again.

"Of all the slitching, vile—" the voice from below growled.

I leaned back against the tree, closing my eyes, reveling in my last few moments of solitude. Those hints of freedom were what I loved most about being able to climb. Going up a tree, out of reach of the things that would catch me.

"Ena," the voice called. "Ena."

I didn't answer.

"Ena, are you going to leave me down here?"

My lips curved into a smile as I bit back my laughter. "I didn't ask you to follow me. You can just go back the way you came."

"I don't want to go back," he said. "Let me come up. At least show me how you did it."

"If you want to chase me, you'd better learn to climb."

I let him struggle for a few more minutes until he threatened to find a pick and crack through the rock wall. I glanced down to find him three feet off the ground, his face bright red as he tried to climb.

"Jump down," I said, not wanting him to fall and break something. I could have hauled him back to the village, but I didn't fancy the effort.

"Help me get up," he said.

"Go south a bit. You'll find an easier path."

I listened to the sounds of him stomping off through the trees, enjoying the bark against my skin as I waited for him to find the way up.

It only took him a few minutes to loop back around to stand under my perch.

Looking at Cal stole my will to flee. His blond hair glistened in the sun. He shaded his bright blue eyes as he gazed up at me.

"Are you happy now?" he said. "I'm covered in dirt."

"If you wanted to be clean, you shouldn't have come into the woods. I never ask you to follow me."

"It would have been wrong of me not to. You shouldn't be coming out here by yourself."

I didn't let it bother me that he thought it was too dangerous for me to be alone in the woods. It was nice to have someone worry about me. Even if he was worried about ghosts that didn't exist.

"What do you think you'd be able to do to help me anyway?" I said.

He stared up at me, hurt twisting his perfect brow.

Cal looked like a god, or something made at the will of the Guilds themselves. His chiseled jaw held an allure to it, the rough stubble on his cheeks luring my fingers to touch its texture.

I twisted around on my seat and dropped down to the ground, reveling in his gasp as I fell.

"You really need to get more used to the woods," I said. "It's a good place to hide."

"What would I have to hide from?" Cal's eyes twinkled, offering a hint of teasing that drew me toward him.

I touched the stubble on his chin, tracing the line of his jaw.

"There are plenty of things to hide from, fool." I turned to tramp farther into the woods.

"Ena," he called after me, "you shouldn't be going so far from home."

"Then don't follow me. Go back." I knew he would follow.

I had known when I passed by his window in the tavern on my way through the village. He always wanted to be near me. That was the beauty of Cal.

I veered closer to the stream.

Cal kept up, though he despised getting his boots muddy.

I always chose the more difficult path to make sure he knew I could outpace him. It was part of our game on those trips into the forest.

I leapt across the stream to a patch of fresh moss just beginning to take advantage of spring.

"Ena." Cal jumped the water and sank down onto the moss I had sought.

I shoved him off of the green and into the dirt.

He growled.

I didn't bother trying to hide my smile. I pulled out tufts of the green moss, tucking them into my bag for Lily.

"If you don't want me to follow you," Cal said, "you can tell me not to whenever you like."

"The forest doesn't belong to me, Cal. You can go where you choose."

He grabbed both my hands and tugged me toward him. I tipped onto him and he shifted, letting me fall onto my back. I caught a glimpse of the sun peering down through the new buds of emerald leaves, and then he was kissing me.

His taste of honey and something a bit deeper filled me. And I forgot about whips and Lily and men bleeding and soldiers coming to kill us.

There was nothing but Cal and me. And the day became beautiful.

Order your copy of Ember and Stone *to continue the story.*

ESCAPE INTO ADVENTURE

Thank you for reading *Viper and Steel*. If you enjoyed the book, please consider leaving a review to help other readers find this story.

Dive deeper into the world of the Guilds on MeganORussell. com/ilbrea, where you'll find exclusive Ilbrean content, a peek behind the scenes, and updates on new books.

As always, thanks for reading,

Megan O'Russell

Never miss a moment of the magic and romance.

Join the Megan O'Russell readers community to stay up to date on all the action by visiting https://www.meganorussell.com/ book-signup.

ABOUT THE AUTHOR

Megan O'Russell is the author of several Young Adult series that invite readers to escape into worlds of adventure. From *Girl of Glass*, which blends dystopian darkness with the heart-pounding danger of vampires, to *Ena of Ilbrea*, which draws readers into an epic world of magic and assassins.

With the *Girl of Glass* series, *The Tethering* series, *The Chronicles of Maggie Trent*, *The Tale of Bryant Adams*, the *Ena of Ilbrea* series, and several more projects planned, there are always exciting new books on the horizon. To be the first to hear about new releases, free short stories, and giveaways, sign up for Megan's newsletter by visiting the following:

https://www.meganorussell.com/book-signup.

Originally from Upstate New York, Megan is a professional musical theatre performer whose work has taken her across North America. Her chronic wanderlust has led her from Alaska to Thailand and many places in between. Wanting to travel has fostered Megan's love of books that allow her to visit countless new worlds from her favorite reading nook. Megan is also a lyricist and playwright. Information on her theatrical works can be found at RussellCompositions.com.

She would be thrilled to chat with you on Facebook or

Twitter @MeganORussell, elated if you'd visit her website MeganORussell.com, and over the moon if you'd like the pictures of her adventures on Instagram @ORussellMegan.

ALSO BY MEGAN O'RUSSELL

<u>The Girl of Glass Series</u>

Girl of Glass

Boy of Blood

Night of Never

Son of Sun

<u>The Tale of Bryant Adams</u>

How I Magically Messed Up My Life in Four Freakin' Days

Seven Things Not to Do When Everyone's Trying to Kill You

Three Simple Steps to Wizarding Domination

Five Spellbinding Laws of International Larceny

<u>The Tethering Series</u>

The Tethering

The Siren's Realm

The Dragon Unbound

The Blood Heir

<u>The Chronicles of Maggie Trent</u>

The Girl Without Magic

The Girl Locked With Gold

The Girl Cloaked in Shadow

<u>Ena of Ilbrea</u>

Wrath and Wing

Ember and Stone

Mountain and Ash

Ice and Sky

Feather and Flame

<u>Guilds of Ilbrea</u>

Inker and Crown

Myth and Storm

Viper and Steel

Tower and Grave

<u>Heart of Smoke</u>

Heart of Smoke

Soul of Glass

Eye of Stone

Ash of Ages

<u>Fracture Pact</u>

The Cursebound Thief

<u>Sorcerers of Ilbrea</u>

Spell and Secret